"I'd love to dance," she said, holding out her hand.

Levi's hand closed around it, and his mouth snapped shut as he led her to the dance floor. He turned to face her, gently placing his free hand on her hip. Elinor's hand went automatically to his shoulder. Habit.

He didn't pull her close, too cautious for that, and she found herself remembering the middle school dance he'd invited her to, when they'd stood with arms extended, elbows locked as they rocked back and forth. He'd been scared to presume too much then, too. He was such a man now, but it had never been more obvious that he was still that gangly thirteen-year-old boy, too.

"People keep talking to me about you," she said when the intimacy of the dance got to be too much. She needed the words to escape the warmth of it, the familiarity of his hands, his scent...

"Likewise," he murmured.

"Everyone's going to be speculating that we're back to-gether. Again." She made a face. "This town. Sometimes it drives me crazy."

"You didn't have to come back after college. You could have gone anywhere."

Irritation flashed fast. That I-know-what's-best-for-you button he always pushed, ready to react to the slightest pressure. "No, I couldn't," she snapped. "My family was here. And even if I didn't have to come back, I *wanted* to. That was the piece you never seemed to get. I never felt forced or trapped. I *wanted* this. I wanted you. And you broke my heart."

To All the Dogs I've Loved Before

Praise for Lizzie Shane and the Pine Hollow Series

To
All
the Dogs
I've Loved
Before

Lizzie Shane

FOREVER
New York   Boston

Copyright © 2021 by Lizzie Shane.

Cover art and design by Daniela Medina. Cover photographs © Shutterstock. Cover copyright © 2021 by Hachette Book Group, Inc.

Bonus novella *I'll Be Home for Christmas* by Hope Ramsay © 2011 by Hope Ramsay.

Forever
Hachette Book Group
1290 Avenue of the Americas, New York, NY 10104
read-forever.com
twitter.com/readforeverpub

First Edition: November 2021

Forever is an imprint of Grand Central Publishing. The Forever name and logo are trademarks of Hachette Book Group, Inc.

The publisher is not responsible for websites (or their content) that are not owned by the publisher.

The Hachette Speakers Bureau provides a wide range of authors for speaking events. To find out more, go to www.hachettespeakersbureau.com or call (866) 376-6591.

ISBNs: 978-1-5387-3594-7 (mass market), 978-1-5387-3593-0 (ebook)

Printed in the United States of America

10 9 8 7 6 5 4 3 2 1

For everyone who believes sometimes love needs a second chance

Chapter One

The chief's on-again-off-again relationship with a certain librarian has been stuck in the "off" position for years now, but several eyewitnesses reported seeing him playing with her dog in the square last Friday. Could these two lovebirds finally be patching things up?

—*Pine Hollow Newsletter*,
Monday, September 27

The dog was a menace.

Some days Levi was convinced she'd been put on this earth for the sole purpose of messing with his peace of mind—and her owner wasn't any better.

Levi mentally cursed the pair of them as he chased the furry troublemaker through the Pine Hollow town square on a sunny Friday afternoon. Again. He'd spent *entirely* too much time running after that fluffy white tail over the last nine months.

The mottled white-and-brown Australian shepherd ran a zigzag pattern through the hay bales set up for the fall festival before leaping up onto the gazebo platform and looking back at him with eager eyes.

Tactical mistake, Levi thought, keeping the critique silent.

He refused to become the guy talking to a dog as if she understood him.

Moving quickly to the base of the gazebo, he cut off her exit. He'd learned his lesson since the first call about a loose dog back in January—the little demon was *fast*, and he'd never catch her if he just followed her.

It was all about maneuvering. And usually about keeping treats in his Explorer, but he'd run out two weeks ago and hadn't remembered to pick up more of the liver-flavored ones she liked.

"Come on," Levi coaxed, creeping slowly closer with the leash—something else he'd started keeping in his glove box—hidden behind his back so she wouldn't spot it.

The little Aussie crouched, watching him eagerly with her mismatched eyes, her tail sweeping back and forth.

"Good girl," he murmured, one hand out to the side to cut off her last avenue of escape. Just a few more inches.

"Hi, Levi!" a cheerful voice called across the square.

Levi didn't react. He didn't take his eyes off the canine menace for a second.

So he had a clear view when she whirled, bounding up onto the railing he'd been certain was higher than she could jump without a running start. He lunged, but she was already scampering along the top of the railing like a high-wire act. When a post blocked her route, she launched herself over the hedges and took off across the open green of the square at breakneck speed.

Levi swore under his breath and jogged down the gazebo steps to give chase, but that chipper voice came again.

"That Elinor's dog you're playing with?" called Linda Hilson, the nosiest gossip in Pine Hollow. "You two back together?"

The blare of a car horn jerked his attention toward the street, where Elinor's menace of a dog was trying to herd cars again. Because *of course she was*.

"No," Levi bit out to answer both questions as he sprinted toward the street before the dog got herself killed. He was *not* back together with Elinor, and he was not *playing* with her pain-in-the-ass dog.

Since Pine Hollow was too small for its own animal control department, calls about everything from bears knocking over trash cans to dogs on the loose went through Levi's office—and even though Levi had two part-time deputies working for him, he always seemed to be the one to hear about it when Elinor's nuisance of a dog got out.

It would be one thing if this were the first time. Or the second. Or even the tenth. But complaints about the dog running amok through town had become almost a weekly occurrence ever since Elinor adopted her last Christmas. The calls had paused during the summer when Elinor was on hiatus from her job as the school librarian and could keep track of her own damn dog, but they'd picked up like clockwork again when the school year started last month.

The calendar hadn't even tripped over into October yet, the town just starting to gear up for the annual fall festival, and Levi could not take another month of this. Elinor needed to find a way to keep the forty-pound fluffball contained.

He made it to the street bracketing the square in time to see the menace in question veer down the alleyway beside Magda's bakery.

"*Thank* you," Levi growled, jogging across the street to block the dog in. The alley dead-ended where the back of the bakery met the back of the historic Pine Hollow Inn—

not to be confused with the Inn at Pine Hollow or the Inn *of* Pine Hollow.

Levi stepped into the alley, scanning the shadows for signs of her. He'd definitely seen that tail disappear back here. She had to be here somewhere. Even Dory the Menace couldn't leap three-story buildings in a single bound. But all he saw were the trash bins tucked against the side of the building—and a swath of graffiti that hadn't been there yesterday on the inn wall.

Levi swore under his breath, momentarily distracted from the pursuit in progress by the new development in his other ongoing headache. There'd been a string of small thefts and minor vandalism around town over the summer. He'd been hoping the new school year would distract the likely underage perpetrators, but the paint splashed across the brick of the historic building told a different story.

Pine Hollow was a quiet town. He'd only had to arrest three people all year—and two of those had been DUIs. His job was mostly about listening to what the town needed and finding solutions before situations could worsen. That was what Elton, the previous police chief, had always taught him, and Levi tried to live by it. The benefit—and the curse—of a small town was that everyone was in everyone else's business. So if he kept his ears open, he could usually catch wind of things before they got too bad. Usually.

Which was what was so frustrating about the times when he couldn't. And about incidents like the vandalism—where no one seemed to have any idea who was doing it. This town was his responsibility, and he had the sleepless nights to prove it.

One of the trash cans rattled, pulling Levi's gaze away from the spray paint and back to the culprit at hand. He rounded the can, squaring off against Elinor's dog. She looked up at him, her ears pricked forward, tongue flopping out the side of her mouth as she panted happily.

"You pleased with yourself?" he grumbled.

She wriggled into a crouch, bouncing up to sit, then back down on her belly, watching him as he approached. He kept his hands loose in front of him like a soccer goalie, ready to lunge if she tried to dart past him. There was no way out of the back of the alley. Just the cans, a brick wall, and the back door to Magda's place. As long as Magda didn't open it to investigate the rattling trash cans, he was home free.

"It's okay...nice and easy..." He stretched out one hand—and the dog bounced sideways with a bark.

Farther down the alley.

"You wanna go that way, we'll go that way. That's a dead end," he said—and then reminded himself that he did not talk to Elinor's crazy dog.

She danced in three quick circles, spiraling out of reach.

"Just come quietly. There's no way out..."

She cocked her head—giving him a look that he could almost *swear* meant she took those words as a challenge. Then she bolted for the closed door. He straightened, not bothering to immediately give chase—where could she go? It wasn't like dogs could open doors.

She bounced up on her hind legs, her front paws pushing down on the handle.

No way.

The latch released, and the door cracked open.

"No, no, no!" Levi lunged—but Elinor's diabolical pet had already wedged her nose into the opening, working it wide enough to dart inside.

He resisted the urge to roar in frustration and flung open

the door, charging into the employees-only area of Magda's bakery—through the dry storage room, chasing the wisp of fluffy white tail into the kitchen and the storefront beyond.

"Levi, what the hell?" Magda yelped as he burst into the front of the shop in pursuit of the fiendish Aussie.

"Sorry." He dodged around the counter.

"Why did you set a dog loose in my bakery?" Magda blocked his path, thunder gathering in her eyes. "Did Mac put you up to this? He'd better not be calling the health inspector."

"Is that Elinor Rodriguez's dog?" asked Gayle Danvers, one hand *holding the front door open*.

"Don't let her out!" Levi shouted, but it was too late. The menace had escaped past Mrs. Danvers back into the square.

He called out another apology to everyone in the shop, slowing down respectfully as he moved past Mrs. Danvers, before breaking into a sprint as he saw the streak of brown-on-white fur vanishing back into the props for the Harvest Festival that dotted the square.

Townspeople watched him race past with amused expressions. He must have chased down Elinor's dog dozens of times by now, but in the past she'd tended to frequent less-populated areas. He'd found her in Elinor's neighborhood or near the school more times than he could count—probably trying to track down her owner. Twice she'd been hanging around the Furry Friends shelter, where she'd lived for a few weeks before Elinor adopted her. And once he'd even found her cavorting around the old mill, a wreck of a building outside town that wasn't safe for anyone, man or dog, though tourists loved to take pictures in front of the crumbling stones. But this was only her second visit to the square.

And hopefully her last.

If Elinor didn't find some way to lock her up, he was going to do it himself. He had an empty jail cell. He'd like to see her open *that* door.

Levi saw a flash of white, only a few feet away, weaving between the hay bales, and desperation drove him into a dive. He landed on his stomach on the hay bale, his arms stretched out in front of him—with no dog to show for it, only the feel of fur brushing past his fingertips.

"What are you doing?"

Levi looked up, silently waving goodbye to the last shreds of his dignity as he met two pairs of curious eleven-year-old eyes. Astrid Williams and Kimber Kwan. School must be out. Which meant he'd been chasing Elinor's menace of a dog for at least thirty minutes. It had been too early when the first call came in about a loose dog to just call Elinor and tell her to get control of her own damn pooch.

"Astrid. Kimber." Levi came to his feet, dusting stray bits of hay off the front of his uniform. "Just catching a loose dog," he said, mentally calculating the likelihood that this wasn't going to get back to his friends and become a source of ribbing at poker nights for the next month.

Considering Ben was Astrid's uncle and legal guardian, he didn't like his odds.

Astrid cocked her head at him, frowning as if he'd said something inexplicable. "You mean Dory? Why don't you just call her?"

"I tried that," he explained, keeping his voice calm and his frustration to himself. "She thinks we're playing chase."

Astrid nodded sagely. "She does that," she said. "Aunt

Elinor said the trick is to offer her a treat. Or a game she likes even better." The girl turned to where Dory was peeking out from behind a hay bale. "Dory want the ball?" she asked in a high-pitched voice, cupping her hand like she was holding an invisible ball.

The dog instantly raced out of hiding, rushing to sit angelically at Astrid's feet, her focus fixed diligently on the nonexistent ball in Astrid's grip.

"You've gotta be kidding me," Levi muttered—but he wasted no time clipping the leash to Dory's collar while the dog was still fixated on the pretend ball. Astrid offered the "ball" to Dory, and the dog licked her empty hand—as Levi tried not to take it too hard that he'd just been out-smarted by an eleven-year-old in under two minutes. Ego was overrated anyway. At least he finally had the freaking dog under control.

Now all he had to do was return her to his ex-fiancée and convince the woman who had been angry at him for three years to do him a favor and padlock her dog inside when she was going to be at work.

No problem.

Chapter Two

No one knows for sure why the chief and the librarian mysteriously called off their engagement three years ago, but many a Pine Hollow resident is hopeful that this could be a sign that our favorite couple will be headed back to the altar soon.
—*Pine Hollow Newsletter*,
Monday, September 27

The downside of living in the same small town as her ex-fiancé was that it was virtually impossible to avoid bumping into him. Particularly when that ex was the chief of police and couldn't resist butting his nose into other people's business. Especially hers.

Elinor groaned as she pulled onto her street and saw the all-too-familiar black Explorer in her driveway, the Pine Hollow Police seal on the driver's door glinting in the sunlight.

It had been such a good day.

Or, more accurately, it had been an absolute crap day during which she'd been hanging on to her good mood by her fingernails.

She'd woken up with the beginnings of a sinus headache.

Then Jeremiah Svec, who seemed to pride himself on being the class clown, had chosen this morning during the before-school hot breakfast program to dump his juice all over her shoes. She was pretty sure it had been intentional, but she pretended to believe it was an accident, even as she squelched her way through the morning classes.

Because Murphy's Law was alive and well, a bear had been spotted not far from the school. So in an excess of caution, recess had been moved to the gymnasium—and the kids obviously hadn't gotten their wiggles out as well as they did outside, because the entire day was an exercise in enforcing the library rules against running and shouting when what she *really* wanted to be doing was fostering a love of the written word.

She loved her job, but even on a good day it was exhausting—and today she was a little ashamed of how relieved she felt that she wasn't on duty for the after-school program and could just go home.

Except, of course, her baby sister had called as soon as she pulled her phone out of her desk and turned the ringer back on—as if Charlotte had a hidden camera on Elinor, letting her know the exact second she could make demands.

She should have let it go to voice mail. She should have known by the fact that it was a call and not a text that Charlotte was asking for a favor. But she'd picked up anyway. And immediately succumbed to the "best of all possible sisters" wheedling.

So instead of going home, she'd found herself at Magda's bakery picking up cupcakes—literally the *only* thing Charlotte had been tasked with picking up for the party tonight.

The traffic around the square had been a mess, thanks to

all the weekend tourists coming up to Vermont for the fall foliage and gawking at the picturesque small-townness— one of the hazards of living in adorable Pine Hollow. Elinor had to park so far away from Magda's she might as well have walked from the school, but she'd pushed away her irritation and squelched her way in her still-moist shoes to the cute little bakery to collect the goodies.

It was Anne Day—a holiday that only existed in her family—and she was determined to be happy. She just needed five minutes curled up with her sweet dog and a good book to reset her mood.

But Murphy's Law ruled her life, so, of course, Levi was sitting in her driveway.

If a man was going to declare that he didn't want to marry you after the world's longest engagement, he ought to at least have the decency to leave town. But no. Not Levi. He'd just moved into a cabin by the old Keller place and loomed over her life.

Though he wasn't in the habit of dropping by for no reason.

Elinor pulled alongside him, and the reason he was there flung herself against the Explorer's passenger window, barking her joy that Elinor was home.

Dory.

Who was supposed to be secured inside the house while Elinor was at work—but who always seemed to find new ways of escaping.

Elinor shut off her car and took a moment to tug the hair tie out of her hair, the thick, dark brown length falling around her shoulders for only a moment before she raked her hands back through it, yanking it back into her standard ponytail—a habit that Levi used to tease her about, saying she did it when she wanted to compose herself, his gray eyes glinting at her in that knowing way.

"This is a good day," she said to herself, smashing the memory and focusing on Anne as she reached for the cupcakes and climbed out of the car.

She automatically glanced toward the house as she heard Levi's door creak open, looking for evidence of Dory's latest jailbreak, but there were no open doors or windows on the front side. She must have made it out the back this time.

Levi rounded his front bumper, unhurried, letting his irritation roll out in front of him in an intangible wave. He held the leash in one hand, and Dory bounced toward Elinor, eager and ridiculously proud of herself.

Elinor quickly set the bakery box on her hood so the cupcakes wouldn't go flying when Dory reached her.

She wasn't a bad dog—in fact, Elinor would argue to the death that she was the best of dogs—but Dory kept finding new ways of getting out, no matter what Elinor did to try to contain her. The only locks that seemed to stop her were padlocks—so Elinor had tried padlocking Dory in her puppy crate. It had worked until she'd come home the following week to find the padlock still attached to the crate door, which had been removed at the hinges and lay discarded on the kitchen floor.

She was pretty sure Dory had snuck out a second-story window that day. One of the neighbors had reported seeing her on the roof.

She just kept getting loose.

And Levi always seemed to be the one to find her. Always with that same disapproving frown on his face when he brought her back.

Not that his frown was noticeable to the naked eye. Levi

was a master of the blank stare. But Elinor had known him since they were seven. She'd always been able to read him.

He was a below-the-surface kind of guy. She'd been intrigued by that when they were kids. Fascinated by his stillness. Dying of curiosity to know what he was thinking because he said so little. Her personal jigsaw puzzle.

When she was thirteen, she'd filled journals with dissertations on every flicker of his eyelashes.

He'd been gangly then, tall for his age and so thin it looked like a stiff breeze would blow him right over, but he'd always had that stillness. That quiet intensity. And he'd always had her. No one had ever caught her attention quite as completely as Levi Jackson.

He'd filled out while she was away at college, his shoulders finally catching up to his height. When she'd come back, he'd been sexy in a way that had actually been a little intimidating. Other girls had stared at him then, gawking at his muscles, fawning over his eerily pale gray eyes and how good he looked in his uniform. But he'd still been her Levi, and they'd fallen easily back into being friends. And then, later, back into being more than friends.

She'd felt sort of smug then. Possessive and proud of the fact that she'd wanted him before he grew into his hunkiness.

Now the sexiness was just salt in the wound. He'd never have trouble finding someone to replace her, especially if he gave a new girl that slow, deliberate look he used to give Elinor.

The look that wasn't even a distant cousin of the one he was giving her at the moment.

Levi, who now met her eyes with absolutely no expression, was currently *pissed*.

"I know. I'm sorry," Elinor said to cut off the lecture she could see in his eyes, kneeling to greet Dory as the little Aussie tried to wiggle in every direction simultaneously to express her joy at their reunion. "I don't know how she keeps getting out."

Those pale, almost-silver eyes she'd once thought were the most beautiful color in the world stayed hard. "I'm not going to spend another school year chasing your dog, Elinor. You have to find some way to contain her."

"It's not like I'm not trying."

"Try harder. I have better ways to spend my time than wrangling your dog."

"Oooh, did Mrs. Glenn double-park again? You'd better get on top of that, or we'll have a crime wave."

The sarcasm popped out, instantly chased by regret. She knew his job was important. She knew he cared about the town and did everything he could to make Pine Hollow a great place to live—but it was hard to focus on that when she was still so *angry* with him.

She could go weeks or even months without noticing it and then *wham*. It would all come rushing back. The anger was always waiting beneath the surface. Dormant but ready to erupt at a moment's notice. He'd been her person, the love of her life—until he'd casually ripped out her heart and walked away without even an explanation. A little anger was warranted.

She reached for the leash, and Levi shifted, holding it away from her.

"I'm not kidding, Elinor. Don't make me take her away from you."

"You wouldn't."

He sighed. "No, I wouldn't," he admitted. "But I am

going to have to fine you if we get any more complaints. She ran through Magda's bakery today. If she'd caused any damage—"

"Then I'm sure Magda would take it up with me." She was a little surprised she hadn't heard about Dory's exploits when she'd picked up the cupcakes—but the bakery had been packed, mostly with out-of-towners. Fall color was starting, after all. Magda had caught her eye and handed over the cupcakes Charlotte had preordered without missing a beat in the conversation she'd been having with the tourist at the front of the line.

"Just keep her inside," Levi said in that deep, rusty growl of his.

"I will."

It wasn't like she hadn't tried. She'd adopted the canine equivalent of Ethan Hunt in *Mission: Impossible*. Or freaking MacGyver.

Elinor reached for the leather leash, and Levi relinquished it after a beat, stepping back. His gaze flicked past her as he surveyed the scene, missing nothing—and landed on the oversized Magda's box she'd set on the hood of her car. Far too many cupcakes for one person.

"They're for Anne," Elinor heard herself explaining, even though she didn't owe him a damn explanation.

A new alertness lit in his eyes, a question sharpening his gaze, and Elinor realized her mistake. He loved her sisters. He worried about her sisters. Always so protective of Anne and Charlotte. It was part of what made it so hard to completely hate him. It would be so much easier if she could just hate him properly.

"Five years cancer-free," Elinor said, and the sharp edge of worry in his eyes instantly eased into relief. "We're having a little celebration. Just family," she amended quickly, before she found herself inviting him. They'd been together through Anne's entire illness, including the terrifying recurrence after nearly two years cancer-free, but that didn't give him the right to come celebrate this milestone with them. He'd given that up when he'd dumped her in the middle of wedding planning.

He glanced back toward his Explorer. "I should go."

"Yep."

Now that Levi was no longer holding her leash, Dory seemed to have decided she desperately needed his attention. She gave a short, conversational bark, her mismatched eyes focused intently on Levi and her feet braced in a sort of half crouch, ready for any game. He rewarded her with a glower.

"Did you know she can open doors?" he grumbled—as if Elinor had taught her to do it to spite him.

"Yeah, I know. She was the resident escape artist at the shelter when I got her, always letting all the other dogs out to play with her."

"Ally has a doggie day care now," Levi reminded her.

"I know." She also knew she couldn't afford to pay to have someone watch Dory every day, not on a school librarian's salary, when she was already strapped to pay the mortgage on the house she'd bought back when she thought she and Levi were going to live happily ever after there.

Charlotte had lived with her for a couple of years, which had helped out with bills even if they'd driven each other crazy, but Charlotte had moved to one of the NetZero Village condos out by the ski resort last year, and since then money had been tight. Elinor might need to look into another roommate.

"I'll figure something out," she insisted, reminding Levi with the hard look in her eyes that her problems were not his to solve anymore. No matter how much he liked to play Savior of the Universe.

He gave a short, jerking nod. "Right," he muttered, *finally* moving back to his SUV.

Dory whined, and Elinor dropped a hand to the top of her head, stroking her silky ears. "He isn't our friend," she told Dory after the Explorer door creaked shut.

Levi started the engine, one wrist draped over the top of his steering wheel as he gave Elinor one last look, then put the SUV into gear and backed out of her driveway. She watched him go, staring after the back bumper of the man she'd been convinced was the love of her life when she was fifteen.

Of course, she'd also thought *Titanic* was the most romantic movie in the world back then. Obviously, she'd been an idiot.

She looked down at Dory, her sweet baby gazing up at her with abject adoration. "All right, Trouble. What are we going to do with you?"

Chapter Three

Some are skeptical that a reunion might be in the works—especially those who speculated about Kaye Berry's involvement in the infamous breakup...
—*Pine Hollow Newsletter*,
Monday, September 27

Levi drove away from Elinor's, glaring over the steering wheel. They couldn't even have a conversation anymore. Her dark brown eyes were hard when she looked at him now, always with that same steady, slightly frowning stare as she bumped up her glasses.

This wasn't how things were supposed to go.

Yes, he'd expected Elinor to be upset initially when they split up, but they'd been friends first and friends when they took a break while she was in college. And she'd always been the logical one in their relationship, the analytical one who thought everything to death. He'd been sure that as soon as she took a step back and realized this was for the best, they would go right back to being friends again.

Except it hadn't worked out that way.

It had been three years, and she was still spitting venom at him. He'd tried being there for her. He'd tried giving her space. He'd tried every damn thing he could think of, and she still seemed to think he was Satan. When was she going to freaking *forgive* him? She had to see by now that he'd done what was best for the both of them.

Levi barely saw the road, only realizing he'd returned to the Pine Hollow Rescue Squad station on autopilot when he pulled into the parking lot. He cursed under his breath, kicking himself for his lack of focus, and headed inside the building.

The combined police, fire, and rescue station wasn't fancy—there was a definite warehouse vibe. A large bay to hold the fire truck and ambulance took up half the building. The other half contained a handful of claustrophobic offices for the police staff, a bunk room for the volunteer fire-fighters to crash when they needed it, a kitchen that hadn't been updated since the seventies, and a lounge area with a flat-screen TV and carpet so threadbare the concrete floor had started to peek out in places.

Levi had an "official" office over at the old courthouse, in the same basement that had housed the Pine Hollow jail for more than a century, but since the jail was almost never occupied and the ancient basement had a tendency to flood whenever it rained more than an inch, he spent most of his time working out of the rescue squad building.

This was where the dispatcher was, where his deputies shared an office, and where he could trade information with the other public servants working to keep Pine Hollow safe. It had been his predecessor's idea to move most of the police department's operations to the rescue squad station. Elton had been a firm believer in consolidating resources.

Levi pushed through the front door, waving to the dispatcher, Kaye, who waved back without looking up from the anatomy textbook open on her desk. She'd recently started taking night classes to become an EMT and studied whenever there weren't emergency calls coming in—which in Pine Hollow was more often than not.

Her hand popped up when he passed, the elbow resting on her desk at a right angle as she held up three sheets torn off her message pad between her index and middle finger, still without looking up. "Messages."

Levi shuffled his bag and his keys, automatically pretending to have his hands full. "What are they?" he asked, as if he was too busy and important to take the scraps of paper from her hand. The habit of a lifetime. Better she think he was an ass than watch him frowning over the words. A thousand tiny coping mechanisms to keep from ever having to read anything in front of anyone.

Kaye rolled her eyes, but she indulged him, like he'd known she would, quickly reading them off. "Another complaint about the dog—did you catch her?" He grunted something in the affirmative, and she continued. "Linda Hilson called to ask how long you and Elinor have been back together." Kaye gave him a sympathetic look as his jaw locked. "I told her the department has no comment at this time."

Oh, he had a comment. It just wasn't something fit to print.

Linda had taken over the town newsletter when his friend Ben had become mayor and needed to hand off the job—which meant anything Levi said was highly likely to end up quoted in what was quickly becoming the town gossip column.

There hadn't been any official complaints filed against

her yet, but he figured a libel lawsuit was only a matter of time.

Kaye flipped to the third message. "And then your mom called to tell me to tell you to return her calls." Kaye was younger than he was by several years, but she fixed him with the how-could-you-disappoint-me-this-way mom glare that all women with children seem to have perfected. "Call your mother."

"Yes, ma'am," he promised, starting toward his office again without taking the messages she wagged at him. He knew his mother's number, and the others would just go in the trash anyway. "Thank you," he called over his shoulder, but Kaye's attention was already back on the anatomy text.

He headed down the hallway to his office, past the open door of the office his deputies shared. They were both so young that they made Levi feel geriatric at thirty-four. Aaron, the twenty-three-year-old ski bum, had been recruited to the search-and-rescue team because of his rock-climbing skills and had taken the part-time deputy job for extra cash.

And then there was Hunter, who had the makings of an excellent deputy, but was only biding his time until he could get his parents on board with his plan to enlist in the military. He was already eighteen. Technically, he could have gone anytime. But he was convinced he could ease his folks into the idea—and he probably wasn't wrong. The kid was persuasive. Levi figured he'd be gone in six months.

Retention was a bitch.

It wasn't unusual for the deputies in a small town like Pine Hollow to keep moving on to better-paying jobs—law enforcement in bigger cities or a completely different career. There weren't that many opportunities for advancement for a part-time deputy in a town that only had one full-time cop. And writing traffic tickets for tourists wasn't most kids' dream job.

Levi had started out that way, taking a job as a deputy right out of high school, learning on the job, slowly racking up more responsibility. He'd worked for Elton for more than a dozen years before his mentor had retired and Levi had been appointed as chief of police. But Levi wasn't planning to retire anytime soon, and he couldn't blame the younger guys for wanting something more.

He heard voices from the end of the hall—the fire captain and EMT who were the co-heads of the rescue squad shooting the shit in the lounge—but Levi turned into his office before he reached that doorway.

It wasn't large—old desk, old file cabinet, a couple of old chairs, and the fancy ergonomic one the rest of the squad had all chipped in to get him for Christmas last year.

And it wasn't empty.

Marjorie Stanhope lounged in the chair behind his desk like she owned the place, reading a book. The silver-haired firecracker looked up when he walked in, instantly closing the paperback. "Levi." She smiled.

"You have your own office," he reminded her.

He headed toward the rickety filing cabinet, opening the top drawer and setting his service weapon in the lockbox there. With Ben's help he'd convinced the town to go digital a few years ago, so now—thank God—there were no more paper files cluttering up the office. He'd always avoided the paperwork side of things, but now at least when he had to file reports he could make his notes with the dictation software on his phone while he was out patrolling the town, rather than being trapped behind a desk spending far too long trying to make sense of the damn forms.

"I'm lying in wait," Marjorie said, rocking back in his chair and making herself right at home. "It works so much better in here."

He arched a brow, resting an elbow on the top of the filing cabinet. "Am I supposed to know why you're lying in wait for me?"

He didn't remember a meeting on the schedule.

Marjorie had joined the Pine Hollow public service team two years ago, at Levi's request. They'd never had the budget for a full-time social worker—and they still didn't—but Marjorie had recently retired from her therapy practice and was looking for a way to give back. She'd been an old friend of Elton's and had sort of become the town grandma—only now she did so in a quasi-official capacity, something Levi had thought of after Elinor had made him listen to a podcast about grandmas on public benches in Zimbabwe helping stave off mental health problems.

Marjorie had taken to the role immediately, and Levi was pretty sure there'd been a decline in mental health crisis calls, though he didn't have the data to back that up. Elinor would have crunched the numbers. She probably would have drawn up a paper on the subject for peer review, but Levi had never been good at that stuff. The academic crap.

He'd barely graduated from high school, but Marjorie had all the master's degrees and fancy letters behind her name that he lacked, and she looked like a professor now as she steepled her hands on his desk. "Have a seat."

He lifted a brow. "You do realize this is my office."

"Yes. It's very impressive," she said, utterly unimpressed by his authority. "Sit."

Levi sank onto one of the two chairs facing his desk, his long limbs feeling too large for the utilitarian chair. He'd never worried about having fancy chairs—he didn't get many visitors—but the damn thing was like sitting on a rock. He shifted awkwardly, trying to get comfortable, and Marjorie leaned forward, bracing her elbows on *his* desk.

"Do you remember when you hired me?" Marjorie asked, in what he was pretty sure was a rhetorical question. "How you told me the plan was to listen to the town and intervene before problems could become problems?"

At her pause, he realized she actually wanted him to answer and jerked out a nod. "Absolutely. What's the problem?"

"You are."

Levi stifled his reaction, limiting it to a slow blink. "I am," he repeated, trusting her to explain.

"Or rather, I don't want you to become one."

He didn't say anything, letting her see the question in his eyes—and she drew a breath to fill the silence he'd left, releasing it on a sigh.

"What happened to Britt Wells was not your fault."

He didn't flinch. But he also couldn't hold her gaze. His jaw locked as he glanced back toward the filing cabinet. It had to be older than he was, but it still worked. Just needed a little WD-40 every now and then to keep going. There must be a lesson there.

"Levi." Marjorie's voice was gentle, but firm.

No, I don't want to talk about it, he silently argued, staring at that filing cabinet, noting the pattern of rust starting to creep along the side. *Don't say that name again.*

"Obviously I can't be your therapist," Marjorie continued—and this time he wasn't sure he hid his flinch.

He could hear his father's voice in his head. *Don't show weakness. Jackson men are strong.* It almost drowned out Marjorie's next words.

"And I thought you might object to seeing anyone here in town, so I reached out to an old colleague based in Stowe. He's very good." She paused, studying him, but her next words were firm. "I'd like you to go see him."

"I'm fine."

"You promised never to bullshit me," Marjorie reminded him gently. "And I'm doing the same."

It wasn't bullshit. He was fine. He'd made a bad call with Britt Wells—a catastrophically bad call—but he was dealing with it. He was being more vigilant, listening to all the audiobooks he could find on strategies to intervene with opioid addicts. It wouldn't happen again.

"Levi. When was the last time you slept? A full night's sleep? July? August, maybe?"

Levi blinked. His eyes felt gritty, but he didn't think anyone had suspected that he hadn't been sleeping. He never showed weakness. He kept it together for the town.

"I'm not saying you have a problem," Marjorie went on when he didn't speak. "I'm asking you to talk to someone before this becomes one."

She extended something toward him. A business card. He stared at it like it might bite him.

Jackson men don't need therapy. His father's voice again.

She wagged the card. "Don't make me call Elton."

His old boss. His mentor. The reason he wasn't in jail right now. A much better guidepost for what he should do than the voice of toxic masculinity that lived rent-free in his head. Elton was a big believer in talking things out. He'd taught Levi that the best thing he could do to keep

Pine Hollow's residents safe was to listen to them, to know them, to know who needed help.

To not miss the warning signs, like he had with Britt Wells...

Elton was a small man with a big smile, and Levi would never be able to fully fill his shoes, to be what Elton had been to Pine Hollow now that he'd retired to Florida. But Elton would want him to talk it out.

He took the card, giving a tight nod.

"Thank you," Marjorie murmured, then rocked back in his chair, the tension that had seemed to fill the office defusing with her movement and her quick, flashing smile. "So what's this I hear about you getting back together with Elinor Rodriguez?"

Chapter Four

...and some report not all members of our
dear librarian's family are as enthusiastic
about a possible reunion...
                              —*Pine Hollow Newsletter*,
                              Monday, September 27

Your mom really had a thing for Jane Austen, huh?"
     Elinor watched as Anne's girlfriend, Bailey, trailed
her fingertips lightly along the spines of the gilt-embossed
hardbacks in their place of honor on her mother's bookshelf.
     "It was her passion. One might even say an obsession,"
Charlotte drawled from her position sprawled on the floor.
     Elinor lobbed a cocktail napkin at her sister's head—since
that was all she could reach from her dad's oversized armchair without disturbing Dory, who was sleeping in her lap.
"She was a big reader," Elinor explained to Bailey. "And Jane
Austen was the pinnacle, as far as she was concerned."
     The party had wound down. Anne had invited a few
friends to join them for the celebration, but it was just the
four of them now—Elinor, Anne, Charlotte, and Bailey—

lingering in the living room long after everyone else had departed. Their father had headed up to bed, smiling fondly at his girls and cautioning them not to stay up *too* late, like they were still kids.

The cupcake box sat open on the floor, empty now, though Charlotte kept snatching stray bits of icing off the sides of the box.

Elinor knew she should go home—it was just a short walk down the street from her dad's house to hers—but Dory had fallen asleep cuddled in her lap after conning every single person at the party into throwing her ball for her, and Elinor didn't have the heart to wake her up to walk her home.

Tomorrow would come early, and she needed to get started on figuring out a new containment system for the dog…but it had been so long since she'd just hung out with her sisters, and she found herself sinking deeper into her dad's old chair.

"She always wanted to go to England," Anne added as Bailey bent to inspect the old-fashioned portrait of their mother nestled among her favorite things. "Walk in Austen's footsteps."

"At least she didn't name you after Charlotte Lucas," Charlotte grumbled from the floor. "I mean *Charlotte Lucas*." She lay on her back, staring up at the ceiling with a plastic champagne flute resting on her stomach.

Bailey glanced over at Charlotte with an anxious frown. "Is it awful that I don't know what that means?" Bailey and Anne had only been dating a couple of months, and she still seemed nervous whenever she was around their family, worried about making a good impression.

Charlotte waved a hand, like the pope granting clemency.

"*Pride and Prejudice.* Charlotte Lucas is like the *worst* character."

"Hey. I like Charlotte Lucas," Elinor protested.

"She marries Mr. Collins. *Mr. Collins.*"

"She's very pragmatic," Elinor argued. "Something you could consider emulating."

"*I* should have been Elinor," Charlotte insisted, pouring the last of the prosecco into her plastic champagne flute. "You can be Charlotte."

Elinor bristled. "Are you implying I'm a Charlotte Lucas?"

"Elinor Dashwood is pragmatic, too," Anne interjected, trying to head off the conflict, but Charlotte was already smirking at Elinor.

"Not so funny when you're the one marrying Mr. Collins, is it?"

"I always thought of you as more of a Marianne," Anne tried again.

"Or a Lydia," Elinor muttered.

Charlotte sat up with a snap. "Excuse me?"

"I'm lost," Bailey confessed, retreating to the couch to sink down beside Anne.

"Elinor and Marianne Dashwood are sisters from *Sense and Sensibility*," Anne explained. "And Charlotte Lucas marries one of the most obnoxious Jane Austen characters ever written because she doesn't think she'll have any better options. Don't worry. None of us expect you to remember any of this. Just because everyone in this family is obsessed with Austen doesn't mean you're expected to be."

"I'm not obsessed," Charlotte argued—as if she wasn't the one who dropped the most Austen references into everyday conversation.

"Anne is from *Persuasion*," Elinor said, "which is my personal favorite."

"At least I'm dating a Darcy," Charlotte declared smugly.

Elinor didn't quite manage to restrain her skeptical snort—not that she tried that hard.

She'd been relieved when Charlotte's dickhead boyfriend had decided not to grace them with his presence tonight. Warren had all the sensitivity of a sledgehammer. The last time he'd met Anne, he'd asked her if she was "the cancer one or the library one." Which was bad enough, but he had met her three times already. Anne's face had flushed bright red—her pale complexion was inherited from their mother, along with the ovarian cancer gene—and she'd stammered until Elinor had stepped in and reminded Warren—again— that *she* was the librarian and Anne worked at the Bluebell Inn.

Dealing with Warren was the last thing Anne needed on the night when they celebrated her fifth year of being cancer-free.

But Charlotte's death glare when Elinor impugned Warren's Darcyness was epic. "At least I date at all. Your girly bits have been gathering dust for three years."

"I date," Elinor protested, her face flushing.

"There's a new physical therapist out at the Estates. I could set you up with him," Charlotte offered. "You should be honored. I'm giving you first dibs at fresh meat, before I even try to pimp him out to Mags and Kendall."

Magda, Kendall, and Charlotte had been best friends since kindergarten, so taking priority over them was a big deal, but Elinor frowned. "I'm not sure if that's an honor or a sign of how pathetic you think I am."

"Not pathetic. Just…needy." At Elinor's glower, she explained sweetly. "Like you need a man."

"A woman needs a man like a fish needs a bicycle," Anne quoted, raising her own plastic champagne flute in a mock toast.

Charlotte rolled her eyes. "I'm not saying you need a man because you're incomplete without one. I'm saying you need a man because you're still hung up on Big Bad Levi."

Elinor glared. "That's ridiculous. I'm not hung up on anyone. And I've dated plenty of guys since Levi and I broke up. Some for months."

"But you weren't into any of them. Frankly, it was painful to watch. You have deeply prudish tendencies—"

"I do not!"

"So I bet you didn't even sleep with any of them. You never got closure."

Okay, yes, she hadn't slept with them, but seriously, what kind of argument was that? "So now I need to have sex with random men for closure?"

"Not random," Charlotte argued. "That's the whole point. Someone *good*. Someone you actually like. You imprinted on Levi like a duckling, and now you can't even *see* other men when they're standing right in front of you."

"I like Levi," Anne interjected gently.

"No." Charlotte stabbed a finger in Anne's direction. "We are not Team Levi in this house. We are Team Closure and Moving On with Your Life."

"I *have* moved on," Elinor snapped.

"Then why did Magda text me that she saw Levi with your dog?"

"She gets out!" The dog in question stirred at the volume of Elinor's voice, so she lowered it, stroking a hand down

Dory's silky side to soothe her back to sleep. "Levi is the one people call when they see her running around, because the animal control number goes to him, but the only time I see him is when he brings her back."

"Fine. Whatever. But I'm not wasting fresh meat on you if you're in denial. I'll give the new guy to Mags."

"I think the new guy might have something to say about that."

Charlotte flapped a hand dismissively and downed her prosecco.

Anne pressed her lips together to hide a smile—and Elinor felt herself smiling because Anne was smiling.

Anne had been fine for years now, but Elinor still found herself watching for any sign of exhaustion, any hint of a symptom. She was sagging a little on the couch now, leaning against Bailey, but her smile was sleepily content as she tangled her fingers with Bailey's.

The two hadn't been together long, but Elinor still felt something warm spreading through her chest every time they looked at one another. Anne was the best of them, and there was something special there. A softness. A care that made her feel like Anne was getting the kind of perfect love story she deserved.

But she still looked tired enough to rouse Elinor's mother hen instincts. "It's getting late. We should probably all get some sleep." She shifted in the chair, gently moving Dory so the dog came awake in her lap, her head jerking up.

"All right, *mom*," Charlotte grumbled. "It's barely ten thirty."

"Some of us have a lot to do this weekend. I think I'm going to have to install security cameras just to figure out how Dory's getting out so I can get Levi off my back."

"You should put a GPS tracker on her collar and track her from your phone," Charlotte suggested, scraping the last fingerful of frosting off the lid of the cupcake box.

Elinor's eyebrows arched. "You know, that's actually a really good idea."

"You don't have to sound so surprised." Charlotte glared over the lip of her plastic champagne flute. "I am smart. I did graduate magna cum laude from med school. Not that anyone in this town cares."

"Hey," Anne soothed, always trying to make peace. "People care. We care. We're proud of you."

"Very proud," Elinor confirmed. She'd always felt like the town was watching her. *That Rodriguez girl, she's going places.* They'd all thought she would cure cancer, put Pine Hollow on the map—but it was little Charlotte who'd become a doctor.

And Charlotte who glared at her now, as if she was being sarcastic.

"No one takes me seriously," Charlotte griped—a familiar refrain Elinor wanted to be sympathetic to, but it had lost its impact after the seven-thousandth repetition. "Mr. Blake kept insisting today that he didn't want me, he wanted a *real* doctor, a *grown-up* doctor. I tried to tell him that I *am* grown-up, and that *old* doctors went to med school in the dark ages before we even knew half the stuff we know now, so I'm *better*, but does any of that matter? Of course not. I am so sick of the Doogie Howser jokes."

"That's what you get for being a genius," Bailey teased— she and Anne the perfect matched set, both so kind, and always trying to put everyone else at ease.

"I *am* a genius," Charlotte groused.

"And modest, too," Elinor drawled, earning a glare.

Elinor couldn't decide whether Charlotte's ego was impressive or horrifying. But then she often walked that line with Charlotte. Her baby sister was brilliant, there was no denying that, but she was also constantly aggrieved that she'd been short-changed by the universe.

Which, admittedly, she definitely had.

Elinor had been fifteen when their mother died. Charlotte had been nine, young enough she didn't really remember a time before their mom got sick. Not like Elinor did. The sound of her mother's voice reading *Sense and Sensibility* to her...the shrieks of laughter as they built a pillow fort in the living room. Charlotte didn't have that.

She'd always been hungry for attention, for praise, but after they lost their mom, it seemed like no amount was enough. When Anne was diagnosed at nineteen—while Charlotte was a senior in high school—everything had become about cancer again. It didn't matter how impressive Charlotte was—valedictorian, National Merit Scholar—no one had the emotional bandwidth for her. Elinor tried to be sympathetic, she did, but they'd *all* lived through it. It had sucked for everyone, especially Anne.

And then Katie...

Elinor pushed that thought away. Refocusing on the happy. Tonight was a celebration.

"It is getting late." Anne pushed up off the couch. "We probably should be heading out."

Charlotte grumbled about Elinor sucking all the fun out of everything, but she also wrapped her arms around Anne and squeezed extra tight as they all gathered up their coats. The late September night had that perfect hint of fall in the air, just chilly enough to feel brisk and invigorating.

Elinor hugged Anne one last time before her little sister

climbed into Bailey's car. Dory sniffed a pine cone, investigating the front yard as Elinor hesitated in the driveway, studying Charlotte, who was swaying slightly as she read something on her phone.

"You sure you're okay to drive?"

"God, could you stop?" Charlotte's head snapped up. "I am an adult, you know. I was just checking to see if Warren could pick me up." Elinor pursed her lips, and irritation instantly flashed on Charlotte's face. *"Don't."*

"I didn't say anything!"

"I can see you thinking it. I don't know why you hate him."

"I don't hate him." *I might hate him.* "He just never seems to be very good to you."

"You're one to talk. You're still hung up on Levi after he practically left you at the altar—"

"I'm not hung up on him! When are you going to stop harping on that?"

"When are you going to stop treating me like I'm twelve? I am an adult, with a great job, a gorgeous condo, and a fabulous man who is everything I've ever wanted, and you don't get to tell me he isn't!"

"What makes him so fabulous? The fact that he's constantly standing you up and can't be bothered to remember anything about your family even though he's met us like five times?"

"He's *busy.* And he has a lot on his mind. Not everyone has an encyclopedic memory for every random-ass detail about this family."

"I just hate seeing you with these guys who keep stringing you along and making you feel like you have to beg for their attention. You deserve so much better, Char."

"Warren is *amazing,*" Charlotte snapped. Her phone

binged and she looked down at it, a flash of something like hurt moving across her face so quickly Elinor almost wasn't sure she'd seen it. Then she spun on her heel, stalking toward the sidewalk. "I'm going to Magda's."

"I can give you a ride home," Elinor called after her, shortening Dory's leash so the dog abandoned the mailbox she'd been investigating. "Or you can sleep in my guest room."

Her sister didn't stop walking, her heels clicking down the sidewalk toward the heart of town.

"Charlotte?"

"I'm fine, Elle. I just don't want to be around you right now. Okay?"

Elinor sucked in a breath at the vivid sense of déjà vu from Charlotte's teen years. Their relationship had always been more than strictly sisterly. Their mom had gotten sick when Charlotte was so small, and Elinor had been determined to help out any way she could that she'd been sort of a pseudo-mom even before their mother passed away.

Their father was amazing, but when it came to the girly stuff, Elinor felt like she'd been the one guiding Charlotte through life. Until a few years ago, when Charlotte had started pushing back against that—hard. Now it seemed like Elinor couldn't say anything without Charlotte taking it as a criticism or a judgment on her maturity. She didn't know how to talk to her sister anymore—and it only seemed to be getting worse.

Katie would have known what to do.

The thought popped into her head out of nowhere, startling her with its power and clarity. Three years later, and the hole Katie's death had left in her life still felt like a gaping void.

Losing her mom had been horrible, but she'd been braced for it. They'd had so long to figure out how to say goodbye, how to accept it. It hadn't been enough—she wasn't sure anything ever could have been—but they'd had time.

But Katie…Katie had just been gone one day. Her best friend for twenty years. The person who knew her in ways no one else ever had. Just ripped right out of her life by the roots, leaving a bleeding hole that never quite seemed to heal.

She had lots of casual friends. People in town knew her, and she got along well with everyone. Her karaoke birthday parties were always packed with well-wishers, but she'd never connected with anyone else like she had with Katie. No one just *got* her.

Even more than Levi, *Katie* had been her soul mate. The person she went to whenever she needed to talk. Whenever she needed to figure something out. And now…

How did you get over that?

Dory bumped against her leg, and Elinor tore her eyes off her sister's retreating form. Her sweet Aussie sat at her ankles, gazing up at her adoringly—as if she'd somehow known Elinor needed to be jostled out of her thoughts.

"Come on," she murmured, ruffling the softest ears on the planet. "Let's go home."

Chapter Five

The Vandal of Pine Hollow strikes again! In the latest of a string of heinous vandalisms, the hoodlum responsible defaced the rear wall of the Cup last week, leaving all of Pine Hollow to wonder who is next. And when will our dear chief catch the responsible party?

—*Pine Hollow Newsletter*, Monday, October 11

Levi stared at the graffiti splashed across the back of the Cup on Friday morning, his arms folded.

At his side, Mac stood with his hands on his hips and a look of grudging respect on his face. "If anything, I'm impressed," the Cup's owner acknowledged. "That's some next-level stealth to tag this entire wall six feet below where I sleep. And the deliveries start early in this alley. Whole thing must've taken, what? Two, three hours?"

Levi didn't comment—and Mac had been his friend long enough that he wasn't remotely fazed by the silence.

"Heard they got the inn a few days ago. How many others are there?"

"Two." No cameras back here. Just like there hadn't been at any of the other spots their budding artist had hit. Levi studied the slashes of red and black. They looked angry to him, but what did he know about art? "You mind if I have Marjorie come down and take a look at it before you repaint it?" He'd already taken photos on his phone, but there was a feel to it in person, and he wanted her take.

"I figured I'd leave it for a while, see if it grows on me." Mac shoved his hands into his pockets, rocking on his heels. "Who knows? Kid could be the next Banksy." He shrugged, as if physically shrugging off any concern about the ten-foot swath of vandalism, and turned to Levi with an easy smile. "You coming to poker night tomorrow?"

Levi jerked his chin up in a nod. "Might be late." He and Mac and Ben usually headed to Connor's for poker night on Wednesdays, but with Ben's schedule shaken up by wedding planning, they'd had to move it to Saturday this week. Levi had an appointment to meet that counselor in Stowe on Saturday afternoon, and weekend traffic could be a bitch this time of year with all the tourists gawking at the leaves.

"I'll see you there," Mac said, already heading toward the delivery door of his diner. "Good luck catching the Vandal of Pine Hollow."

His final words were spookily melodramatic, and Levi shook his head, fighting a grin. At least Mac had taken the vandalism better than the owners of the Pine Hollow Inn. There'd been no shortage of hand-wringing and bemoaning the possibility of *permanent* damage to the *historic* bricks. The word *defacement* had been used so many times that it would have made an excellent drinking game.

Levi wasn't sure he found the graffiti to be as much of an insult to history as the owners of the inn, but neither was he as cavalier as Mac. Someone was running around town vandalizing private property, and even if it was just a bunch of teenagers, they couldn't go unchecked.

Taking one last look at the paint, he headed toward the mouth of the alley, pulling out his phone to text Marjorie. He lifted it to use the voice-to-text feature, pausing to glance back over his shoulder. It might just be a meaningless prank. Some kids with too much time on their hands. Harmless. But his Spidey sense was twitching, and he had a feeling there was more to the story.

Or maybe that was just sleep deprivation talking.

Either way, he needed a second opinion.

Then he turned back around and saw a flash of white-and-brown fur streak across the mouth of the alley.

Dory.

It had been two weeks. He'd almost started to think Elinor had managed to keep the damn animal under lock and key.

More the fool he.

Levi swore under his breath and broke into a run.

🐾

"I see Elinor's dog got out again."

"Don't start," Levi grumbled, walking past Kaye with Dory heeling angelically on the leash Elinor had dropped back at the station's front desk the morning after Dory's last escape act.

"Linda Hilson still wants a comment on your relationship status!" Kaye called after him as he headed down the hall.

"Tell her to stop texting and driving, or I'm going to

have to give her another ticket!" he shouted back without pausing.

He opened the door to the interrogation room, which tended to get more use as a drunk tank when someone needed to sober up, and ushered the dog inside before unclipping the leash and quickly shutting the door. She whined, the high-pitched sound perfectly calibrated to play on his sympathies—but after chasing her halfway across town, he didn't have any sympathy left. Even when she started a high, yelping bark. He was tough. He could withstand her.

"*Stay,*" he said through the door, heading back to his office.

It wasn't even noon yet. She'd gotten out early today. Usually it was nearly three before he got the first loose dog call. It would be hours before Elinor got off work and he could read her the riot act for letting the damn dog get loose again. And he had that freaking therapy appointment.

The doctor had texted him earlier, as he was returning to the station, to say an appointment had opened up in the afternoon today if that was better for him, and he'd accepted it before it had sunk in that he'd have Elinor's dog all day.

He should take her to Ally's shelter. Ally had taken over Furry Friends last year and added a doggie day care service, so he knew she could handle the dog—but she was friends with Elinor. She would undoubtedly call her as soon as school was out, and Elinor would pick up the dog and Levi wouldn't be able to see her. To impress on her how completely unacceptable this pattern was.

Maybe he could leave the dog in the interrogation room while he ran up to Stowe and back. He wouldn't be gone long—

"Why is there a dog on the fire truck? Did we get a new mascot?"

No.

The interrogation room door didn't have the kind of push handle she'd opened at Magda's. It was a freaking *knob*. She didn't have *thumbs*.

Levi was on his feet before Marjorie finished speaking, moving quickly toward the engine bay, where, sure enough, Dory was perched happily on the roof of the cab, tail wagging, her shoulders lowered in a come-play-with-me crouch.

"Hey, Levi," Dean, the fire captain, called conversationally. "That your dog?"

"Elinor's." He frowned up at Dory, wondering how he could lure her down. He still hadn't replenished his treat supply.

"That's right. I heard you two were getting back together."

"We're not back—" Levi bit off the sharp denial. "Her dog is a public nuisance," he forced himself to explain more calmly. "She was running loose, herding cars on Main Street. I locked her in the interrogation room, but she got out somehow."

"Uh-huh," Dean said—without an ounce of belief. And Levi had to stop himself from grinding his molars. Why did people believe everything they read in that newsletter?

First priority was getting the damn dog down before she hurt herself. What had Astrid done the last time?

Feeling like a fool, he lifted his hand up in the air, cupping it like he was holding a tennis ball. "Dory, uh, want the ball?"

The Aussie's ears instantly pricked forward. Her eyes sharpened on his hand.

And she leapt.

Marjorie let out a little shriek. Levi lunged forward—as if he could catch her in midair. But she was already airborne, and there was no way he'd get to her in time.

The dog seemed to fly in slow motion. He'd seen her jump over and off things before—benches, gazebos—but the roof of the fire truck was several feet above his head, at least eleven feet in the air, and she'd gone full Superman, on a trajectory straight toward the unforgiving side of the ambulance and the hard concrete floor.

And he was the one who'd called her, who'd encouraged her to fling herself off the truck, kamikaze-style.

Visions of telling Elinor he'd killed her dog flashed before his eyes. Dory was going to slam into the ambulance any second—

But she somehow pivoted against the side of the ambulance, bouncing off it with a neat little flip—her entire body going upside down for a moment—before landing deftly on the ground on all fours and racing toward him without so much as breaking stride. She didn't stop until she reached Levi's feet, gathering herself up in a perfect sit, gazing attentively at the hand he hadn't realized was still cupped as if it held a ball, all of his muscles locked immobile by dread.

"Jesus," Levi whispered—as Dean let out a bark of laughter.

Aaron—the deputy who wasn't even on shift today, since it was Hunter's day, but always seemed to be hanging around anyway—whooped. "That was awesome. How did you train him to do that?"

"Her," Levi corrected absently. As if his heart hadn't just stopped.

She was still staring at his hand, waiting for him to throw a ball that didn't even exist.

Remembering what Astrid had done, he lowered his hand and relaxed his palm, showing the waiting dog that he wasn't holding anything. Dory didn't seem to mind, licking his fingertips and wagging her tail. Thankfully, he still had the leash in his back pocket, and he clipped it quickly to her collar.

"I'm not letting you out of my sight," he told the dog, who gazed up at him adoringly.

He turned to find Marjorie watching him entirely too closely. He cleared his throat, fighting the heat rising to his face. "Did you have a chance to look at the new graffiti?"

See? All business.

Marjorie smiled gently. "I did. Shall we talk?"

"My office."

She trailed after him, still smiling when she sank into one of the chairs he now knew wasn't nearly as comfortable as it looked. He should really think about replacing them. He shut his office door, taking his own chair—and frowning at the dog. What was he supposed to do with her?

"Down," he tried.

The little Aussie instantly dropped to her stomach, gazing at him like he was her personal deity.

"Uh...good dog."

"She's smart, that one," Marjorie commented.

"Too smart," he grumbled. "So what do you think of the vandalism?" he asked, bringing the subject back to something he actually felt equipped to handle. "Bored teens?"

"Probably," she agreed. "But I do find it strange that no one seems to have seen or heard anything. The local kids aren't usually quite this good at covering their tracks. I can put out some feelers. See if anyone comes forward. It's probably nothing to worry about."

He studied her eyes. "But?"

"But I'll feel better when we know who's doing this, and why, so we can redirect those artistic impulses in a more constructive direction."

Levi nodded, in complete agreement.

The owners of the Pine Hollow Inn were eager for him to file charges against whoever had defaced their precious historic site. To them, whoever had done this was a bad seed and needed to be punished. He knew that mentality. He'd been that bad seed, growing up. The one so many people had been so quick to wash their hands of.

Who knows what would have happened to him if he'd broken the rules in any other town, but he hadn't. He'd gotten picked up trying to break into a car in Elton's town. And, thankfully, Elton hadn't taken one look at him and seen trouble. He'd worked as hard as he could to keep as many kids out of the system as possible. To listen to the kids who thought no one was listening and turn them in a different direction.

Levi tried to run his town the same way. Though he never felt like he was living up to Elton's legacy. How could he?

An alarm buzzed on his phone, alerting him that he needed to start toward Stowe if he was going to make it to his appointment on time. Dory perked up at the sound. He needed to figure out what to do with her.

He glanced at Marjorie. "Do you think you could keep an eye on her? I have that appointment in Stowe..."

She brightened when he mentioned the therapist, puffing up with a pride that made him almost wish he hadn't told her. "Why don't you take her with you?" Marjorie suggested. "She seems to love riding around with you, and you said you didn't want to let her out of your sight."

Of course she'd heard that. "I can't just leave her in the car—"

"So take her in with you. Eugene's very relaxed. I'm sure he won't mind."

Levi glanced down at the dog. If he was honest, he didn't really want to leave her here to get into God-knew-what trouble before he could get back. At least if she was with him, he knew she wasn't herding traffic. He was responsible for this dog until Elinor was done with work, and he should be back well before the after-school program she helped with let out.

So he found himself loading Dory into the car five minutes later. He cracked the window for her to stick her head out and queued up his audiobook for the drive. "I hope you like Ludlum."

Chapter Six

Sources at the chief's office have refused
to comment on his relationship with a
certain librarian, but one has to wonder
why he would bother to deny something
so obvious when he's clearly been teaching
her dog new tricks.

—*Pine Hollow Newsletter*,
Monday, October 11

Elinor stared at the empty dog crate as realization sank through her and landed in her stomach in a pool of dread.

She was going to have to call Levi.

For two weeks, Dory had been an angel. No more escape attempts. No more pissed-off chief of police.

Elinor had actually started to wonder if her dog was somehow smart enough to *know* she was on camera and had given up when Elinor installed the motion-activated system.

No such luck.

Fortunately, thanks to the cameras and the recorded feed she had accessed on her phone, she now knew exactly how Dory had gotten out this time—she'd popped the spring-loaded hinge on the crate door, opened the mudroom door with the quick moves of too much practice, jumped up onto the countertops, and wriggled out the kitchen window above the sink Elinor was *sure* she'd locked, and then, in the backyard, dragged a lawn chair Elinor had been convinced would be too heavy for her to move across the patio to use as a launching pad to leap over the eight-foot fence.

Unfortunately, the GPS tracker Elinor had ordered for Dory's collar hadn't arrived yet. So she had no idea where her escape-artist dog had gone after she hopped the fence.

Usually, when Dory got out, by the time Elinor got home from school, there was either a text on her phone from someone saying they'd found her or Levi's Explorer waiting in her driveway with a tall, frowning man in the front seat with her dog. But today her driveway was empty and there was no message.

Worry whispered in her ear. What if something had happened to her? What if she'd gotten lost? Elinor hadn't realized how much she'd come to rely on Levi bringing Dory back from her escapades until he wasn't there.

Astrid was supposed to spend the night tonight. Ben and Ally had a premarital counseling session with the minister officiating their wedding, and Elinor had volunteered for some extra Astrid time—but if her goddaughter arrived when Dory was missing, she would be panicked. Then they'd *both* be panicked, and that wouldn't help anyone.

She had to keep it together. And call Levi—no matter how galling it was going to be to go groveling to him for help.

Or maybe she could call the town dispatcher. Levi would still get the message, but she wouldn't have to beg him directly—

The sound of a car pulling into the driveway cut off her thought, and Elinor bolted toward the front door, her tablet with the video evidence of Dory's escape still clutched in one hand. She burst out the front door, and there he was, calm as anything in the driver's seat of his Explorer with Dory on the passenger side, her little paws braced on the dashboard.

Relief crashed into Elinor—with a heavy anger chaser.

Had he done this on purpose to teach her a lesson? To make her worry? Hadn't he threatened consequences if she couldn't keep Dory penned? Was this his way of following through? To scare her? To remind her that he had the power?

Levi opened the car door, and Dory bounced out.

Elinor charged toward them, every molecule vibrating with anger. "Where have you been?"

He didn't react to her anger other than a slow upward slide of one eyebrow. He'd never reacted when she got mad, and that infuriating calm inevitably threw gasoline on the fire of her rage. How could he just *stand there*?

"I had an appointment," he said, so freaking calm she wanted to scream. "Figured she could ride along with me. Unless you'd rather I'd left her herding cars."

Her anger cracked, reason shining through the crevices to remind her that he *had* found her dog and brought her back. Again.

Dory wriggled with delight, silently begging for attention, and Elinor crouched down to greet her properly.

"Thank you," she forced herself to say as she straightened. She lifted the tablet she still held in one hand. "It looks like I need better locks on my kitchen windows."

He eyed the tablet as the video footage she'd been

reviewing played on a loop. After a beat of silence, he said, "Your grass needs mowing."

And there it was again. Anger. Bright and shining.

"My lawn is fine," she snapped. He had given up the right to comment on the state of her lawn the second he broke up with her. "The mower is on the fritz. Besides, it's going to snow soon."

She could almost swear he muttered "Not that soon," but he didn't even move his lips, so she couldn't be sure.

"So that's your solution?" he asked louder. "Cameras?"

"The cameras show me where I have weakness in my defenses. I ordered a GPS for her collar so I can track her with my phone, but it's on back order."

"Don't suppose you'd share that GPS link with me. Since I'm the one who always ends up tracking her."

It was a reasonable request, but she was still too annoyed with him to simply agree. "I'm hoping that won't be necessary once I remove her avenues for escape."

"She can open doors."

"Yeah, I know."

"Not just the push-down handles," he insisted. "Actual knobs."

"I know."

Levi frowned. "She doesn't have thumbs."

"Not that I know of. Though it would explain a lot."

"Hi, Uncle Levi. Hi, Aunt Elinor. Hi, Dory!" Astrid called, advancing up the driveway, her voice getting brighter and more excited with each greeting. Levi was still holding the leash, and Dory nearly choked herself in her excitement to get to Astrid.

"Hi, Astrid," Elinor called back, fixing a glare on Levi. "Just let her go. She's not going to run off now that Astrid and I are here. She only escapes because she doesn't like being left alone."

Irritation moved stealthily behind Levi's blank cop stare, but he unhooked the leash. Dory instantly scrambled the last few feet to twine around Astrid's legs, making the girl giggle.

"Why don't you and Dory head inside," Elinor suggested. "I'll be right there."

"Can we watch more *Doctor Who*? He *has* to see Rose Tyler. They wouldn't have teased that she was able to get out of that parallel universe if she wasn't coming back."

"After homework," Elinor reminded her. "Go on in and get started. I'll make us an after-school snack in a minute. Bagel bites sound good?"

"Yes!" Astrid bounced, making Dory yip with excitement. "Come on, Dory."

Astrid and Dory raced into the house, Elinor taking her eyes off Levi to watch them go. He spoke while her back was still turned.

"You guys are watching *Doctor Who*?"

Tension gripped Elinor's shoulders, but she forced them to relax as she slowly turned back to face him. "We're on Donna's season and just got our first glimpse of Rose, building up to the big finale. Astrid's very invested in the love story. Trapped in parallel universes makes for big unrequited drama."

"You always liked that part, too—"

"I've matured," Elinor snapped, cutting him off before he could show off how well he'd once known her. That wasn't who they were anymore. "I like Amy and Rory now. The sweet, uncomplicated guy who *talks* about his feelings and isn't so busy being all brooding and *this is for the best* that he sabotages both of their happiness just because of a little rift in the space-time continuum. *Rory* shows up—even after they kill him off."

"Fine. You like Rory." Levi held up his hands in surrender. "How long have you been showing Astrid *Doctor Who*?"

"She's old enough for it," Elinor argued, defensive.

"I never said she wasn't, Elinor."

She caught the threads of her animosity, reining it back in. "Sorry. A few months. We started in the summer. It was Katie's favorite."

"I remember."

Elinor swallowed over the knot of emotion that was suddenly clogging her throat.

Of course he remembered. Levi had sat through countless dinners that had devolved into debates over the relative hotness of David Tennant and Matt Smith, or which season had the best storylines, or which companion was the most badass.

"She would have loved that there's a female Doctor," Levi commented—and Elinor had to look away. Because she would have.

Elinor considered it her duty to introduce Astrid to all her mother's obsessions. It had been vitally important to Katie that Astrid knew she was in *love* with *Doctor Who* and *Star Trek: The Next Generation*—and that she'd thought *The Lord of the Rings* was excruciatingly boring and could deliver sermons on how Drusilla was the most underutilized character on *Buffy the Vampire Slayer*.

So Elinor showed Astrid the shows, and they talked about her mom. Astrid was always hungry to know which characters Katie had liked. Which ones she'd complained about. They'd worked their way through the X-Men canon last spring—even watching the new ones Elinor hadn't been able to bring herself to watch without Katie, who'd been obsessed with superpowers—and then started on *Doctor Who* in the summer.

There were still shows that were hard for Elinor to watch—some that hadn't even been out when Katie was alive. Elinor would be sitting there, watching *The Mandalorian*, and suddenly she'd be crying because Katie would have loved the show so much and she'd never see it. Just like she'd never see how awesome Astrid was now that she was in her tween years. It wasn't fair.

Elinor kept her face averted, working to get her freaking emotions under control. She didn't show this stuff to Levi anymore. He'd forfeited his right to know what was going on in her heart.

For a while, Astrid had come over while Ben had poker nights with Levi, Mac, and Connor. But lately a lot of those poker nights had turned into "girls' nights" so Ally could spend some special time with Astrid and get to know her better—which was great. Ally and Ben were getting married, and they both wanted to make sure Astrid was one hundred percent on board with that, but Elinor still wanted to hold on to that last piece of Katie as tight as she could. When Ally and Ben had started going to premarital counseling on Friday nights, Elinor hadn't been able to volunteer fast enough to take Astrid for the night.

And now her night was wasting.

"I should get inside."

"Doggie day care," Levi reminded her, the tone sounding a lot like an order. "Or at least get her an obstacle course to slow her down. She was herding cars, Elinor."

"I'm working on it," she snapped, the words a little sharper than she'd intended, but she still felt exposed after going a little maudlin about Katie in front of him. He saw *everything*, and he knew her history.

Sometimes she wished she'd just been able to erase all that history the second he broke up with her—or at least his memory of it, *Eternal Sunshine*–style. It wasn't fair for him to know every little thing she'd ever told him when she trusted him, now that they were over.

His hands had been slowly coiling and uncoiling the leash as they talked, but now he tucked it into his back pocket, giving her a farewell chin jerk and heading back toward his Explorer.

As if he knew she was too brittle to argue anymore. As if he knew her.

She pivoted on her heel and stalked back into the house, pausing in the foyer to redo her ponytail and toe off the shoes she hadn't gotten around to taking off when she got home and found Dory missing.

Astrid was already set up at the kitchen table, her math homework spread out in front of her as she hunched so close to the table that her nose practically touched the paper.

She took after her father, with his reddish hair and his features—but the posture, the way she moved, her *expressions*, sometimes those were so Katie that it took Elinor's breath away. The flicker of mischief in her smile. The skepticism in her sideways looks.

The way she hunched over her paper when she was working on something, so focused that her nose practically touched the paper. How many times had Elinor looked over in class during a test and seen Katie *exactly* like that?

Emotion caught in her throat.

"Are you and Uncle Levi getting back together?"

Well, that effectively banished all her sappy feelings.

"No," Elinor said, her tone brooking no uncertainty. "We are not. Bagel bites?" She moved around the island as Dory perked up from her position at Elinor's feet and came to investigate the wonders of the refrigerator.

"Yes, please," Astrid answered, bending back over her homework. Then she glanced up, out of the corner of her eye, and that mischievous Katie grin flickered. "Are you sure?"

Elinor rolled her eyes. "Yes, I'm sure. Now hurry up with that homework. I wanna watch *Doctor Who*."

Astrid giggled, and turned back to her math.

🐾

Levi drummed his fingers on the steering wheel, glowering at the road and barely seeing it. He couldn't stop thinking about Elinor's overgrown lawn.

His therapist would probably have a field day with that.

Not that the guy he'd talked to today in Stowe was *his therapist*. Just someone he'd talked to one time, to humor Marjorie. He'd done his part.

Words penetrated his thoughts, and he noticed his audiobook was still playing in the background. He flicked it off, raking a hand through his hair and swearing under his breath as he realized where his autopilot had taken him.

The old mill had been run-down when they were kids. It had looked like it was on the brink of falling down twenty years ago, and the last few decades hadn't been kind. Levi pulled his Explorer in front of the dilapidated building and cut the engine, staring through the fall twilight at the crumbling structure. A slow drizzle coated the windshield in mist, blurring the view.

Hunter was still on shift, and Levi had checked in when

he got back from his appointment. Kaye would call him if they needed him. He could afford a minute to get his head together. Staring at the wreck of the mill.

How many times had he and Elinor come out here when they were kids? Fifty? A hundred?

Not that it mattered now. It had become a fitting sort of metaphor for their relationship—a crumbling ruin.

Levi drummed his fingers on the steering wheel again, the video of her yard vivid in his mind. He should have been focused on Dory's gravity-defying leap over the fence, but instead all he could think was that no one was taking care of Elinor.

No one ever had, except him. She'd been the strong one for her sisters—even for her parents, when her mom was sick. She was always taking care of others. But who took care of her? That freaking grass was driving him crazy.

The smug therapist would probably remind him that her grass was none of his damn business.

Not that the therapist had been smug. He'd been calm. Neutral. Annoyingly neutral. Levi was the neutral one. He'd never considered how obnoxious it was to say things to someone who accepted them so calmly. It had felt like an argument, that calm acceptance.

What brings you here? The therapist had asked after he'd gotten settled and apologized for bringing Dory, who proceeded to sleep through the entire appointment.

A colleague I respect asked me to come, he'd explained—and the therapist had nodded, his pencil scratching loudly in the unnatural quiet of his office as he made a note.

The note seemed to scratch on forever, until Levi— who knew the power of silences better than anyone—found himself explaining, *She's concerned about me.*

Oh?

That I'm not sleeping.

How long have you been having trouble sleeping?

Since the summer. That pencil. Scratching. *I made the wrong call.*

He hadn't meant to say it. That was all he'd said, but the man had nodded as if it he'd said more. As if those words were a confession. And maybe they were.

He didn't explain about Britt Wells. About how he should have done more. How he'd allowed her to die on his watch. The little boy she'd left behind.

The cost of his mistake had been a life. But they didn't talk about that. They'd talked about nothing for the rest of the session. Nonsense. How much he worked and what his hobbies were. They might as well have been talking about the weather.

But he still kicked himself the entire drive back to Pine Hollow. He still felt that creep of shame inching up the back of his neck. His father's voice filling his head. *Weakness.*

He couldn't allow himself weakness. There wasn't room for it.

He'd kept his calm at the session, his cool veneer only cracking once when the therapist had asked him if he was ever really *off* the job. He'd snapped something about Marjorie telling him that, and the man's eyebrows had arched up gently as he scratched on that paper, and he calmly—always so calmly—explained that Marjorie hadn't told him anything.

Levi had been good at shutting it off a few years ago—hell, even a year ago, he'd been able to turn off the job—but ever since this summer...

He knew he scheduled himself for too many shifts, but he

didn't want anything else falling through the cracks. Any*one* else. There were worse things in the world than being all work and no play when the safety of his town was at stake.

He didn't really have time for more sessions.

He'd never been a big talker anyway. It felt uncomfortable. Talking for an hour. All the psychobabble nonsense. He knew it worked for other people, but he didn't need it. He could handle himself. He always had.

The sleeping thing was just a phase. He'd power through. He was stubborn. Too mule-headed to let his problems win.

That stubbornness had gotten him in trouble more times than he could count. Back in school, when he would refuse to answer his teachers, staring them down. None of them had appreciated the battle of wills with an eight-year-old, but he'd learned early to keep his mouth shut. Silent wasn't dumb. Better to be the bad kid than the stupid one.

Jackson men aren't weak.

And they didn't need a therapist telling them that they worked too hard. Working hard was good. It was a virtue.

Levi had kept his word. He'd talked to the guy. Now he could get back to focusing on work. Figuring out who was tagging walls around town. And catching Elinor's damn dog.

And if her yard was a disaster, it was none of his business.

As he turned back toward the road, his headlights panned over the FOR SALE sign, and Levi ignored the strange kick of *something* in his chest. It was just an old wreck of a building. And he had work to do.

Chapter Seven

The fall color was out in full force this weekend, leading to many a traffic jam as tourists flocked to our fair town, and many a packed hiking trail in our gorgeous mountains.

—*Pine Hollow Newsletter*,
Monday, October 18

R ise and shine, sunshine!"

Elinor flinched at the cheerful bellow and tried to hide beneath the covers, but they were whisked off her, forcing her to acknowledge the horrifying reality that her youngest sister was standing in the middle of her bedroom. "Charlotte?" She reached blindly for her glasses, fumbling on the bedside until her fingers closed on the familiar shape.

"Basic recognition. Excellent start." Charlotte clapped her hands as Elinor slipped on her glasses, and her sister's blurry form sharpened. "Come on, sleepyhead. Fall color waits for no woman!"

Elinor shied away from her enthusiasm, retreating to the opposite side of the bed in search of some covers that hadn't been snatched away by the sibling most likely to be murdered at seven a.m. on a Saturday morning. "What are you doing here? How did you get in?"

Dory barked and jumped up on the bed, coming to wiggle next to Elinor in her excitement that they had a visitor—and making it that much less likely that she would be able to get back to sleep. She'd been dimly aware of Dory leaving the bed, a vague sense of the loss of the warm little body pressed against her knees, but it hadn't registered enough to fully wake her up—and Dory hadn't barked. Shouldn't she have barked if there was an intruder? But Dory adored Charlotte, who could never seem to spoil her with enough cuddles and treats.

"I still have a key," her sister reminded her. "And I'm here because we need to get an early start, or all the good hikes will be overrun with tourists. It's peak fall color!"

Elinor belatedly noticed the skintight athletic gear Charlotte was wearing. From head to toe she was all Lycra and muscle, like an ad for a high-end lifestyle brand. Whereas Elinor's physique was more of the reading-is-my-favorite-cardio shape. Hiking with the zero-body-fat Energizer Bunny sounded like pure hell. "You're terrifying, you know that?"

"I do," Charlotte declared cheerfully. "Come on. The leaves are *perfect*, but it's supposed to storm tomorrow, and the wind's going to strip all the trees. It won't be this gorgeous again."

"Until next year," Elinor grumbled. "When it all happens again."

"Come on," Charlotte wheedled. "You know you don't want to say no to me."

"Why are you even here? You don't even like hiking with me. You're always waiting for me to catch up—"

Elinor broke off as she woke up fully and the pieces clicked together. "He stood you up again, didn't he?"

Charlotte's sunny smile flickered into a pout. "This isn't about Warren."

"It's always about Warren."

"I forgot how mean you are before coffee."

"You broke into my house!"

"Is it really breaking in if I have a key?"

"Go away." Elinor huddled deeper beneath the covers. "I'm taking back your key."

"Come on, Elle," Charlotte coaxed. "It's the most perfect day. You'll regret not coming with me. You know you will."

No, *Charlotte* would regret it if Elinor didn't come with her. Because Charlotte hated doing things by herself. "Can't you take Magda or Kendall? Or Anne?"

"Magda and Kendall both have to work, and Anne hates hiking."

"*I* hate hiking."

"But not *really*," Charlotte insisted. "And you'll do it for me. I know you will."

"I have other things planned today. I have a dress fitting for Ally's wedding. You can't just expect me to drop everything because your dickhead boyfriend stood you up again and the people you'd *rather* do stuff with are all busy. I have my own life. You can't just assume I'm always sitting around with nothing better to do than obey your commands."

"I wasn't assuming. I was inviting. I guess I won't do that again."

There was a sulk in her voice, but Elinor's instinctive response was pure snark. "Is that a promise?"

Something flickered in Charlotte's eyes, so like hers it was like looking in a mirror, though Charlotte had always been the pretty one. The one people wanted to do things for. The one people spoiled. Even Elinor.

But not before eight in the morning on one of the few days when she was actually able to sleep in. She loved working at the school, but mornings had never been her friend. And even on non-school days, Dory tended to wake her up at dawn. Was it really so wrong to just want to be allowed to sleep as late as humanly possible?

"Enjoy your fitting." Her sister spun on her heel—and Elinor's satisfaction that the human alarm clock was no longer in her room lasted about three seconds before it was swallowed up by guilt as her sleep-lagged brain finally processed what had flashed in Charlotte's eyes.

Hurt.

Crap.

"Charlotte!" Elinor hissed a curse under her breath and scrambled out of bed, Dory bouncing eagerly at her heels. But the next sound she heard was the front door slamming.

🐾

"Why do you look amazing and I look like a preteen playing dress-up in her mom's closet?" Deenie turned in front of the mirror, heaving a defeated sigh. "Though it might have something to do with the fact that you're built like a forties pinup and I'm built like a stick."

Elinor rolled her eyes at Deenie's attempt at humor. "You look amazing."

And she did. While Elinor was short and curvy, Deenie had the tall, willowy build of a model, and the hot-pink streaks in her blond hair somehow perfectly offset the rich burgundy of the bridesmaid dresses they were both wearing.

Ben and Ally had met and fallen in love last Christmas, so they'd decided, when they got engaged, that a Christmas wedding would be perfect. They were actually getting married the weekend before Christmas—so friends didn't have to choose between the wedding and spending Christmas with their own families—but even with that accommodation, only a few of Ally's New York friends would be able to make it.

Which was why, Elinor was sure, she had been tapped to be a bridesmaid alongside Deenie and Ally's friend Adriana from New York. Not that she didn't adore Ally. And Ben was one of her oldest friends. He was Katie's brother, and Astrid would be in the wedding. She was practically family. But she wasn't close to Ally the way Deenie and Ally were close.

Deenie and Ally had clicked from the word *go*, whereas Elinor always felt like she was slightly outside their bubble, looking in. She liked Ally, but there was always that distance.

But Ben had Levi, Mac, and Connor on his side of the aisle, and Ally needed three bridesmaids if they wanted to keep things even. So here she was, two months before the big day, trying on the bridesmaid dress that had just arrived and waiting for her turn with the seamstress who was fitting each of the dresses.

Ally's dress had arrived as well, along with the junior bridesmaid dress she'd picked out for Astrid. The bride had wanted to make a party of it, all of them getting their fittings together. Ally didn't have much living family—and Elinor knew that feeling, going to try on your wedding dress for the first time without your mom. So how could she say no when Ally invited her?

Ally's grandmother had come along as well and was currently talking to the seamstress with Astrid, who had already been pinned while they waited for Ally to finish being buttoned into her gown.

Deenie gave a little twirl in front of the mirrors. "The pockets are pretty fantastic."

"I do love a pocket," Elinor agreed. And the tea-length dresses with full skirts and white satin sashes were pretty adorable. The kind of bridesmaid dress she might actually wear again.

Elinor sipped the sparkling water they'd been given upon arrival at the bridal shop, and silently congratulated herself for not being even a tiny bit maudlin—even though this was the same shop where Katie had helped her buy her own wedding dress for the wedding that had never happened. Pine Hollow only had one bridal boutique.

Her lack of sentimental moping might have had something to do with the fact that she was still irritated with Charlotte and constantly—guiltily—checking her phone.

She'd sent Charlotte a text olive branch.

And her sister, in true Charlotte form, had ignored it.

Because of course she had. She couldn't just let something go without drama. Yes, Elinor had been ugly to her this morning—in her defense, it was before she had had any coffee or was even fully awake—but Charlotte had a master's degree in making mountains out of molehills. Elinor was kicking herself for saying the wrong thing, but it was hard to take all the blame when Charlotte *always* reacted as if she'd said the wrong thing, even when what she'd said was perfectly innocent.

She'd texted she was sorry for being grumpy that morning.
No response.

She'd asked Charlotte if she wanted to grab lunch as a peace offering.

Nothing.

For two hours. From *Charlotte*, who never had her phone more than two inches from her hand.

Deenie's soft gasp pulled her from her thoughts, and Elinor turned, her glass of sparkling water freezing halfway to her mouth as Ally stepped out of the dressing room.

Ally had swept her hair up in a twist, the style she planned to wear on the big day, and Lily Evans, the head seamstress and owner of Sweet Hollow Bridal, had placed a veil on her head. The ballgown was off-the-shoulder ivory with a wide burgundy sash accenting Ally's waist. The sash tied in a large bow, the ends trailing all the way to the end of the dress's short train and adding that splash of Christmas color.

The classical music playing softly in the shop seemed to swell as Ally stepped onto the pedestal in front of the mirror and smiled self-consciously. "Well?"

"Oh, Ally, you look so beautiful!" Deenie gushed, rushing toward her.

"Like a fairy tale!" Astrid agreed eagerly, dancing up to Ally's other side in her own white dress with a wide red ribbon.

Elinor could only nod in agreement, her throat suddenly tight. A single thought seemed to ring in her head. *Katie would love this.*

She should be here. Katie would have loved Ally, and it was just so wrong that they would never meet.

"Elinor?" Ally asked, nerves peeking through the uncertainty in her voice. "You don't think it's too much?"

She swallowed down the clog in her throat, forcing a smile she hoped didn't wobble too sentimentally. This was Ally's moment. "No. It's perfect. Ben won't know what hit him."

Ally's smile was even more radiant than the dress. "I told him that I was going full Mrs. Claus, so I doubt he'll be expecting anything so subtle. The guys should be about done picking out their tuxes, so as soon as we're all finished being pinned and tucked, we can meet them back at the farmhouse to address envelopes so the invitations are all ready to mail—unless you have to go?"

Elinor dropped the cell phone she'd been absently checking into her dress's very convenient pocket. "Nope. I'm all yours." She hadn't always been good at living in the moment, but she was determined to do her duty as a bridesmaid and make Ally's day as perfect as possible. "But we should probably keep Mac away from the envelopes. His handwriting is atrocious."

Lily had been hanging back to let them ooh and ahh over Ally, but she took that as her cue to step forward. "I'd better get started if we're going to get you out of here before Mac is let loose on the invitations."

She had a pincushion strapped to one wrist and half a dozen fabric clips attached to random places on her apron, and she quickly set about pinching and pinning the bodice of Ally's gown.

And if Elinor was silently dreading spending the rest of the afternoon stuffing envelopes with Levi, she kept that dread to herself. Lately their girls' nights had been all wedding stuff all the time, and Elinor had kept a smile on her face the entire time, carefully avoiding the topic of her previous engagement. She didn't want Ally to feel anything other than giddy about her big day. No sympathy for Elinor. No awareness that sometimes happily-ever-after didn't work out.

So she smiled, sipped her sparkling water, and waited her turn with the pincushion.

Chapter Eight

Ever since word spread that our beloved
mayor would be marrying the proprietor
of our favorite dog shelter, speculation
has been rife about who will make the cut
to attend the wedding—a mystery that
should soon be answered, as a little bird
tells me the coveted invitations are set to
go out this week!

—*Pine Hollow Newsletter*,
Monday, October 18

Stacks of envelopes embossed with holly leaves lay piled on the table. Levi frowned at the towers of fancy invitations. "How many people are you inviting?"

"The whole town," Ben groaned. "At least that's what it feels like. Ally doesn't want to disappoint anyone, and between my parents and Ally's grandparents, there's a lot of 'Oh, we just *have* to invite so-and-so' going on."

"You'll be happy to have everyone there," Connor reminded him, handing Ben and Levi each one of the beers he held, while Mac sat on the floor playing with the dogs. "You love the community shit."

"Yeah, as long as I don't declare bankruptcy first."

"I thought Ally's grandparents wanted to pay for it," Mac

said at the same time Connor asked, "So I take it no offers on the house yet?"

"They want to," Ben said to Mac, "but we're already not paying them as much rent as this place is worth, and their place out at the Estates isn't cheap. Ally doesn't want to eat into their savings too much, and we were supposed to buy the farmhouse from them, but we can't afford to do that until Katie and Paul's place sells, and I don't know if we have it priced too high or if we overbuilt for the neighborhood or if the market is just bad—"

"Breathe," Levi interrupted. "It's gonna be fine."

The four of them had returned to Ally's grandparents' old farmhouse after arranging the rental of their suits for the wedding—Connor being the only one among them who actually owned his own tux. It had been all burgundy vests and holly boutonnieres. Ally and Ben were going full Christmas for their nuptials. It was going to be great. As long as Ben didn't hyperventilate.

"I just feel like I'm playing a giant shell game. If I can just keep robbing Paul to pay Peter, no one will notice that the ship is slowly sinking."

"I think you mixed your metaphors there." Connor lifted the hand holding his beer, pointing with one finger.

Before Ben could respond, the dogs all perked up, barking and rushing toward the front door. Tires crunched on the gravel driveway outside, and Ben's hand shot out to bar them from moving toward the door. "No one tells Ally I'm stressed about the money."

Levi refrained from pointing out that he was pretty sure Ally already knew. She kept insisting that it was her dream to get married outdoors. In *December*. So they could hold the—very quick—ceremony in the town square beneath the massive Christmas tree with as many people as could cram into the square watching, before retreating back to the rec center, which would be decorated for the slightly smaller reception. She insisted the rec center was *perfect* because if the roof hadn't collapsed on it last year, she might never have met Ben, and clearly it was a *sign*—but it was also the cheapest place they could find that would fit the number of people they wanted to be there to celebrate with them.

No, Ally definitely knew that money was tight—but Levi just lifted his eyebrow in Ben's direction as the door opened and the women burst into the house in a rush of noise. "Isn't lying to your spouse about money one of those things they discourage in those premarital counseling sessions you signed up for?"

Ben glared at him—and went to greet his bride.

Levi hung back, a silent oasis in the chaos of the house. Everyone had brought their dogs, since Ally's grandfather had volunteered to stay at the farmhouse with the animals while everyone had their various fittings. Between Ally's Saint Bernard, her grandparents' two dogs, Astrid's bulldog, Deenie's yappy little pocket pooch, and Connor's dopey wolfhound, there were entirely too many canines underfoot—and that didn't include the dogs that lived across the driveway at the Furry Friends shelter that Ally ran.

Or the entirely-too-familiar white-and-brown Aussie who sat at Levi's feet, gazing up at him expectantly.

He pointed his most intimidating frown down at Elinor's annoying dog, but she just stared at him, her ears forward, eyes alert.

"Have you been sneaking her treats?"

He lifted his gaze from the dog to her owner, and the sight hit him like it always had.

Elinor had always been the most beautiful girl he'd ever seen, and that beauty had only grown over the years, because it wasn't her physical features that had always stopped his heart. It was her expressions, the intensity of her intellect, the way the blade of her mind seemed to have sculpted her features, sharpening the curves. His breath caught—but he hid the reaction. "I don't think it counts as 'sneaking' when the only time I give her treats is when I need to get her into my car so she stops terrorizing the town."

Elinor's eyebrows arched high over her glasses. "Terrorizing? Really?"

"She's a menace." But there was no heat behind the words.

Elinor pointedly dropped her gaze down to the dog, who sat angelically, still gazing at him with fixed devotion. "She does look menacing."

"All right, everyone!" Ally called, clapping her hands. "First off, thank you so much for being here and being part of our wedding. We love you all so much and are so incredibly grateful for you. And to you. All the gratitude. I've set up some stations so we can assembly-line this and not take up any more of your time than absolutely necessary. One station will address the envelopes from the list of addresses, the next will check the name on the envelope against the master list to see if they get just the wedding invite and RSVP, or if they also get the invite and RSVP to the rehearsal dinner. Then the next station stuffs the necessary pieces, and the last one seals and stamps. I figure there are enough of us to have two lines going and we can knock this out in no time. Sound good?"

Connor and Deenie immediately began squabbling over which of them had the best penmanship—since arguing was their foreplay—until Mac told the couple to get a room and Ally informed them they could both address the envelopes. She volunteered to join them—since that station would likely take the longest and needed an extra volunteer. Astrid and Ally's grandparents claimed stamping and sealing...and distracting the dogs. Mac claimed one of the master lists, and Ben sat beside him to start stuffing— which left Levi to choose between the master list and envelope stuffing.

He headed toward the stuffing station, but Ally grabbed his arm, handing him the first neatly addressed envelope. "Here, you can man the master list."

Levi looked down at the letters, momentarily at a loss as to how to get out of this. Saying no to the bride seemed like bad form, but there was no way—

"Oh, no, I think not," Elinor declared suddenly, plucking the envelope from his lax fingers. "If there's a master list, it's mine. Levi can go stuff it," she said with exaggerated sweetness.

He held up his hands in surrender, as if they were bickering like always. As if she hadn't just saved his ass.

It wasn't that he couldn't read. He'd learned—though much later than everyone thought he had. It had been habit to avoid it. To hide anything that he couldn't do. Better to be silent and be thought stupid than to speak and remove all doubt, right? He'd been the defiant kid. The bad kid. And somehow managed to never let anyone know about the dyslexia. He hadn't even been diagnosed until middle school.

Elinor had always covered for him. They never talked about it, but she'd figured it out somehow. Always so observant, even when they were kids. He didn't want to wonder exactly how long she'd known, if she'd always been humoring him when she told him she liked to read aloud. He hated to think she might have pitied him, but it was the only explanation that made any sense.

"Are you going to stuff those or not?"

Levi jerked, his hands moving automatically as he realized he'd fallen behind, and the conversation had moved on without him. The discussion seemed to center on the upcoming Pine Hollow Halloween Festival. Deenie was working the haunted house—which seemed incongruous with her sunshine-and-rainbows persona, but apparently she'd gotten involved with a local theater troupe that was planning some epic scares inside.

"Just try not to give anyone a heart attack," Levi requested. "I'm on duty all weekend, and I'd rather not deal with the paperwork."

"No promises. We are *very* scary," Deenie—the least scary person on the planet—declared cheerfully.

"I should have signed up for the haunted house," Elinor said. "I waited too long and ended up on the hayrides— which means hay poking through my jeans all night."

"It could be worse," Mac argued. "Last year I made the mistake of signing up to run bobbing for apples. Watching people drooling into a vat of produce haunted me for months."

"Is that why you took the apple crisp off your menu?" Ben asked. "It was so good."

"Flashbacks." Mac shuddered theatrically. "I couldn't do it. It's a sign of how much I love Ally that I'm willing to do those little apple tartlets for your wedding."

"You aren't having a cake?" Elinor asked.

"We are," Ally confirmed—glancing anxiously at Mac, who rolled his eyes.

"It's all right. I know Magda's making your wedding cake. I choose to strategically ignore your betrayal."

"The tartlets are for the rehearsal dinner," Ally explained.

"Okay, I have to ask," Deenie said suddenly, leaning toward Mac in her chair. "Why do you hate Magda? Because she's actually very sweet, and I know it's a whole loyalty-feud thing with you two, but I'm not sure I can give up her raspberry cream cheese croissants. Even for you."

"The better question isn't why I hate Magda, but why Magda hates me," Mac countered. "Aren't I beloved by all who know me?"

"Oh, very," Connor agreed dryly.

"Am I not a pillar of this community? Blessing this town with gourmet coffee and farm-to-table deliciousness?"

"I don't know about *pillar*..."

"Okay, so why does Magda hate you?" Deenie asked.

"It's one of the great mysteries of Pine Hollow," Mac declared. "A grievance from so long ago that no one even remembers."

"Oh, I remember." Elinor didn't look up from the master list in her hands.

Mac barely glanced in her direction. "No, you don't."

"No, I definitely do." Elinor looked up, catching Mac's gaze. "Charlotte and Magda have been best friends forever. I heard *everything*."

Deenie bounced in her chair. "Oooh, what happened?"

Mac shot Elinor a hard look—the ice in his gaze out of place on his always-smiling face. "Nothing."

Elinor studied Mac for a long minute while the entire table watched, suspense building, as an unspoken battle of the wills passed between them—until she glanced away with a shrug. "I guess nothing."

Deenie sighed theatrically. "Great. Now I'll have to wait for Linda Hilson's exposé on the subject."

The declaration was met with a round of groans.

Mac turned to Ben, eagerly taking up the new topic. "I realize you're too busy being all mayoral now to keep doing all the stuff you used to do, but of all the duties you had to off-load, did it have to be the newsletter? And did it have to be to Linda Hilson?"

Ben shrugged. "She was excited to do it."

"There was your first warning sign." Levi accepted an envelope from Elinor, ignoring the tingle through his skin when their fingers brushed. He really shouldn't be so aware of her after all this time.

"She only wanted to do it so she could turn it into a gossip column," Mac argued.

"It's a volunteer position. Beggars can't be choosers," Ben argued. "And we track the stats—it's a lot more popular since she took over."

"People like gossip. Shocking," Levi deadpanned.

"It's not just gossip. More people are reading the town notices, too."

"Come for the gossip. Stay for the information about the next town hall agenda," Mac quipped.

"It's all fun and games until the town gets sued because of her," Levi grumbled.

"Feeling litigious?" Connor asked, his gaze flicking pointedly between Levi and Elinor. Levi manfully resisted the urge to flip him off.

"She doesn't use names," Ben pointed out.

"Everyone knows who she's talking about," Mac insisted—his own eyes going to Levi and Elinor, who had been featured far too often in the newsletter lately.

"She's been watching too much *Bridgerton*." Ally handed an envelope to Elinor. "She's convinced she's Pine Hollow's answer to Lady Whistledown."

"Lady who?" Mac asked.

"The Regency gossip columnist from a Netflix series," Ally explained.

"But whereas Lady Whistledown was anonymous, everyone knows Linda Hilson, and we all know you can't believe everything she writes." Deenie *also* glanced at Levi. "So there's no point in suing her. You'd only be giving her credibility."

"Can we please stop talking about someone suing the town?" Ben groaned. "That is the last thing I need."

The discussion continued, but Elinor's phone buzzed—and Levi was so attuned to her that he immediately tuned out the newsletter/lawsuit debate to focus on her as she fished her phone out of her bag.

"I never knew you knew why Mac and Magda hated each other," he murmured beneath the conversation.

She shot him an irritated glance. "Why would you?"

Because we knew everything about each other, he almost said, but common sense kept his mouth shut. Then she looked at her text notification, and a very specific brand of irritation flashed in her eyes.

Levi's mouth twisted sympathetically. "Charlotte driving you crazy again?"

Elinor looked up from her phone screen, her dark eyes narrowing behind her glasses.

🐾

God, he was annoying.

"You don't know me as well as you think you do," Elinor

snapped—keeping her voice down so they didn't draw attention from the rest of the table.

Pine Hollow was a small town. They were forced to be together in social situations all the time—and they almost always ended the evening arguing. She'd been so determined not to interrupt Ally's wedding preparations with a fight.

"So that isn't Charlotte?" Levi asked, his expression barely changing, but his skepticism peeking through.

Elinor glared. Because, of course, it was Charlotte.

Her sister, who had been ignoring her texts all day, had finally responded with *It's fine.*

When they both absolutely knew that it wasn't fine. When Charlotte was obviously sulking.

"She okay?" Levi asked.

"She's fine," Elinor snapped—and then got irrationally annoyed all over again because she'd used the same words Charlotte had. Her phone buzzed again.

I went on my own. No cell service in Smuggler's Notch.

A spike of worry shafted through her. She barely stopped herself from texting back *Alone???* Because somehow she didn't think her baby sister would take her concern for her safety as it was intended after Elinor had refused to go with her this morning.

She nibbled on her lower lip, trying to compose a response that would safely navigate the minefield of her sister's sensitivity. She finally settled on *I'm glad you got to enjoy it* and hit Send, almost immediately wishing she'd sent something else. It felt so distant. So formal somehow. But she didn't know how else to be without setting Charlotte off. Everything she said seemed wrong these days.

She half-expected Levi to still be staring at her when she looked up from her phone, but she must have spent longer dithering over what to say than she thought because he was in the middle of a conversation with Ben, their voices raised across the table amid several active discussions—and a single word jumped out at her.

"What did you say about the mill?" she asked Ben.

He quickly looped her into the conversation. "The Kellers are selling the land. Levi said they'd put up some *For Sale* signs when he was out there the other day."

Elinor barely stopped herself from looking at Levi. *He was at the mill? Their mill?*

Ben continued, oblivious to the questions pinging around in her head. "I was just saying Mr. Keller's heirs are trying to get a zoning variance from the town so they can ask for more money from the developers who are interested in the land."

"Wait, developers?"

"Like the folks who did the NetZero Village condos out at the resort. It's a big stretch of land with the river running right through it. Gorgeous views. I'm surprised there aren't more companies gunning for it already."

But they'll tear it down.

Her mill. *Their* mill.

She knew it was just an old building. A crumbling pile of rocks. But suddenly her heart was beating too fast. She could feel her pulse thrumming against the thin skin of her neck.

"Excuse me," she whispered, pushing her chair back. "I just need to…"

She didn't finish the sentence, and thankfully no one asked her what she just needed to do, because she had no idea.

Elinor retreated to the back of the farmhouse. She'd started toward the bathroom, but then kept walking until she reached the shadowy room at the end of the hallway.

It had been Mrs. Gilmore's art studio, but now it seemed to hold a mishmash of storage—all the things that hadn't quite gotten moved when Ally's grandparents moved out to the Summerland Estates retirement community.

Someone was tearing down the mill.

She gulped down a breath, reaching blindly for something to steady her—when a deep voice that had always steadied her spoke from behind her.

"Elinor?"

Of course he'd come after her. He'd always known when she needed him. They'd always been so attuned to one another.

But they weren't together now. He shouldn't be here. "Go away, Levi."

He didn't listen. Why should he start listening now?

"Are you all right?"

Maybe if she ignored him he would leave. He was always doing that obnoxious silence thing. All brooding and intense. She could do that. She kept her back to him, staring into the shadows of the room, and used all her Jedi powers to get him to leave the room.

"I should have told you about the mill."

"I'm not upset about the mill!"

Okay. That was a little too loud. And definitely didn't work with the obnoxious silence plan.

Levi cleared his throat—and then he was the one doing the obnoxious silence thing. Great.

"Is Charlotte…?" he finally began, and she whipped around, since apparently her Jedi powers weren't working at *all*. Stupid faulty Jedi powers.

"Levi. I'm fine. Everything's fine. I don't want you here. And I don't know how to be any clearer about that."

"Right," he murmured. But he didn't move. For a long moment he just stared into her eyes—she'd always thought his focus was one of the sexiest things about him. No one concentrated like Levi Jackson. Little tingles broke out along her arms.

Even in the low light she could see the silvery glint of his eyes, studying her. Reading her. Then, after what felt like forever, "How's your writing going?"

"Oh my God! That's none of your business! Nothing about me is any of your business anymore." And she wasn't writing anymore. It had felt so pointless after Katie died. Not that she was going to tell him that.

"I'm still your friend—"

"No, Levi. You aren't."

She pushed past him, back toward the front of the house. He was tall and strong and could have stopped her with barely any effort at all, but instead he shifted slightly out of the way so she didn't have to brush him as she walked past.

Thank goodness. Because she probably would have clipped him like an offensive lineman, given the chance.

She stalked back to the kitchen—where the assembly line had finished up and the last of the invitations were neatly stacked and ready to be mailed. Ally's grandparents had apparently gone back home with their dogs, and Astrid was on the floor, playing with Dory and Partridge and Max, while tiny JoJo watched their antics with skeptical eyes from a safe distance and barked. The Saint Bernard, Colby, was fast asleep.

Ben and Connor were arguing about something, while Mac needled them both—but since Ben and Connor delighted in aggravating one another and Mac was a gleeful instigator, Elinor took that as situation normal.

She yanked down her hair, immediately snatching it back up in another ponytail.

"Mimosa?"

Deenie and Ally formed a cautiously smiling barricade, and Ally extended a pastel orange drink in her direction. "We went lazy on the cocktails."

She loved champagne. It was her absolute favorite. But she'd avoided drinking it—even when they offered it at the bridal salon this morning—because it always, *always* made her think of Levi. But Levi was just freaking *everywhere* tonight anyway, so why not indulge?

She accepted the glass. "Thank you."

Levi reentered the room behind her. She was immediately aware of him, like the air pressure in the room had changed, an airlock opening, but she hid her reaction. Or at least she thought she did, until she noticed Deenie's gaze flicking avidly between her and Levi as he made his way across the room to join the guys.

"Okay, I know there's an unwritten rule that we aren't supposed to ask, but what's the deal with you and Levi? Do we need to beat him up?"

Elinor had been braced for the first question, but the second startled a laugh out of her. "No beating up," she assured them. "And there is no deal. We were together and now we aren't. End of story. It's just awkward sometimes, because we live in the same small town and know all the same people."

Ally and Deenie exchanged a quick glance. "So... that's it?"

"That's all it will ever be," Elinor vowed, pointedly *not* looking at the man across the room. They were over. And nothing was going to change that.

Chapter Nine

A certain chief's denial of a certain relationship would be so much more believable if he weren't constantly spotted at the home of a certain librarian... as he was just this Monday...
—*Pine Hollow Newsletter*, Wednesday, November 3

Her yard still hadn't been mowed.

Levi shoved down the flash of irrational frustration at the sight and drove past without pausing. It was his day off. He'd worked all weekend at the Halloween Festival, which had been over the top in true Pine Hollow fashion. He'd spent the entire time keeping the peace and trying to keep his mind off Elinor.

Not that his attempts to ignore her did much good, with her organizing the hayrides. She seemed to be everywhere. For someone so small, she took up a disproportionate amount of his attention. But then she always had.

He cruised slowly through the heart of town, automatically scanning the streets and sidewalks as he drove. Not that he was patrolling on his day off. He was just going for a drive to unwind. Listening to an audiobook. This was relaxing. It wasn't work. He wasn't incapable of turning off the job, or whatever that guy up in Stowe had implied. Even if the audiobook was a dry one about policing practices and not the latest Grisham.

The audio cut out, replaced by the trilling of his phone through the SUV's speakers. Levi's gaze flicked to the console to read the caller ID and one hand fisted on his lap. The other gripped the steering wheel as his shoulders automatically tensed.

It wasn't that he was avoiding his mom's calls. He just didn't want to have to feel guilty about the soft edge of worry in her voice. His parents were from North Carolina, and they'd moved back there a few years ago—right after he and Elinor broke up but before he got the promotion to chief of police—and his mother had been worrying over him from afar ever since.

Guilt had him tapping to connect the call. "Hey, Mom."

"Levi! Am I bothering you? Is this a bad time?"

She always asked that. As if he wouldn't let it go to voice mail if he was actively arresting someone. "No, it's fine. What's up?"

"Oh, well, I was talking to your father, and I just wanted to check with you to see if you'd had a chance to think any more about whether you might want to visit us for Thanksgiving?"

For his mother, that was practically a demand. She was the most indirect person on the planet—which he supposed was a coping mechanism for living with his father for the last thirty-odd years. "I don't think I can make it this year, Mom. My deputies are both young and part-time—"

Which was why Levi had worked out a deal with a

neighboring town's police department that they would cover for one another when the chief needed to be away.

But *I can't get away from work* made a much better excuse than *I just don't want to spend a weekend with you fussing over me, and Dad telling me life isn't fair*.

"It's a crime the way they work you so hard. Elton got vacation days."

"Elton had me." A streak of white flashed through the edge of his vision, and Levi's head snapped in the direction of the movement. "Mom, I've gotta go. Something just came up. Love you."

"Don't work too hard!" she called, but he was already disconnecting the call and turning down the narrow road that led out to the mill. The trees bent over the pavement, making it feel like a tunnel, and Levi scanned the brush. He was sure he'd seen…

There.

Another blur of white-and-brown fur.

Right in front of his bumper.

Levi slammed on the brakes to avoid flattening Elinor's dog, the rear end of the SUV fishtailing slightly at the sudden stop. Thankfully, no one was behind him.

He put on his hazard lights and threw the Explorer in park, then opened the door, intending to climb out and lure Elinor's dog to him on foot. But before he could even finish unbuckling his seat belt, a bundle of fur bounded onto his lap. Dory squirmed excitedly, licking his face.

"Off! Off!" Levi commanded, but she ignored his attempts to shove her away until her contortions brought her wiggling butt into contact with the horn.

At the loud *beep* she barked—right into Levi's ear—

and leapt to the passenger seat, her paws braced on the dashboard as she alertly scanned their surroundings for the source of the horn.

"That was you, genius," Levi grumbled, shutting the door so she couldn't go for the easy escape—though she seemed perfectly happy where she was. She turned in a circle and sat on his passenger seat, her head cocked to the side as if asking where they were going. "You proud of yourself for getting out again?"

It wasn't even noon. Hours before he could hand her off to Elinor.

He could always take her to Furry Friends—Ally had mentioned last week that she would make space for her.

But he couldn't stop thinking about the damn lawn.

Elinor used to tease him that he had an overactive sense of responsibility—but that yard still felt like his. She hated yard work, so even before he'd moved in with her, back when she first bought the house, he'd been the one to build that fence and fertilize that grass. It kept bugging him, thinking she was just going to let it grow wild until the first snow came and covered it up.

Levi glanced at the dog beside him.

Returning her was the perfect excuse. Elinor was at work. She wouldn't even have to see him, and her yard would get mowed. Really, it was the neighborly thing to do.

Levi put the Explorer in gear.

🐾

The fence was locked.

Levi had expected the latch—he'd installed it, after all. But he'd thought he'd be able to reach over the top and flip it open. He hadn't expected a combination lock to be holding the latch in place.

Levi narrowed his eyes at the Australian shepherd, who was seated patiently at his feet, watching him. "You figured out how to unlatch the gate, didn't you? Before you started using the chair as a launching pad."

Dory opened her jaws in a canine grin, clearly pleased with herself.

He'd put the leash on her, but she seemed in no hurry to run away—like Elinor had said. She just didn't want to be alone. All those times she'd run from him before had apparently been a game, but one she thankfully didn't seem interested in playing today, fascinated instead with this new game of breaking into her yard.

"Okay, Houdini," he said to her, "you're so good at getting out. How do we get in?"

She cocked her head, as if considering the problem—and Levi realized he was talking to a dog.

"I'm losing it," he muttered, looking around for another way into the backyard.

He didn't actually want to break into Elinor's house to get into the backyard—somehow he didn't think she would take that well—but he wasn't ready to give up. She usually kept her lawn mower in the tiny shed out back. If he—and Dory—could get into the backyard, he could fix the mower, mow the lawn, and be gone before she got home from school. But first he had to get in.

He had a ladder back at his place...but that would stretch the credible limits of the "oh, I was just being neighborly" excuse.

If he could find something to stand on, he could boost himself over the fence—but there was no guarantee Dory would sit still while he did that. She could be halfway to the town square while he'd be trapped in Elinor's backyard.

If he stood on something, he might be able to see the numbers to work the lock—but he still didn't know the combination.

Though he knew Elinor.

He glanced at the garage door. It had a number pad on it so it could be opened from the outside. He'd known the combination, once upon a time.

If she hadn't changed the combination, that was a sign, wasn't it?

"This might be a bad idea," he told the dog.

He punched in Anne's birthday. And the garage door lumbered upward.

Dory scampered inside, pulling at the leash in her eagerness to explore the one-car space that Elinor had always used for storage, even when he'd fussed at her about how much better it was for her car to be inside out of the elements. Levi closed the garage door and navigated the miscellaneous boxes blocking the door that opened into the backyard. Shifting one box slightly, he managed to wedge the door open wide enough for him and Dory to slip through.

The dog danced around his feet until he fixed her with a look and she instantly sat, gazing up at him.

"You gonna be good if I let you off the leash? No jumping over the fence?"

Dory stared at him, trembling with adoration, and he bent to unclip the leash. "No running," he reminded her as he straightened.

He started toward the shed, wading through the too-tall grass—and Dory raced ahead, circling back to him when he was too slow and then ahead to spin circles of joy at the shed door. The lawn was free of doggie land mines, so at least Elinor was keeping up with the poop scooping. When he reached the shed door, he saw that this one was, thankfully, not padlocked, and the lawn mower was right where he'd always left it back when he'd taken care of the lawn.

Everything was right where he'd left it. Three years had passed, and even the tools he'd left behind still hung on their hooks, gathering dust.

Dory sniffed the mower curiously, scampering back when he crouched to examine it. "Let's see what's wrong here," he said to her—and then kicked himself.

He really needed to stop talking to the dog.

🐾

He might have been a little too confident of his ability to fix the mower in five minutes.

It took two hours, five Google searches, and one trip to Mr. Wells's hardware store with Dory riding shotgun before he had the mower running again. But it was running now, and if he worked quickly, he should be able to finish the lawn and leave before Elinor even knew he'd been here.

Though the mowing would go a lot faster without Dory's brand of "help."

He started at the back corner, pushing the mower in a long diagonal line—and Dory raced in front of him and dropped a bright red rubber ball directly in the mower's path.

"Move it or lose it," Levi warned.

The dog danced back and crouched, head down, butt up, her tail wagging wildly as she watched to see what he would do.

"I'll shred it," he promised, pushing the mower a step forward.

Dory didn't budge.

And Levi knew he was going to lose this battle.

The rubber would probably jam the mower, and then he'd be right back where he started. "You're Satan," he reminded Dory as he rounded the mower and grabbed the ball from the ground, tossing it onto the patio and out of the way—and Dory went leaping after it, springing like an antelope to snag it out of the air.

Levi returned to the mower and pushed it another five feet—until the ball landed in his path again. So much for nice, neat lines. He turned the mower ninety degrees—and Dory snatched up the ball, racing to deposit it in front of him again. He turned again—and she grabbed it again, this time putting it close enough that he'd have to drag the mower backward to avoid shredding the ball.

"We aren't doing this," he informed her.

She didn't seem impressed by his pronouncement.

He was losing a battle of wills with a dog.

Levi bent and grabbed the ball, resuming his position behind the mower. He tried putting the ball in his pocket, but Dory stood on top of the mower and stared him down, so he threw it to the farthest corner of the yard, skipping it along the ground like a stone on a pond to make it harder for her to snatch out of the air. He pushed the mower as fast and far as he could before she could trap the ball and race back with it again to block his path.

Over and over again.

Thankfully, Elinor's yard wasn't very big. And Levi quickly discovered that rolling the ball underneath the lawn furniture would keep Dory distracted for minutes rather than seconds. But he was still starting to feel a slight twinge in his left arm from throwing the ball so much by the time he tucked the mower back into the shed.

"You were no help," he informed the dog, who, tired after the game, lay on her belly on one of the patio loungers, the ball braced between her front paws as if to guard it from anyone who might dare to steal it. Her little ears flipped forward happily at his voice.

He checked the time, then frowned at the dog. "If I leave you here, can I trust you to stay for fifteen minutes?"

He could put her on the leash and pin the other end beneath the barbecue grill, which would at least slow her down—but he didn't want her choking herself as she tried to get free. If he left her in the garage, she'd probably destroy half the boxes in the fifteen minutes before Elinor was due home.

"The house it is," Levi decided—and then reminded himself to *stop talking to the dog*.

He shoved open the back door to the garage and Dory instantly perked up. "C'mon, Devil Dog," he called, angling his shoulders through the narrow opening as Dory grabbed her ball to follow.

The garage was dark without the overhead light that had come on automatically when he opened the garage door before. He couldn't close the back door all the way without shutting off the last of the sunlight, so he left it open as he picked through the boxes to the door to the house.

He expected to have to trick Dory through the door, but as soon as he opened it, she raced inside. He closed it again before she could change her mind and opened the garage door to let himself out. He closed everything up, leaving it exactly as he'd found it—only with the dog *inside* the house—and climbed quickly into his Explorer to get away before Elinor came home and got pissed at him for doing something nice for her.

Because God forbid he act like her friend.

I'm still your friend.

No, Levi. You aren't.

He pushed away the burn of those words, tucking the leash back into his glove box. You didn't just stop caring about someone. And he didn't just stop taking care of the people he cared about. Even when she was mad at him. Even when he deserved it.

Chapter Ten

Love was certainly in the air at the Halloween Festival, and not just for the mayor and his bride. Could we be hearing wedding bells soon for some of our other dear residents?

—*Pine Hollow Newsletter*, Wednesday, November 3

Um, Ms. Rodriguez?"

Elinor reluctantly tugged her gaze away from her computer screen. Her thoughts were slower to abandon the story she'd been reading, but when she saw who had whispered her name so tentatively, she blinked back to reality in an instant. "Bailey! You know you can call me Elinor."

Her sister's girlfriend flushed to her white-blond hairline. "I know, sorry, I just, I wasn't sure if—in *school*, you know, if it would be disrespectful?" Her hands twisted as she stood at the edge of Elinor's desk like a kid being called up for disciplinary action. "I thought class was out already," she whispered, casting a quick glance over her shoulder at the kids working at the library desks, their heads bent close to their laptops and notebooks in concentration.

"It's an after-school program," Elinor explained, her own voice pitched automatically to a low murmur after years of practice. "They're all working on novels for NaNo."

"NaNo?"

"National Novel Writing Month. It's an online event every November where people all over the world try to write a novel in a month. I thought it might be fun for the students, so I opened up the library computers for writing time before and after school for anyone who's interested. We had quite a few takers."

Elinor wasn't expecting all of them to stick it out all the way to the end of the month, but day one had been a hit, and it was wonderful to see so much creative energy in the room. There were about two dozen students in all, mostly fifth and sixth graders. She'd expected a lot more giggling and whispering, but so far they seemed to be taking their creative efforts very seriously.

"Cool, cool," Bailey said, her eyes flicking to Elinor's open laptop. "Are you...?"

"Oh." Elinor waved one hand dismissively, using the other to put her computer to sleep. "That's just an old story of mine I haven't looked at in ages." *Pay no attention to the man behind the curtain.* She straightened to face Bailey. "What can I do for you?"

Bailey flushed again, fidgeting. "I, uh, I wanted to... This is going to sound weird—"

"I sincerely doubt that. I'm an expert at unusual questions. A kindergartner asked me today why grapes are round. I'm ready for anything."

Bailey smiled, soft and relieved and still a bit anxious. "It's actually about Jane Austen? I know Anne says it isn't a big deal that I don't know anything about literary stuff, but she loves it, and you guys talk about it all the time, and I guess I just...I wanna learn about it because it matters to her?"

Bailey had a tendency to make every statement a question, but by the end of her uncertain little speech, there was no question: Elinor's heart was mush. She smiled. "You came to the right place."

"A library?"

"Well, that and I also happen to know a ridiculous amount about Jane Austen—and more importantly, the particular works of Jane Austen that are woven into our family lore." And she would walk across fire to help Bailey learn whatever she wanted. Anything for Anne. "The big three, as far as Anne's concerned, are *Pride and Prejudice*, *Sense and Sensibility*, and *Persuasion*. Our mother absolutely hated *Emma*—for reasons that have never been entirely clear to me. And you can read *Northanger Abbey* and *Mansfield Park* if you *really* want to impress her, but let's start with the Rodriguez family canon."

Bailey was nodding along, and Elinor glanced at the students to make sure she wasn't disturbing their creative genius at work before leaning closer to Bailey and lowering her voice another notch.

"This might be sacrilegious, coming from a librarian, because obviously the book is always better than the movie, but there are actually some really good film and television adaptations of the books. Do you think you could swing by my house this evening? I'm supposed to meet Ally and Deenie for some wedding thing, but if you have time, I could give you a stack of stuff—I have extra copies of all the books, and I'll lend you the Colin Firth and Jennifer Ehle *Pride and Prejudice* DVDs...though Anne might kill me for giving them to you. She might want to be the one to indoctrinate you into the cult of BBC Austen."

"I'll take the books and DVDs," Bailey said eagerly. "I want to surprise her. *Thank* you."

"It's my pleasure." Not everyone who dated a member of the Rodriguez family cared enough to learn about their collective Austen obsession. Levi had never read a single one, as far as Elinor knew. He was more of a spy-mysteries-and-thrillers guy.

She and Bailey arranged a time to meet up later. By the time Bailey departed, the after-school session was almost over, and Elinor debated whether it was even worth it to wake her computer back up again.

She didn't know why she'd dug this particular story out of the dusty cellar of her unused computer files. She refused to admit that it might have been because of Levi. Or that his question the other night might have had anything to do with her sudden decision to do a NaNo project at school. It had just been good timing. NaNo always started November 1. And if she hadn't done it since Katie died, well, maybe it was time.

The kids seemed to love it, most of them fixated on their computers, though shy Brayden Wells was drawing what looked like a very elaborate graphic novel—when he wasn't sneaking covert glances at Kimber Kwan. Astrid and her best friend sat together at the closest table, each deep in the process of crafting their own fictional world—and it was hard not to get a familiar pang when Elinor looked over at them. She and Katie had been just like that—though it had been handwritten manuscripts in spiral-bound notebooks for them, all in swirling purple ink.

Katie had been one of the only people in the world

who knew how badly Elinor wanted to be a writer. They'd shared all their stories with one another—Katie's always about superheroes and magic powers, and Elinor's about dystopian worlds. The writing had been her escape when her mother was sick, a way of feeling like she could control *something* when she could control the happy ending for her characters. It had gotten her through the toughest times of her life, but when she lost Katie, it was like that part of her had gone to sleep, an entire chunk of her core identity going completely dormant for three years.

Elinor tapped a key to wake the computer up, the screen instantly filling with the last book she'd attempted to write. This had been Katie's favorite. The one she kept encouraging Elinor to submit to agents and editors.

Elinor only intended to glance over a few more pages until it was time to send the kids to pickup, but she'd forgotten that this story was actually *good*. She quickly found herself sucked back in. Her eyes raced over scenes she didn't even remember writing, the hair rising on her arms with the realization that *she'd written this*. And it was *exciting*.

The alarm rang on her phone, making her jump, and she stood up, quickly closing the file. "And that's it for today! How did everyone do? Lots of good words?"

Kids around the room emerged from their own fictional worlds, the noise level rising rapidly as everyone chattered eagerly about what they'd done. Brayden flushed when Kimber complimented his sketches, ducking his head and darting out of the library. Elinor lingered to talk to anyone who wanted a few extra minutes of encouragement or advice.

By the time the last student left, she only had time to hurriedly gather her things if she wanted to get home before she was supposed to meet Bailey—when all she wanted to do was dive back into her story and see if it was actually as good as she thought it was.

Why had she stopped writing? How had she forgotten this feeling?

Bailey's car wasn't in her driveway when she got home—and thankfully neither was Levi's Explorer.

She rushed into the house, calling out a hello to Dory—and instead of a bark from the mudroom where Dory had her crate, she heard the clicking of Dory's nails on the tile floors as she came racing around the corner with her red ball in her mouth.

"Hey there, Trouble! On your way to escape again?" Elinor knelt and Dory dropped the ball to bounce at her feet so she could receive her hello cuddles and respond with appropriate quantities of puppy kisses all over Elinor's face.

"That's an outdoor ball," Elinor scolded gently. "How did you get that in here? Did you open another window?"

She headed toward the back of the house to investigate, but didn't immediately spot anything amiss. Windows closed. Doors closed. Patio furniture neatly arranged. Grass neatly cut—

Elinor froze. *Grass neatly cut.*

"He wouldn't."

But apparently he would.

She grabbed her tablet, hurriedly pulling up the video feeds while Dory barked at her ankles, picking up on her sudden agitation.

Elinor scrolled quickly through the motion-activated video log, seeing it all in black and white. Dory's escape. Then forty minutes later—according to the timestamp—Levi's arrival. The garage door opening. Levi in the backyard.

Coming and going as if he owned the place. Fixing her freaking lawn mower. Mowing her lawn. Playing with her dog. As if he had any right.

She looked down at Dory—who had apparently spent the entire freaking day with her new best friend. "I'm going to kill him."

Chapter Eleven

Some men send flowers. Some bring
chocolates. Others perform yard work.
—*Pine Hollow Newsletter*,
Wednesday, November 3

H e *mowed* my *lawn*."

"The *bastard*!" Deenie gasped with satisfying horror, before ruining it with "Though can someone explain
why this makes him a bastard? Because I'm confused. Do
we not like short grass? Anti-mowing? Back to nature?"

Elinor, Ally, and Deenie were sitting at one of the tiny
café tables in Magda's Bakery after hours, alone except
for the baker herself, who was periodically appearing with
additional slices of cake from the back. Ally had enlisted
Elinor and Deenie to help her with the final wedding cake
decision after her first attempt with Astrid and Ben had
ended with the three of them agreeing that they were all
delicious and they needed all of them.

"It *is* a little high-handed," Ally said, before breaking off to groan at the lemon cream in her mouth. "Okay, I was wrong. *This* one was my favorite."

"They were all your favorite. That was the problem," Deenie reminded her, before grabbing a forkful of chocolate and turning back to Elinor's drama with avid interest. "So it was the macho take-charge-y aspect we hated?"

Elinor searched for the words to explain. Levi had always been high-handed. He'd always wanted to jump in and fix everything. That wasn't new. But this . . . this was more . . . this was . . . "He acts like he has the right to oversee my life."

Ally and Deenie both *ooh*ed, nodding their understanding.

"It's like, remember last spring, when he gave me *permission* to date Connor?"

"I do, in fact, remember that," Deenie, Connor's then and current girlfriend, commented dryly. "He gave Connor permission, too."

"No one needs his permission!" Elinor snapped. "I am my own person. I get to decide who to date. He doesn't get a say. *He* broke up with *me*."

It wasn't until Ally's eyes widened slightly that she realized she'd never admitted that part to them before.

"Okay." Deenie set down her fork, cake forgotten. "We've been trying not to pry, but I'm dying here. What happened with you two? Because whatever it is, it doesn't seem like it's over."

"Oh, it's over," Elinor insisted, viciously stabbing the raspberry chiffon, which crumbled satisfyingly under the assault.

Ally reached out and caught the hand that wasn't dismembering raspberry chiffon. "What happened?" she asked gently.

Elinor heard Katie's voice whispering in the back of her

mind. Droll and knowing. *They're never going to know you if you won't tell them anything.*

She knew it was just her subconscious, but it sounded so much like Katie that she felt a pricking at the back of her eyes. And that fake-Katie voice was right. She'd spent the last three years feeling lonely because her person was gone—and pushing away everyone who tried to get close to her.

Charlotte, with her two ride-or-die besties, was always saying that "best friend" wasn't a person, it was a tier. And it wasn't locked. It was flexible. There was always room for more best friends. But Elinor had never had a tier. She'd had Katie. The one person who had always understood her brand of weird. And the idea of replacing her had felt unthinkable.

Elinor met the eyes of the two women around the table. Deenie was walking sunshine, but her life wasn't all rainbows and Skittles. She'd lost the person who meant most to her in the world to Alzheimer's just a few months back. Ally's only living relatives were her grandparents, and she worried about them constantly. These two had shared their worries with her over countless margaritas during the last ten months—while Elinor had evaded all questions about Levi and Katie and anything real.

They wanted so badly to be there for her. Maybe it was time she let them.

"We were engaged," she admitted—and two pairs of eyes widened. They were both relatively new to town, but still. "I thought you knew—if not from town gossip, from the newsletter."

"That's Linda." Ally waved her fork. "No one believes everything she writes."

"Well, in this case, she's actually accurate. My history

with Levi goes way back. Like, elementary school. He was the first boy I ever kissed. My first everything. We dated off and on through high school. He's eight months older than me, but I was two years ahead in school." *Skipping grades. Always trying to be perfect for Mama.* "So we were sixteen when I graduated. We sort of agreed to split up when I went away to college, but Dartmouth isn't far from here, and I still saw him all the time, because I was always coming back to see my family. School was good, but I was younger than everyone else, and Pine Hollow was the only place I really felt comfortable." She shook away the memory of that awkward time.

"Anyway, we were friends, and that was it, until a couple of years after I moved back. By then we were in our twenties, but it was still there, you know? That thing we always had. It felt so inevitable that we would get back together. And we just sort of did. But then my little sister got sick, and I told him I couldn't handle a relationship on top of everything. So we went back to friends again—but about a year later, we sort of slid back into being a couple. Like gravity." No one had ever made her *feel* the way Levi did, the sheer volume of emotion. "When he proposed, it was the easiest question I'd ever answered. Of course. It was always Levi, right? I didn't want to tell anyone until Anne had been in remission for at least two years—her cancer had already come back once. So we didn't start actually planning a wedding until about three years ago. It was always this someday thing. When the time was right. And then it finally seemed like the time was right. Anne was good. Everyone was good. It could be about us. Finally."

She stopped, her throat tightening as if the memory was still fresh and not years old.

"But?" Ally prompted softly.

"He just *ended* it. It was suddenly over, and he wouldn't tell me why. 'Trust me. This is for the best.' That's it. That's all the explanation I got. After a freaking *lifetime* together. 'Trust me.'"

"That's it?" Deenie asked incredulously.

"He's never been a big talker."

"You can say that again," Deenie muttered.

"But I always felt like we understood each other—like I knew him so well it didn't matter that he didn't say much. It didn't matter that he never seemed to have any opinions about the wedding or talked about his feelings, because I knew what he meant, right? I knew what he felt. Because I felt it, too." That volume of emotion. "But then afterward, I couldn't stop second-guessing. Had I built this entire relationship in my head? Had it always been one-sided, and I just filled in the blanks for what I thought he was feeling?"

"I'm sure that wasn't—"

Elinor shook her head over Deenie's soothing words. "There were all these rumors around town after we broke up—about other women. I felt like such a fool. Classic idiot—and not just because I hadn't seen it, but because he was my friend and I thought I knew him."

"Are you sure he cheated?" Ally asked. "The rumors in this town are insane."

"And that doesn't really seem like rules-rules-rules Levi," Deenie agreed.

"I didn't think so either, but he never denied it. Even when—" She broke off, the words snapped off by the vise in her throat. *Even when Katie died.*

He'd been there for her.

He'd shown up at her door and pulled her into his arms, silent and *there*. Holding her together. He'd held her when she sobbed like her soul had been ripped out of her body. He'd been the only one she could stand to see for days. But then when the first fog of grief had lifted a little, she'd done the stupid thing. She'd asked him outright if he'd been with other people while they were together. And she'd seen guilt on his face before he'd said he had to go and walked out the door.

Why else would he look so guilty?

Elinor shook her head, hard enough to dislodge the memory. "It doesn't matter. He broke off our engagement without even giving me the respect of an explanation. And now, what? He has the right to break into my house to mow my yard whenever he feels like I'm not doing a good enough job keeping up with it?"

"Okay, don't hate me," Ally said with a wince, "but are we absolutely *sure* there wasn't a good reason he couldn't explain why? I mean, he is a cop. Maybe there was some undercover thing and he was only trying to protect you."

"A dangerous undercover sting operation," Elinor reiterated, her voice dry as dust. "In *Pine Hollow*."

"It could happen."

"In a movie, maybe," Deenie argued, so thankfully Elinor didn't have to.

Elinor shook her head. "Occam's razor. The simplest explanation is usually the correct one. And the simplest explanation is that I'd been projecting this romantic ideal onto Levi, and he wasn't who I thought he was. So when push came to shove and the wedding got real, he bailed."

"I don't know if *that's* the simplest explanation." Deenie picked up her fork again, poking at the vanilla chiffon. "And

I know it sounds boring, but this vanilla is about the best thing I've ever tasted."

"Right?" Ally agreed. "There is nothing vanilla about that vanilla."

Elinor took a bite of the cake in question, grateful for the break from talking about her past—and even more grateful for the silky sweet deliciousness in her mouth. "My God," she mumbled. "How is that so good?"

"I have a theory that she's secretly sneaking crack into the croissants, but I think this is even more addictive than those."

"One last thing about Levi," Ally said.

Elinor groaned. "Could we not? I already feel like I can't escape him. I can't go two weeks without him showing up with my dog."

"That's actually what I wanted to ask—if you guys can't stand each other now, why is he watching Dory for you? You know we would take her at the doggie day care, free of charge. You're family."

"I can't ask you to do that. And he isn't watching her. Dory keeps escaping, and he's the one who tracks her down."

"You aren't asking me," Ally said. "I'm offering. And I remember exactly how clever Dory is. We had to padlock her inside her pen just to keep her from letting all the other dogs out."

"I could take her, too," Deenie offered. "Connor and I both work from home, so she wouldn't be alone. She could play with JoJo and Maximus."

"I've got a new system. We're good," Elinor assured them—as if Dory hadn't broken through the new system that very morning.

Deenie and Ally exchanged a glance, but any attempt

to press their case was delayed when Magda returned from the kitchen.

"Any decisions?"

"All of them," Ally said, at the same moment Deenie and Elinor chorused "The vanilla."

Ally pointed at them. "What they said."

Magda grinned. "Vanilla it is."

She and Ally began discussing tiers and delivery timing while Deenie snitched all the rest of the samples and Elinor stared blindly at the array of cake flavors. Nothing had been resolved, but she felt *lighter* somehow.

That's what happens when you don't hoard your problems to yourself, the Katie voice in her head muttered.

But Elinor had never been good at relying on anyone but Katie. And Levi. She had to be strong for her dad, for her sisters, for her mom, and for the entire freaking town, which expected so much from her. They'd always said she would be the one to put Pine Hollow on the map, but she'd just come home and become a librarian. She'd given up her writing. She'd forgotten how to dream.

When had that happened?

She'd put away a piece of herself.

Elinor thought back to the dusty story on her computer. The one she'd kept getting sucked into.

Maybe it wasn't too late to get that part back.

Chapter Twelve

As romantic gestures go, I'd rather have jewelry than short grass, but perhaps the way to a certain librarian's heart is through her lawn mower...

—*Pine Hollow Newsletter*,
Wednesday, November 3

omething you want to tell us, Romeo?"

Levi tapped his cards into a neat stack before fanning them out—and it wasn't until the silence stretched that he realized *he* was supposed to be Romeo. He looked up, arching a brow at Connor, who had asked the question.

"Elinor?" Connor prompted.

He kept all reaction off his face, patiently waiting for Connor to spell out whatever it was he clearly wanted to give him shit about.

"You were seen mowing her lawn," Ben supplied.

"By Linda Hilson," Mac added gleefully—and at that Levi did flinch.

"Jesus."

"You really should keep up with the town newsletter,"

Mac suggested cheerfully, rocking back in his chair—and somehow Levi resisted the urge to flip that chair onto its back with his foot.

"That woman is going to get sued," he muttered.

"She's harmless," Ben insisted.

"You only say that because she isn't writing about your love life."

"Yes, she is. Just not as much as she's writing about yours."

"It's all in her head," Levi growled.

Connor arched a brow. "So you're saying you *weren't* seen coming and going from Elinor's garage on Monday and that you didn't, in fact, spend the entire afternoon of your only day off mowing her lawn and playing with her dog?"

Levi locked his jaw. How had she known? He hadn't seen anyone, and the backyard was totally fenced.

"It's been three years. Are we allowed to ask yet how you screwed up the best thing that ever happened to you?"

Levi glared at Mac. "I didn't screw it up," he insisted— and if he just kept saying that, he could drown out the whisper of doubt in the back of his mind that he had *completely* screwed it up. "I did what I had to do."

"You seriously aren't going to tell us what happened?"

"It doesn't matter now." Levi could usually shut things down with only the heavy authority in his voice, but this time they weren't letting him off the hook.

"So you guys are what?" Mac asked. "Dating again?"

"I'm surprised it took this long." Connor rearranged the cards in his hand. "We all figured you guys would get back together, but you've certainly dragged it out."

Levi held up a hand to stop him. "We're just friends. We've always been friends."

"I don't think you can call the last three years 'friends,'" Mac said. "She hated your guts."

"Still does, according to Ally," Ben chimed in. "I'm not sure the lawn-mowing gesture was the way to win her back."

"I'm not trying to win her back," Levi snapped, the words a little too sharp. "Her lawn needed mowing. I mowed it. End of story."

Connor's eyebrows arched upward. "You really think that's the end of the story?"

"Did you cheat on her?"

They all frowned at Mac.

"What?" he demanded. "We all heard the rumors. And you could have denied them, but you didn't. I'm not going to pretend I'm on your side just because of some bro code. I am fully Team Elinor, and if you cheated on her, I will definitely find a way to kick your ass, even if you are bigger and meaner than me."

Levi tried to stare him down, but, for once, the jovial diner owner wasn't backing down. The eyes that met Levi's were surprisingly serious. Frankly, it was a miracle Levi had avoided this conversation for this long—but the last few years had seen a lot, and somehow his screwed-up relationship status had never gotten top billing.

"I didn't," he finally said. He watched the tension in Mac's shoulders unknot—and a stray ember of jealousy embedded itself in his gut. "Why does it matter so much to you?" Was Mac interested in Elinor?

Mac rolled his eyes. "Relax, Tarzan. It matters because she's my *friend*, and honestly, most of the time, I like her more than I like you."

"Tarzan?"

"Because you're all 'Me Tarzan. Elinor mine,'" Mac grunted brokenly. Levi slowly lifted an eyebrow, and Mac flicked a poker chip at him. "Shut up. It was a good metaphor."

"Deenie thinks you're still in love with Elinor," Connor commented—always stirring the pot.

"Because I mowed her lawn?" Levi glared at the table at large. "Are we playing cards or not?"

"I'm fine with 'not' if you need to talk about your feelings," Connor drawled, reaching for the beer at his elbow.

"I don't have feelings," Levi snapped—and the guys exchanged a look, a look that made him want to throw down his cards and stomp from the room like an overgrown toddler.

Connor's wolfhound, Max, groaned loudly in the heavy silence and rolled over on his dog bed in the corner of the game room.

"I just wanted to do something nice for her. Okay?"

He'd kept thinking about the look on her face when she'd gotten that text from Charlotte. The way she'd chewed on her lip, like she'd always done when she was concentrating. The worry pinching between her eyebrows. He'd just wanted to take one of her worries away. Like he'd always done.

Ben cleared his throat. "You should probably know Ally says she's pissed about the yard."

Of course she was. He should have known she would be. Even when they'd been together, she'd always pitched a fit when he'd tried to do things for her. The time he'd installed a remote starter in her car had been a fight for *years*. Just when he'd thought she was finally over it, it would come up in another argument.

Though if he was honest, he *had* known she would be mad.

Even when he was mowing the yard, he'd been trying to do it before she got home—which was definitely a sign that he'd had more than a hunch that she wasn't going to love it.

But that didn't mean he stopped taking care of her. She'd be glad it was done, even if she hated him for doing it. He could take her hate. He just needed to take away one little burden. Was that really so horrible?

"Can we just play cards?"

🐾

The therapist's office hadn't changed. Not that he'd expected it to. It had only been a month, after all.

Levi hadn't expected to come back. And he had a feeling the therapist hadn't expected him to either, though the man hid it well as he smiled and welcomed him in.

Dr. Park.

Levi needed to stop thinking of him as *the therapist*, the nameless adversary in his mind. His name was Dr. Eugene Park.

He was a bit older, with silver threaded through his black hair and wrinkles in starbursts around his calm eyes. Somehow this time the calm didn't bother him quite so much. There was something almost soothing about it. Accepting. Levi wondered if they practiced that look in therapy school, then mentally kicked himself for being defensive. He'd told himself, on the drive up here, that he was going to be open and honest and all the things Marjorie was always going on about.

"No dog today?"

"She's not mine," Levi explained as he settled on the chair.

No couch, thank goodness. That was a little too clichéd for him. "She belongs to my ex. The dog keeps getting out, and I just had her with me last time because I didn't want to leave her unsupervised."

"So you and your ex share custody of the dog?"

"No, Dory's her dog. And she's a menace. I just don't want her getting hurt. Not that Elinor would ever thank me for it. I can't do anything for her without her getting mad at me."

Dr. Park's pencil scratched along his notebook, his expression placid. "Why do you think she's angry?"

"I know why. Because she didn't ask for my help. She'd say I'm interfering. But you can't always wait for someone to tell you what they need. If you see something, you have to do something. And I know what you're going to say— that I'm not responsible for the whole town. But I am. It's my job. And if I fail to do my job it can cost—" He broke off before he said the word *lives*.

Dr. Park just nodded. Calmly. "Have you always been a perfectionist?"

Levi snorted. "I'm not perfect. Far from it."

"But you think you need to be? If you fail, what happens?"

Britt Wells dies.

The words froze in his throat—and Levi became aware of how freely he'd been talking.

When Levi pressed his lips together in a tight line, the therapist—*Dr. Park*—tried another tack. They talked for a while about work, and he occasionally dropped in questions about Elinor. It felt strange explaining things to him. Everyone in town knew their history. There were no secrets in Pine Hollow, as Linda Hilson had aptly proven.

Except his. His big secret.

He'd hidden the fact that he wasn't a reader his entire life. But he wasn't about to tell the therapist that.

It was much later when the conversation turned back to Elinor again.

"You keep talking about taking care of her—whether she wants you to or not." Dr. Park's calm voice filled the room. "Have you considered that taking care of your ex is you trying to feel in control in a world where you can't save everyone, no matter how perfect you are?"

Levi tensed, fighting the instinct to stand up and leave. "That's not what this is."

"All right," Dr. Park acknowledged, his calm never wavering.

"It's not about control." Even if he never allowed himself more than two beers. Or even too much of that cold medicine that made him feel foggy. He just didn't like being weak. *Jackson men aren't weak.* "I just want to take care of her."

"But you aren't together anymore."

"No."

"And why is that?"

"It's complicated."

Dr. Park's smile was saturated with understanding. "It usually is." The timer on his phone went off. "And it looks like we'll get into that next time."

There won't be a next time. Levi shoved down the thought, hiding his eagerness to retreat as the session wrapped up.

He flicked off the audiobook in the Explorer as soon as he turned on the engine, his thoughts too busy for outside words.

His fingers drummed on the steering wheel as he drove back toward Pine Hollow. He wasn't a control freak. And he certainly wasn't using Elinor to feel in control of his life. He'd never been able to control how he felt about her. That love had always controlled him, not the other way around.

The therapist didn't know what the hell he was talking about. Calling him a perfectionist was laughable. You had to be within striking distance of perfect to be a perfectionist, and Levi had always fallen far short of that mark.

Nope. Dr. Park was full of shit. And he didn't know the first thing about Elinor and Levi. She wasn't a way to feel in control. She was the inevitable, gravitational force he'd never been able to resist. She was the planet he orbited around. That was just physics. And he'd been locked into orbit much too long ago for any of that to change now.

Chapter Thirteen

Rumor has it there might be other candidates vying for the heart of our fair librarian...

—*Pine Hollow Newsletter*,
Wednesday, November 3

On Saturday morning, Elinor sat on her couch, drinking her coffee, watching Dory play with a pine cone she'd brought inside and contemplating the fact that she might actually be a freaking amazing writer.

She'd forgotten that feeling. The combination of the post-book sigh and *I can't believe I actually wrote that*.

Katie had always told her she was good, but Katie was biased, and Elinor had never felt ready to submit to agents or publishers. There was always one more editing pass to do, one more tweak that would make it perfect, one more reason this wasn't the right time. But it had never been the right time, and somehow taking three years away—unintentional as it had been—had left her with a foreign new feeling.

The book might be ready.

The doorbell rang, and Dory levitated off the floor,

barking wildly as she ran to the door, her toenails clattering down the hall.

Elinor followed more slowly, her fuzzy slippers slapping against the floorboards. Dory sat, her tail wagging as she gazed expectantly at the door.

Elinor's sisters stood on the doorstep. Anne huddled beneath a red scarf, still looking groggy from sleep, while Charlotte had that I-just-jogged-three-miles-and-I'm-on-a-mission look that Elinor had learned to fear.

"Did I know you were coming?" Elinor asked.

"We're staging an intervention," Charlotte declared, pushing past her into the house holding a pastry box from Magda's.

"Charlotte's staging an intervention. I'm just here for the crullers," Anne clarified, trailing Charlotte toward the kitchen.

Elinor shut the door and followed them to where Charlotte was already making herself at home at the Keurig. Dory had positioned herself as close to the counter as possible, in case cruller crumbs might be in her future.

"Do I want to know what this is about?" Elinor asked Anne under her breath, but it was Charlotte who answered.

"Every time I think you're over him, you go sliding backward."

Realization dawned. "I'm not back with Levi," Elinor insisted. *That damn newsletter.*

"He was seen *mowing* your *lawn.*"

"It's not like I asked him to!" Anne had just opened the pastry box and distracted her by shoving a cruller into her hand—and Elinor reined in her volume as she continued. "You know what he's like. Remember the remote starter?"

"How could I forget?" Charlotte picked up her coffee—

taking it black, which was an insult to taste buds, in Elinor's opinion, but Charlotte had always been a little crazy.

"I thought that was sweet," Anne commented, getting out a mug for herself while Elinor set her cruller on a plate and put the kettle on for tea.

"It was not sweet," Charlotte argued. "It was overbearing."

"It was also kind of sweet."

Charlotte glared at Anne. "Stop it. We aren't getting them back together. This is a reality check. Team Closure."

Anne unwrapped a tea bag and grumbled something that Charlotte pretended not to hear.

"We just want you to be happy," Charlotte insisted, though her glare made the words sound more like a threat than sisterly love.

"I am happy," Elinor insisted. "I'm perfectly capable of synthesizing my own happiness."

Charlotte frowned, her coffee cup pausing midway to her mouth. "What does that even mean?"

"I bet it's a podcast thing," Anne said.

Elinor glared at both of them. "Just because I heard about it on a podcast doesn't mean it isn't valid. People need to take responsibility for synthesizing their own happiness regardless of what life hands them, rather than waiting for the universe to grant them perfect good fortune."

"Is that like making lemonade? Are you just using fancy words for making lemons into lemonade?" Anne asked around a bite of cruller.

Charlotte snorted. "Synthesized lemons or whatever, you can't get back with Levi."

"I'm not going to!" Elinor protested.

"But you aren't actually doing anything to move on, either."

"I'm on dating apps." Admittedly she hadn't checked them in a while. She'd actually gotten a notice that one of them was deactivating her profile due to lack of use.

"When was the last time you went on a date?"

Elinor flushed. Okay. It had been a while. Probably since summer. But the school year was her busy time, and her last few dates had been so *awkward* she'd just wanted a break from it all. But she knew better than to say that to Charlotte. "It's almost the holidays," she argued instead. "Everyone's busy—"

"Oh my God, would you stop with the excuses? I'm setting you up with George."

"George?"

"The residents at the Estates cannot stop gushing about how wonderful he is."

"Is this the new physical therapist? I thought you were giving him to Magda."

Charlotte waved a hand. "Oh, you know, apparently he has celiac, and gluten is her love language."

"Amen," Anne muttered around a blissed-out bite of a Magda cruller.

"There's always Kendall—" Elinor suggested.

"Stop trying to give him to my friends when I'm trying to give him to you! Take the gift PT and say thank you."

"Have you asked the gift PT if he wants to be given? He might be in a relationship. Or gay."

"He's single and straight. Trust me. The biddies at the Estates had his relationship status and sexual orientation nailed down in less than twenty-four hours. There was a bridge tournament to determine who got first dibs for their hetero granddaughters, but I'm their favorite doctor, so I can jump the queue."

"That poor man."

"He's doing fine. I'll set you up—are there any days you can't do?"

Elinor shook her head. "I didn't agree to this."

"But you will, because you love me and you know I'm right."

"One of those things is true."

Charlotte made a face—but it rapidly transitioned to *the look.* The we-both-know-I'm-right look. "Come on, Elinor. He's *nice.*"

Elinor caved. "Fine! I'll go out with him."

She needed to date more anyway. She'd gotten on Match last year because she wanted to meet someone. She might as well meet Charlotte's someone.

Though Charlotte wasn't exactly known for her excellent taste in men.

Still. Even if he wasn't Mr. Perfect, Elinor needed to get out of her rut. She was so good at rationalizing why she and her various online matches wouldn't work out, she never actually went out with most of them. It was time to try again.

In more ways than one.

It might be time to research agents and actually chase the dream she'd put away. Katie would be so mad at her if she knew how she'd stagnated for the last three years. Katie had always pushed her, and these last few years she'd forgotten how to push herself.

Yes. It was definitely time.

🐾

George Leneghan was cute. He was nice. He was funny. Elinor could easily see why the octogenarians at the Estates were lining up to set him up with their grandchildren.

And she felt nothing.

The big nada.

He had longish sandy hair that he was constantly flick-ing out of his eyes, and dark brown eyes behind his thick Clark Kent glasses. His front teeth were a tiny bit crooked, one overlapping the other just slightly, but if possible that made his smile even more endearing. He leaned forward when he spoke, talking with his hands, and listened—really listened—without interrupting whenever he asked her a question.

And they had zero chemistry.

She was pretty sure George noticed it too, though his charm never wavered for a second.

They'd met up for drinks at the Tipsy Moose. Elinor preferred coffee for a first date, but since the best coffee in town was served at the Cup, which was also the worst gossip hub in a fifty-mile radius, Elinor had persuaded Charlotte to arrange her blind date for drinks instead. The Tipsy Moose was a casual pub, all dark wood and scarred booths, with none of the starched-tablecloth formality of the Grill at the Pine Hollow Inn, which Charlotte had originally suggested.

Elinor wanted someplace she'd be comfortable, some-place they had more than a snowball's chance of being left alone. The Tipsy Moose was quiet on the Monday night before Thanksgiving—no trivia, no karaoke, and no rowdy darts tournaments. Just the jukebox in the corner playing a random assortment of classic rock. The high backs of the booth gave them the illusion of privacy. The bartender, Iain, gave them the occasional glance, but they were as alone as they could be in public in Pine Hollow.

The perfect place to get to know each other.

George was from Colorado. He had four older sisters, and he'd moved to Pine Hollow to take the job at the Estates because he loved the outdoors and had always heard Vermont was breathtaking. He'd liked the fall color, thought their mountains looked more like the hills where he came from, and he did not, in fact, have celiac disease.

When she'd expressed concern that there would be gluten in the pretzel bites he suggested they share, he'd thought *she* had a problem with gluten, which had led to a distinctly awkward moment and the overwhelming desire, on Elinor's part at least, to murder her sister.

But she couldn't blame Charlotte for the lack of fireworks. She couldn't really blame anyone.

Except perhaps the podcast she'd listened to over the weekend that had claimed it was possible to manufacture love—that there was a set of questions you could ask on a first date that would make people fall in love. Like love was just a matter of asking the right question in the right order—though with Levi it had never been about questions. Never about what they said to one another. They'd known one another for so long the questions would have been redundant—but she'd been wrong about him. Maybe the questions were the way to go.

"Do you think it's possible to make people fall in love?"

George's jaw loosened slightly—like it wanted to drop, but he managed to catch it before it got far. "I'm sorry?"

Elinor felt her face heating and shoved her glasses higher on her nose in an attempt to distract from the blush. She hadn't meant to blurt that out. It probably wasn't the reply he'd been expecting when he asked her about her favorite books, but they'd been getting to know one another for an hour now. Endless small talk—and she'd always been terrible at small talk. She didn't want to talk about what she liked and what he liked and how many siblings they each had and whether they'd done any interesting traveling.

If he was going to get to know her, he might as well know that her brain jumped all over the place—especially when she was uncomfortable or impatient—and she had a tendency to drop random non sequiturs into conversation.

"I was listening to this podcast," she explained, the words quick and staccato. "About some scientists who wanted to grow love in a lab, so they came up with this series of questions that are supposed to create a sense of intimacy and make you fall in love, even if you've just met some-one. But is it even love if you did it on purpose? Or is it just people who *want* to be in love convincing themselves that they are? How would you even measure that? I mean, with something so subjective, how can there be any kind of scientific rigor? Are people self-reporting love? And how in love are they? Are some of them more in love than others? It's like pain. They have those pain scales at the hospital— but how do I know my two isn't your six?"

A small dimple appeared in his left cheek. He only had one. Lopsided. Cute. "Have you spent a lot of time thinking about this?"

"Just in the last five minutes," Elinor admitted, awkward-ness swelling up from the floor to envelop her. "Sorry. I don't mean anything by it. I'm always blurting out stuff like that. I know it's weird."

"Don't apologize." That crooked smile quirked again. "Weird is awesome. The sexiest thing you can be is at home in your own skin."

It was the right thing to say, but it still felt wrong.

Maybe because she didn't feel at home in her own skin.

She knew that was what people saw when they looked at her—someone confident, maybe even a little intimidating. She knew that she was good at things. She knew that she was smart.

But she was also pretending. She was a thousand broken pieces held together with super glue and string, and she wanted someone who loved the broken pieces. Someone who didn't make her feel like she had to put on the show that everything was okay.

"Thanks," she muttered, disengaging from his eye contact by taking a sip of her drink.

"Do you wanna try it? Answer the questions?" he asked, and his face was so open and willing that she felt awful for the fact that no, she didn't want to try it.

Elinor chewed on her lower lip, leaning back in the booth. "I don't know. It takes a long time." And she'd have to talk about stuff. Real stuff.

She hadn't said a word to George about Katie or her mom or Anne's illness. She'd redirected the small talk whenever the conversation had drifted too close.

She'd have to talk to him about those things eventually if they were going to date.

Anyone she met now would never know her mom or her best friend. Maybe that was part of why it had been so hard to completely let go of the idea of Levi. He knew her history. All of it. Katie. Her mom. All the people whose memories shaped her, but who were only memories now.

"I've got time," George offered. "You gotta make time to give love a chance, right?" he teased with a sweet, no-pressure, I'm-game-if-you-are smile.

Except she wasn't game. And she felt guilty that she'd brought it up at all.

She knew he was only a couple of years younger than she was, but there was something so boyish about that smile, as if nothing bad had ever happened to him, and in that moment she felt *old*.

This was why she sucked at dating. She didn't want to talk about the real stuff—for almost a year she hadn't been able to bring up Katie's name without crying—but small talk made her stir-crazy.

Charlotte was right. George was wasted on her. Her sister should have saved him for Magda, after all.

"Maybe some other time," she hedged. "I try to save psychological experiments for the second date."

He laughed, deep and easy, and she jumped a little at the sound. "Fair enough." His kind eyes took in her flinch, and he rocked back in the booth a little, reverting back to the neutral territory of small talk. "So you said your sister Anne is the sweet one and Charles is the bossy one—which I totally see—so which one are you?"

Elinor's eyebrows popped up. "Charles?"

George laughed at himself. "Sorry. Force of habit. The first time I saw her name it was written on a medical file and the end was cut off, so it was just Dr. Charl Rodridguez. I made an assumption."

"I bet Charlotte *loved* that."

"Shockingly, you would be wrong," he said mildly, pretending not to notice her sarcasm. "For some reason she wasn't a fan. But nevertheless, the nickname stuck."

She smiled at the dryness in his voice. "I have a feeling you made it stick."

"I admit to nothing."

"And yet she still set you up with me. I'm suddenly wondering if she's mad at me."

He laughed, but then his smile seemed to freeze awkwardly in place, his eyes flicking to the left and behind her. "Okay, this might sound crazy, but I think someone's watching us. Don't look—" he started to say, but she was already twisting around in her booth.

And there he was.

She hadn't been thinking of Levi—she'd been doing an excellent job of *not* thinking of him—but she must have known on some level whom she was going to see, because when she locked eyes with him what she felt was more grim acknowledgment than surprise.

He leaned against the bar near Iain, his long build propped against the mahogany with a lazy permanence like he'd been there all night, though his hair still glistened from the rain outside. He didn't even look embarrassed to have been caught stalking her on her date. He met her eyes, lifting one shoulder in a guess-you-caught-me shrug.

Elinor's heart began to pound.

How *dare* he? This was worse than mowing her lawn without her permission.

He'd broken up with *her*. She was just trying to date, trying to move on with her life, and it was already hard enough because no one else would ever be him. Nothing had ever felt like they did. She hated him a little bit for that and now he was going to *supervise* her dates?

No. Not happening.

"Someone you know?" George asked, his voice breaking into the rage bubbling up from her core like lava en route to an imminent volcanic eruption.

She yanked her glare off Levi and spun back to face her kind, charming date. "I'm sorry. Could you excuse me for a moment? There's someone I have to go kill."

Chapter Fourteen

And may I just say, jealousy looks good on our dear chief.

—*Pine Hollow Newsletter*,
Wednesday, November 24

Levi had been on the receiving end of Elinor's death glower enough times to predict that this was going to be a spectacular explosion. He should have known better than to trust Linda Hilson's claim that there was an "emergency" at the Tipsy Moose.

Elinor stalked across the bar, her gaze never leaving his as steam practically poured from her ears.

He'd always thought she was gorgeous when she was angry—but that thought had never done him any good. Her dark eyes were fiery behind her glasses, and her mouth was drawn into a tight, angry bow. Slim black brows pulled down angrily, and her ponytail swung with each aggressive step.

She'd worn a midnight-blue dress for her date—it had

been obvious it was a date from the second he walked in the door—and the skirt swished around her thighs as she stomped toward him. The bodice was snug, and the gold cross her grandmother had given her seemed to point straight down toward the shadow of her cleavage. Which was probably sacrilegious to think, but if the Almighty was going to create something as gorgeous as Elinor, the least Levi could do was appreciate it. Even if she currently looked like she was getting ready to break some Commandments. Specifically the ones prohibiting her from killing him.

"Get out," she snapped when she was close enough that her angry growl could be heard without raising her voice.

He lifted one eyebrow. "It's a public place."

"Not for you it isn't. Get out." Her palms smacked onto the curve of her hips. "What are you even doing here? You never come here."

It would be more accurate to say he never came here without her. She was the one who loved karaoke and team trivia nights. When they'd been together, he'd only come along to rock back in his chair and watch her and Katie laugh themselves silly.

He could have conceded that this was her territory, that she'd gained custody of the Tipsy Moose in their breakup, but instead he heard himself asking, "Is that why you brought him here?"

Her eyes narrowed dangerously. "That is none of your business."

It felt like his business. Elinor had always felt like his business. "I'm just here investigating a call. Someone called in suspicious activity at the Tipsy Moose."

"Are you kidding me?" She hissed something under her breath laced with expletives. "I don't belong to you."

"I know."

"They have no right to *tattle* on me just because I'm having a perfectly nice date with a perfectly nice man."

Levi's gaze flicked involuntarily behind her—to where her date was watching their conversation with tense interest. He looked ready to intervene if Elinor needed him but was hanging back to let her fight her own battles until then. And the fact that he was handling the situation exactly the way Elinor would want him to made Levi hate him a little bit.

He should run a background check. People with nice faces could be serial killers, too.

"You can't break up with me and keep lurking in my life." Elinor's sharp statement brought his full attention back to her. "That's just wildly unfair."

"I'm not lurking."

"What would you call it?"

"Looking after a friend."

"We are not friends, and I do not need you looking after me. I look after me. You forfeited your right to look after me when you broke up with me. You can't just do these things. Checking up on my dates. Mowing my lawn."

"I should have known you would make an issue out of me doing anything nice for you."

"It's not nice!" she snapped. "It's overbearing! You don't ask. You just take over. No discussion. No consideration that I might have had a plan to do it my own way in my own time—"

"And now you don't have to plan. The mower's fixed. Your lawn is done. You're welcome."

"I'm not thanking you! You're not listening. It doesn't matter if you think it's good for me. It's my life. My choice—"

"So leaving your lawn overgrown is a lifestyle choice now?"

"It's *my* lawn. This is just like the remote starter."

"You were irrational about that, too."

The look she gave him made him feel lucky she wasn't armed.

"It was my car," she hissed in a voice right out of a horror movie.

"Your garage was always full and your car was sitting out in the cold in the middle of winter. At least with a remote starter you didn't have to get into a cold car every day."

"So you just steal my car one morning and have a remote starter installed?"

"It was a surprise. Lots of women love surprises."

"Then go date one of them!" she shouted. "Weren't you supposed to be dating half the town?"

Levi studied her face, the evidence that she'd believed the rumors stinging more than he'd expected. She'd asked once if they were true, but this was the first time she'd ever thrown the rumors in his face. And yes, he'd never done anything to disprove them, but he'd also thought Elinor knew him better than that.

"Go supervise someone else's love life. Or better yet, leave us all alone. But either way, I'm allowed to date whoever I want."

"I never said you weren't." He'd been watching her date other men for three years, hadn't he? "I told you to date Connor. He would have been good for you."

"Seriously?" she yelped—and if there had been any heads in the place that weren't already turned toward them, they would have turned at her volume. "Connor is in love with Deenie!"

"Well, he is now. But before—"

She didn't let him finish. "You don't get a say in who I date! How many times do I have to say this? You don't get a say in anything I do. What did you think was going to happen when you broke off our engagement?"

"I thought we'd be friends. We were always friends."

"And you broke my heart."

His throat closed. There was no answer to that.

The steam seemed to drain out of her, the anger leaving a sadness in its wake that pricked at him. "Are you okay?" he asked softly. "Is there something else going on—"

"Of course I'm okay," she cut him off, but the words were weary rather than sharp. "I'm always okay. And it's none of your business if I'm not, is it?"

"It could be," he offered low. "You know I'd always help you."

"You wanna help? Help me file a restraining order against the chief of police."

His head reared back. "Is that what you want?"

Elinor took a long, slow breath before shaking her head. "No. I just…I need you to not be here, Levi. I know we're both in the wedding, and we can be grown-ups about that, but other than that, I need you to stay away from me. You broke up with me, but it was like you never let me go. You have to let me go."

"I didn't come to bother you. I didn't even know you were here—"

"No, but the town knew, and everyone is assuming we're back together because you're running around *mowing my lawn*."

"People already thought we were together because of your dog, and I wouldn't have thought to mow it at all if Dory hadn't gotten out again—"

"Dory will be staying with Ally or Deenie while I'm at work from now on. You won't have to worry about that. So stop dropping by my house. Stop *helping*. And maybe this town will figure out what I did three years ago. That we are *never* getting back together."

His heart shuddered. He'd known. Hell, it was what he'd wanted, but it still felt like a blow.

Levi nodded tersely. "I'll leave you to your date."

"Good," she snapped. Arms folded as if she wanted to watch him leave before she moved.

Levi nodded again and pushed away from the bar. Elinor's date immediately tensed at the movement and Levi barely resisted the urge to get involved in an alpha staredown. He walked out of the Tipsy Moose without a backward glance, moving without pausing to his Explorer and climbing in.

He sat behind the wheel, staring blindly into the night and rubbing a hand over his chest. They'd been broken up for three years, so why did this hurt? Why did it feel like he was losing her all over again?

Had he been lurking in her life? Casting a shadow over her dates and making it impossible for her to move on? If he was really honest with himself... he probably had. Not intentionally. Not consciously. But he had. And he needed to stop.

The problem was he'd never really *wanted* to let her go. He'd done it for her. Because it was best for her. Because he had to. And she'd never appreciated it.

"Did you tell her why?"

"What?" Levi shifted uncomfortably in the very comfortable chair, while Dr. Park gazed at him calmly.

"Did you tell her *why* you let her go, as you put it?" the therapist asked again.

Levi knew why he'd come back—he'd already had the appointment scheduled, and it felt rude to cancel at the last minute—but he didn't know why he'd started talking about Elinor. Marjorie had wanted him to talk about his feelings about Britt Wells, but instead he was stuck in his feelings about Elinor.

"No," he admitted. "She would have only argued with me."

"So you made the choice for both of you."

Levi instantly tensed. "It's not like the lawn. Or the freaking remote starter."

Dr. Park nodded, tapping his pencil against his pad. "Levi…when you talk about your ex, you always refer to breaking up with her as 'letting her go' or 'setting her free.' Do you think Elinor was trapped with you? That she had no choice but to be with you?"

Good for you, kid. You found a woman way too good for you and too nice to ever leave you. Chip off the old block.

"No. Of course not," Levi insisted, pushing away the echo of his father's voice. "It was just for the best."

"The best for whom?"

"For her." Obviously.

"But you made that choice for her."

"Elinor always does what she should do. She steps up. Takes care of people. Puts herself last. It's what she's always done ever since we were kids. She never had a chance to chase her own dreams, and she wasn't going to leave me."

"But you thought she should? That she couldn't have those dreams and you?"

"You're twisting things. I did it for her."

"And she's been angry at you ever since?" Dr. Park asked mildly.

"Sometimes people don't know what they need."

"But you know."

"I'm not saying I know. I just know Elinor, and..."

"And?" Dr. Park prompted.

"She was too good for me, okay?"

The timer on Dr. Park's watch went off, and he glanced down at it. "We're out of time, but I just want to give you one last thing to think about before our next session."

Would there even be a next session? "Yeah, okay."

"Have you ever considered whether you didn't break up with her for her? If instead, you might have been afraid she was too good for you and someday she would figure it out and leave you, so you left first because that way it was in your control?"

Levi's jaw locked. "That isn't what happened."

"Just something to think about."

Levi flexed his hand on the steering wheel as he drove back toward Pine Hollow, his audiobook once again silent. He needed to find a therapist closer to home. The drives home were killing him, his thoughts circling in a downward spiral.

Good for you, kid. Chip off the old block.

Those words had never been good, coming from his father. Sarcastic. Bitter. All the ways they were alike seemed to be ways he was failing to measure up. Failing in school. Getting into fights. Breaking his arm senior year right before the scouts were supposed to come watch him play.

Chip off the old block. Translation: Look what a loser you are. Just like me.

Levi remembered with crystal clarity the day his father had said Elinor was too good for him. It wasn't like it was a shock. He'd always known. But that day the words had slipped into a different part of his brain, embedding themselves there, burrowing deep.

His parents had been moving to North Carolina. He'd been helping them pack, and his mother had been bemoaning the timing. She'd wanted to be around to help with wedding planning. Elinor had so much to do and no mother of her own to help her. His mom wanted to stay, just a few more months, but his father wanted to go right away—and they all knew whose preferences would win.

Elinor had come over to help, calling his parents Mr. and Mrs. Jackson with that stiff formality she always had around them, no matter how many times his mother had asked her to call her Sheila. His father had watched Levi watching Elinor with his mom and clapped him on the shoulder.

Good for you, kid. You found a woman way too good for you and too nice to ever leave you. Chip off the old block.

And Levi had nearly been sick.

He'd never seen the parallels before between his relationship with Elinor and his parents' marriage. He'd never wanted to see them. His mother was a saint. His father far from it—but his mother stayed. For as long as he'd been old enough to be aware of his parents' marriage, he'd wondered why his mother stayed.

And in that moment he'd started to wonder why Elinor stayed.

He didn't realize she would be better off without him right away. It was weeks of thinking about it and having his suspicions confirmed by the person who knew Elinor best in the world that had finally tipped the scales—and even then he hadn't been able to bring himself to do what he knew he needed to do for another week after that.

Elinor been talking about the wedding, about whether they wanted to write their own vows, and he'd realized he couldn't do it. He couldn't make her promise to stay. He couldn't let her make that vow. He had to take it back. End the engagement.

He just hadn't realized their entire friendship would unravel. He hadn't thought that far. He'd only been thinking one step ahead.

And it wasn't because he was scared she would leave him later or trying to control an uncontrollable situation. It was because he was scared she *wouldn't* leave him when she needed to. So he'd forced her hand. And maybe it had been an asshole thing to do. She hated when he made decisions for the both of them, but it had been the only way to get the necessary result. And the result had been necessary. He might be a chip off the old block, but there was no way in hell he was letting Elinor turn into his mother.

His mom always tried to hide how unhappy she was, but he'd seen the strain. As a kid, he'd heard her crying on the nights when his father didn't come home. He'd never forgotten that sound. When he was older, when he'd moved out and stopped being so certain his mother had only stayed because of him, he'd come right out one night and asked her why she didn't leave his dad. The answer had been evasive and indirect—but it hadn't been about love or happiness. It was about keeping her word. About not believing in divorce. About his father *needing* her. And about not giving up when things were hard—because it seemed like they were always hard with his dad.

Dr. Park had accused him of trying to be the savior of the entire town? Fine. So he had a savior complex. He'd saved Elinor. And he'd do it again. Because he loved her too much to let her screw up her life for him.

Chapter Fifteen

As we settle down to feast this weekend,
don't forget we've opened up a tip line...
just in case you hear anything particularly
juicy as you're passing the gravy.
—*Pine Hollow Newsletter*,
Wednesday, November 24

Happy Turkey Day, Rodriguez family!"

Anne and Elinor exchanged a grin at Charlotte's
bellow as their baby sister burst through the front door.
They sat curled on the couch in front of the Macy's parade
with fresh pastries on their laps. Dory lay on the floor at
Elinor's feet, her chin propped vertically against the couch
so she could watch for any falling crumbs.

Charlotte paused in the process of unwinding her scarf,
her nose twitching. "Are those medialunas?"

Elinor managed a single word around the pastry shoved
into her mouth and pointed toward the kitchen, where their
father could be heard singing to himself. "Kitchen."

Charlotte squealed and disappeared through the swing-
ing door into their father's domain, where they could hear

her shouting "Happy Thanksgiving, Papa!" and their father's more muted response.

Matias Rodriguez loved to cook, and holidays were his Olympics—always kicking off with the fresh Argentine pastries his mother had made for him growing up. But the highly organized engineer couldn't stand having his daughters underfoot while he was cooking—he had a *system*, and they didn't understand the system—so it was no surprise when Charlotte was kicked out of the kitchen less than two minutes after she went in.

"Hello, gorgeous." She cradled the pastry plate in her hands and cooed at it lovingly, only paying attention to her sisters after taking her first bite and closing her eyes with bliss. "Did Snoopy come out yet?" she asked, flinging herself onto the couch in between Anne and Elinor.

"Not yet," Anne answered. "The Rockettes just did their thing."

Charlotte nodded as she took another bite and groaned orgasmically. "I love carbs." As the next marching band appeared, she nudged Elinor with her foot. "So? How was the date?"

Elinor narrowed her eyes at her baby sister. "Funny you should mention carbs. He isn't celiac."

"What?"

"George. The PT. You said he was allergic to gluten."

She frowned, visibly confused. "I never said that. How would I even know?"

Elinor glared. "You said he couldn't date Magda because gluten was her love language!"

She snorted. "Obviously I wasn't serious."

"It wasn't obvious, and when I asked him about it, he thought I was crazy."

"Whatever." Charlotte flapped a hand dismissively. "You should be thanking me for knocking the dust off your girly parts. Is he a good kisser?"

Elinor huffed, keeping her gaze fixed on the parade in progress. "I wouldn't know, because I didn't kiss him."

"Why not? Is he secretly a dick? Because I need to tell the biddy grapevine that he's a sleaze if he isn't going to treat their granddaughters well."

"He's not a sleaze. He's very sweet. He just—"

"Oh God," Charlotte groaned. "*Sweet*. Kiss of death. You friendzoned him."

"I didn't friendzone him! I just didn't jump into bed with him on the first date like you seem to think is appropriate behavior."

"Has it occurred to you that you worry a little too much about what appropriate behavior is?" Charlotte asked. "If you like a guy, jump his bones."

"What a beautiful sentiment. Maybe I'll put that in our vows."

She could *feel* Charlotte roll her eyes. "It's not always about romance and candlelight. Sometimes you just need to get your world rocked, and if your grumpiness lately is anything to go by, it has been far too long since anyone has rocked your world."

Levi had rocked her world—but he had no place in this conversation, or her thoughts. The obnoxious lurker.

"I don't need a man to make me happy," Elinor declared.

"No, but certain parts of them are very useful—"

"I'm a grown woman. My mood is not dictated by dick."

Anne snorted. Charlotte went on as if she hadn't spoken. "I teed you up. He's sweet—your words. He's cute—"

"So *you* jump him."

"I'm taken."

"And where is dear Warren?"

"Oh, look, Snoopy," Anne suddenly interjected.

Charlotte glared at her now-empty medialuna plate. "You try to do something nice for someone," she muttered—not nearly under her breath enough to avoid being heard.

Elinor felt an unwelcome glimmer of guilt. Charlotte was pushy, but she was also trying to help. This was how she showed she cared—obnoxious though she could be.

As Snoopy made his slow way down the street on television, Elinor reached over and interlaced her fingers with Charlotte's. "Thank you for setting me up with the cute PT. He really is a very nice guy, and I might have kissed him good night if the end of our date hadn't gotten kind of weird."

Charlotte instantly perked up, intrigued by the hint of good gossip. "Weird how? Is he secretly kinky? And if so, what kind of kinky?"

"I didn't have the chance to find out. Levi showed up."

Charlotte groaned, sliding off the couch and dramatically onto the floor in a puddle of disappointment—which Dory thought was wonderful. She immediately began climbing all over Charlotte and licking everything she could reach.

"This was supposed to be a Levi-free date," Charlotte complained, somehow managing to deliver the scold with a dog all over her chest.

"It's not like I invited him. Some helpful townsperson called in 'suspicious activity' at the Tipsy Moose, knowing he'd have to come by to check it out."

"And you couldn't just pretend you didn't know him?"

"I only talked to him long enough to tell him to leave me alone, but after that the dynamic was different." Not that there'd been much of a romantic vibe before that, but after Levi's departure Elinor hadn't been able to entirely put away her irritation with her ex. It had made the rest of the evening strained.

Charlotte sighed. "Well, I guess if George is scared off by one six-foot, fully armed ex-fiancé, then he isn't for you."

"I don't think we can blame this one on George."

"Well, I can't blame you. You're my sister. Obviously George was lucky to get a shot at you," Charlotte said, with the absolute conviction that made it hard to be annoyed by her, even when she was at her pushiest. "Can we blame Levi?"

"Yes. Absolutely."

A doorbell rang on a commercial on the television, and Dory launched herself off Charlotte's chest to race toward the front door, barking frantically at the phantom intruders. Charlotte grunted at having her rib cage used as a canine springboard and rolled to her feet.

"Did you bring up the Christmas stuff yet?" she asked, the topic of Elinor's love life apparently shelved for now—thank goodness.

"It's all still in the basement," Anne said. "We were waiting for you."

"Well, come on, then." Charlotte clapped her hands, heading for the stairs. "This house isn't going to decorate itself."

🐾

By the time their father announced that the turkey he'd faithfully tended all afternoon was ready to eat, the house looked like Santa's workshop had exploded inside it.

Their family had always taken the holidays seriously, and their collection of Christmas decorations seemed to grow every year. The sheer density of Christmas cheer didn't even seem to be impacted much by the fact that Charlotte, Anne, and Elinor had all migrated most of their ornaments to their own places. Astrid was coming by later in the weekend to help Elinor put up her own tree and deck the halls, but at the moment her dad's house was Christmas perfection.

They all stuffed themselves with too much turkey, and after dinner, Anne sat at their mother's piano, softly playing Christmas carols. Charlotte lay on the floor on her back with her head beneath the Christmas tree, staring up at the lights—and she'd spent so much time on the floor today that Dory didn't even seem to think it was a game anymore.

Most days Elinor would be on her back right next to Charlotte, staring up at the tree with her glasses off so all the colored lights blurred together in a glorious impressionist montage—but instead she sat curled on the couch, leaning her shoulder against her dad's while Charlotte kept checking her phone every ten seconds and frowning. It didn't take a genius to see Warren was being Warren again.

Their dad had muted the television so he could listen to Anne play, but he flipped through the channels, muttering something about looking for football scores. As if they didn't all know he was going to end up stopping on the cheesiest made-for-TV Christmas movie he could find and watching the whole thing because he "just forgot to change the channel."

He was such a softie. He never said much—not that it was easy to get a word in edgewise in a house with three daughters—but he was always there for them, a silent, steady presence in their lives. No wonder she'd fallen so hard for Levi's strong-and-silent routine when they were younger. Though Levi was nothing like her father. Matias Rodriguez was a total marshmallow, tearing up at sentimental commercials and Hallmark Channel movies. Whereas Elinor didn't think she'd ever seen Levi cry. Not once. She couldn't even be positive he had tear ducts.

Her dad had stopped on a movie where a young city girl returns home to her picturesque small town to save the family inn before Christmas. Anne finished her song and came to join them on the couch, turning on the sound as she passed the remote. Charlotte glanced up at the sound and rolled onto her side to watch, though she kept messing with her phone.

Elinor opened her mouth to say something, but Anne sat beside her and bent close to her to whisper. "Do you really think it helps? Giving her a hard time about him?"

Elinor sighed, giving Anne a look that said, *No, obviously I'm aware it doesn't help, but how do you not say something when he's awful to her and she just takes it like she can't do any better?*

Anne smiled gently. "She has to figure it out on her own," she whispered.

Elinor closed her mouth.

All the wisdom seemed to have skipped right over her and landed on her sister. Though it wasn't like she didn't *know* what Anne knew. She simply found it hard to act on. Especially when it came to Charlotte.

It was hard not to feel responsible for her. She knew Charlotte was an adult now—Charlotte certainly told her often enough—but Elinor had practically raised her. Her sisters were a huge part of why she'd wanted to stay so close to home for college. And why she'd come back. Though she couldn't imagine being anywhere else. Pine Hollow was home. Her mother had loved it here, working at the welcome center as long as she was able, telling visitors all the best things about their town.

Everyone had always told Elinor she was going to put Pine Hollow on the map. That she was going to go off and achieve great things. But she'd always just wanted to be here, with her family. It was Charlotte who'd gone to med school. Charlotte who almost hadn't come back. And now that she was back, it was hard for Elinor to turn off that protective instinct. On some level, her sister would always be that little girl who needed her. Nine years old and small for her age, clinging to Elinor's hand as they stood in the church, lined up to receive condolences at her mother's funeral.

They watched the movie in silence—which was odd for them. It was rare for all of them to be in one house and for no one to be talking. On screen the heroine's widowed mother kept receiving deliveries from the handsome older florist in their small town—and Charlotte kept sneaking glances at their dad.

When the movie went to commercial, Elinor wasn't at all surprised when her younger sister rolled over and propped her head on her hand. "You know you could do that," she commented to their father. "Pick up some cutie at the inn. You've got the whole silver fox thing going on."

Their father's ruddy cheeks flushed as he shook his head. "Don't be silly." The words were touched by his soft accent, a by-product of moving to the States when he was eleven.

"Why is it silly?" Charlotte argued. "You're a catch."

Their dad appealed to Elinor and Anne with a look, and Elinor shrugged. "She's not wrong. You know you can date, right? We all want you to be happy. Mom would have wanted you to be happy."

"I know." His gaze strayed over to the angel their mother had crafted for the top of the tree, as if he could see her there. "She told me she wanted that for me—not to be alone—and I don't want to let her down. But my heart isn't ready. Not yet." The movie came back on and he shushed them, turning back to the screen. "Now let me watch my movie."

Elinor hugged his arm and settled back in to watch, but something about the words stuck in her brain, tugging at her thoughts and making it impossible to fully concentrate on the show.

It was so simple, and yet she'd never thought of it that way. Whether her heart was ready.

She wasn't still heartbroken. She'd gotten over that feeling long ago. Which was why it had always driven her crazy when people implied she wasn't over Levi. She wasn't pining. She wasn't broken.

But she was still angry.

And she wasn't sure her heart was ready.

The words teased at the edge of her brain, making it impossible to sleep that night after she got home. In the morning she found herself up before dawn, even before Dory, making herself a cup of coffee and staring blindly into her backyard.

Fog hung low over the trees in the hollow for which Pine Hollow was named. There was something almost magical about mornings like this, right before fall tipped fully into winter, when the morning frost clung to the leaves.

On impulse, she called out to Dory, quickly pulling a sweater over her pajamas and shoving her feet into boots.

The fog would lift soon, burned away by the sunrise, but there was something she wanted to see before it did.

The mill had been their place. It was the first place she and Levi had ever gone together, just the two of them, back when everything was new and she was still so nervous that he would realize she wasn't as awesome as he thought she was and decide he didn't want to be her boyfriend, after all. He'd taken her hand to help her over a pile of rocks that had once been a wall, and she'd felt that touch all the way to her toes.

She'd practically dared him to kiss her, that first time. *Are you gonna kiss me or what, Levi Jackson?* she'd challenged him, brave with him in a way she'd never been with anyone else. She'd seen the surprise in his eyes, the pleasure, and then his lips had brushed hers—closed and careful. And it had felt like the most perfect moment ever in the history of the world.

They'd come back to the mill dozens of times. Walking barefoot along the rocks in the river in the summer and hiding from the winter snows inside—where they were lucky the ancient roof hadn't fallen down on them. The mill was condemned now. Had been for years. The old wheel was broken down and tilting sideways in the water. But it was still the most beautiful place she'd ever been.

She pulled into the driveway, staring for a moment at the FOR SALE sign before climbing out of her car. Dory leapt out after her and darted in circles as she made her way toward the riverbank.

There were so many memories here, layered over one another in the collage of a life, and all of them included Levi. She'd sat on that rock the day after her mother's funeral, Levi's arm around her. They'd dipped their toes into that water on another day, the one when he'd told her they should take a break while she was at college because he didn't want her to feel tethered to Pine Hollow—as if anything could have broken that tether. He'd proposed to her right over there—on another misty morning. Valentine's Day.

No wonder she hadn't been able to let him go. She'd been in love with him for more than half her life. And angry at him ever since.

It was the anger that held on.

It wasn't even the fact that he'd broken her heart—it was that he'd betrayed their friendship by not telling her *why*. How was she supposed to move on if she was always wondering what had changed? What had happened? What she'd done?

She was lonely and hanging on to the past just like her father—but she wanted someone to share her life with, and she couldn't get that with the Ghost of Fiancé Past looming over her like a dark shadow.

She'd complained that he hadn't let her go. But *she* needed to let *him* go. *Really* let him go.

Which meant—galling as it was to admit—Charlotte was right.

"I need closure."

Charlotte gasped as if she'd just been offered a Black Friday deal on the Prada bag she'd been drooling over online. "Are we talking about what I hope we're talking about?"

Elinor had gone back to her house and gotten dressed, just in time for Anne and Charlotte to show up for their annual Black Friday shopping blitz. All three Rodriguez women had been raised with a deep appreciation for a deal, and Black Friday was a necessary ritual. Anne had texted that she was running late, and Elinor had barely been able to wait for Charlotte to get in the door before her epiphany burst out.

"If you think we're talking about Levi, then yes. We are. You were right."

"Oh my God, I love those words." She held up her phone. "Could you maybe just say them one more time into the microphone so I can make them my ringtone?"

Elinor shoved the phone away. "I just realized I've been waiting for an explanation for three years. For an apology. I can't believe I put myself on pause."

"Of course you did," Charlotte flapped a hand as if it was the most natural thing in the world to get stuck for three years. "You and Levi broke up, what? Three *weeks* before Katie died? How could you process anything when what happened to Katie and Paul swallowed up everything else? And then you had Astrid to worry about, and Ben trying to figure out the whole dad thing—of course you got stuck. So what are you going to do now?"

Elinor chewed her lip. "I have to talk to him."

Charlotte immediately began shaking her head. "He isn't closure. Closure is inside you."

"Closure may be inside me, but there are some things I need to ask him. It's not that I want him back. I just need him to tell me why. He owes me that."

Charlotte sighed, her face twisting. "Levi's never been big with the words."

"No," she agreed. She'd never minded that before. He'd never had to say a word for her to feel like they were perfectly in sync—which had made her doubt herself even more when he left. "But I've been driving myself crazy for the last three years, wondering if I was always wrong about him, if I built a relationship out of thin air and wishful thinking. I stopped trusting myself because I had trusted him so much. And now I just need to hear him say it. I need him to tell me *why*."

Charlotte wrinkled her nose. "He probably won't say what you want him to."

"I know. But I need to confront him. Now. Today."

"Today?" Charlotte's eyes flared wide. "But it's Black Friday. It's tradition."

"I know. But now that I know I have to do this, I have to do it."

Chapter Sixteen

Dear Reader, when I set up the tip line, I had no idea our dear chief and dear librarian were going to give us quite so much material for our anonymous tipsters to discuss. Talk about a Black Friday special!

—Pine Hollow Newsletter,
Monday, November 29

Elinor went first to Levi's cabin, which looked as run-down and inhospitable as ever. He wasn't there, of course, because he was never there. She tried his office next—both the old one at the courthouse and the main one at the rescue squad station—but his Explorer wasn't parked in front of either place. She cruised through the center of town, scanning every side street for signs of his SUV. With no luck.

It figured that the one time she actually *wanted* him to be everywhere she looked, he was inconveniently invisible.

She finally returned to the rescue squad office and walked in the front door—*knowing* that it meant she was going to be the subject of Linda Hilson's next gossip newsletter, but unable to wait any longer. She didn't want this feeling, this sense of purpose, to go away. She finally knew what she had to say to him. It was running through her head in an endless loop, and she needed to get it out before she could think about anything else.

Kaye Berry looked up and blushed when Elinor walked through the door, though she didn't flinch from meeting her eyes.

Elinor had never known Kaye very well. She was Anne's age and had gotten pregnant and married in high school, while Elinor was away at college. Her son was one of Elinor's favorite students, and Kaye had always seemed nice enough—so Elinor did her best to ignore the rumors that had flown during Kaye's messy divorce—rumors that had all included Levi's name.

"Hey, Elinor," Kaye said, closing what looked like a textbook on her desk and shoving it under some papers. "What can I do for you?"

"I need to talk to Levi. Do you know where he is?"

"He's out keeping an eye on things. You know Levi. Do you need me to call him back?"

"No, it's not important. Do you know when he's off duty?"

Kaye glanced at a chart on her desk. "I think he's not technically on duty now. Hunter wanted to pick up some extra shifts."

So he was only patrolling because he was physically incapable of letting anyone else be the savior and protector of Pine Hollow. That sounded like Levi. "You know what? In that case, yes. Can you get him back here?"

"Do you want me to tell him you're here?"

"No, no just...whatever you would usually..."

Kaye nodded and reached for her phone, pulling up some kind of walkie-talkie function on it. "Hey, Chief, can you come on back to the office?"

The phone beeped. And then they heard Levi's voice saying he was on his way.

And suddenly Elinor didn't know what to do with herself. She thanked Kaye. She looked around the bland foyer, eyeing the waiting area. They really should decorate in here. At least for Christmas. The whole warehouse chic thing was kind of depressing.

She paced toward the front window, wondering how far away he'd been. Pine Hollow wasn't huge. Even if he was on the other side of town, it would only take twenty minutes to drive across—and that was assuming he got caught in the tourist traffic at the square. But twenty minutes suddenly felt like an eternity. And not nearly long enough.

She knew what she wanted to say. She'd driven here riding a wave of determination, but suddenly nerves were flattening that wave.

She realized she was chewing her lip and forced herself to stop, glancing back at Kaye, who was pretending not to watch her.

It felt like a lifetime, but it was probably only five minutes before Levi walked through the front door, concern instantly flashing through the controlled blankness of his face when he saw her. "Elinor. Is Dory okay? Did she get out again?"

"No, she's fine. She's with my sisters." Anne and Charlotte had insisted on waiting for her when she'd told them she wanted to confront Levi. Apparently her personal drama was more entertaining than Black Friday shopping. "I just wanted to—" She broke off, her gaze flicking toward Kaye. "Can we talk?"

"Of course." Levi glanced toward Kaye as well—who was doing her best to look like she wasn't listening. "My office?"

"Great. Yes." She agreed quickly, thinking only of getting away from interested eyes and ears. It wasn't until she was following his broad shoulders down the hallway that she realized she'd given him home field advantage. Though maybe that would help. Maybe he would be more honest if he was someplace he felt comfortable.

He paused at the door, waving her inside in front of him. She stepped into his office—and curiosity had her eyes roaming across every surface. He'd still been a deputy when they broke up. *Correction: When he broke them up.* This had been Elton's office, and it had been perfectly tidy.

As Levi's, it was a disaster.

Clutter had accumulated on top of every flat surface. She knew there would be a system. He would know exactly where everything was, but to the untrained eye it was chaos. And so Levi. He never took care of his own space. The town, her yard—those things might drive him crazy if they weren't perfectly tended, perfectly tidy, but Levi's personal space was always one step away from needing a hazmat suit.

"Is everything okay?" He moved behind the desk. She didn't sit, and neither did he, but he shuffled some of the clutter into vaguely neater stacks. Connor would have a heart attack if he saw Levi's office. He hated mess. To Elinor, it just made the small room feel even smaller.

Or maybe that was Levi, the weight of his presence. Or the unspoken words sucking up all the available space. The words she needed to get out.

Needing something to do with her hands, she gripped the back of the chair facing his desk.

"Can I get you anything?" he offered. "Coffee?"

She opened her mouth to answer, and the words she'd needed to say for three years fell out. "I'm angry at you."

Levi met Elinor's eyes—unsurprised by the words, but surprised that for the first time in three years she didn't *sound* angry. There was no hatred in her eyes today. She sounded like she was reciting trivia, using that voice he'd heard in class when they were tiny, before she started skipping grades.

Montpelier is the capital of Vermont. Fact.

I am angry at Levi Jackson. Fact.

"I'm sorry about the other night. I swear I wasn't checking up on you—"

"This isn't about the other night."

Anxiety spiked. Had she decided she really wanted that restraining order? "I've been staying away—"

"This isn't about that," she interrupted again, gripping the back of the chair so hard her knuckles were turning white. Her gaze held his, unwavering. "I need you to tell me what happened."

He shook his head. "I don't underst—"

"What changed?" she demanded. "What did I do? Was it cold feet? Was I just always wrong about you? Had I invented the fact that you ever cared about me?"

The last question was a punch in the gut. "Elinor."

"What happened, Levi? Why did you break it off?"

"I told you—"

"No, you didn't. Because I think the worst part was that you never gave me a good reason. *That* is what I can't forgive you for. I need to know. I need to know so I can stop wasting so much energy wondering why and being mad at you. I need to put this behind me. So what changed? What did I do?"

Anxiety tightened in his chest. "You didn't do anything. Nothing changed."

"Something changed. You dumped me."

He shook his head. "That isn't what happened—"

"I was there. I'm pretty sure I remember you breaking up with me."

His throat felt tight. "It was for the best."

"That isn't an answer!"

"I couldn't hold you back anymore."

She hadn't been moving, but at that she seemed to freeze. He could practically see her ears pricking up. "What do you mean? I need you to explain that."

He shook his head. "It's nothing."

"It wasn't nothing!" she snapped. "It was *everything*. And you owe me the truth."

He wasn't sure he even knew what the truth was anymore. But he could give her at least the part of it he understood. "It was something Katie said."

Elinor flinched. "What?"

"She said you always sacrificed your own goals for other people. That you could have conquered the world if you weren't always putting your dreams on hold for someone else."

"You thought I was putting my dreams on hold for you?"

"Katie knew you better than anyone. She said you always did what you thought you should."

"Why would she say that to you?"

He shook his head. "Don't be mad at her. She didn't mean anything by it. She was just talking about how much you could have done if you hadn't felt like you had to come back here. But it got me thinking about how you'd agreed to marry me when we were fifteen and how you'd keep your word no matter what—"

"Are you talking about that promise ring? We were kids! And we broke up after that! Twice. You thought I was only marrying you because I was too honorable to go back on a promise I'd made when I was *fifteen*?"

"I didn't want to trap you."

"You never trapped me, you idiot! I wanted to marry you. I *loved* you."

He didn't miss the past tense.

"And I would have told you that if you'd just talked to me." She released the chair, stalking toward the file cabinet before she was forced to pivot in the tight space. "But no. You just decided you knew what was best for me."

"I didn't know...I just knew it wasn't me."

"Why?"

"Because I knew you wouldn't leave me even if it was the best thing for you." And he'd been willing to break his own heart to protect her. Worse, he'd been willing to break hers.

"So you broke up with me because I *loved you too much*?"

"No. Because you were too good to leave me when you should."

"Levi!" She gripped her skull as if trying to hold her exploding brain together with the palms of her hands. "That wasn't your call. You didn't get to make that decision for the both of us. You should have told me what was going on."

"I know. But it was simpler to let you hate me. Easier." It had been a sort of relief when she'd been so angry. It made it clean. Impossible for him to win her back, so he didn't try to hold on when he shouldn't.

"Easier for who?"

"For me," he acknowledged. "If you hated me, then I knew it was over."

"It was only over because you ended it! God, do you hear yourself?"

He'd done the right thing. He had to believe he'd done the right thing. It was the only thing that had made hurting her worth it. "You're my best friend. I will always watch out for you. I'd stand guard for two thousand years, if I had to."

Her eyes narrowed dangerously at the reference.

She'd made him watch all of *Doctor Who*. He knew the story of Rory, who had literally come back from the dead and guarded a box for millennia because he loved Amelia Pond so much.

But she shook her head. "You can't be my Rory, because you *broke my heart*." She turned away, spinning back almost immediately. "And you know what, I don't think you did this for me. You say you're always trying to protect me—which is insulting enough, because it implies I can't protect myself—but I think that's really just an excuse to protect yourself. You were always waiting for me to leave you, always joking that I was too good for you, always watching for the other shoe to drop—and when it did, I bet you felt so smart, because you were right all along. But *you dropped the shoe*, Levi. You made this happen. I never wanted you to feel like you weren't good enough for me. I just wanted you to love me. I always saw how amazing you were, how lucky I was, and now all of this, we broke up because you were too insecure to believe me?"

"Katie—"

"Katie didn't know everything!" Elinor shouted. "She didn't know me as well as she thought she did. And I am so sick of people making decisions for me." She threw herself onto that uncomfortable chair. "Do you know why Katie gave Astrid to Ben and not me? She left me a letter, as part of her effects. She wrote it when Astrid was tiny, when Anne was still in treatment. I'm sure she never thought—none of us thought—one car accident changes everything, right?"

"Elinor…"

"She asked me to make sure Astrid knew who she was. She told me she needed me to keep her memory alive for her daughter, but she couldn't ask me to raise her. She never wanted me to feel 'guilted into being the mom again.' That's what she said. But she never asked. I would have wanted Astrid, and it wouldn't have been about guilt. And yes, Ben is amazing with her and now she's got this wonderful family with Ally and she's so happy. But Katie didn't ask me. She made the call for me, and I'm so *mad* at her. For dying and for not asking me." Tears were bright in her eyes, but the words kept coming in a rush. "And I hate myself for being mad at her because I'm never going to see her again, and I miss my best friend."

He took a step toward her, and she launched out of the chair, backing toward the file cabinet. "Don't touch me. You can't fix this."

"I know," he murmured. But he couldn't watch her hurting and not want to help. It was why he'd stayed with her after Katie and Paul's accident, even though he and Elinor hadn't been together anymore. He hated this helpless feeling.

Levi stood by uselessly as Elinor pulled herself together, brushing at her eyes, her shoulders squaring before she finally lifted her gaze and met his eyes.

"Was that really all it was? You being stupidly noble? Everyone in town thought you had someone else."

"I know." He'd never refuted it, because the town seemed to need someone to be the bad guy in their breakup, and he never wanted anyone thinking it was her.

"I felt like such a fool."

"Elinor, I never meant to—"

"You know what? It's ancient history."

🐾

Elinor said the words—and for the first time realized she actually meant them. This conversation hadn't gone at all as she planned. She couldn't pin down how she felt with everything so tangled up inside. She needed to get away from him, to think, to process everything. But first, there was just one more thing she needed to know.

"Did you really…?" She broke off, shaking her head as she restarted, asking the question that had been pulsing behind all the others. "Was it real?"

"What?"

"Between us. Was it real? Or was it all in my head? Did I really know you like I thought I did, or was I just projecting who I wanted you to be?"

His expression was motionless, giving away nothing—but then his throat worked and his eyes…When she looked into that pale gray, she saw entire galaxies of emotion.

"It was real," he whispered.

She believed him. Something that had been dormant for years inside her chest shifted, and her breath caught. Suddenly she was Elinor again and he was Levi, and everything they'd always been to each other was there, just beneath the surface, just beneath her breath. And she wasn't prepared for any of it.

So she did the only thing she could think of. She ran.

Chapter Seventeen

With so many conflicting reports of exactly what happened in the last week, one can only speculate as to whether our chief and librarian are off or on again.
—*Pine Hollow Newsletter*,
Monday, November 29

She'd forgotten her sisters were waiting at her house, eager to hear how her confrontation with Levi had gone. Elinor sat in her driveway and stared at their cars, trying to work up the gumption to go inside. She'd left on a mission for closure, eager for a fight, but now...she didn't know how she felt anymore. Somehow hollow and overflowing at the same time.

Their breakup made sense now in a way it never had before. She should have known Levi would get some twisted idea of what was best for her and sacrifice himself. He was always doing things for her, whether she wanted him to or not. It was practically his defining trait.

He'd broken up with her before she left for college because he hadn't wanted her to feel held back by him. She should have seen the pattern. She should have figured it out—but she'd been too busy nursing her broken heart and feeling like a fool. And then too busy grieving Katie.

For the first time in three years she felt like herself again, like she could trust her judgment again. But she still had no idea what these feelings were, twisted and tangled inside her.

The front door burst open, and Dory raced out to the car to greet her. Evidently, Elinor had waited too long, and her sisters' curiosity had overruled their patience. They stood on the front step, craning their necks as they tried to get a good look at her face and figure out how it had gone.

Elinor opened the car door—to Dory's delight—still not entirely sure how it had gone herself.

"Well?" Charlotte asked when she was still ten feet away. "Did you find him?"

"I found him." At least that question she could answer.

Inside, she paced in the living room—which Dory thought was a wonderful game—as she explained everything that had happened to her sisters. Saying it all out loud, it made sense again, and she found herself arguing Levi's position—obviously he was still an idiot, but she knew *why* now and what he'd done was so *him*.

"I knew he hadn't cheated," Anne declared from her position on the couch where she and Charlotte were watching Elinor pace.

Charlotte glared at her. "We don't know that. We only know that he said he didn't. I still think it's awfully convenient that Kaye Berry's marriage broke up at exactly the same time he decided to break things off with Elinor."

"Then why aren't they together?" Anne demanded. "It's been three years. Both Levi and Kaye have been single for ages. If they were madly in love, wouldn't they have owned up to it by now?"

"I'm not saying they were madly in love. People do stupid things."

"That isn't his brand of stupid," Elinor argued, her gaze focused on the bookshelves that lined her walls, the sight of the books somehow soothing the chaos inside her. Levi had baggage about cheating. He'd never wanted to be anything like his father. It was part of what had never made sense about their breakup.

Charlotte groaned. "You're getting sucked back in. It's all over your face. I knew this was a bad idea."

"This was *your* idea! You were Team Closure."

"Yeah, but closure as a you thing, not as a him thing. I wanted you to burn his stuff in the backyard and roast marshmallows on the memories until you didn't even think of him anymore."

"I couldn't do that until I did this. And I think it wasn't just him. I never really processed my grief for Katie. I hoarded it. Like somehow I could change the past and bring her back if I just never let it go."

"Honey." Anne crossed the room and pulled her into a hug.

"I'm so mad at her for dying," Elinor whispered, her eyes welling. "And Levi...I don't know. It all got tangled up."

"So what happens now?" Anne asked—and Charlotte glared at her.

"They are *not* getting back together."

"No. We aren't," Elinor agreed. She didn't know how she felt exactly, but she knew what came next. "And now I move on."

Chapter Eighteen

The annual tree lighting is always one of the highlights of the Pine Hollow Christmas celebrations, and this year was no different, with plenty of cheer, led by our dear mayor and his blushing bride, who have lots of reasons for joy with their wedding only a few more days away.

—*Pine Hollow Newsletter*,
Monday, December 13

Merry Christmas, Pine Hollow!" Ben's voice rang out over the square, amplified by the speakers set up on each side of the massive evergreen that was about to be lit, and every face in the crowded square turned toward the sound.

Every face except Levi's.

He scanned the crowd, telling himself he was checking for anything amiss, doing his job. Not looking for a certain face he hadn't seen in two weeks. Elinor never missed the tree lighting.

He'd kept busy the last couple of weeks. The town was kicking into high gear for the holidays, like it always did. The first snow had hit the Sunday after Thanksgiving, and

Levi had been occupied digging out those who needed help and towing tourists out of ditches.

The Vandal of Pine Hollow, as everyone insisted on calling their amateur artist, hadn't struck again. Levi wasn't sure whether to credit the colder weather for making it less hospitable for outdoor painting, the snow for making it harder to get away without leaving tracks, or the likelihood that the newsletter coverage had tipped off their vandal and sent them into hiding.

Whatever the reason, Levi was glad for the reprieve going into the busy holiday season.

Ben's wedding was only a week away—which meant the groom was in full panic mode. Though there wasn't much left to do other than go to the bachelor party tomorrow, the details of which Connor was being annoyingly evasive about.

Ally and Astrid stood with Ben on the platform in front of the town Christmas tree, both of them bursting with holiday cheer—and even Ben looked reasonably festive as he started the traditional pre-lighting countdown.

The numbers echoed through the square, townspeople joining in. "Five...Four...Three..."

When they reached the end of the countdown, Ben, Ally, and Astrid's stacked hands smacked down on the ceremonial button. The tree lit. The town gasped. And the choir began to sing some Christmas carol.

Elinor loved this part. Not that it was any of his business what Elinor loved.

Around the square, townspeople put their arms around one another, gazing upward and singing along. Near the gazebo, Connor bent his head close to Deenie's, whispering something in her ear that made her roll her eyes. Levi's gaze kept moving.

Where *was* she?

"It's just *so*...beautiful."

Levi turned his head at the theatrically overemotional declaration to see Mac pretending to dab a tear from his eye.

"Our boy has come so far," Mac continued, voice quavering. "To think, we used to call him the town Scrooge, and now he's Mr. Christmas, lighting the tree. Love really does conquer all."

Ben was lighting the tree because he was mayor, not because he was in love, but Levi just grunted, absently scanning the crowd again.

"Looking for someone?"

Levi stopped scanning to fix Mac with a pointedly disinterested look. "I don't know what you mean."

Mac snorted. "Uh-huh." Luckily he was distracted by a sudden influx of customers at his cocoa cart before he could give Levi shit.

Levi automatically resumed his scan of the square.

It had been fourteen days since everything he'd never had the guts to tell Elinor had come out. He'd been numb afterward, like all his higher functions had shut off to get through it, but since then he'd had time to process. Time to regret. And he hadn't seen a trace of her.

He had no idea how she was. She'd practically run from his office. Before, at the pub, she'd told him to stay away from her. He could only assume she still wanted that, and he wanted to honor her wishes. But he also desperately wanted to know she was okay.

He just hadn't had a good excuse to seek her out. He'd hoped Dory would get loose. To give him a reason to see Elinor. But she never did.

He kind of missed the furball.

Uneasiness twisted in his gut. Even if he missed Elinor at the tree lighting, he was bound to see her with all the wedding stuff coming up. The rehearsal dinner, the wedding itself.

He needed to talk to her before the ceremony, make sure they were all good before Ben and Ally's big day. Not that either of them would do anything to disrupt their friends' wedding, but he wanted to see her.

He'd spent so long being certain he'd done the right thing by breaking off their engagement, but now the certainty felt hollow, and he couldn't remember why he'd been so sure. He'd thought setting her free was the best thing he'd ever done. His moment of nobility. But now... Had it really been his biggest mistake? Had he used that certainty as a shield?

Maybe Katie hadn't been omniscient. Maybe she hadn't known what was best for Elinor. Maybe he'd just been looking for a reason to pull the rip cord and bail out before she did.

His therapist had said something about that, when he'd told him about the confrontation with Elinor—about causing pain he could control in an attempt to avoid that which he couldn't—and now he couldn't stop thinking about it.

Dr. Park might have been right about one or two things. Not that knowing that did him any good. He couldn't undo the past. Though he might need to apologize for it.

"Levi? You still with us? Does someone need to reboot you?"

Levi frowned at Mac, who was no longer conveniently distracted by a crowd at his cart. "Reboot me?"

Mac shrugged, unapologetic. "You looked like you'd gone into RoboCop mode. I was concerned."

"Sure you were."

Connor appeared in front of them, rubbing together his leather gloves like a cartoon villain. "You guys ready for this weekend?"

"It would be easier to *get* ready for this weekend if you would actually tell us what we're doing," Levi grumbled as Ben approached.

"I second that. As the groom, I feel like I should have veto power on the bachelor party," Ben said before turning to Mac. "Can I get a couple of cocoas for Ally and Astrid?"

"Two for me and Deenie after that," Connor requested before facing Ben. "If you planned it, we'd stay home and play poker."

"I don't see what's so terrible about that. We finally have someone interested in looking at the house on Sunday—plus there's the Christmas Fair at Astrid's school and all the usual town stuff, not to mention a million last-minute tasks for the wedding. I don't have time to take a whole weekend away."

"It's not the whole weekend," Connor argued. "I pick everyone up tomorrow morning and drop you all back off Sunday morning. Twenty-four hours. You can spare that much for the only bachelor party you're ever going to have. We're doing this right."

"Yeah, but what are we doing?" Levi asked. "'Dress warmly' isn't exactly specific."

"Trust me. You'll love it." Connor grinned.

Levi glowered—and he wasn't the only one. "I'm not doing some crazy reenactment of *The Hangover*."

"No roofies, I promise. You will remember every minute and cherish the memory."

Ben clearly wanted to balk at the entire idea of the

bachelor party when Mac handed him two cups of cocoa. "Just don't make me regret this." The mayor lifted the cups. "I'd better go deliver these."

Levi watched him go and then turned a hard look on Connor. "It's stressing him out not knowing what we're doing."

Connor snorted. "Stressed is his natural state. Ben's always overdoing it—which is why tomorrow is important. If I tell him what the plan is, he'll find some way to get out of it or sneak in some work for the town or for the wedding. This way, he just has to go with it—one day, totally unplugged. Just what the doctor ordered."

"I take it you're the doctor in this situation?"

"Don't be jealous because he picked me to be best man."

"I'm not jealous," Levi said. "I'm relieved."

And he was. Planning a bachelor party, giving a speech— the thought of all that stressed him out. He wanted to support his friend—he'd stand wherever Ben asked him to and do whatever Ben wanted for the wedding, but the idea of performing their friendship as the best man sounded excruciating. He hated being on display.

It was the same reason every time Elinor had asked him what he wanted for their wedding he'd told her whatever she wanted. Not because he didn't care, but because he didn't really want any of it. He'd wanted quiet. Private. Just them and a judge, saying some words. But far more than he'd wanted that, he'd wanted her to have the wedding she'd always dreamed of, so he'd told her to pick whatever she wanted.

Had that been a mistake as well?

"Just dress warmly," Connor reiterated, accepting a pair of cocoas from Mac. "And be ready at eight a.m. sharp."

He walked off, and Levi's gaze followed him before roving absently over the crowd.

"She's by the roasted chestnuts," Mac said without looking up from the disposable cup he was filling.

"What?" Levi glanced in the direction Mac had mentioned—and there she was. Elinor.

She'd brought Dory—and her whole family, by the look of it. She stood between her sisters, laughing at something her father said. Anne's girlfriend, Bailey, stood with them, and Charlotte looked annoyed, frowning at her phone.

She was with her family. This wasn't a good time.

"Here." Mac shoved two cups of cocoa at him. "Don't say I never did anything for you."

"I don't know." She looked so happy. He didn't want to infringe on that. But he did need to apologize...

"Go." Mac gave him a little shove. "Take her a peace offering. Do it for Ben and Ally, so you guys have practice pretending you can stand each other for their wedding."

Not being able to stand her had never been the problem.

But Levi accepted the cocoa and started across the square.

He was halfway there when the knot of people around Elinor shifted to make room for a new arrival. Charlotte's smile grew positively massive as she gleefully shoved the newcomer toward Elinor. The man in the puffy winter jacket turned—

And Levi recognized the man from the Tipsy Moose. Elinor's date.

His steps immediately turned—a sharp right turn before his conscious brain even realized he was changing direction.

He spotted the Johnsons, a sweet older couple who'd lived in Pine Hollow forever, and handed them the cocoas, as if he'd been bringing them to the older couple all along.

They smiled and thanked him, gushing over his kindness, and he nodded to acknowledge the words, already moving toward the edge of the square.

Suddenly he couldn't stop remembering the exact tone of Elinor's voice when she'd accused him of lurking in her life. And he needed to get out of here before she spotted him.

He would see her at the rehearsal dinner. That would have to be soon enough.

Chapter Nineteen

And speaking of the big wedding, rumor
has it the bride and groom were both
whisked off to undisclosed locations for
their bachelor and bachelorette parties
this weekend…

—*Pine Hollow Newsletter*,
Monday, December 13

Have I mentioned how glad I am that you're here? And
not just because we'd probably still be stuck in that
escape room without you." Ally sank down beside Elinor on
one of the overstuffed couches in the Escape Adventures
party room. She wore a white sash with BRIDE written on it
in bright pink letters and a glittery tiara with a scraggly veil
coming loose on one side where it had caught on something
in the dark of the room they'd just escaped.

"I think you would have made it out." Elinor grinned,
raising her margarita to clink against Ally's. "Eventually."

Deenie, as maid of honor, had arranged for them to have
the "Ball and Chain" package—which included their entire
group being locked up in an old-fashioned jail-style escape

room, followed by cupcakes and cocktails in the party room after they escaped.

"I'm not so sure," Ally hedged, sipping her own fruity pastel drink. "I've never seen anyone work a puzzle as fast as you did. Are you sure you've never done an escape room before?"

"Never. But I think I might be addicted," Elinor admitted. She'd always loved puzzles and riddles—and the adrenaline rush of having to solve one on a clock had been electrifying. She was still riding her nerd high. "It was easier once we figured out they'd customized some of the clues to be about you and Ben. Using his birthday on that last combination lock was pretty clever."

Ally lowered her voice so it wouldn't carry to the rest of the group, where everyone was still rehashing the escape room experience around the cocktail tables on the other side of the room. "Thank you for dropping that hint to Astrid, so she could be the one to figure it out. I was a little worried at first that as the only kid in the room she would feel like she wasn't being heard, you know?"

"I had a hunch she might be good at puzzles like this. In some ways, she really is her mother's daughter. Katie would've loved this. We always talked about doing an escape room, but there weren't any nearby for the longest time."

"I wish Katie could have been here," Ally murmured. "Ben really misses her."

Elinor nodded and was a little surprised that her throat didn't immediately close off with emotion. She could actually think about Katie, *talk* about Katie, without feeling like she was drowning. "She would have really liked you."

Ally's face lit with a shy smile. "Yeah? Ben says she could be pretty all-or-nothing about people. You were either her favorite or she couldn't stand you."

Elinor grinned. "That might be a little bit true. But if she loved you, she *loved* you. And she would have loved you. If for no other reason than you're so good for Astrid and Ben. Though you're also pretty awesome in your own right." Ally blushed, looking down, and Elinor changed the subject. "Are you nervous? About the wedding?"

"I feel like I should be. Ben is. I'm just…impatient, I guess. We've done all the prep, ticked off all the boxes, and now I'm just ready to do the thing. To be married already. I feel like I've been ready for this for longer than I even knew it was a possibility. Like this was always who I was going to be, and I just had to get here." She flicked a quick glance at Elinor, uncertainty moving across her face. "Honestly, the part I'm most nervous about is Astrid. I don't really know what I'm doing with the whole stepmom thing. I don't want her to feel like I'm taking over or trying to take her mom's place, but I want to be her mom as much as she wants me to be, you know?"

Elinor's throat tightened. "You love her, right?"

"Yes, *absolutely*."

"Then you're gonna do fine." She swallowed around that knot in her throat. "You wanna know a secret? Something even Ben doesn't know?"

Interest flickered in Ally's eyes. "About Katie?"

"Mm-hmm." Elinor leaned closer, lowering her voice. "Astrid wasn't planned. Don't get me wrong. Katie *loved* being a mom—she'd always wanted to be one, and she had this whole Supermom thing going on that I think frankly intimidated some of the other mothers—"

"That's how Ben talks about her. Like she was terrifyingly perfect."

Elinor smiled. "It's not a bad description. At least of how

she wanted the world to see her. But she obsessed over her screwups just like anyone else. She was so nervous when she got pregnant. Happy, but really scared. She felt like it happened before they were ready—before *she* was ready. But life does that. It happens before you're ready for it. And you just do your best and hang on tight. And love 'em like crazy." She gently bumped Ally's arm. "So now that's what you do. With Astrid."

The tinge of nerves on Ally's face softened. "How'd you get so wise?"

"I listen to a lot of podcasts." A startled laugh popped out of Ally, and Elinor grinned. "And I always try to learn from my mistakes."

Concern shifted in Ally's eyes, and Elinor realized too late where the conversation was heading. They hadn't talked about Levi since the cake tasting, but she could see it building in Ally's eyes.

"I'm sorry," Ally said softly. "This must be awkward for you. All we ever talk about is wedding stuff and—"

"Don't," Elinor interrupted. "I never want you to censor yourself because of me. I'm so happy for you and Ben. You know that, right?"

"I do. I just feel bad that I'm asking you to stand across the altar from a man you were once engaged to."

"Hey. You guys are family. I'm happy to be a warm body balancing out the wedding party." It might be awkward. She hadn't even seen Levi since that explosion in his office, but they were both perfectly capable of being adults and behaving at the wedding.

Ally's brow scrunched. "You know Ben and I couldn't care less about even numbers, right? I wanted you up there with me because I couldn't imagine our wedding without the woman who showed up with eggnog and common sense when I needed her most. You made me feel like I fit here. You and Deenie and our girls' nights are part of what made Pine Hollow *home*."

Now the emotion that she'd controlled earlier hit her in the throat. Elinor smiled, but it felt wobbly. "It was good eggnog," she acknowledged.

"It was lighter fluid," Ally corrected. "But I loved it. And I know we haven't known each other for decades, but you're one of my favorite people, and you guys were there for me when I needed you. So I want to be the same for you." Ally grinned, catching her hand. "And I'm patient. If I have to wait a long time to repay the favor, I can do that. But you were not, in any way, an add-on to fill out the wedding party. Just so we're clear."

Elinor met Ally's eyes, feeling foolish. She needed to stop comparing everything to Katie. Yes, no one had ever known her like Katie did. She missed just *talking* to her, the way they built on one another, pyramids of ideas, reaching places neither could have gotten on their own.

She *liked* Ally and Deenie, but she kept holding herself distant from them, convinced that if it didn't feel exactly like it did with Katie, then it wasn't a real, to-the-bones friendship—but it was like Charlotte said. Best friend was a tier, not a person, and she needed to stop closing herself off to other friendships because she'd lost someone.

"I'm sorry," Elinor murmured, squeezing Ally's hand. "I've been kind of an idiot."

"Nah." Ally grinned. "Just a little dense sometimes," she teased.

Elinor huffed out a soft laugh, dabbing at the corner

of her eye. "Ugh. Who knew bachelorette parties were so sappy and emotional?"

Ally laughed. "Right?"

"You guys aren't being serious, are you?" called out one of Ally's New York friends, her voice ringing through the room.

There were four women who'd made the drive up from New York for the bachelorette party—most of them as kind and fun as Ally herself. Crystal was the only one Elinor wanted to vote off the island. Since it was Ally's day, she forced herself to smile—or at least keep her mouth shut.

Crystal tripped over to them, swaying on her heels just enough to indicate the cocktail in her hand might not be her first. "I can't believe we're both getting married the same year!" she gushed to Ally. "I bet we're going to be pregnant at the same time, too." She thrust her pink drink into the air. "To Ally and Ben! Who are going to have the most adorable babies!"

Everyone else chimed in with toasts to Ally and Ben, but Elinor scanned the room behind Crystal, frowning when she didn't see Astrid. The other women at the party were crowded around Ally now, and Elinor excused herself with a quiet word, moving toward the door.

"Have you seen Astrid?" she asked Deenie, who pointed toward the hallway.

"Bathroom. She'll be right back."

Elinor nodded, but set down her drink and headed toward the hallway. As soon as she stepped into the hall and saw the Converse sneakers poking out around the corner at the end, she was glad she'd trusted her instincts.

The escape room building had an odd layout, with lots of little hallways jogging in various directions around the strangely shaped rooms. Astrid sat in a little dead-end hall-way with her back against the wall and her feet sticking out straight.

Elinor lowered herself onto the linoleum floor beside her. "Hey. You okay?"

"Yeah."

"Just looking for some quiet?"

Astrid shrugged one shoulder—and Elinor nodded, taking a page from Levi's book and letting her silent presence coax whatever was bothering Astrid out.

Finally, Astrid mumbled, "That Crystal lady kept talking about Ally and Uncle Ben having babies. And I want them to. Merritt Miller's baby brother is so cute, and it'd be fun to have a little brother, but if they have their own kids..."

She trailed off, and Elinor wondered if it was bad luck to murder a bachelorette party guest a week before the wedding. Though it wasn't really Crystal's fault. She'd just been oblivious.

Elinor waited, but when no more words came, she filled in softly, "You're worried it'll change things?"

Astrid sniffed. A small nod. "It's just...where do I fit?"

"Honey. They love you. And they are never going to love you even a tiny bit less. No matter what. A funny thing happens when you get younger siblings. I happen to know about this. I'm kind of an expert. And what I figured out is that your parents' hearts actually get bigger. And so does yours. To make room for all that new love inside. And it isn't just love for the new baby. It's for you, too."

"But I'm not really *theirs*."

"Yes, you are. Always. Am I your aunt?"

"Yeah, I mean, of course."

"But we don't share any blood," Elinor reminded her.

"Katie wasn't really my sister. But I'm always going to be your aunt. And Ben…he's another dad for you now. And Ally is *so* excited to be your new mom. She had Deenie plan this whole bachelorette party for something she thought *you* would like."

A little smile. "It was pretty fun."

"Right?" Elinor grinned, gently nudging Astrid's shoulder with her own. "I feel like we need to do more of these. Maybe on your birthday. I heard a rumor about a *Doctor Who* one. We might have to make a pilgrimage."

Astrid's face lit. "Oh wow, that would be amazing."

Elinor smiled—and wondered if this place had gift certificates. She might have just found Astrid's Christmas present. "You ready to head back in?"

"Yeah," Astrid mumbled and they climbed to their feet.

Elinor walked a couple of steps behind her as they headed back toward the party room, feeling a little guilty over how glad she was that Astrid still needed her.

She wasn't the nice one, like Ally. Or sunshine and sparkles, like Deenie. She'd always been a little sharper. A little less patient. But Katie had been, too, and she'd made her feel like it was okay to be a little acerbic. Deenie and Ally liked her just the way she was, but they didn't share her bite.

But maybe that was okay. Maybe they still needed her.

She could get used to that.

Chapter Twenty

No one knows where exactly the gentlemen went, but sources tell me they were spotted getting into a helicopter at the resort.

—*Pine Hollow Newsletter*,
Monday, December 13

Okay, you have to admit this was a good idea."

Levi looked up at the mountains all around them—the undisturbed snow, the heart-stopping blue of the sky, the crisp winter air bright and sharp in his lungs—and did, in fact, have to admit this had been a brilliant idea.

Connor had gone over the top, in true Connor fashion, and rented a helicopter to take them heli-skiing—along with a pair of guides to make sure they survived the experience, since they were all a little rusty on skis and snowboards. They'd all skied and boarded together as kids, but it had been years since any of them had the time to go regularly—though muscle memory had kicked in pretty quickly, and they'd been racing through the powder before long.

He was going to hurt tomorrow in muscles he barely remembered he had, but they were miles away from cell phone service, and the snow and rush of winter air had washed away stress he hadn't even realized he was carrying.

"It's all right." Levi shrugged, just to mess with Connor, who flicked snow at him.

"It's *genius*," their ringleader insisted.

Ben skidded to a stop beside them, his snowboard chattering on an icy patch as he came to rest with a teeth-baring grin on his face.

Connor and Levi had always been the most competitive, flinging themselves down the mountain as fast as they could. Mac was the most cautious, always bringing up the rear, with Ben falling somewhere in the middle, alternating between racing with Levi and lollygagging with Mac.

"This was an *amazing* idea," Ben declared, shoving up his sunglasses, as Mac arrived in a spray of snow.

"See?" Connor bragged to Levi. *"Amazing."*

"Provided we don't get stuck out here," Levi commented. "We've got half the search and rescue team with us, so if someone needs to come looking for us, we're screwed." His deputy, Aaron, was one of their guides, along with Tomas, who volunteered as a firefighter and part of the rescue squad when he wasn't teaching ski school.

"That's just negative thinking," Connor declared. "We've got half the search and rescue team out here with us, so we're the safest we could possibly be if something happens."

"Can we just avoid a scenario in which something happens?" Mac requested.

"You can't avoid Mother Nature when she's coming for you," Connor argued. "Did you see that Will Ferrell movie with the avalanche?"

Mac groaned. "Why are we talking about avalanches?"

"It was either that or ask Levi what the hell is going on with him and Elinor."

"Who's ready for the next section?" Levi asked, looking down to where Tomas had disappeared down the next slope. He pushed off, throwing his body into motion before anyone could say anything else.

"You can't avoid me forever!" Connor shouted.

No, but I can try.

Connor always pushed, always needled. It was what he did. But Levi didn't know what was going on with him and Elinor. He didn't know where they stood. And he didn't want to talk about it. He just wanted to fling himself down the mountain, feel the powder hit his face, the cold waking him up and making him feel more alive than he had in years.

Heli-skiing had been a freaking amazing idea.

But his reprieve lasted only until the chopper picked them up and dropped them back at the Pine Hollow ski resort.

Connor, never one to do things by half measures, had rented out the entire rooftop lounge, where the non-skiing members of the party were already waiting with aged Scotch and cigars, keeping warm around the scattered fire pits.

There were cheers on Ben's arrival—and shouted toasts to the groom and to Ally. Levi instinctively hung back, watching over things, but in retrospect, he should have made himself part of the crowd, because it would have been harder for Connor to corner him.

"All right, what's going on?" Connor asked as he handed Levi one of the two Scotches he was carrying. "Deenie keeps asking me what the deal is with you and Elinor, and I need to have something to report."

"There's nothing to report."

"So you didn't have a screaming fight in your office on Black Friday?"

Levi's head wanted to snap in Connor's direction, but he forced himself not to move—only the slightest flinch betraying the impulse. As far as he knew, their discussion in his office wasn't public knowledge. Yet.

"We aren't getting back together."

"I'm not saying you are. Though if you're still completely in love with her, I have to admit I'm confused why you broke up with her in the first place."

"It was for the best."

Connor groaned, not unsympathetically. "Oh God, please tell me you didn't actually say that to her."

Levi stared into the fire and sipped his Scotch.

"You're an idiot, you know that?"

Levi tensed, a knee-jerk reaction to being called out for the moron he was. "Everyone says if you love something, set it free."

"That is literally the worst advice in the history of advice," Connor argued. "Who told you that? Because that person is an idiot, too."

It hadn't been a person. It had been a freaking meme, a platitude—and a defense mechanism. But before he could respond, Mac appeared at his other side.

"Who's an idiot?" Mac asked as Ben joined their fire pit, rounding out the group.

Connor lifted his glass mockingly in Levi's direction. "Levi told Elinor that their breakup was for her own good."

"Ouch." Mac winced, and even Ben cringed.

"Was this recently? Or back when it happened?"

"Does it matter?" Connor asked. "The last thing any

woman wants to be told is that she doesn't know what's best for her, but the big, strong man does."

Levi glared. "Yeah, I got that."

"So how are you going to fix it?"

"I'm going to apologize," Levi explained. Just as soon as he was able to talk to her without being accused of lurking in her life.

"Oh, no." Connor shook his head. "You need to do better than that."

Mac nodded. "Big romantic gesture. That's your only shot to win her back."

"I'm not trying to win her back," Levi insisted—and he was pretty sure a big romantic gesture wasn't going to help—but his friends looked at him as if he was nuts.

"But you're still in love with her," Ben said, as if it was a fact and not a question.

Levi didn't bother denying it. They wouldn't believe him.

At his blank expression, they all nodded and began talking about him as if he wasn't there.

"He needs to do something big."

"Ben already did the make-an-idiot-of-yourself-in-front-of-the-whole-town thing."

"Hey," Ben protested.

"Not knocking it," Connor assured him. "It worked. As evidenced by the wedding next week. So maybe Levi could give that a shot—"

"No." Levi's refusal was flat.

"Or there's always my method. Whisk her away to another continent. You'd need a passport, but we could watch Dory for Elinor—"

"Guys," Levi tried again—and they kept talking as if he was invisible.

"Serenade?" Mac suggested. "She loves music."

"Have you heard Levi sing?"

"Okay, so maybe just a recording of her favorite song. Do you have a boom box? You could go the whole *Say Anything* route. It's a classic."

"Cheesy," Ben protested. "And totally clichéd."

"Says the man who used *puppies* and *mistletoe*," Connor countered. "The music idea isn't bad. But it would have to be the perfect song."

"Stop." Levi held up a hand. "I'm not trying to win her back."

Three identical frowns turned in his direction.

"So you're saying you're not still in love with her."

"I'm saying we're friends." *Or I'd like us to be.* "And I owe her an apology."

They all exchanged another unreadable look, and Ben sighed. "Just try not to piss her off on my wedding day. I don't want Ally trying to kill you in the middle of our reception. It's hard to get blood out of wedding dresses."

"I'm not going to piss her off." *I hope.* "I'm just going to talk to her. And I won't do it at your wedding."

Which was a great plan. A freaking brilliant plan.

Unfortunately the gods were laughing at him.

The week conspired against him with inconveniently timed town headaches. The temperature kept fluctuating around freezing—which meant icy roads and a string of fender benders. Then on Thursday evening—right when he'd decided he was going to go by Elinor's house and take his chances—all the wet snow in the next pass came down in an avalanche, blocking the main access road to nearby Woodland. The Pine Hollow Search and Rescue had a partnership with Woodland's—so Levi's team was called out to clear the road and help the Woodland residents for the next thirty-six hours.

He missed the rehearsal and the dinner, feeling guilty the entire time, though Ben insisted he understood and Mac promised to tell him where to stand on the day. So Levi pushed down what he wanted to do and did what he needed to instead.

And woke up on the wedding day, achy and tired—and without having spoken to Elinor in three weeks.

Chapter Twenty-One

The square was packed for the ceremony
this weekend—and even those who would
have complained about holding a wedding
outdoors in December were warmed by
the obvious joy of the bride and groom.
—*Pine Hollow Newsletter*,
Monday, December 20

Have I mentioned how much I love you guys?"

Elinor grinned at Ally's gushing. "Only about twenty million times."

Ally had been telling everyone how much she loved them all morning—and she hadn't even seen Ben yet. It would have been a little ridiculous if not so heartfelt.

The ceremony was due to start any minute, and Ally looked like Christmas in her gown with its deep red sash, clutching a bouquet with sprigs of holly and evergreen mixed in with red and white roses. Her makeup was perfect and every hair was in place, but it was her smile that stole the show.

Elinor swallowed, her eyes a little misty. She'd known she might feel something today—it was the first wedding she'd been to since the one she'd had to cancel—but she hadn't expected it to be envy. Or maybe not quite envy, but a sort of happy sadness. A poignant achy joy.

"I know outside in December is insane," Ally said for the fifteenth time. "I promise the ceremony is quick."

The bridal party crowded together in Magda's Bakery, which had been closed for the occasion, along with the street out front. One of the benefits of marrying the mayor was that the permits to shut down the street for half an hour had flown through the town council. The plan was for the bridal party to emerge from Magda's—which was apparently where Ally and Ben had first met—and cross the street to the town square, where a trellis arch had been set up in front of the Christmas tree and Ben would be waiting with the wedding guests. A wide red carpet—borrowed from the local community theater for the occasion—stretched from Magda's door to where Ben waited, so Ally's hem wouldn't brush the snowy street for even a second.

Ally was clutching Astrid's hand when her grandmother poked her head inside Magda's Bakery and beamed. "It's time. We're ready when you are."

Elinor glanced at Ally, who gave her an eager nod, and moved toward the door.

Elinor was first, since they'd decided to go in height order. She stepped outside and immediately heard Pachelbel's Canon in D playing from the square. She timed her steps to the music, her heels soundless on the carpet as she crossed Main Street. She shivered a little, but the soft white stole around her shoulders—and her own nerves—kept her from feeling the cold too much.

At the edge of the square, Mac was waiting on one side of the carpet with the other groomsmen. Elinor very purposefully looked only at Mac, taking the elbow he offered as the two of them walked down the aisle created by the rows of guests. Ben stood at the end of the aisle—looking like he might pass out from nerves at any moment. He was rocking slightly back and forth, puffing out breaths that made little clouds around his face.

Mac and Elinor separated at the arch, taking their places on opposite sides, and she turned in time to see the couple behind her coming down the aisle.

Levi and Adriana from New York.

Her eyes hit his for a moment—an inevitable clash—and there was something in the storm-cloud gray that made her breath catch in her throat. They'd nearly done this. Not outside in the cold, like these mad people, but the white wedding, the Canon in D, the vows.

She almost never saw him in a suit—prom had probably been the last time, and he hadn't filled out the shoulders the same way back then. Now her heart clutched at the sight of him—tall, and strong, and looking like he could carry the weight of the world. Like he would, for her.

Levi took his place opposite—and Elinor forced her gaze away from him. Might-have-been didn't matter right now. Deenie and Connor had just reached the arch, taking their places, and then came Astrid, carrying a smaller replica of Ally's bouquet and Partridge's leash.

The little bulldog waddled pendulously down the aisle to the delighted murmurs of the guests. Ally's Saint Bernard, Colby, was already lying at Ben's feet—since Ally had wanted him to be there, but they'd all agreed that the lazy-bones would only slow the ceremony down if they had to drag him down the aisle, and no one wanted to be out in the winter cold for longer than absolutely necessary.

Astrid took her place. Then the music shifted, the wedding march began, and Ally appeared, flanked by her grandparents, all three of them smiling so broadly it almost made Elinor forget the cold. She stole a quick glance back at Ben—whose nerves seemed to have vanished into thin air. He watched Ally coming toward him with such adoration that Elinor found herself instinctively looking away from that private moment.

And her gaze snagged on Levi's.

He wasn't watching Ally. Or Ben. He was watching her.

His face was expressionless. Classic blank cop face. But she knew him. And her heart squeezed tight.

He would have looked like that on their wedding day. All somber and stoic. He didn't smile when he was happiest. He just got this look, this concentration, like he was trying to memorize the feeling, save it in a box.

The way he was looking at her now…

She pulled her gaze away from him, trying to force herself to focus on the ceremony, but suddenly she couldn't hear a word over the pounding of her heart.

Of course today was confusing. She'd always known it would be, tangled up as it was in might-have-beens and pointless longing. It didn't mean anything. It was just an echo. An afterimage on her eyelids of the love that had been burned into them when she was young. A memory of a feeling, not the feeling itself. She wasn't still in love with him. That wasn't what this was. It was just an emotional reflex, brought on by the day.

It would pass.

Thank goodness the ceremony was brief.

"If you don't want everyone to think you're in love with her, you should probably stop staring at her."

Levi frowned at Deenie, who grinned back, cheerfully unfazed. She was covered in glitter. It even seemed to be in her pink-streaked hair. But then, that was Deenie. "I don't know what you're talking about."

"Of course you don't." She lifted her glass of champagne, blue eyes sparkling. "Enjoying yourself?"

"Yeah. Of course."

Ally and Ben had just finished their first dance to "I'll Be Home for Christmas." They'd gone a little too all-in on the Christmas theme, as far as Levi was concerned, but what did he know about weddings? They looked so happy, it had to be the right choice.

He'd missed his window to talk to Elinor before the wedding, and he'd promised Ben that he wouldn't stir things up and risk upsetting Ally, but he hated that he still didn't know how things stood with her—and that he still hadn't been able to apologize to her. He knew the apology was three years late, but it was the last three weeks that had been killing him.

"You could always ask her to dance," Deenie commented lightly—and he realized his gaze had drifted back to Elinor again. It seemed to be pulled there every time he didn't guard himself.

She looked gorgeous in the bridesmaid dress, with her hair twisted into some kind of fancy knot with little tendrils resting against the sides of her face—but that wasn't why he couldn't stop looking at her. She looked happy. Lighter, somehow. And he wanted to be close to that happiness. He'd always been in orbit around her, warmer when her sun shone on him.

"I shouldn't," he said—far too long after Deenie made the suggestion.

She made a face. "I hate the word *should*. But if you'd rather pine for her longingly all night, I'm not going to stop you." She chucked him on the arm. "Hang in there, Levi. I'm secretly rooting for you."

Then she was off, bouncing into the crowd to sow her chaos elsewhere—and leaving him with a single sentence lingering in his brain.

You could always ask her to dance.

It was a terrible idea, but he found himself navigating his way toward Elinor, drawn in by her gravitational force, but moving slowly so as not to spook her.

She'd been avoiding him for weeks, but she was chatting with Ben's mom on the edge of the dance floor and either didn't notice his approach or was softened by the mood of the wedding to give him a chance. He was hoping it was the latter.

Ben's father joined them briefly, and then Mr. and Mrs. West drifted onto the dance floor, leaving Elinor standing on the edge of the crowd, watching the couples sway to a love song. He wouldn't get a better chance.

"Hey."

Her chin jerked up toward him, the surprise in her brown eyes telling him he might have been overly optimistic in his hope that she was giving him a second—third, twentieth—chance. She just hadn't seen him coming. But he was here now, and he'd been trying to find a way to talk to her for weeks.

Apologize, a voice in the back of his brain whispered, this one sounding like Marjorie. *Do it now.*

But the words that slipped past his sudden nerves

were "Would you like to dance? That is, if you don't still hate me?"

Elinor frowned slightly—an irritated little bunch of her eyebrows. She had the most expressive eyebrows, telegraphing whenever she was annoyed. His nerves ratcheted up another notch. But being nervous around Elinor had been a semi-regular state when he was thirteen, so there was something familiar about the fear as he waited and met her frowning eyes.

🐾

Levi hated to dance.

They both knew it. School dances, proms, even the one time he'd put on music out at the old mill and they'd swayed to it—it had all been for her. Because he knew she loved it.

She didn't want to be thinking about that right now, remembering all the things he'd done just to make her happy, all the things that had melted her heart. Not when she was already feeling this confusing knot of might-have-been twisting through her.

But there was something so vulnerable in his eyes. So she found herself admitting, "I never hated you, Levi. That was the problem."

Something shifted in his eyes, and he opened his mouth, but suddenly she didn't want him to speak, to ruin this moment with whatever serious thing had taken over his face.

"I'd love to dance," she said, holding out her hand.

His hand closed around it, and his mouth snapped shut as he led her to the dance floor. It was only a couple of feet, not far to go before he turned to face her, gently placing his free hand on her hip. Her hand went automatically to his shoulder. Habit.

He didn't pull her close, too cautious for that, and she found herself remembering the middle school dance he'd invited her to, when they'd stood with arms extended, elbows locked as they rocked back and forth. He'd been scared to presume too much then, too. He was such a man now, but it had never been more obvious that he was still that gangly thirteen-year-old boy, too.

"People keep talking to me about you," she said when the intimacy of the dance got to be too much. She needed the words to escape the warmth of it, the familiarity of his hands, his scent...

"Likewise," he murmured.

She flicked a glance around the room. Most people were watching Ally and Ben, but there were several eyes on them. "Everyone's going to be speculating that we're back together. Again." She made a face. "This town. Sometimes it drives me crazy."

"You didn't have to come back. You could have gone anywhere."

Irritation flashed fast. That I-know-what's-best-for-you button he always pushed, ready to react to the slightest pressure. "No, I couldn't," she snapped. "My family was here. And even if I didn't have to come back, I *wanted* to. That was the piece that you and Katie and everyone else who kept pushing me to chase this idea you had of my potential never seemed to get. I never felt forced or trapped. I *wanted* this. I wanted you."

Chapter Twenty-Two

The bride and groom weren't the only ones who looked right at home in each other's arms...

—*Pine Hollow Newsletter*, Monday, December 20

Wanted. Past tense.

He'd screwed it up. He'd missed his shot. Because he hadn't listened when she told him he was what she wanted—or he had listened, but he hadn't been able to believe it.

Contrary to what everyone in this nosy town seemed to think, he wasn't trying to win her back. He knew he'd long since missed his window for that. But he still felt a compulsion to make amends. To fix this. Not romantically, but because this was Elinor and he needed her to be okay.

"I'm sorry."

She shook her head, brushing away the words. "I am, too. I don't want to fight. Especially not tonight."

"No, I... that's not what I meant. I need to... explain. Do

you think we could...?" He glanced around the crowded rec center, which had been decked out like a Christmas ballroom for the reception. "Is there somewhere we could talk?"

Elinor hesitated. He could feel her reluctance through his hand on her side. They'd barely been swaying before, and he kept forgetting to dance, moving side to side whenever he realized the music was still playing.

He stopped moving. "Please," he said softly. "I just...I want to explain. If you'll let me."

She chewed on her lower lip, the familiarity of the uncertain gesture hitting him in the gut. "Okay," she whispered.

He took her hand and started to lead her from the dance floor, but Elinor quickly freed herself. "Everyone will think we're sneaking off together," she hissed at him. "Just...meet me on the balcony in ten minutes."

The rec center had a second floor that provided a jogging track and a viewing area for the main floor below. It was a useful overflow space for the various craft fairs and farmers markets held at the center when the weather wasn't hospitable at the town square, but no one was up there tonight.

Levi had hoped for somewhere a little more private, but he would take what he could get. He nodded, and Elinor slipped into the crowd without looking back.

He smiled at a few wedding guests without seeing them, going through the motions until he could disappear without rousing suspicion. Deenie and Connor were dancing—looking like they invented it. The show-offs. Astrid danced with Ben, while Ally chatted with his parents. No one seemed to be paying any attention to Levi, so he ducked through the double doors to the stairwell and headed up.

The balcony was all shadows. Levi paused at the top of

the stairs to let his eyes adjust. The bleachers that rolled out for viewing sports events had been only partially shoved back after the last time they were used, and the bottom two rows stuck out onto the jogging track. Levi headed toward them, forcing himself to sit rather than stare over the railing, incessantly searching the crowd below for Elinor and wondering if she was actually going to come.

His palms were sweaty, and he rubbed them down the pant legs of the rented suit. His collar suddenly felt too tight. This was what he'd wanted. To clear the air. But now that it was time, he might be having a small panic attack.

The door at the far end of the balcony opened. Levi stopped breathing.

He stood, jerking to his feet like a marionette.

Elinor walked toward him slowly, the sound of her heels muted on the rubbery material of the jogging track. "At Last" had begun playing below, but his nerves rang so loudly in his ears he barely heard it.

"I wasn't sure you'd come," he admitted as soon as she was close enough that she could hear him without his voice carrying over the balcony to the party below.

"I almost didn't." A wry smile.

"I'm glad you did."

She stopped a few feet away from him, hugging the stole she'd worn for the outdoor ceremony around her as if she was cold, though if anything the balcony was warmer than the area below. Levi was about to sweat through his suit.

"What did you want to say?" she prompted.

He nodded. *Right. Moment of truth.* "I'm sorry."

Her face shut down, the spark of her withdrawing, and he rushed to explain.

"I'm not saying that to get you back. I know that isn't happening. I don't want—That isn't why..." *God, stop talking, you idiot. Slow down.* Levi took a jagged breath. "I want to explain. I know I didn't do a good job of that before. Or ever. But I need you to understand. I never would have—I never wanted..." He stopped. "Can I start over?"

Elinor's closed-off posture softened, and she moved toward the bleachers. She sank down on the lowest level and clasped her hands in her lap, still several feet away, but no longer looking like she might bolt at any second. "Okay. Explain."

"This isn't an excuse. I'm not trying to excuse—I never meant to hurt you, but I know intentions aren't always—Shit." He broke off, rubbing both hands down his face. So much for his fresh start. She'd always been the one who was good with words. He'd loved to listen to her talk, especially when she got excited and the words seemed to trip over one another, like she couldn't get them out fast enough. When he talked too fast, he was a bumbling idiot. "I've been talking to this therapist—"

"You have?" She interrupted before he could interrupt himself.

He flushed. "I know. What's more shocking? That I'm talking at all, or that I'm going to a therapist?" He rocked, trying to contain his body's sudden need to pace. "Marjorie and Elton wanted me to go. I'd been, you know, not sleeping great since the stuff this summer, and they were worried."

"Levi..." Sympathy touched her face, and he spoke quickly to head it off.

"I didn't mean to talk about that. That's not what I—God, I'm bad at this."

"It's okay."

But it wasn't. He needed to say this right, and he was screwing it all up. *Chip off the old block.* His father's voice flashed in his mind, bitter and dry.

And in that moment he knew exactly what to say.

"I *knew* I was going to be a shit husband to you."

"Levi." No longer sympathetic, her tone was aggravated. Sharp.

"I only had my parents as a model. I was going to screw things up for you. I knew it." *Chip off the old block.* "They got together young, just like us. She was miserable, but she stayed, even when he was awful to her, even when he cheated."

"Levi, you aren't your father."

"I know, but I had an awful example of what a marriage is supposed to be, and *he* saw them in us. He told me I'd done exactly what he did—found someone who was too good for me and made her promise to stay. I was going to be this anvil, dragging you down, and I know you're pissed at me for making the call without you and for listening to Katie and my dad"—*and my own insecurities*—"but if I'd talked to you about it, you would have stayed."

"And it never occurred to you that it might be because I *wanted* to stay?" There was heat in her voice now.

"You had all this passion. All this purpose. I never had that, and I didn't want to be the reason that you didn't go after something."

"Did you ever think it might have been *easier* to go after what I wanted with your support? That you might have *helped* me achieve my dreams?"

"No," he admitted. "I spent my entire childhood watching my father chip away at my mom, listening to her defend him, feeling guilty because the only reason they got married in the first place was because she was pregnant with me. I couldn't do that to you."

"Levi, we aren't your parents! It wouldn't have been the same. You were there for me. You were the best thing in my life, aside from Katie and my family, and the only thing stopping us from being happy together was *you*."

"I'm sorry," he said. The only thing he could say. "I didn't want to fight with you tonight. I just wanted..." His throat closed off and he swallowed until he could make the words come again. "Maybe I was wrong. Maybe it was the biggest mistake of my life. But I wanted you to know why I did it."

Because I love you. Because I never stopped loving you. Because you have always been better off without me.

"I do know," she said softly, her gaze on her hands in her lap.

"Elle..."

Her chin lifted on the nickname he hadn't let himself use in years.

"I'm sorry."

She nibbled her lower lip, one corner of her mouth quirking up sadly. "Me too."

He didn't know what to say after that. The words seemed to have drained away, leaving him empty. He held her eyes, something invisible in the air seeming to draw close around them, and the first few guitar notes of a familiar song floated up from below.

His breath caught.

It had been their song, once upon a time. The country ballad they'd danced to at their first-ever middle school dance—when she'd already been in high school but he'd screwed up the courage to ask her anyway. He'd swayed with her, and it felt like something was clicking into place, something so perfect he knew he didn't deserve it, but that had only made him want to hold on tighter.

She'd teased him later that there couldn't have been a better first song for them to dance to, since it was called "When You Say Nothing at All," and Levi had never been much for talking.

He'd played it for her out at the mill the day he'd given her that stupid promise ring when they were fifteen. Her mom had been sick—not like she had been for the previous several years, but in the hospital for long enough that they all knew it was bad. They knew what was coming. Levi had needed Elinor to know she wouldn't be alone, that he would always be there for her. The promise ring had seemed like the perfect thing when he was fifteen. Before he'd realized how much he could hold her back.

The female singer's voice rose up plaintively—and Levi knew Elinor heard it too when she turned her face away, unable to hold his gaze. She had a voice like that, the kind that knocked people back when they first heard it. She'd sing to herself when she was happy and rule karaoke nights without even trying. She'd never pursued it, but she could have been a star if she wanted. She could have done anything. Valedictorian. The pride of Pine Hollow.

And he'd been the tone-deaf kid who'd barely finished high school. Who probably would have wound up in prison if Elton hadn't grabbed him by the collar and shoved him onto the right path. He'd never been right for her. But Levi would rather have cut off his own arm than hurt her. And he hated himself for breaking her heart—even if it had been the right thing to do.

And it had been.

Hadn't it?

Standing there, listening to that song, he wanted to ask her to dance, like he had that afternoon at the mill all those years ago. He wanted to sway and pretend nothing else in the world mattered more than how much he loved her.

But that wasn't this world. And he'd told her he wasn't trying to win her back. He wanted to make her feel better—not put her in a position where he might hurt her again.

He'd said his piece.

Levi pushed his hands into his pockets, rocking back on his heels. "I guess I should go."

Elinor's gaze snapped to his, but she didn't say a word. And Levi nodded. That was it then. The end of them.

Alison Krauss was still singing when Levi walked away.

Elinor couldn't make herself move, watching the stairwell door close behind him.

She'd thought, when she came up here, that she owed him this. She'd ambushed him on Black Friday, and after all the things he'd done for her in the last twenty years, she could do this for him. But now she didn't know what to think.

The song below changed, some up-tempo eighties power ballad, but Elinor didn't move. She should head back downstairs, back to the reception, but she needed a few minutes to collect herself.

That was how it felt. Like she was a jar of marbles that had spilled out and she needed to find all her missing pieces and get them back in order.

She'd thought she had closure three weeks ago, but *this*

felt final. This felt like goodbye. The end of an era. The Elinor-and-Levi years.

And it was sad.

She hadn't been sad like this when they first broke up. That had been sharp and angry and wronged. This was soft and worn-down and resigned. An ache, deep below the surface. A regret. That longing for what might have been. Because she'd finally accepted it wouldn't be.

She could love Levi. He could love her. But she couldn't make him see that she was better off with him if he was determined to see himself as an anvil dragging her down. So they were really done.

The music shifted again, the emcee announcing it was time for the bouquet. Elinor moved to the railing to watch. On another day, she might be in the pack crowding together to jump for the bouquet, but today her heart wasn't ready.

Ally laughed as she threw the bouquet and the pack leapt en masse, tumbling to the ground in a heap. After Deenie emerged from the pile with the bouquet clutched triumphantly in one hand, Elinor pushed away the lingering sense of melancholy and started back downstairs.

She didn't see Levi anywhere—but she told herself she wasn't looking. Today was about Ally and Ben. Two of her favorite people. Getting married. And she didn't want to miss another second of it because she was in her head.

Ally found her within three minutes of her reappearance downstairs. "You okay?" the bright-eyed bride asked, linking their arms together. "I didn't see you when I threw the bouquet, and I saw you dancing with Levi earlier…"

"No, yeah." Elinor smiled. "I'm good. I'm really good," she said, and was surprised by how much she meant it. "But I don't think I'm quite ready for the bouquet. Not yet."

"Okay." Ally's smile brimmed full of relief. "It's probably for the best. Deenie was taking no prisoners."

"I saw that. We're lucky there were no injuries."

"She's tenacious." Across the ballroom, Deenie was dragging Connor toward the dance floor as he laughed. "I never would have predicted those two, but the universe moves in mysterious ways." Ally squeezed her arm. "And it's coming for you. I can feel it."

"That sounds so ominous."

"Nonsense. We're coming up on the year of Elinor. You'll see."

Elinor smiled at Ally's conviction. A few months ago she'd thought she was in a good place. She would have insisted she didn't need a year of Elinor, but now it was like a valve she'd closed in herself three years ago had finally opened and she was ready to let light in again—and let her own light out.

"You know, I think you may be right," she told Ally. "The year of Elinor. I like that."

And maybe, finally, her heart was ready.

Chapter Twenty-Three

Happy New Year, Pine Hollow! As always, there were many New Year's Eve parties of note around town, but the real question isn't who attended which party, but who was seen kissing whom when the clock struck midnight?

—*Pine Hollow Newsletter*, Monday, January 3

The New Year's Eve party at the ski resort was always the biggest party of the year. Elinor hadn't attended in ages, but this year would be different.

The year of Elinor.

White twinkle lights had been strung around the perimeter of the rooftop lounge, and partygoers were already crowded around all the fire pits even though midnight was still hours away. At nine o'clock the lights would all be turned down and the gas-powered flames on the fire pits lowered so everyone could watch the annual torchlight ski parade down the mountain, followed by fireworks for the families who didn't want to stay out until midnight. But the party on the rooftop would only continue to grow until the New Year arrived.

And, for once, Elinor planned to be there for every second of it.

Ally and Ben had flown off to Jamaica for their honeymoon two days after Christmas. If Elinor peeked over the edge of the rooftop, she'd see Astrid below in front of the lodge, running in a pack with some other local kids as they waited for the torchlight parade. Ben's parents were down there as well. They were staying at Ben and Ally's place with Astrid while the newlyweds were away, and would head there after the fireworks, but Deenie and Connor had booked one of the VIP tables on the rooftop and insisted Mac and Elinor join them.

Deenie was in manic pixie mode—though Elinor couldn't tell whether it was excitement over the new year or excitement over the giant rock that was currently sitting on her left hand. Apparently Connor had popped the question at the wedding—or Deenie had, Elinor wasn't clear on the details—but this was Deenie's first night wearing the diamond.

Anne and Bailey swung by their table to say hello, and Deenie immediately sucked them in with her enthusiasm, along with Charlotte and Kendall and anyone else who came into range—though Charlotte seemed distracted by her phone and Kendall kept getting pulled away for minor resort emergencies. Magda, the third member of her sister's little trio, was nowhere in sight, and as much as Elinor had always liked Magda, she was a little relieved, since Mac was seated to Connor's left. The last thing she wanted tonight was drama. No skirmishes between Mac and Magda. No thinking about Levi. Just the new leaf she was turning over.

Which would have been easier if people would stop asking her where Levi was.

She'd barely been at the party fifteen minutes and had already been asked twice where the chief was. Deenie was the third, craning her neck to scan the rooftop as she asked, "Where's Levi?"

At least she was asking the group at large and not giving Elinor pointed looks.

Elinor blamed Linda Hilson and her damn newsletter, but lately everyone in town seemed to think she and Levi were back together.

Which they absolutely weren't.

But things felt different now. The past looked different now. Like they might be able to be friends again.

"He's probably working," Connor answered, lounging on one of the overstuffed couches.

"On New Year's Eve?" Deenie—who had declared herself Master of the Fun—was suitably appalled. She wore a sparkly black tutu—an actual tutu—and had silver hair tinsel woven through her pink-streaked hair, but somehow the princess-party planner made it work for her. Everything seemed to work for Deenie. She could carry off any style with a smile.

Unlike Elinor, who always seemed to forget to think about her appearance. Her mom hadn't been well enough to show her how to put on makeup or style her hair, so she'd deprioritized those things. As long as her face was clean and her hair was in a shiny ponytail, she was good to go. The best of what she had to offer was on the inside anyway, but maybe if she was going to start dating in her "new year, new you" plan, she might want to check out some of those makeup tutorials Charlotte was so addicted to.

"Levi always works on the holidays," Connor explained while Elinor was distracted by fashion musings.

"That's so sad." A stray firework popped in the distance, and Deenie twisted toward the sound, but the tall trees and mountains blocked their view.

"Don't feel sorry for him," Elinor said. "Levi works even when he isn't on shift. Gotta keep Pine Hollow safe." Even when they were together, he'd never made it to New Year's Eve parties. The only holiday that was different was Valentine's Day. "The man has an overdeveloped sense of responsibility."

A deep voice spoke behind her. "Still misquoting *The Princess Bride*, I see."

"Levi." Elinor twisted quickly on her chair as Deenie bounced off hers.

"You made it! I was just wondering where you were. Happy New Year!" She spun back to Connor. "Now that everyone's here, can we tell them?"

Connor's grin was wry as he flicked a glance to the planet-sized rock on Deenie's finger. The thing probably had its own gravitational field. "I think most of them have figured it out already."

"I know, but it's so fun to *say*." Deenie thrust her hand over the center of the table, waving the ring. "We're getting hitched! And *I* get to plan everything. Ambush wedding! No spoilers, but it will be an elopement and there will be very little warning, so brace yourselves."

Mac turned a skeptical look on Connor. "*You* are giving up planning control?"

"We made a deal." Connor shrugged, holding his hands up in defeat, but he was smiling hugely.

"Congratulations," Elinor said—though she'd already congratulated Deenie, one on one. Her words set off a round of congratulations and shuffling as everyone moved to hug the happy couple.

When they were all settled again, Levi had taken the empty chair at her side—which only made sense. There weren't that many empty chairs. But she couldn't help thinking of what Linda Hilson's stupid newsletter would think of it. Someone was probably calling the tip line right now.

He had that blank face on again—but this time it seemed cautious. Like he was waiting to take his lead from her.

Elinor grabbed for the lightest, most inoffensive olive branch she could find. "I didn't misquote, for the record. I was *referencing*. It was an homage."

"Ah." He nodded. "Should have known. I take it you're still obsessed with that movie."

"It's the best movie ever made," she said. "It's not obsession. It's just good taste."

"I stand corrected."

She glanced over at him. "You're really not working tonight?"

"Later," he admitted. "We set up free rideshare services with all the places holding events, but there's always someone who thinks they're okay to drive and pushes their luck."

And they both knew how dangerous the twisting mountain roads could be when a driver was impaired or distracted. "Be careful," she murmured.

"Always," he promised. He nodded toward Connor and Deenie, who was performing an exaggerated pantomime of showing off her ring, which had Mac cracking up. "Did you know?"

"About the engagement? Not until I saw the ring tonight. Deenie said she's been dying to tell people. I guess it's been a couple of weeks."

"Yeah. At the wedding reception, apparently," Levi

confirmed—but there was something off about his expression.

"You aren't happy for them?"

"No, of course. I just didn't know they were on that path."

"All your friends getting married and leaving you behind?" she tried to joke. "Gosh, if only someone would have made an honest man of you."

Embarrassed awareness shifted in the gray of his eyes. "I didn't mean..."

"I'm teasing you, Levi." She smiled. "It's a new thing. I'm trying it out."

Relief replaced the embarrassment. "I like it."

"Good. I plan to do it mercilessly."

His lips twitched in that little involuntary whisper of a smile that had always made her feel like she won the lottery. "How's the writing going?"

Two months ago the question had made her want to bite his head off, but she felt like a different person now. "It's really good, actually. I did NaNo with some students this year and decided to keep the after-school sessions going for any of the kids who wanted to keep writing or to revise what they've done. It's sort of become a creative writing club, and I've been working on some of my own stuff at the same time. Mostly rereading and revising. Katie used to give me a hard time because I never thought anything was done."

"I remember."

"I just always wanted to do one more revision before I showed anyone—but I don't know. This feels different." *She* felt different.

She had been fiddling with her drink as they talked, but now she looked up and caught him watching her with that steady, attentive concentration of his. There was something so familiar about it, so comfortable, that she found herself confiding in him.

"I've been thinking about what Katie told you," she admitted. "About how I don't prioritize myself. And I'm *not* saying your reaction was justified, but I think she may have been right, a little bit. I think I got in the habit of trying to be perfect for everyone when my mom was sick. Perfect daughter. Perfect big sister. Perfect student. And then it just kind of swelled. Like I had to be perfect for the whole town. And it was easy to be perfect when I was younger. There was this set path, you know. You just ace every test and get all the scholarships and go to the best college—but then what? Because I wasn't really happy there. I was homesick, and I didn't like premed, and it was Katie who convinced me I didn't have to become a doctor just because I thought I should. I couldn't save my mom." She swallowed. "And then I couldn't save Katie. And I know that was out of my hands, that there was nothing I could have done, but when people have been telling you your whole life that you can do anything, it's hard to accept that some things are out of your control. And it's hard to make yourself try again when you realize you can't control the outcome."

Levi and Katie had been the only people she felt comfortable being herself around—imperfections and all. They'd also been the only two people she'd talked to about her writing dreams, but then it felt like she lost them both, back to back, and that part of herself had gotten lost somewhere along the way.

"Anyway, that's kind of a long, disjointed way of saying I'm going to start submitting my book to editors and agents." She used to dream of taking the world by storm. And now, finally, maybe she would. "I've been doing some research the last few weeks while we're on break, trying to teach myself how to do it. And psych myself up." It was weird without Katie cheering her on, but it was time. "I set myself a deadline. Five queries before the next semester starts."

His eyebrows arched. "That's Monday."

"I know. And I'm sure their inboxes are all going to be flooded after the holiday, and everyone else on the planet is also making New Year's resolutions to finally submit their book, but if I don't start now, I'll never start. So I'm starting. New year, new me."

Elinor smiled, and Levi couldn't look away. She was breathtaking. He knew she didn't realize how much she lit up when she was talking about something that excited her. He'd long since fallen completely in love with the absent way she would push her glasses farther up on her nose as she leaned forward, as if proximity could help pass her passion on to him.

He wanted to tell her that she didn't need to be a new her, that he was still in love with the old her, but he knew better. They were finally good. She was finally talking to him again. Friends. Thank God. And he couldn't screw this up. Not again. So he smiled, and said what a friend would say. "That's awesome. Good for you."

She grimaced. "Well, I haven't done anything yet. I can't seem to stop tweaking my query letter."

"Do you want a second opinion?" he offered, before his brain caught up with how stupid that suggestion was. "I don't know anything about query letters."

"No, I—thank you. That's very sweet, but I think..."

"Of course." He was the last person whose opinion she would want. For a dozen different reasons.

The lights on the rooftop suddenly dimmed, and they both looked instinctively toward the mountain. Connor had reserved them a space near the stone ledge that wrapped around the edge of the roof, and as soon as the lights lowered, people started shifting and angling to get better views. Levi stood, offering his hand to Elinor. He didn't think she was even aware she grabbed it, her focus entirely on the mountain.

The lights around the resort flicked off in sequence—the lodges, each of the chair lifts and gondolas—until the only light was from the stars and the tiny sliver of a moon that sat in the sky tonight. The snow reflected that whisper of light back at them, so it wasn't completely dark. The hush of winter was broken only by the excited murmurings of the crowds on the rooftop and down below, who were all staring eagerly up the mountain.

Then the music began to play.

It was some sort of classical thing. Elinor probably knew what it was. All he knew, as the first of the torches appeared at the top of the mountain and began gliding downward, was that it was beautiful.

He'd skied in the parade, back when they were younger. Lots of kids in town did, when they were too old to be awed by it like the little kids but not old enough yet to get into any of the parties that served alcohol. He hadn't seen the parade in decades, and never from the rooftop vantage point with the music playing—and Elinor's hand in his.

He should have done this every chance he got.

The torches wended lazily down the hill, creating a gliding trail of light zigzagging down the mountain as the music floated through the night air. The crowd watched in silence—and Elinor's fingers brushed gently against his, a tiny twitch of movement.

The music picked up tempo as the first of the skiers and snowboarders reached the base of the mountain, and the crowd gathered in front of the lodge began to cheer the torchbearers. Deenie leaned over the balustrade, adding her voice to the shouts, and soon everyone in their group was hooting and cheering as well—except for Levi and Elinor, who exchanged a fleeting smile and then turned their eyes back to the parade.

As the last few torchbearers reached the final stretch above the darkened chairlift, the first fireworks exploded in the air above them. Everyone gasped, reflexively turning their faces to the sky.

Everyone except Levi.

His favorite part of fireworks had always been the faces of the people watching them. He looked down as flashes of color lit the snow—and watched those same flashes of color lighting the planes of Elinor's upturned face. She'd bitten her lower lip as she watched the spectacle, and in the darkness he could occasionally see the shapes of the fireworks reflected on her glasses.

His heart squeezed tight in his chest as he told himself he'd made the right call. And even if he hadn't, there was no going back now. Regret could suck the life out of you. He'd seen who his father had become, riddled with might-have-beens. He wouldn't do that, even if part of him whispered that he'd made a mistake. The worst mistake.

The music swelled, building to the final crescendo as the fireworks painted the sky above. The cold night air pressed against his exposed skin, colder now with all the fire pits and braziers lowered for the fireworks. He saw Connor tuck Deenie against him, and Anne and Bailey huddling closer for warmth. Mac had found someone to cozy up to—but the only person Levi wanted to put his arm around was Elinor, and that felt like a step too far. The truce was too new between them. Too tentative.

On another night, in another world, he would have held her close. He would have tipped her face toward his as the last fireworks filled the starry sky. He would have kissed her now, and at midnight, and everything would have felt like it did before.

But tonight the last fireworks faded, the last notes of the music sounded, and there was a beat, a moment of quiet before the lights all came back up and applause swelled through the crowd.

Elinor's hand slid away from his with a final brush of her fingers as she raised her hands to clap. And he forced himself to look away. At anything but her.

During the post-fireworks buzz, everyone moved back toward the table, huddling closer to the fire, but Levi held back, lingering by the stone railing. Kendall appeared at their table with a bottle of champagne in each hand.

"Champagne?" She wagged the bottles. "On the house—and by house, I mean preordered on Connor's credit card."

A server approached behind her with a tray of glasses as Deenie looked to Connor. He shrugged with a grin. "What? We're celebrating. You love celebrating."

She smiled at him as if he'd personally hung the stars in the sky for her.

And Levi was reminded again of how much he'd given up, the way Elinor used to look at him. The biggest-mistake-of-my-life hypothesis was starting to feel more and more accurate.

As Kendall began passing around glasses, Levi caught Elinor watching him, a question in her eyes. He glanced at his watch. "I should get going. But congratulations, Connor. Deenie. And happy New Year, everyone."

Choruses of "Happy New Year!" answered him as he picked up the hat and gloves he'd set on his chair when it was warmer on the rooftop than he'd anticipated, before they lowered the fires. He glanced back at Elinor, expecting her to be avoiding his gaze, pretending he was already gone like she would have for the last few years whenever they were forced to be in the same place, but instead she was smiling. It was a small smile, sort of distantly friendly, but he would take it.

"Be safe," she told him.

He nodded. And walked away from the best thing that had ever happened to him.

Chapter Twenty-Four

The chief may have missed out on midnight kisses, but multiple sources have reported there was some very cozy handholding going on during the torchlight parade.
—*Pine Hollow Newsletter*,
Monday, January 3

E linor?"

Elinor jumped guiltily and jerked her gaze away—as if by moving quickly no one would notice she'd been gawking after Levi, when, of course, everyone in the freaking town had noticed. And would be speculating about it for the next week.

Deenie stood at her elbow, holding a brimming glass of bubbly. "Champagne?"

Elinor reached for the glass, but Charlotte's voice interrupted the action. "Don't waste a full glass on Elinor. She'll only pretend to drink it anyway."

It wasn't so much the words as the tone that stopped Elinor's hand in midair. The extra edge.

Elinor had avoided champagne for the last few years—

which was a stupid, self-sabotaging thing to do, considering she loved the stuff, but it had always made her think of Levi. Her first taste of it had been when he snuck a bottle of it out from under his parents' noses so he could bring it out to the mill and make a toast to her getting into Dartmouth. The taste and the bubbles and Levi had all gone right to her head that day. When he'd been so happy for her and so proud of her and everything had felt so wonderful. So right.

All of the milestones of her life were marked by champagne and Levi, but she wasn't trying to bury her past anymore. "Actually..." Elinor took the glass Deenie was holding uncertainly. "I will take a full glass. We're celebrating."

She lifted the glass to her lips for a sip, the bubbles bursting across her tongue.

Charlotte's lifted eyebrows were skeptical—but before she could comment, her phone buzzed and her attention jerked to it desperately. Elinor wanted to yank the thing out of her hands, but Charlotte was already turning away, moving quickly to the stone balustrade, seeing nothing but the message on her screen.

Deenie frowned after her. "Okay, what is her problem tonight?"

"Her boyfriend, the *wonderful* Warren, was supposed to be here, but it looks like he's standing her up again, which shocks absolutely no one, including Charlotte."

Deenie winced. "Ouch. This was why I never did relationships. The expectations are killer. Especially on the High Holy Days of Romantic Relationships."

"Says the woman with the giant rock on her finger."

Deenie shrugged, her gaze moving across the fire pit to her fiancé. "Connor's different. He's my person."

"I think Charlotte is still trying to convince herself that

Warren is her person, no matter what he does to prove he doesn't deserve the title."

"I've been there. Though for me it was usually trying to twist myself into knots to prove I matched the person I thought I wanted to be my person," Deenie said—and Elinor felt like a brat because Deenie was more sympathetic to Charlotte in five minutes than she'd managed to be in the last three months. She just wanted her sister to wake up and smell the arrogant dickwad.

"This thing with Warren was all whirlwind romance at first, and she became convinced he was her Mr. Darcy— Jane Austen is a whole thing in my family—"

"Oh, no, I get it," Deenie assured her. "Ms. Jane is a major deity in my pantheon."

"He always struck me as the kind of guy who threw money around so no one would call him on it when he was being a dick."

Deenie's eyebrows popped up. "Mr. Darcy?"

"No, sorry, Warren. It's always, 'I can't make it tonight, Charlotte, but pick out any diamond bracelet you like.'"

"So he commemorates standing her up with jewelry. Classy."

Elinor snorted. "Charlotte says his love language is gifts, and he wants her to know she's important to him—but her love language has always been attention, or quality time, I guess it's called, and he never gives her any. But, as Anne would remind me, it's not my call. Not my relationship. And the more I piss her off about it, the worse things get between us. But how do you watch someone treating your baby sister like crap and just encourage her to take it?"

"There might be a halfway point between giving her a

hard time and encouraging her to take it," Deenie suggested dryly and Elinor grimaced.

"I know. I'm not good at rational and measured with her. We push each other's buttons. We always have."

"That's what happens when you're so alike."

"Alike? Charlotte, the Energizer Bunny fitness junkie who hikes mountains for fun?"

"No, you're right," Deenie reply dryly. "Type A. Strong willed. Stubborn. You guys have nothing in common."

"We can't all be glitter and rainbows."

"But we could be!" Deenie declared dramatically. "Everything is better with sparkles."

Elinor grinned. "Your wedding dress is going to be bedazzled, isn't it?"

"No spoilers," Deenie singsonged. "But glitter is my love language, so all bets are off."

At the stone railing, Charlotte swore and smacked her phone down, lifting her champagne glass to drain it in a single go.

Deenie followed Elinor's gaze and made a face. "Free advice?" she offered.

"Sure." Elinor lifted her own glass, taking a sip.

"As someone who always felt like my decisions were being questioned by my family? Them picking at me never helped. And if you push her, make her feel like she has to choose between you and him, she might choose him just because he isn't the one making her feel bad. Or because she doesn't want to admit you were right."

"I know," Elinor murmured. But it was so hard not to want to defend Charlotte—even to Charlotte.

She was the big sister. It was her job to look out for them. Always.

Kendall appeared at Charlotte's side at the railing—
which was probably for the best. If Elinor tried to offer
comfort, she would inevitably say something that would set
her sister off, but Kendall would know what to do.

"Total change of topic?" Deenie asked at her side.

"Please." Elinor turned toward the fire so she would stop
watching her sister.

Deenie linked their arms together and tugged her down
onto the couch facing the fire pit. "I was trying to think of a
subtle way to slip this into the conversation, but I'm failing
completely, so I'm just gonna bulldoze my way through it.
I promise I wasn't trying to eavesdrop, but I kind of heard
Levi ask you something about your writing, and I had to
stop myself from squealing and leaping on top of you. Are
you secretly a writer?"

"No," she protested instinctively. "I'm just messing around
while helping some students with their writing projects."

"But you wrote a book."

Elinor flushed. "Yeah, but I haven't actually done anything with it..."

"But you're a writer!" Deenie squealed, bouncing on
the couch cushion. "I don't think I've ever met a writer—
I can't even wrap my head around how you would hold a
whole book in your head, but I'm a huge reader. What do
you write? Please say romance. Whatever you say will be
awesome, but I will die if it's romance."

Elinor smiled in spite of herself. It was impossible not
to be charmed by the tidal wave of Deenie's enthusiasm.
She'd always kept her writing secret. Levi and Katie knew,
but she hadn't wanted to expose her fragile eggshell dream
to the blast furnace of the town's attention. They would all
be rooting for her. And the pressure would crush her. But

somehow Deenie's giddiness didn't feel like pressure. It felt like pure delight.

"Actually it's young adult," she admitted, her voice low.

Deenie squeaked, unable to contain her glee. "That's my other favorite genre. Is it, like, dystopian or contemporary...?"

"Kind of more dystopian." Deenie squeaked again, and Elinor's cheeks began to ache from smiling. "I don't know if it's any good. I just, I guess I wanted to get back into it...Writing was always something Katie and I did."

"Ally said Astrid's mom was a huge reader. So you guys wrote together?"

"Not *together* together. We each worked on our own projects, but it made it feel more possible, having her want the same thing."

"Well, I'm not a writer, but I would crawl over hot coals to read anything you wrote, so if you're ever looking for a test reader, I'm very willing."

It was instinct to say no. Habit. She'd been hoarding her words for so long that the idea of sharing them was terrifying. But she trusted Deenie. And this was a new year. The year of Elinor.

"You know, I might take you up on that."

Deenie squeaked, clapping her hands. "Okay, so tell me more. I want to know *everything*."

Elinor laughed—and tried not to notice Charlotte refilling her champagne glass at the other side of the table.

She spent the next two hours trying not to notice her little sister's unhappiness as the band played, everyone danced, and Charlotte laughed a little too loudly at the edge of the dance floor, as if trying to prove to everyone that she was having the time of her life.

As the clock ticked toward midnight, the lines between their group and those around them melted away, the party becoming one giant Pine Hollow celebration. Magda arrived—which sent Mac to the opposite side of the dance floor—and Kendall was called away to deal with some guest emergency at the party down in the ballroom, the fancy one all the tourists paid to attend.

Around eleven thirty, they were joined by some of her coworkers from school and several of Charlotte's coworkers from the Estates. Including George—who thankfully didn't seem to hold it against her that their date had ended with her yelling at her ex in the pub. He really was a nice guy, and he'd deserved a much better date than she'd been.

Deenie and Connor were on the dance floor, doing some kind of cha-cha and making everyone else look clumsy by comparison, when Elinor found herself back at their table, rehydrating with her sisters and Bailey.

Anne's face was flushed with happiness as she chugged an entire glass of water. "We haven't done this in far too long," she said when she came up for air.

"What? Dancing manically on a rooftop in the middle of the night?" Charlotte teased. "I do this every week."

"'To be fond of dancing was a certain step towards falling in love,'" Bailey quoted—and all three Rodriguez sisters turned to gape at her.

"Did you just quote *Pride and Prejudice*?" Anne asked, the same way someone else might ask *Did you just turn water into wine?*

Bailey blushed, her eyes uncertain. "Did I get it right?"

Anne grabbed her by the collar of her fitted jacket and kissed her until they broke apart, laughing and flushed. "C'mon. Let's dance, since it's a certain step toward falling in love." Anne giggled, pulling her girlfriend back onto the dance floor.

Elinor watched them go, feeling a balloon of delight swelling up inside her. They hadn't had many New Year's celebrations like this. Their mom had been sick, and then Anne had been sick, and then Katie had died. Each New Year's Eve, depending on which part of the cycle they were in, looking into the new year had been an act of desperate hope or fearful relief or trying not to fixate on the absences. This was the first time in a long time it was just another new year. And Anne was so happy. She deserved to be this happy.

"Bailey's been reading up on Austen to surprise her," Elinor told Charlotte as she watched the pair, their smiles enormous as they danced. "She's so good for Anne."

"And Warren's horrible. I get it, Elinor."

"What?" Elinor yanked her gaze away from Anne and Bailey and frowned at Charlotte, who glowered at her. "I never said…"

"You didn't have to." She grabbed an empty glass, re-filling it from one of the mostly empty champagne bottles that littered the table.

"Maybe you should take it easy."

"Maybe you should lighten up and stop trying to control everything I do."

"I'm not—" She bit off the denial. It wouldn't do any good. Anne and Deenie and everyone who had told her Charlotte needed to come to her own conclusions about Warren were right. Charlotte wouldn't hear her now.

But a little voice kept whispering in the back of her head that Charlotte wasn't happy, that Warren wasn't good to her, and maybe missing New Year's was the straw that would break Charlotte's seemingly endless tolerance for his bullshit. Maybe this was the perfect time to say something because it was the only time she would listen.

Elinor knew she should keep her mouth shut.

But…

"I just want you to be with someone who values you. Someone nice. Someone like…" She flailed, looking around and her gaze landed on a likely candidate. "Like George."

Charlotte rolled her eyes. "You're one to talk. I hooked you up with a *nice* guy, with *George*, and you're still hung up on Levi even after *everything* he's done. I saw you talking to him tonight."

"He's my friend."

"He wants you back. We can all see he wants you back. And you're eating it up. But don't expect me to be there to pick up the pieces this time when he dumps you again."

Elinor's eyebrows flew up. "You? Pick up the pieces?"

"Like that's so funny? Like the idea of me being able to do anything for you is just hysterical because I'm the baby? I'm not a *child*, Elinor."

"I never said—"

"I *idolized* you when I was little, and everything was great as long as I did everything you wanted me to, but as soon as I became my own person with my own opinions, you didn't know what to do with me. Everything I do is wrong because it isn't what you would have me do."

"That isn't fair—"

"I'm twenty-seven years old. Why can't you just see that I'm an adult and my own person? Why can't you accept that I might actually know what's right for me, and maybe, just maybe, it might be Warren?" She spun on her heel.

"Charlotte!" Elinor shouted after her, but her sister was already moving quickly through the crowd.

She knew it was stupid, knew she should let her go, but the worry that always lurked under the surface grabbed hold of her and she followed, needing to know that Charlotte was okay.

She caught up with her in the stairwell, where Charlotte was rushing down the steps. "Charlotte! Where are you going? It's almost midnight!"

"I'm going to Warren's," Charlotte snapped, without slowing.

"You'll be on the road at midnight!" Her sister didn't stop, if anything taking the stairs faster. "You shouldn't be driving!"

"I'm getting a Lyft!" Charlotte shouted over her shoulder. "I'm not an idiot. Can't you give me any credit at all?"

"Charlotte, come back upstairs."

Her sister hit the last landing and spun to face her. "I know what I'm doing, Elle. I'm not a child, and you *aren't my mother*. Could you just trust me for once?"

"I do."

"Then just *stop*."

Elinor forced herself to stop and not move again as she watched her sister continue down the last half-flight of stairs and out the door at the bottom.

She stood there, held immobile by numb uncertainty. She couldn't imagine going back up to the party. Any minute now everyone would be counting down to the New Year, but her "year of Elinor" plan felt wrong now. Like a clock with the gears knocked out of alignment.

Instead of going up, she headed down to the lobby and ducked behind one of the lodge's decorative Christmas trees to watch the circular drive where Charlotte was waiting for her Lyft. Apparently, Levi wasn't the only one with an overdeveloped sense of responsibility. Though even he would have told her to stop stalking her sister and go upstairs.

But he didn't know that feeling, like the people she loved the most could be taken away from her at any moment, and she had to do everything she could to protect them. Even when it drove them crazy.

Or maybe he did. Maybe that had been their problem all along.

Both trying to save everyone around them, trying to control the things they couldn't control.

Music drifted from the ballroom, along with laughter and the buzz of excited conversation. It was almost midnight, but Elinor didn't move. Not until Charlotte got in a blue SUV and was driven away.

"Everything okay?"

Elinor yelped, spinning, and nearly tumbled into the Christmas tree she'd been hiding behind. "George!"

He reached out to catch her, but she'd already caught her balance and his hands stopped short of touching her. "Sorry. Didn't mean to startle you. I saw you and Charles rush out a little while ago, and when you didn't come back I thought I'd come see if everything was all right."

"You're gonna miss the countdown."

"It's just a countdown. There'll be another. You okay?"

She shook her head—more to decline his concern than to answer his question. "It's just my sister and me driving each other crazy. Situation normal."

In the ballroom, the crowd began chanting toward midnight. *"Ten...nine..."*

She flushed, guilty that he was missing the party. "You didn't have to come down..."

"I know. I'm gonna go back up now. You coming?"

His final words spilled over the shouts of "Happy New Year!" from the ballroom and a small smile quirked his lips. "Happy New Year," he said, conversationally.

"Happy New Year." She studied him. "You're a very low-drama human, aren't you, George Leneghan?"

"I don't know about that. But you forget. I have four older sisters. I am well versed in sibling drama. And when to strategically ignore said drama."

"Smart man."

"I am," he agreed with mock arrogance. "In fact, I'm so brilliant you should probably go out with me again, just so you can appreciate my genius."

She shook her head, smiling, as they headed toward the elevators. "You still want to go out with me after what happened last time? I'm not sure if I should be impressed or reconsider my opinion of your intelligence."

He shrugged as the elevator doors opened and extended a hand to hold them open so she could precede him inside. "Everyone has history. You live in a small town. I figure some of it's bound to be right around the corner. Doesn't mean you don't have a future. And maybe I'm in it. You seem like someone I would like."

She pushed the button for the roof as he let the doors close. A future sounded wonderful. It sounded like the year of Elinor. And maybe low-drama George was just what she needed in her life. She really did owe him a better date.

"You know what? I'd love to go out again. If the offer is still open."

His single lopsided dimple popped as he grinned.

Chapter Twenty-Five

> Those who saw a certain librarian with
> a certain town newcomer on New Year's
> Eve might be surprised to learn that a
> certain chief was seen with said librarian's
> dog several times this week...
> —*Pine Hollow Newsletter*,
> Monday, January 10

When Elinor's text arrived at three fifteen on Tuesday afternoon, Levi felt a sudden, unmistakable swell of relief.

Not only because it was the first time Elinor had voluntarily texted him in three years, or because she could easily have reached out to someone else—but also because, if he was honest, he really missed that dog.

The GPS Elinor had attached to Dory's collar had pinged her phone with an alert that the dog was loose. Elinor was tied up with the after-school program for at least another hour. Ben and Ally were still on their honeymoon, which explained why Elinor hadn't dropped Dory at the puppy Club Med that was the newly improved Furry Friends Animal Shelter and Doggie Day Care.

Levi pushed back from his desk and the paperwork he'd been looking for an excuse to avoid, and voice-texted a reply that he was on it. Elinor's response was instantaneous. A THANK YOU GIF and a link to the GPS tracker.

"Dory's loose again," Levi explained to Kaye as he walked past so she'd know she could reach him in his Explorer if anything urgent came up.

As soon as he climbed into the driver's seat, he popped his phone into its holder and pulled up the GPS tracker. At first the little dog icon looked like it wasn't moving, but then he realized the technology wasn't quite at the same level as *Mission: Impossible* movies, and the site was slow to update. The little dog blinked in one place, then thirty seconds later jumped to a new location. Levi watched until he could get a sense of which direction Dory was heading, and then turned on the engine, shut off his audiobook, and pulled out of the parking lot to give chase.

Dory, in true Dory fashion, led him on a zigzagging path through town—his pursuit complicated by the fact that nearly half the streets in Pine Hollow were one-way—but after about fifteen minutes of chasing the blinking dog icon, it veered toward a familiar country road and stopped.

Dory had returned to the mill.

Levi glanced down at the GPS tracker every thirty seconds to check that she hadn't moved on, but the tracker icon stayed put as he drove out to the mill. He wasn't sure how accurate the GPS was, so he kept his eyes peeled as he pulled into the gravel drive and cut the engine. He didn't see any sign of a fluffy white tail as he climbed out of his car, the ice-crusted gravel crunching beneath his boots.

"Dory want the ball?" he called, but the only reply was

a scrambling sound like a cascade of tiny rocks from inside the mill.

"It's not safe in there, dog," he called, hoping the sound of his voice would lure her out and he wouldn't have to go into the condemned building after her. Reaching through the open car door, he stretched across the center console and pulled a bag of treats out of the glove compartment. He gave the bag a shake and heard another scramble of rocks from inside—but no Dory emerging in a fluffy rush from the stone archway where the door had long since fallen off the hinges.

He should board that up so kids and curious dogs didn't get themselves crushed by falling beams in the derelict old building. There was a NO TRESPASSING sign, but that wouldn't have stopped him as a kid, and it certainly hadn't stopped Dory.

The land hadn't sold yet. There had been holdups regarding the zoning reclassification. Some anonymous citizen had requested a public hearing on the subject, and the town council had been so busy with the Christmas rush that it hadn't been scheduled yet. Which meant the mill wasn't a developer's problem yet, and Levi needed to make sure no one got hurt in there.

"Come on, Dory," he coaxed, shaking the bag as he approached the half-crumbled arch. When he was close enough to see inside, he realized that the interior wasn't as dark as he'd expected. A third of the roof must have fallen in with the last snow, though you couldn't tell from the road. Light streaked through the gaps in the ceiling, and snowdrifts had gathered on the floor inside.

And a streak of white fur raced through the shadows.

"Dory!" Wind gusted, making the entire building creak as Levi stepped over the threshold. "This isn't a game, dog."

But she just scampered to the back corner and turned in an excited circle before racing along the outer edge of the building and up a half-rotted staircase to the last remaining ledge of what had once been the second floor.

The very unstable second floor.

Levi took two steps toward her in an instinctive rush before he remembered she would only think he was playing and run away. He stopped and shook the bag. "Dory, want a treat?"

The little dog's ears perked up. Wind made the building groan again—and then the rotted wood beneath the dog's paws shifted as she launched herself off it and landed on a hill of crumbled bricks, sending little pieces cascading toward the floor in a mini avalanche.

She danced over and sat for a treat, her tail sweeping through the rubble.

"This is not a good place to play," Levi informed her. He reached into his back pocket for the leash—but as soon as she saw it, she danced away. "Come on, dog," he growled.

Something loud dropped behind him, and Levi spun toward the open-air part of the building, his entire body tensed—and his jaw dropped at the sight that greeted him.

Apparently Dory wasn't the only one who thought the decrepit mill was a great place to play.

Graffiti covered one entire wall of the ruins, the paint stretching up well above his head. Dozens of footprints marked the snow at the base of the wall, and there was even a ladder leaning against it that looked like it might fall down in the next stiff breeze.

"I'll be damned."

Levi turned in a circle, seeing other splashes of spray paint in the dark corners of the building, now that he knew to look.

Their vandal hadn't stopped working when the snow had come. They'd moved out here.

Moving carefully over the uneven flooring, Levi went closer to the ladder. The paint looked fresh. He touched the wall, his fingers sticking slightly to the tacky surface. "Hello?" he called. "Anyone here?"

"Who were you expecting?"

Levi spun toward the door. Elinor stood just inside the crumbled stone arch, bending to greet Dory, who wriggled with delight. "I thought you had the after-school program."

"Just finished." She gave the dog one last pat and straightened, looking past Levi to the wall. "Wow. How long has that been there?"

"Since I'm not in the habit of entering condemned buildings unless I'm chasing your dog, no idea." He turned his back to the graffiti wall. "Speaking of which. We should get out of here. This isn't safe."

"It's never been safe. It's been falling down since before we were born, but that didn't bother us when we were kids."

"Half the roof hadn't fallen in when we were kids."

Elinor came farther into the building, her attention on the spray paint behind him.

"You're trespassing," he reminded her—though he didn't move to cut her off. It felt good to be out here with her again. It had always felt like anything was possible when it was just the two of them at the mill.

"You never used to be so hung up on the rules."

"I wasn't the chief of police then."

"Big Bad Levi, protector of Pine Hollow—and all its ordinances." She tipped her chin back to study the wall. "These are kind of pretty." A line formed between her brows as she frowned at them. "Do they seem familiar to you?"

"They match the graffiti someone was leaving around town all fall, if that's what you mean."

"No, it's something else. I feel like I've seen…" She trailed off. "I don't know." She nodded toward the nearest wall. "Looks fresh."

"I think we just missed our artist. Or scared him off."

"Him?"

He shrugged. "Just a guess. Could be a girl. Or a group. Though Marjorie thinks it's probably a lone tagger. No group is this good at keeping a secret." He pulled his gaze off the graffiti—which, he had to admit, now that Elinor had mentioned it, was sort of pretty. "Come on. Let's get out of here before the rest of the building comes down."

This time, thankfully, she didn't argue. Dory came with them, racing through the doorway in front of them and doing a sprint around his Explorer before bounding onto the hood in a single spring-loaded leap. She crouched to watch him, her ears pricked forward.

"I think she missed you."

I missed her, too, Levi thought—but he kept the words to himself. Just because he kind of liked having the dog riding shotgun beside him didn't mean he should admit how attached he was. Dory wasn't his. Just like Elinor wasn't his. She'd probably been kissing someone else at midnight New Year's Eve. That guy. The one from the tree lighting.

"How was the rest of the New Year's thing?" he asked, because he couldn't stop himself.

Elinor made a face, her glasses slipping as she scrunched her nose. "Minor explosion with Charlotte."

He tried to make his face sympathetic, when what he really felt was relief that she hadn't immediately started telling him about the guy.

"It's so frustrating. I can't say anything to her without her taking it the wrong way. The whole thing started because I said Bailey was good for Anne. Because Bailey's been reading all these Jane Austen books to try to understand Anne better and I thought that was really sweet and Anne is so happy and if anyone deserves to be happy it's her, but then as soon as I say that, Charlotte makes it about Warren and me hating Warren—which, yes, I kind of do, because he has consistently been a dick to her and she just *takes* it. He's *insufferable* and arrogant, but that would be fine if he didn't also stand her up on New Year's Eve—which makes her freak out and yell at *me*."

Levi just nodded—he could easily picture the explosion she described. Elinor and Charlotte loved each other more than anything—but they also drove each other crazy.

"So then she starts accusing me of trying to control her and never treating her like a grown-up." She turned to him. "You've seen us. Be honest. Do I treat her like a baby?"

Levi winced. "Am I going to get in trouble for answering honestly?"

The mask of righteous indignation on Elinor's face cracked and she groaned. "Damn. I do. Don't I?"

"Sometimes."

"I just want what's best for her! I'm the big sister. I'm supposed to watch out for her."

"Yeah. But she's not eight anymore."

"I never said she was!"

He lifted his hands in surrender. "Hey, I'm on your side. But it's her call if she wants to date someone who isn't good enough for her. We all make mistakes. That's how we learn, right?"

"I don't want her to make mistakes. I don't want anything to hurt her. I'm supposed to—" She broke off, laughing almost bitterly. "I was going to say protect her. Which is exactly what you're always doing for me—taking care of me, doing things for me—and it drives me nuts because I just want you to ask me first and not assume I can't put a remote starter in my own damn car if I want one." She sent him a halfhearted glare. "Why did you have to make me see it from her perspective? Now I have to apologize."

He laughed softly. "I'm sorry to be the bearer of bad news that you aren't infallible. That must be a new feeling for you."

She rolled her eyes. "You know me better than that. This town only *thinks* I'm perfect."

"Better than the alternative."

She frowned at him. "You know no one thinks of you like that anymore."

"The bad kid?"

"You were never the bad kid. Just like I was never the perfect one. There's always this disconnect between the image people want to put on you and who you really are—especially in a town like this one, where everyone has an opinion about everything. But you were the one who saw the imperfect side of me—and I saw the perfect side of you."

She was delusional, but he loved her.

The words rang in his head with absolute simplicity. A bald fact. He loved her. He'd never stopped. He never would. Even if this was what they were now. Friends. Even if this was for the best.

"Did you send off those queries?" he asked, pushing away from the topic of their relative perfection.

She sucked in a breath—nervous. "I did," she admitted, the words reluctant.

"And?"

She flushed. "I got a response already."

"That's fast."

"I know. I didn't expect to hear anything for weeks, or maybe months. It can take a long time, right? Everyone says that. And then today, two days after I sent my query, there it is in my inbox."

"What'd they say?"

She groaned, squeezing her eyes shut. "I don't know! I couldn't look. It came in right after I sent you that text about Dory getting out, and I was just staring at it and thinking, 'As long as I don't open it, it isn't a rejection.'"

"I don't think that's how it works."

"It's like Schrödinger's email. As long as I don't open it, it's both a rejection and an offer. It's the best and the worst at the same time, but as soon as I open it, it's one thing. As soon as I know, it's final. And what if it's a rejection?"

"What if it's an acceptance, and you're making that poor agent wait before you tell them you're going to grace them with your genius?"

She shook her head. "It's too fast. They would only reply this fast if it was a no. They probably didn't even read the sample pages."

"Maybe they read fast. Maybe something about your idea caught their attention and they got sucked in."

"Don't try to make me feel better," she complained. "I'm

a mess, and I haven't even opened it yet. I'm no good at this. I'm not good at failing."

He snorted. "You just haven't had as much practice at it as I have."

"Levi." She glared at him. "Stop. You aren't a failure."

"And neither are you. At least not until you open that email."

She laughed through her groan. "Too soon."

"You know you're going to have to look at it eventually."

"Do I, though?" she asked.

"Only if you actually want to be a writer."

"Do I, though?" she repeated, and he laughed.

"I don't know. It's only been your dream since you were twelve. I'm sure it's just a passing phase." She glared at him and he grinned. "Look, from what I've heard, every writer on the planet gets rejected at some point. Except maybe Stephen King, but I'm pretty sure he sold his soul to the devil long ago, and I'm not sure you want to take that route."

"Ha-ha."

"It's a rite of passage. And we learn more from our failures than our successes. You can learn—"

"That I'm a terrible writer who has no hope of ever becoming published?"

"You can learn how you take rejection for one thing—which doesn't look like it's very well, so far. You can learn if rejection is something you can handle as part of your life, or if you'd rather hoard all your books on your hard drive and never show them to anyone who might be critical. Or if you'd like to know how you can be better. The Elinor I know was all about being the best—but you worked hard to get there. Are you really not willing to work for this? You just want it to be magically handed to you? Because I have to say, if that email is an acceptance, I think it's going to be very bad for your character to get it so easily. You could use a little failure."

Elinor smiled, shaking her head. "Are you trying to synthesize my happiness?"

He blinked. "I have no idea what that means."

"It's a podcast I heard."

"Of course it is."

"Do you want to know or not?"

"Always." Elinor was a magpie for information, constantly collecting random tidbits, and he was endlessly fascinated by how her mind worked.

She looked grumpy but no longer wallowing in antici-pated rejection as she explained, "There's this professor from Harvard, I think, who talks about the concept of synthe-sized happiness. So natural happiness is when something good happens to you—like winning the lottery or landing your dream job—but the high of that doesn't last. And what apparently correlates more to long-term happiness is the ability to frame things for yourself in a positive light. To see the upside, and see the adversity as something that shapes you into who you're meant to be. Like how glad I am that I got waitlisted for Stanford, because if I'd gotten in, I might have gone there just because my mom had always told me she wanted me to go somewhere adventurous for college, but Dartmouth was so much better for me because I was able to stay close to my family."

"You cried for three days when you got waitlisted at Stanford."

"Yeah, but now, looking back, I'm really glad I didn't get in. And not just because Dartmouth was a better fit for me, but because everyone had always told me I could go wherever I wanted, and I needed the reality check that even being the star pupil didn't mean you always got everything you thought you wanted. And sometimes it's better not to."

"So are you going to open that email? See if this is one of those character-building it's-better-not-to-get-it moments?"

"Now?" Her voice squeaked. "In front of you?"

"Why not?"

Chapter Twenty-Six

Is it just pet-sitting among friends? Or
something more?
—*Pine Hollow Newsletter*,
Monday, January 10

Elinor studied Levi's steady, unshakable expression and
suddenly couldn't think of a single reason not to open
the email. With anyone else, opening it would have been
horrifying. She would have flatly refused and hidden to have
her moment of euphoria or mortification in private.

But this was Levi. She didn't have to put on a good face
for him. She didn't have to worry about reacting the right
way or managing his expectations if it was good news, or
reassuring him that she wasn't bothered if it was bad.

She pulled her cell phone from her jacket pocket, moving
quickly before she could lose her nerve. She opened her
mail client and there it was.

The familiar subject line. The name on the reply.

Her dream agent.

She'd been scribbling stories since she was a kid, since she sat down on the other end of the couch in Katie's basement and the two of them had written their dreams into curling, childish cursive. She'd wanted this for so long—and it had never felt closer. Or further away.

Schrödinger's email.

She didn't have to open it.

She'd sent out a dozen queries in all, feeling ambitious. But this one—the one that had somehow, miraculously come back first, was the one she'd really wanted. The agent with a podcast she listened to religiously, whose words always sounded like the gospel of publishing. One who represented the authors she most admired and aspired to be.

And she'd replied.

Elinor didn't look up at Levi. She just took a breath— and tapped the screen.

Disjointed words seemed to jump out at her.

Regretfully decline... didn't connect with the voice... just didn't grab me... so difficult to break out in the current market...

It was a nice letter. A kind letter.

And a rejection.

"Shit."

It was Levi who spoke, reading the truth on her face.

She grimaced, looking up at him. "I guess it's character building."

"What did they say?"

She shrugged. "The publishing equivalent of *it's not you, it's me*. Trying to be nice while saying she doesn't love it."

And one sentence that kept digging at her. A perfectly innocuous sentence about needing something really fresh and original to break out these days. It wasn't *directly* saying she was hackneyed and unoriginal, but it felt like that.

The words seemed to blur and fold into one another, but they all added up to one thing.

No.

And it hurt.

She'd been so sure the book she'd sent was the best thing she'd ever written. So certain that her publishing idol would recognize that. That she would be one of the success stories the agent talked about on her podcast. The next big thing.

The disappointment was cavernous—a great hollow space opening up inside her chest with a cold wind rushing through it.

"So are you giving up writing forever?"

Her brows snapped together. "What? Of course not."

"Then I guess you survived your first rejection. Congratulations. We should frame it."

"We absolutely should not frame it."

"It's going to be a collector's item one day. The first rejection the great Elinor Rodriguez got—before she became the biggest thing in books."

She rolled her eyes. "I don't need cheering up, Levi."

"Who's cheering you up? I want a copy of that email. It's gonna be worth something. Could you sign and date it for me?"

She smiled, shaking her head. "You're ridiculous."

"You okay?" he asked, gently.

"Yeah," she replied, just as softly.

She'd wanted to change the world with her words. As a school librarian she got to turn kids on to the magic of books. She was a firm believer that kids who didn't love books just hadn't found the right books for them yet. She got to see the way a story could change the way they saw the world, open them up to entirely new ideas and possibilities. She'd wanted to do that. To create something that left that kind of mark.

But one rejection didn't mean she couldn't.

She'd always felt such incredible pressure to live up to everyone else's expectation for her. If she wasn't perfect the first time, it felt like she was letting everyone down. It was why she never told anyone about her writing. It felt too raw. Too risky. But Levi was different. He'd seen all of her imperfections and still looked at her with complete confidence that she could be what everyone else told her she was. The girl who would put Pine Hollow on the map. He'd made her feel invincible. And he'd known exactly what to say.

"When did you learn so much about rejections?"

His smile was self-deprecating. "Other than my own personal expertise?"

"Levi." She narrowed her eyes. She hated when he made jokes at his own expense.

"I listened to a podcast," he admitted. "Couple of 'em."

He was downplaying. She wasn't sure how she knew, but she was positive he'd listened to at least half a dozen. "Why?"

He shrugged. "You're doing this. We're friends. I want to know what you're up against."

That was so Levi, always trying to anticipate what she would need. But it didn't bother her so much right now. In fact, her heart softened.

She couldn't meet his eyes, and when she turned her head, the FOR SALE sign loomed in front of her. "I still can't believe they're selling it," she said. "Tearing it down to make condos. It was always a wreck, but I thought it would be here forever, you know?"

"What would you think if I bought it?"

Her eyes snapped back to lock on his. "What?"

"Put a trailer on it. Live there while I build a house. I'm just renting now. Could be nice."

"You want to buy a broken-down mill?"

He met her eyes. Shrugged. "Maybe."

He was lying.

He had an amazing poker face, but he'd never been able to lie to her. She wasn't sure what he was lying about—wanting to buy the mill?—but he was hiding something. His eyes seemed to be testing her, searching for a reaction.

Did he want her to tell him to buy it? Because it was theirs? Did he want her to live with him at the mill where they'd fallen in love?

That vision of the future felt so far away right now.

There was no reason that thought should make her sad. They were over. They'd been over for a long time. But her heart didn't seem to remember that.

His phone buzzed while she was standing there staring at him.

He glanced at it, then back toward his Explorer, where Dory had fallen asleep sprawled on the hood. "I should get back."

"Right. Thanks for coming for her," Elinor said as she woke Dory and urged her off the hood.

"Any time," Levi offered. "In fact, if you want to just drop her by the station, I'll keep an eye on her for you during the day. Until Ally and Ben get back."

"Oh, I couldn't—"

"Saves me time chasing her down."

She smiled. "I'll think about it."

Dory jumped down, and Levi paused with his hand on the car door, looking over the hood at Elinor. "Did it ever bother you that I didn't..."

"What?" she prompted when he trailed off.

"That I never read those Jane Austen books like Bailey did."

Elinor blinked. "No. Of course not."

"Because you know I'm not a reader."

She frowned. "Yes, you are. You read more than almost anyone I know. You just always liked spy thrillers and Stephen King. I didn't think Jane Austen was your taste."

"Audiobooks don't really count."

"Says who? You're still taking words and turning them into an entire world inside your mind. That sounds like reading to me."

He shrugged, climbing into the Explorer.

As he closed the door and drove away, Dory whined softly in her throat, and Elinor crouched down to pet her. "You miss him, huh? Is that why you ran off today?"

Dory cocked her head in the listening posture that made Elinor think she really understood, and Elinor bent her face close to the dog's. "Yeah. I miss him too," she whispered.

🐾

Dory got out again on Wednesday—and on Thursday. On Wednesday, Elinor turned her phone on after school to find a text from Levi letting her know he had Dory and she was safe before she even saw the alerts she'd gotten an hour earlier. On Thursday, she got a text at lunch—Levi had swung by to check on Dory and caught her in the act of escaping.

On Friday, Elinor gave in to the inevitable and brought Dory by the station on her way to work—where the dog was hailed as their mascot and welcomed with cheers from the entire staff.

They were all so happy to see her that even after Ally and Ben got back from their honeymoon on Sunday, Elinor rationalized that they would be too jetlagged to watch Dory on Monday and brought her to the rescue squad station instead. Then Dory seemed so comfortable with their new routine that she just kept doing it.

She dropped Dory off each morning, chatting with Levi for a few minutes before she had to go to work, and came back after school each day to pick her up, often getting sucked into conversation with him again. It was...comfortable.

But at the end of the week, when she walked into the rescue squad building for the second Friday in a row to pick up her dog, instead of the patter of paws on the floor and the sight of Dory rushing to greet her with Levi strolling behind her with that lazy gait, there was only Kaye hunched over another of her textbooks.

Kaye looked up, smiling a tentative welcome. "She's still out with Levi," she explained. "He's had her riding around with him all day. It's the sweetest thing. Aaron even heard him talking to her this morning—a full conversation. From *Levi*." She shook her head. "He sure loves that dog."

Elinor bit her lip, unsure how to respond to that. "Do you know when they'll be back?"

"Should be any minute. You're welcome to wait. There's coffee. Though it's Aaron's day to make it, so I wouldn't get your hopes up on the quality."

Elinor decided not to risk the coffee and glanced toward the waiting area, which consisted of a couple of chairs, a side table, and a stack of magazines that looked like they hadn't been updated since the late nineties.

"Actually, I was kind of hoping I'd have a chance to talk to you," Kaye said, before Elinor could decide which of the two chairs looked more stable.

"You were?" Elinor asked, wary.

"I wanted to tell you. I never...I never slept with him. Levi. When you guys broke off your engagement. I know everyone thought—but that never...He didn't. Just so you know, nothing happened."

Was there anything more awkward than the woman your ex had supposedly cheated on you with trying to clear his name? "It's ancient history."

"I know, but Levi's a great guy, and he was a really good friend to me at a time when I needed it more than I ever have in my life. I don't know what I would have done without him, but it wasn't romantic. I know I should have told you ages ago, but I got so caught up in my own drama, and then I was so nervous around you because I knew what you must think of me—but Levi never thought of me that way. And I did kind of have a crush on him, and maybe I hoped it would become something, but I think I always knew that was just wishful thinking. No one else existed for him when you walked into the room. And these last few weeks...we've all seen a change in him. I just thought you should know that."

"Kaye, Levi and I aren't together. I actually have a date tonight. With someone else." She and George, finally doing their second take.

"Oh." Kaye's expression fell, but she rallied quickly,

plastering on a smile. "Well, good for you. And either way, the facts are still the facts. And you should know that no matter what people said back then, Levi is probably the most loyal, faithful person I've ever met."

"I know," Elinor agreed. But that didn't mean they could just erase everything that had happened in their past.

Thankfully, the front door opened and Dory rushed in before Kaye could keep singing Levi's praises. Dory raced to Elinor, dancing in circles around her and wriggling with delight before sitting to receive a pat of hello. As soon as Elinor had stroked her head once, Dory's butt popped up again and she sprinted down the hall toward the fire truck bay, where Dean could be heard greeting her before she ran back toward the front and bounced up to put her paws on Kaye's lap. As soon as Kaye gave her a hello, she was down again, checking all the offices to make sure she hadn't missed out on greeting anyone, darting into Marjorie's twice for good measure, though the de facto social worker was apparently out. Then she was back in the front, circling Elinor and then running to circle Levi, who had come in while she was completing her circuit of joy.

He looked good in his uniform. So confident and at ease. Elinor's heart thudded—and she firmly reminded it that she was about to go on a date with *someone else*.

"Hey," he said to Elinor. "Sorry to keep you waiting. We got a call up at the Estates that took a little longer than I expected."

"Everything all right?"

"Yeah, it's all good."

"I don't suppose you saw Charlotte?"

His eyebrows pulled together. "She still ghosting you?"

"I apologized to her voice mail and nothing."

"She'll come around. She never holds a grudge against you for long."

He was right, but this time felt different. A lot of things felt different now. Different but familiar—which appeared to be a dangerous combination.

"I should go." She clipped on Dory's leash. "Thanks for looking after her today."

"My pleasure."

Elinor hurried out the door, determined to get him out of sight so he would get out of her mind. She was supposed to be meeting George in an hour. They were grabbing dinner, starting over. He was a great guy who deserved her full attention. Who deserved a real chance.

As soon as she climbed into her car, she shuffled through the podcasts saved in her favorites on her phone, finding the one she'd been telling him about on love. The one that had those questions that could grow love in a lab, make anyone fall in love with anyone.

She just needed to remind herself that science said she could make herself fall in love with absolutely anyone.

Maybe it could make her fall out of love with the wrong person the same way.

Chapter Twenty-Seven

Could Pine Hollow have a new love triangle brewing? The chief, the newcomer, and the librarian were all spotted at the Cup last Friday night...
—*Pine Hollow Newsletter*,
Monday, January 17

H e genuinely hadn't meant to stalk her date.

Kaye had told him—with sickening sympathy in her voice—that Elinor had a date tonight, and so Levi had made a concentrated effort *not* to lurk in her life. He'd figured she would take her date to the Tipsy Moose or some other place in town for drinks. Mac's restaurant had never gotten a liquor license, so he'd thought the Cup was safe.

Then Levi had walked through the door and seen Elinor and that guy sitting at one of the tiny tables in the Cup's overcrowded dine-in area.

He'd almost walked out again—but he'd already called in a takeout order, and half the patrons of the Cup had already seen him. If he turned around and walked back out, it would be even more of a scene than if he just went to the takeout counter and pretended to be oblivious.

So pretend he did.

Not that Elinor would believe he was oblivious. It wasn't exactly in his normal repertoire. He was always hyperaware of his surroundings. Hyperaware of her.

Which was how he knew it was the same guy. The one from the Tipsy Moose and the tree lighting. He didn't know why that should make it sting more, that Elinor was going on multiple dates with the same person—especially when Levi had checked him out and he'd come back clean.

He hadn't flinched when Kaye told him Elinor had a date tonight. He'd told himself he wasn't jealous. He was happy for her. Pulling for them.

But the reality wasn't so evolved.

He was so jealous he could hardly see.

It was busy at the Cup, as it always was on a Friday night. He was second in line, and one of Mac's usual servers must have called in sick, because the wait staff were scrambling. The restaurant wasn't really built for heavy dine-in traffic anyway. It had started life as an espresso shop, but Mac kept experimenting with new "specials" and adding them to the menu until it had become one of the favorite eateries in town.

It was always crowded, stocked with fresh coffee—and fresh gossip. Which made it about the last place Levi would have chosen for this particular tableau to play out, but he'd honestly thought he was avoiding Elinor's date when he came here.

He could feel everyone watching them, and from the corner of his eye he could see Linda Hilson—who wasn't even bothering to pretend she wasn't staring.

He very purposefully didn't look toward Elinor, but he could tell the moment she noticed him there in the takeout line. The air seemed to shift around him, tightening with awareness. Conversations around the room hushed with anticipation.

He was here.

Elinor didn't know how she felt about that, but it wasn't as angry as she should be. The last two months had shifted everything, and all she was now was tangled up and confused.

And distracted.

She tried to focus on George.

He was such a nice guy. They really had quite a bit in common. And maybe, under other circumstances, she could have made herself fall in love with him. Or at least convince herself she had. She'd listened to that podcast again while she was getting ready—the one about love—but she hadn't heard it the same way this time. Maybe she hadn't really listened before, or maybe she just understood it differently now because she was different now. Either way, a single phrase had jumped out at her.

Love is a collaborative work of art.

She'd never thought of it that way. She was half convinced she hadn't even heard those words the first time she listened. She'd always thought of love as a force as much as a feeling. An external, inevitable thing. Love had crashed into her, sudden and inescapable, when she was still a girl, and made her dance like a puppet ever since—or so she'd thought. Now she couldn't help but think that was a very childish—almost cowardly—way of looking at it.

Love had always been this thing that existed, often

beneath the surface, uncontrollable, frequently driving her actions—but the idea that she had to tend it, to create it with another person as a team, was never how she'd thought of it.

If love was an overwhelming force, a power that swept her up and made her dance to its tune, then it wasn't her fault when things crashed and burned; that was just the course of true love. But if it was a piece of art that she was crafting with another person, a collaboration, then she might actually have a say in the outcome. A responsibility.

She and Levi both had a few controlling tendencies—Charlotte would say more than a few—but their relationship was the one thing she was pretty sure neither of them had ever felt in control of. Because they'd been looking at love all wrong.

"Elinor?"

She jerked to attention, refocusing on what George was saying—and realizing that she had no idea how long she'd zoned out. "I'm sorry—"

Before she could come up with a good excuse, George twisted around, glancing over his shoulder—and immediately spotted Levi. Understanding filled his face, which only made her feel less deserving of his compassion.

"Would you like to go somewhere else?" he asked gently when he'd turned back to face her.

"No, of course not." It would be ridiculous to run from Levi—especially when he was only getting takeout and would be leaving any minute.

And, if she was honest, she'd been distracted long before she spotted her ex.

That damn podcast, the one she'd listened to in order to encourage herself to really give this date a chance, had been messing with her mind all night. Making her rethink things she'd thought were settled.

Behind George, Levi spoke with Mac for a moment at the counter, then walked to the small hallway that led to the bathrooms. His order must not be ready.

"—don't you think?"

Oh no. Elinor refocused on George with a sudden sense of panic. She hadn't been paying attention. She made a noncommittal *mm*ing noise as she debated the relative merits of admitting she was hopelessly distracted and begging his forgiveness, or playing it off like she was always this spacey.

George met her eyes, and his own softened. They were so gentle. So kind. He was *such a good guy*. Why couldn't she just fall in love with him?

"I'm glad you agree, because I really do like you, Elinor."

Oh no. Oh God. What had she just agreed to? She didn't want him to really like her. The last thing she wanted was to lead on a perfectly lovely guy like George. "I—"

"And I meant what I said on New Year's."

God, what had he said on New Year's? Why couldn't she remember?

"You and I could have a great future—"

No no no no.

"—as friends."

Wait. What? Realization was late—but quick when it came.

He was letting her down easy.

Thank God.

"I'm sorry," she murmured. "The last thing I wanted to do was lead you on."

"And you didn't," he assured her. "You have nothing to

apologize for. Sometimes there are sparks—even when you don't want there to be—and sometimes there aren't."

Curiosity nudged her to ask, "If you didn't feel sparks, why did you ask me out again?"

He shrugged. "There's more to love than instant chemistry. Sometimes things take longer to develop. I thought we might grow on each other, but I'm kind of getting the feeling that you aren't looking for a love connection." His gaze flicked toward the bathroom hallway. "At least not with me."

"I'm not *not* looking..." she protested, but the words faded into nothing. She didn't know what she was looking for anymore. "Anyway, I'm pretty sure you're too nice for me."

"Maybe," he agreed with a good-natured grin. "But don't tell your sister I said that. She thinks you walk on water and I should be thanking my lucky stars I got to bask in your presence as long as I did."

Elinor shifted uncomfortably on her chair. Somehow she didn't think Charlotte would have that same opinion if George asked her about Elinor now. Her little sister was still ignoring her calls and texts.

"What are you waiting for?" When Elinor gave him a blank look, George smiled. "You're obviously dying to go talk to him."

"I'm not..."

"I'd go now. If you wait until he comes back out here, you're going to be in full view of that woman who's been taking notes on our date."

Elinor glanced automatically toward Linda Hilson—who did appear to have a tiny notebook she was scribbling notes into. "I can't just leave you sitting here—"

"I've got this." George waved to the two coffees in front of them, which was all they'd gotten around to ordering before Levi came in. The Cup was slammed tonight, and neither of them had been in a hurry, so they'd told their server they could wait. George leaned across the table, his brown eyes warm. "Don't tell your sister, but I'm secretly a romantic, and I'm pulling for you and the big guy."

Elinor was almost insulted that George had been so uninterested in her that he was pulling for her and Levi...but she hadn't exactly been interested in him, either. Love may be more than just that zing of instant chemistry, but it was hard for the guy with the definite friend vibe to compete with the one who'd always made her feel more alive just by walking into the room.

"Are you sure?"

George rolled his eyes. "Go! Before the investigative journalist over there decides to stake out the bathrooms."

Elinor stole one last glance at Linda Hilson—who, miraculously, seemed distracted by the entrance of her arch-nemesis Gayle Danvers—and darted quickly toward the bathroom hallway while she wasn't looking.

The hallway wasn't long—half a dozen feet with three doors off it—single-stall men's and women's rooms, and a third door marked STAFF ONLY. There were no windows, and the light was always dim back here—but she clearly saw the large silhouette leaning against the far wall as soon as she burst into the dark hallway.

"Oh!"

Levi straightened suddenly from where he'd been tilted against the wall. "I'm sorry. I was trying to wait out of sight," he explained. "Mac's backed up, and my order isn't ready— and I swear I didn't follow you here. I was trying to avoid you. Kaye said you had a date, and I figured you'd go back to the Moose, or maybe the inn. The Cup seemed safe."

"No, it's fine. I didn't think you were..."

"Lurking?"

She flushed. "I'm sorry I said that—"

"No, you were right. I wasn't doing it consciously, but I think I'll always have to fight the urge to watch over you." He cleared his throat. "He seems nice."

Elinor studied Levi's face—and almost laughed at what she saw there. "You ran a background check on him, didn't you?"

"Just a little one."

At that she did laugh, a soft huff of humor.

"You're not mad?"

"I don't know what I am anymore," she admitted. Things had been so much clearer when she was trying to hate him. Now it felt like the only thing she knew was that she didn't.

"I know he seems like a nice guy," Levi said, his gray eyes inscrutable. "I just wanted to make sure he was a Bingley and not a Wickham."

Elinor's eyes widened. "Did you read *Pride and Prejudice*?"

"It's not really reading. I'm just listening to the audiobook—"

"Levi, it's reading. It doesn't matter that you're dyslexic." She realized she was snapping at him and bit her lip. "You really listened to Jane Austen?"

She couldn't tell in the low light of the hallway, but she could swear Levi was blushing. "Dory likes them. The narrator's accent is really soothing, and it relaxes her when we're riding around."

He'd listened to Jane Austen with her dog while driving around Pine Hollow. Her knees melted a little.

"Thank you," she whispered, not even entirely sure what she was thanking him for. Driving Dory around? Listening to her mom's favorite author? Still caring enough to do both?

Levi met her eyes in the shadowy hallway. It was one of his enigmatic looks. The ones no one else ever seemed to be able to read. But when he looked at her like that, she'd always felt like a window was opening up and she could see right inside him.

And right now he looked...*fierce*.

Possessive. There was fire there. All the things he was trying not to feel. And Elinor felt her mouth go dry.

She didn't think he would say anything. He never did. This was Levi. He was a master at keeping it all inside. But then the silence stretched for a beat and Levi opened his mouth.

"I hate seeing you with him."

She sucked in a breath and forgot to let it out.

And then something inside her shifted.

She wasn't sure who reached for whom. All she knew was that it happened fast. One second he was looking at her—the way he looked at her, like she was everything he'd ever needed in the world—and the next she was kissing him. Or he was kissing her. The lines always blurred where one of them ended and the other began.

It was familiar—so familiar. The feel of his arms pulling her close. The solid bunch of muscle along his shoulders where her hands gripped. The scent of him—*God*, the scent of him, always with that hint of evergreen, like the pines they'd grown up with had seeped into his skin. She knew it was just his soap, but it *killed* her. Tears were in her eyes before she was even aware that this was more than just lust and impulse and heat.

It was Levi. It was always going to be more.

One of his hands cupped her jaw, and her mouth opened automatically beneath his. Ten thousand kisses had taught him exactly what she liked—and he proved he remembered every detail as his tongue slanted against hers.

God, she'd missed this.

Elinor knew she had a tendency to overthink things, to overanalyze. Levi was the only one who'd ever been able to suck her into a moment so all she could do was feel. So she completely forgot who she was supposed to be and what she was supposed to do, and just *was*. And what she was felt *good*.

She ran her fingers through the soft short hair at the top of his neck.

Door hinges creaked.

"Oh! Sorry!"

The door slammed, and Elinor jerked back. Levi instantly released her, and she dropped from her tiptoes down to flat feet with the thudding sensation of coming back to earth.

What were they doing?

He broke off their engagement. He broke her heart. She had no reason to think anything had changed.

"Elinor..." His voice was low. His eyes pleading. One hand palm up in supplication.

"We can't do that again."

The words rushed out—and then so did she. Out of the hallway, out of the Cup, without looking back.

Chapter Twenty-Eight

Our librarian looked very flushed when she raced out of the bathroom hallway where she was heard "speaking" with the chief… Could it be she's made her choice?

—*Pine Hollow Newsletter*,
Monday, January 17

Levi knew he shouldn't have kissed her, but he couldn't make himself regret it.

He leaned against the wall where he'd been hiding when Elinor found him, taking a moment to compose himself before returning to the dining area. It was undoubtedly too much to hope that half the town hadn't figured out he and Elinor were back here, but he could at least wait long enough to give them plausible deniability.

He was still trying to slow his racing heartbeat when the STAFF ONLY door that had interrupted them opened again. Mac stood on the other side, glaring at Levi—and holding a bag that looked like his takeout order.

"Come on," Mac offered grudgingly. "You might as well sneak out the back so Linda Hilson doesn't get a picture of you on her phone." Mac pivoted without checking to see if Levi was following, leading the way through the tight confines of the kitchen, toward the side delivery door.

It hadn't been Mac who had caught them—the voice squeaking with surprise at finding them making out in the hallway had been undeniably feminine—but the server must have run straight to her boss if the irritation on Mac's face as he opened the exterior door was anything to go by. He thrust Levi's food at him in a *take-it-you-asshole* silence.

"What?" Levi snapped, snatching the bag from Mac's hands. "Should I check this for arsenic?"

"What are you doing?" Mac demanded, and Levi was surprised by the force of the words. "I thought you weren't trying to win her back."

Mac was the easygoing one. It was strange to see him pissed off. Strange enough that Levi actually shelved his own irritation and answered genuinely.

"It wasn't planned," he admitted.

Mac's jaw shifted. "I don't want you to hurt her again. Last time... Levi, last time was shitty."

"I know. I'm sorry. And I should have talked to you guys back then. I just... I guess I felt like if you hated me a little, it was okay because I deserved it. Because I was ashamed."

Mac stared at him as if he'd started speaking in tongues.

"I know," Levi grumbled. "I don't usually talk about the feelings shit, but I guess this therapy stuff really works. No stopping the mushy confessions now."

"No shit. You're really seeing someone?"

"Yeah." Levi swallowed down his discomfort.

"Damn, man. Good for you. That's awesome."

Levi flushed. He hadn't expected to be praised for it.

Mocked, maybe. Teased mercilessly at the next poker night. He'd expected to be ashamed, kind of thought he should be, but the way Mac reacted, like he'd actually done something *admirable*, caught him off guard. Maybe he had been a little too quick to hide behind his *Jackson men are strong* persona.

"You're a good friend," he said to Mac—something that had always been implied, but he didn't think he'd ever actually said aloud. Mac would bend over backward for the people in his life, always with a smile on his face. He was the grinning glue that bound them together. And Levi should have told him that. "I'm sorry I stonewalled you guys back then. You know my dad…"

"Conditioned you to be repressed? Yeah, I know. But I'm glad you're doing the manly thing and owning your feelings now."

Levi snorted. "Just don't go expecting me to burst into song."

"You're missing out on the musicals," Mac insisted, smiling again. "Highest form of art. I'm just saying."

"Agree to disagree."

Mac's grin flashed, but then his smile faded into something more serious. "Levi, what's going on with Elinor?"

"Honestly, I don't know. But I think I might be trying to get her back."

❧

Elinor Rodriguez was quietly losing her mind.

By Wednesday afternoon, she was a basket case.

After the Kiss That Lived in Infamy, she'd retreated home on Friday night, hugged Dory, and curled up on the floor with her. She tried to read, but her thoughts kept spinning in circles, making it impossible to focus. On Saturday, she managed to avoid thinking about Levi and how twisted around she was by spending the day marathoning *Doctor Who* with Astrid—but even the show kept reminding her of him.

Everything reminded her of him. Even the rejection email that arrived on Sunday morning.

She'd been surprised to receive a reply on the weekend—but even more surprised by how badly it had made her want to reach out to Levi. Not that she couldn't, but she wanted to know what she wanted before she talked to him. She needed to be clear.

But clarity wouldn't come.

On Monday, she agonized over whether to take Dory to Levi or to Furry Friends. Ultimately, she chickened out and dropped her at Ally's. Then she spent the day wondering if she'd screwed things up by not pretending that nothing had happened. How were they supposed to go back to being friends now?

If that was even what she wanted.

By Wednesday, she was desperate for girls' night. Ally and Deenie would talk it through. She'd get the clarity she needed. All she had to do was wait until Astrid's bedtime, then her friends would sort her out over margaritas. It was what they did.

Astrid's bedtime took forever to arrive. She adored Astrid. She never wanted to get rid of her, but tonight she was counting down the seconds.

They were in the farmhouse living room—and the second Astrid headed upstairs, Deenie turned to Elinor with an expectant stare. "Okay, what happened?" she demanded—

proving Elinor hadn't done nearly as good a job as she thought of pretending everything was normal.

She groaned. "Am I that obvious?"

"Yes," Deenie and Ally said in unison.

Ally started for the kitchen area to blend one of her fruity adult concoctions, as she always did on girls' nights when Astrid headed upstairs, adding, "We were also tipped off by the fact that the entire town is talking about some kind of *event* at the Cup ever since the newsletter came out— though I was pretty sure my grandmother's gossip source out at the Estates was confused when she said you'd had a three-way in the bathroom."

Elinor groaned again, covering her face with her hands. "Why did I come back to this town?"

"Because you love it," Deenie said simply. They all paused for a moment as Ally ran the blender. As soon as silence reigned again, Deenie bounced in place, impatiently urging, "So what happened? Spill."

"I kissed Levi," Elinor admitted. "Or he kissed me. Someone kissed someone. But it wasn't intentional. I don't think he meant to, and I certainly didn't—"

"Okay, a kiss happened," Deenie cut in to stop her babbling. "Through no fault of anyone involved in said kiss. No charges will be filed." She leaned forward on the couch. "Then what happened?"

"I told him we could never do that again and bolted."

"This was in the bathroom at the Cup?" Ally asked as she handed out glasses of something a pale peach.

"The little hallway in front of the bathrooms," Elinor clarified, taking the peachy drink and a grateful sip of what tasted like a Bellini. "Which is the stupidest part of the whole thing. The entire town has been speculating about us for months, and we go and make out in public where anyone could just walk up and see us?"

"So it was 'making out'?" Deenie asked, accepting her own Bellini. "We're not talking a brotherly peck."

"*Not* brotherly."

Deenie nodded. "I didn't think so, but it's important to get all the details. And it was...good, I assume?"

Elinor felt her cheeks heat. "Chemistry was never our problem."

"Right. So on a scale of *that was nice* to *my panties just combusted*—"

"It was good, okay?" *Total panty inferno.*

Deenie eyed Elinor over her drink. "Were you really on a date with someone else when you kissed him?"

Elinor groaned. She'd almost managed to make herself forget that part. "George. But we'd already broken up—not that we were ever really together. We went on two dates. My sister coerced him into the first one, and he sort of asked me out again in the spirit of *why not*. He's really great, but I can't seem to stop letting things with Levi ruin my chances to ever be with anyone else. I keep convincing myself that I don't still have feelings for him and my heart is ready to move on and I got closure and all the things you're supposed to get, right? And then I go backsliding, like Charlotte said. I just can't—"

"Quit him?" Deenie provided helpfully.

"Stop. This isn't a movie. And he isn't some brooding romantic hero. The whole strong, silent thing isn't nearly as sexy as he thinks it is."

"Yes, it is," Deenie and Ally said in unison—and then shared a grinning toast as she glared at them.

"What?" Deenie asked at her glower.

"You're engaged. And *you're* married," she reminded Ally.

"And neither of us is dead. The strong, silent thing is hot."

And it was. Damn it. "Fine. But this isn't one of those awful books where the hero is this distant, brooding asshole who treats the heroine like crap and she still pines for him for years because apparently *that's* what love was if you were a Brontë. This isn't *Wuthering Heights*. I'm not a Brontë!"

"You're an Austen," Deenie snarked.

Elinor just groaned. "That was the worst part. He read *Pride and Prejudice*."

"How dare he!" Deenie gasped in feigned shock—and Ally smacked her on the arm.

"How is that the worst part?" Ally asked.

"I said something to him about how Anne's girlfriend, Bailey, was reading a bunch of Austen because she knew how much it meant to our family and she wanted to be in on all the jokes, be closer to Anne—and then the next thing I know, he's making Bingley references. But he's never actually said he wants to get back together. He just *does* things, and it's confusing!"

"Like kissing you?"

"And putting ice melt down on my front walk!"

Ally and Deenie shared a confused look.

"He did it while I was at work on Tuesday. I wasn't home to actually witness it, but the security cameras caught him," Elinor explained. "And how do you get mad at someone when he's doing all these sweet, considerate things for you, but you just want to scream at him to *talk to you*, but if you do, then you're terrified that maybe he *will* talk to you, and you'll have no excuse not to face that he really does want you back, and then you have to figure out whether you want him back, too?"

Ally blinked. "That's a lot."

"So Levi's love language is acts of service, huh?" Deenie asked, sipping her Bellini.

"Big time," Elinor confirmed. "And sometimes it drove me crazy because he can be so overbearing and it's like he can't turn it off, but then there were other times when it made me feel so safe and cared for in a way no one else has ever made me feel. And I *want* someone else to make me feel that way. I don't want to be the stupid girl who goes back to the guy who broke her heart. I hate that girl! But then I can't help thinking, what if it's different this time? What if we're different? *I'm* different. But is that enough? I don't want to change him, but how can I trust him not to make another sweeping decision about what's best for me and yank the rug out again?"

Ally and Deenie exchanged a look that said neither of them had a good answer for that.

"I know I'm overthinking this. I overthink everything—"

"Everyone overthinks love."

"Do they?" Elinor asked.

"Okay, probably not. A lot of people leap first and look later." Ally put her hand over Elinor's on the table. "But it's perfectly okay to be cautious."

"I don't want to be cautious. I just want this settled. I feel like I've been in self-imposed limbo for years. And now...I don't know what I want. I'm all tangled up, and Valentine's Day is right around the corner—"

"It's nearly a month away," Deenie pointed out. "Is that some kind of deadline? Did he give you a schedule for making up your mind?"

"No, but...It was our day. Valentine's was always special to us, and it feels like this looming thing, approaching."

"You guys have a lot of history," Ally said gently.

"Exactly. He's been there for every significant moment of my life. He knows me better than anyone on the planet. That's never going to stop being powerful. Our history can trump anything. But our future has to be worth it, too. And I just don't know what that looks like."

Chapter Twenty-Nine

A certain librarian's dog was spotted last week at the Furry Friends Doggie Day Care. Could this be a sign of love on the rocks with our dear chief?

—*Pine Hollow Newsletter*,
Monday, January 24

Levi didn't know what the hell he was doing.

He hadn't seen Elinor or Dory in about a week. He'd seriously considered going over to Elinor's house and breaking the dog out, just so he'd have an excuse to talk to Elinor face-to-face. But then Ben had mentioned she was leaving Dory with Ally during the day. So that took away that option.

He didn't have the first freaking idea how he was supposed to win Elinor over.

He wasn't in the habit of asking for dating advice. Or any kind of advice, really. His friends already knew he'd screwed up. It wasn't like admitting he didn't know how to fix it would make him look any worse in their eyes than he already did.

Which was why there was no rational reason for the fact that he'd blown off poker night to schedule an extra session with Dr. Park. The therapist had made time for him after hours—and with the sun setting so early in January, it was pitch-black by the time Levi climbed the steps to the Stowe office.

He'd meant to explain about Elinor. To get expert advice. But as soon as the pleasantries were over and he was settled into his usual chair, the first words out of Levi's mouth were on another topic entirely.

"My folks got married young. They were high school sweethearts, and right after graduation, my mom got pregnant with me and they just accepted their fate. Got married. Got jobs. Started a family."

Once the words started, they came quickly. Things he hadn't even realized he wanted to say. "My mom is sweet. Total pushover. Too nice for her own good. And my dad...I guess he wasn't always an asshole. I want to think he wasn't a total dick when she fell in love with him. He never got what he wanted out of life. Mad at the world. I don't know if he blamed me..." Levi shook his head. "Anyway, they moved up here because she wanted to and he was having trouble finding work—though it wasn't any better here. When he did get a job, it was always one he hated, and he never had it for very long—which wasn't a tragedy. He was such a dick when he was working, using the stress as an excuse, so it was easier for all of us when he wasn't." He grimaced at the memory. "My mom didn't seem to mind taking care of everything—bringing in the money, taking care of the house and me—she'd bend over backward to make things better for us. And *I* didn't make it easy on her. I was the bad kid. Always getting in trouble in school. Not with the other kids—I got along with everyone—but I defied my teachers. Disrupted class."

"Problem with authority figures?" Dr. Park prompted when Levi paused.

"No, I...I guess, but defying them was how I proved I wasn't stupid." A rare reaction showed on Dr. Park's face, and Levi forced himself to explain. "I wasn't a reader." *Understatement of the century.* "Dyslexia. Didn't get diagnosed until middle school because I was so good at convincing everyone that I *knew* the answers but was just refusing to give them. 'Better to be silent and be thought a fool than to speak and remove all doubt.' My dad loved that quote. I can still hear his voice in my head, even though we almost never talk anymore."

"You described yourself as bad. Did you think of yourself that way?"

"I don't know. Trouble, I guess. More trouble than I was worth. My dad was always telling my mom, 'I don't know why you waste your time with him.' But she was stubborn. She took me out to the Elks Club, where some of the members taught my friends and me to play poker. I'd stare at the cards, and everyone said I had this great poker face— and I was just trying to make sure I'd read them right. But that's where I met Elton. My mentor. He's the reason I became a cop. I didn't think that was even an option. I thought I'd have to do something like construction. Something where it was about how good you were with your hands. My dad was always telling me the world wouldn't do me any favors—I'd need a *skill*—but Elton saw something different in me. I've been trying to live up to that ever since."

"It sounds like you have."

Levi shook his head. "No. I keep screwing everything up. That thing with Britt Wells this summer…"

"Wasn't your fault."

"But I could have done more. And now with Elinor…"

"Has something happened with Elinor?"

He grimaced, admitting, "Part of me wants her back, but I want what's best for her more than anything."

"And you don't think that could be you?"

Levi let the doc see the skepticism in his eyes. "My dad cheated on my mom. Probably my whole life, but I only found out when I was in high school. She knew—I think she always knew—but she never left him. I don't know if she stayed for me or…"

"You know you aren't responsible for your mother's choices. You didn't make her stay with him."

"But she was with him in the first place because of me. They got married because of me."

"They got pregnant without your help. And they might have gotten married anyway."

"He didn't think so. He joked with me a few years ago that I'd trapped Elinor just like he'd trapped my mom—but I'd done it with promises, and he'd done it with me. He always said we were so alike."

"Was he dyslexic as well? It can be passed down genetically."

The question seemed to ring inside his mind, and Levi went silent to listen to the reverberations of it. How had he never wondered that? It would explain the bitter way his father always commented on their similarities. His trouble holding a job—always telling off managers over imagined slights. Was he just doing what Levi had always done with his teachers?

God, were they really alike, after all?

He'd never wanted to be like his father. His mother always wanted him to see the good in his dad, but Levi hadn't been able to. Because they were too alike? Because they both hated the things in the other that they hated in themselves? The weakness. The fear that someone would see through their act and think they were stupid.

"I don't know," he answered finally.

"Either way, your mother made the choice to stay with him, whatever her reasons. And Elinor made the choice to be with you. No one was trapped. And if you want to decide what's best for Elinor—whether that's you or someone else—you're going to have to talk to her. You can't figure that out without her. Love isn't something we do *to* other people. It's something we do *with* them."

"And if she doesn't want to talk to me?"

"Then that might be your answer." Dr. Park's eyes were sympathetic. "But however things turn out with Elinor, you aren't your father."

"I know," Levi said—but the words were too quick. Even he didn't believe himself.

Dr. Park's voice was low and calm. "You've described him as quick-tempered, never able to hold down a job. While you're so even-tempered and contained that you're almost impossible to read. You've worked at the same place since you were eighteen and devoted yourself to the town. There may have been similarities at one point, but you've made yourself into a different person, and it doesn't matter that you and Elinor first got together when you were young. Did you cheat on her?"

"No, God, I would never."

"And is Elinor your mother? Would she make all the choices your mother has made?"

"No, of course not." He remembered the fire in Elinor's eyes when she argued with him, the way she never bowed down to him. No. She wasn't remotely his mother.

"Then why would you judge your relationship with Elinor by your parents' relationship? Why would you let that get in your way?"

Because I was scared.

He'd been scared of being his dad. Scared of losing Elinor. Scared of not being worthy of her. And he hadn't known how to handle that fear. He'd never known how to handle fear. Or failure. No matter how many jokes he made to Elinor about his endless practice at failing. He'd never been able to accept his failures.

"I screwed up," he admitted, hating the words. "And I don't know how to fix it."

"You may not be able to," Dr. Park acknowledged. "There's only so much we have control over. All we can do is try to learn from our mistakes and become better. Not perfect. No one is perfect. But better—we can achieve that." He met Levi's eyes. "So what can you do to be a little bit better?"

Chapter Thirty

Batten down the hatches, Pine Hollow.
A big snow is coming, and we all know
what havoc that can wreak on our fair
town...

—*Pine Hollow Newsletter*,
Thursday, January 27

On Thursday afternoon, Elinor was no closer to knowing what she wanted when she picked Dory up from Furry Friends and drove home as the first fat snowflakes began to drift lazily down from the sky. She'd always loved the snow, especially when it came down in thick blankets and the whole world fell under its spell, all hushed and peaceful. Charlotte could wax poetic about the fall foliage as much as she liked, but for Elinor's money, winter was the reason to love Vermont.

The thought of Charlotte snagged at the fragile lace of her good mood, tearing a hole in it. Everything was so unsettled. She just wanted one relationship that wasn't a mess. But her sister still wasn't answering her texts.

She took Dory home and fed her, watching her chase

her dish around the slippery kitchen floors in her enthusiasm. The snow was coming down harder by the time Dory curled up for her post-dinner nap. Elinor's cell phone rang, and Dory didn't even perk up, proving how exhausted she was. There must have been activity at Furry Friends today, because she usually only slept like that when she'd been playing all day. She'd been downright docile after riding around with Levi all day, obviously so happy to be his sidekick—but Elinor pushed that thought aside when she saw her sister's name on the caller ID. Anne. Not Charlotte.

"Hey. What's up?" she asked as she answered, staring out the kitchen window into the backyard, where the snow was coming down in sheets, the heavy clouds darkening the late afternoon.

"Can you run over to Dad's?" Anne asked. "He wants to set up his new generator in case the snow knocks out power, and it's a two-person job—but I'm still at Bailey's, and I'm not sure I want to drive in this."

"No, of course," Elinor assured her. "I'll walk over. You stay put. And say hey to Bailey for me."

After Anne agreed and wished her luck, Elinor hung up—and considered Dory. Her paws were twitching in little puppy dreams, and she didn't even open an eye when Elinor piled on her snow gear and asked in a bright voice, "Dory wanna come, too?"

Normally that would send her into a frenzy of energy where she couldn't get to the front door fast enough, but she must have been seriously exhausted from her day, because she slept on, curled up on the doggie bed in front of the fireplace.

"Okay," Elinor finally said aloud, "you catch some Zs and

I'll be right back." Her dad's house was barely five minutes up the road. Even if the snow slowed her down, she'd only be twenty minutes.

There was no barking, no excited scamper of feet on the hardwood floors after Elinor exited out the front, which she took as a sign that her absence had yet to be noticed by the curious Aussie. She'd be there and back literally before Dory knew it.

The air was heavy with snow even before she stepped out from beneath the overhang on her porch. A hush had already descended over the town. It was probably approaching sunset, but there were no swaths of color in the sky, just unrelenting white reflecting off the streetlamps as Elinor tromped toward her father's house. There were already several inches of accumulation, but it was easy to move through, the flakes fluffy and light as she kicked a path down the sidewalk—or where she knew the sidewalk should be.

Her dad's porch light was on, and Elinor let herself in, knocking the snow off her boots on the doorframe before stepping onto the mat. "Dad?" she called—not wanting to bother stripping off her snow gear if she was going right back out again. The generator would need to be set up beside the shed in the back, away from the house. They'd had one there when she was a kid, but it had died a couple of years ago, and apparently her father had finally gotten around to replacing it.

When he didn't reply, she made her way back outside and tromped around to the shed—to find him already hunched over beneath the tilted awning he'd built years ago to keep the generator from vanishing beneath piles of snow.

"I thought this was a two-person job," she called out.

He turned, stepping out from beneath the awning enough to straighten. "Wanted to see if I could do it."

"And could you?"

Her father grimaced. "Let's just say I'm glad you're here. Can you get that end?"

For the next several minutes, they worked mostly in companionable silence. Her father had never been one to waste words. Thankfully, it didn't take them long to get the new generator set up, since the original generator cords were already hooked into the transfer switches. When they were done, her father stood back, dusted the snow off his hands, and jerked his head toward the house. "Tea?"

"Sounds perfect." She'd have preferred coffee, but her father had stopped drinking coffee in the afternoon since it stopped him sleeping, and she was happy to have whatever he was having. She could warm up for a few minutes and then head home.

Her dad waited until she had a warm mug cradled between her hands and was perched at one of the stools at the island before he launched his sneak attack. "Do I want to know what you and Charlotte are fighting about?"

Elinor resisted the urge to groan. Barely. "Just the usual. I'm trying to apologize, but she won't even take my calls."

He sighed. "She's so like your mother sometimes. So good at holding a grudge."

Elinor stared at her father, the words refusing to compute. Her memory of her mother was faded by time, but she'd always thought of her like Anne. Gentle. Kind. Quiet. It was the memory formed by a child—but when she tried to picture her mother angry the image seemed to flicker. "Mom held grudges?"

"Like a champion. I think that's why she wanted you to

all have names she called 'practical influences.' Because she knew she could be so volatile and wanted to try to counter-program you."

Elinor chewed her lower lip. Now that she thought about it, other memories started to filter in. Little whispers of who her mother might have been, in addition to being her mom.

That was who she'd been in Elinor's mind. Mother. Invalid. But she didn't really know who she'd been as a person.

She didn't really know how she was like her.

And she was the lucky one. She'd been the oldest, had the most time with her. But even then, they hadn't had a normal relationship—at least not what she thought of as one from the books she read and family dramas she'd watched. There had been such an emphasis on not upsetting her when she was sick. The few times Elinor had yelled at her like a normal hormonal teen, she'd felt miserable afterward, haunted by the idea that *that* would be her last memory with her mother. Things had been careful in their house, with a care brought on by equal parts love and fear.

"I wish I'd been able to know her as an adult," she said softly.

Her dad put his hand over hers on the countertop, gently squeezing her knuckles. "Me too. She would have been so proud of you."

That was what she'd wanted. What she'd *always* wanted. To make her mother proud. But would she be? If Charlotte wasn't even speaking to her and Elinor couldn't figure out what she wanted?

Part of the appeal of Levi had always been that her mom had known him. Not that it was the only reason Elinor had loved him—not even close—but there had been something comforting about knowing that her mother had met the love of her life. She'd been so sad when she realized whoever dated her next wouldn't have that connection. But that was no reason to be with him. It was just another drop in the buckets currently weighing on the should-she-or-shouldn't-she scales.

She set down the last of her tea. "I should get back before the snow gets too deep."

Her father walked with her to the front door as she put her coat back on, staring out at the snow when she opened the door. "Be careful. It's really coming down."

"I will be," she promised, hugging him and wishing him a good night before starting into the snowstorm.

It was harder to see now, the wind picking up enough to make the flakes swirl blindingly. It wasn't quite whiteout conditions, but it wasn't far from it, and the forecast had predicted the snow would only get heavier throughout the night.

Thank goodness she didn't have to be out in it.

Her thoughts drifted to Levi and the rescue squad as she walked through the increasingly heavy drifts. She sent out a quick little prayer that there wouldn't be any calls tonight to pull cars out of ditches or go searching for lost backcountry snowboarders who tried to sneak in a few extra runs in spite of the weather. She may not know how she felt about Levi, but she didn't want him out in this.

Pushing against the wind and trudging through snow that was already halfway up her shins, the walk home took twice as long as usual, and she was relieved to duck safely onto her porch, out of the elements. She took a moment to brush herself off and stomp the snow from her boots before stepping into the entry.

"Dory! I'm home!" she called as she stripped off her parka. She expected the clatter of puppy nails on hardwood with Dory racing to greet her, but the house echoed with silence. Could she still be sleeping?

Elinor struggled to toe off her boots, stumbling against the wall as her heel finally came free—and still Dory didn't come to investigate the thud. Her jeans were soaked above the boots—she should have taken the time to put on snow pants, but she hadn't expected to be gone long enough for the snow to pile up and reach the tops of her boots.

She was thinking longingly of changing her clothes, starting a fire, and curling up in front of it with a warm dog, a good book, and a cup of something warm—preferably with something extra warming added to it—as she headed down the hall to see if Dory was still snoozing in front of the fireplace.

But when she flicked on the light, the living room was empty.

"Dory?"

A little whisper of fear rose up and she quickly pulled out her phone to check the GPS. She only took a deep breath again when she saw the locator light blinking happily over her house. So Dory was here. But where?

She searched the house quickly, calling out to the dog—but she wasn't in the bedrooms, the garage, the basement, or the kitchen. She tried the bathrooms and even the closets—just in case the curious dog had somehow locked herself in one, but still, nothing. She checked the tracking signal again, but it hadn't moved—thank goodness. She had to be here somewhere.

Finally realizing the signal wasn't exactly precise, Elinor

grabbed her boots and coat and headed out to check the backyard. Maybe Dory somehow got into the toolshed.

Flashlight in hand, Elinor stepped back into the snow. She automatically searched for tracks and there weren't any recent ones, as there should have been if Dory was romping around the backyard—but there was a spot where there was a suspicious dip in the snowbank—like a medium-sized dog had walked through and her tracks had been filled in by snowfall a while ago.

Elinor shone her flashlight along that dip—hoping to see Dory curled up against the fence. She had to be close.

The flashlight reflected off something bright and metallic. "Dory?" Elinor moved quickly—was that her collar? Had she burrowed into the snow so that was all Elinor could see? Was she stuck? The snow was light, but it was already deep. If she'd fallen into it...

But when Elinor reached the metal flash, it wasn't Dory.

It was just her collar. Frayed and ripped, and dangling from a hinge on the gate. She'd gotten caught and wriggled out of it. Elinor reached for the collar, her heart beating fast as realization hit.

The GPS was here.

But Dory was missing.

And the snow was only getting worse.

Chapter Thirty-One

...and remember, if you find yourself
trapped in the storm, call on the rescue
squad...

—*Pine Hollow Newsletter*,
Thursday, January 27

Levi? I need you."

Levi had been waiting to hear those words for
weeks, but the waver in Elinor's voice instantly brought him
to attention. "What's wrong?"

"It's Dory. She's gone."

Two minutes later he was in his Explorer, the windshield wipers working at maximum speed to keep up with
the snow.

Elinor was standing on her porch when he arrived, already bundled up in her mismatched winter gear. She raced
down the steps and leapt into the Explorer as soon as it
shuddered to a stop. He was backing out even as panicked
words filled the car.

"I only went over to my dad's for a minute—and she was

fast asleep when I left. Even if she woke up, I didn't think she'd have time to get out, let alone wriggle out of her collar. She's never done that before. And now we have no way to find her and we can't even *see*."

"Breathe," he coached. "We're gonna find her. I've been tracking her for months. I know all her usual routes."

A bitter laugh slipped out of her mouth. "I never thought I'd be so grateful that she's been driving you crazy." A little half sob. "She's just so *small*. I know she's got a lot of energy and seems bigger than she is because she's always in motion, but she only weighs forty pounds. If she falls into a snowdrift, she could just vanish—"

He stopped the SUV at the entrance to the square and turned to face her.

"Elinor." He made his voice hard enough to stem her panic. Her frantic gaze flicked to lock on his. "We're going to find her."

"Okay," she whispered, staring into his eyes as if he could make his promise come to life. Then she turned to squint through the blinding white of the snowstorm. "Do you see her?"

"Look for movement," he coached. "That's usually how I spot her."

"What if she's trapped—"

"No what-ifs. Just look."

Elinor nodded, the motion a little too rapid, and did as he asked.

There were no other cars on the road in this weather to care as the Explorer crawled through the square inch by inch. He rolled down his window, shouting for the dog, straining his eyes and ears for some trace of her. On the other side of the cab, Elinor did the same.

His radio crackled with an update from Kaye. The entire rescue squad had been called in before the storm came in, everyone ready to help citizens who found themselves caught in it. Aaron had been on a call when Elinor contacted Levi—and Kaye had just heard back from him that Gayle Danvers was back home safely, though her car would be stuck in the ditch until the roads were clear enough for the tow truck to drag it out. And neither Aaron nor Gayle Danvers had seen a trace of Dory.

It had been a long shot. Gayle was on the other side of town, but Levi was a firm believer in using all his resources.

And he was worried about the dang dog.

The animal had tormented him ever since Elinor got her, but somewhere between chasing her over hay bales in the square and driving around town with her riding shotgun, her little paws on the dashboard and her ears pricked forward as she surveyed her terrain, he'd started to care about the furball.

He kept it all ruthlessly inside, but he was nearly as worried as Elinor was. The sun had already set and the temperatures were dropping. It was supposed to snow through the night, with as much as two feet of accumulation.

He didn't want to say it, but if they didn't find her soon, they probably wouldn't. Not in this storm. The best they could hope for was that she would make her way home safely on her own.

But Levi still scanned the square and the nearby alleyways that Dory had made her playground over the last few months.

They checked all her usual haunts—the preschool playground, where she tried to herd the children, and the town square, where she tried to herd the cars. The school, the animal shelter, and the area around the rescue squad building—all the places where her people worked.

Nothing. And the road conditions were getting worse.

Levi didn't want to say it, but even his four-wheel-drive SUV with the best winter tires was going to start having trouble before long. He wanted to find Dory, but he didn't want to put Elinor in danger to do it. In another few minutes, he'd need to convince her to let him take her home so he could go on looking without worrying about driving his Explorer off the road with her in it. But first he had one last place to try.

"She likes the mill," he said, turning down the county road that was a little too narrow for his comfort tonight. Snow made the tunnel of trees even more cave-like. "Maybe she took shelter inside when the snow got bad."

Elinor didn't speak from the passenger seat. Her lips were pressed together, her expression tense and worried in the dashboard light.

"It'll be okay. I'll find her," he promised, hoping he wasn't lying.

There were no streetlights out here. The mill was a hulking shadow in the snow when Levi pulled up in front of it. He didn't see any tracks in the swath of snow illuminated by his headlights as he pointed them toward the building, but the snow was coming down hard enough now that tracks were erased almost as quickly as they formed.

"I'll go check inside," he volunteered, putting the Explorer in park but keeping the engine on so the lights would stay on and Elinor would stay warm.

Elinor opened the passenger door. "I'm coming with you. She might come if she hears my voice."

Levi didn't bother arguing, though not because he doubted Dory would come to him. In the last few weeks, he and the dog had come to an understanding. She now knew the difference between his "okay, you rascal, we can play a little" tone of voice and his "this is business, get in the car" tone. But even if he knew Dory would come running if she heard him, he also knew that Elinor needed to look for herself. It was why he'd picked her up rather than simply assuring her he was looking and going to do his job on his own, as he would have with any other concerned citizen.

It was supposed to get colder throughout the night, but for now the snow was still the thick, heavy flakes that fell when the temperature was right around freezing. They waded through it, and Levi automatically reached out a hand to help Elinor when her shorter legs struggled through the snowdrifts.

Through the arch of the mill doorway, he could see snowdrifts forming inside from the gap in the roof. The light from the headlights shone through the cracks in the crumbling building, but it was dark enough inside that Levi pulled out his Maglite and flicked it on before stepping inside, kicking a trail in the snow for Elinor.

"Dory?" she called as he panned the light around the graffitied walls. The beam illuminated the snow drifting through the hole in the ceiling. It seemed lazier inside, not swirling so much in the wind. It would have been magical, those flakes floating on the light, if he wasn't so worried.

"Dory!" Elinor shouted again.

A scuffing sound.

Levi's head snapped to the left and he trained the Maglite on the sound. A flash of white—*not* snow. A tail. A very familiar tail.

"Dory!"

Elinor rushed forward as Dory wriggled from the cover beneath the rotting steps. Relief flashed through him in a knee-weakening rush as Elinor fell to her knees in front of the dog.

And then another flicker of movement from the hidey-hole. A pale face.

Elinor froze in the process of making sure Dory was okay when Levi's flashlight shone on that face.

"Brayden?"

🐾

"He's out like a light. I think he'll be okay."

Levi looked up from the fire he'd been stoking when Elinor came into the main room of his cabin. The power had gone out, as predicted, but if he kept the fire going, the snug little cabin would stay warm enough through the night.

Brayden Wells was fast asleep in his bed, underneath a pile of blankets to keep him warm, with Dory sprawled over him like an extra, very protective blanket. Thankfully, the kid had been able to take a hot bath to warm up before they'd lost the power to the water heater. He had to have been out there in the cold for hours, and Levi's first priority had been making sure he didn't need medical intervention for hypothermia.

The roads were a nasty mess—which was the only reason Brayden wasn't currently at home or back at the rescue squad house being fussed over by Kaye and Marjorie. After a quick call to dispatch and Brayden's grandparents, they'd all agreed that getting Brayden warmed up fast was more important than the three of them trying to cross Pine

Hollow in the current conditions. Levi's cabin was closest. And he was still on the radio if anyone needed him for an emergency through the night.

"He's lucky Dory got out." Levi straightened as Elinor settled down at one end of his ratty overstuffed couch. It wouldn't be comfortable for her to sleep on, but it would be better than the floor, which was where he planned to be. "Without her body heat, things could have been a lot worse. Kid wasn't dressed for this weather."

Levi settled onto the opposite end of the couch. He'd been dreaming about spending the night with Elinor, but never in these circumstances.

She'd shed her down parka, tucking it over her lap like a blanket. "I thought his grandparents might be struggling with him, but I didn't realize..." She trailed off. "Did you see the spray paint cans under the steps where he was hiding?"

"I think we found our vandal. He probably got the paint from his grandfather's store. I have to admit, I thought it was teens. I wasn't expecting a ten-year-old."

"I think he's eleven. Same grade as Astrid."

"Britt Wells's kid." He scrubbed a hand down his face, dry-washing the familiar grit of guilt.

"He lived with his grandparents even before..." She swallowed and they both heard the words she didn't say. *Before his mother died.* "And he never makes trouble. He's so quiet. I should have known."

"So should I. But there's no point dwelling on that. All we can do is learn from our mistakes and be better," Levi said, repeating Dr. Park's words as he looked toward the closed door of the cabin's single bedroom. "So how can we be better for him?"

"I could try to get him back into the after-school program. It's nothing earth-shattering, just a place for the kids to hang out and do some projects, but it helps make them feel like they're part of something. Engages them with the town, making floats for the parades…"

"It takes a village?"

"Don't be flip." She glared at him, shoving her glasses up her nose irritably. "You had the Elks."

"I know. And I wasn't being sarcastic." Elton and the other members out at the Elks had probably saved his life. They'd certainly turned him into the man he was. A bunch of middle-aged men and retirees teaching him to play poker had meant more than he could ever explain. Though Elinor already seemed to know that as her expression softened.

"Have you ever thought about doing something like that?"

"Playing poker?"

She rolled her eyes. "You know what I mean. Something with kids. Like, I don't know, Junior Rescue Squad. Some kind of cadet program."

It wasn't a bad idea. Marjorie would probably love it. And Kaye's son was about the right age. Levi would have to give it some more thought, talk to Ben and the town council…

"Kids all want to grow up so fast, all trying to be like the adults in their lives. So it's up to us to model for them," Elinor said. "Give them good examples. It could be great— kind of a Big Brother thing."

She wasn't wrong, but he wasn't ready to make any promises. "You think Brayden…?"

"Would be interested?" she finished for him. "I don't know, honestly. I only see him when his class comes for library hours, and he always keeps to himself. I don't really know what he's interested in."

"He's quite the artist." Maybe Peg, who ran the arts and crafts shop in town, would be interested in taking him under her wing. Of everyone in town, she was the most likely to appreciate the graffiti.

Elinor knocked on her forehead with her knuckles. "I should have put it together. I thought the graffiti looked familiar. He came to my NaNo club—just the first week. He was drawing the whole time. I thought it was a graphic novel, but then he stopped coming, and I just didn't think. I can't believe I didn't recognize his work—"

"From the one time you looked over his shoulder?"

"I knew that I knew who our artist was, but I wasn't thinking Brayden. He's just a kid."

Just a kid who had lost his mom.

The guilt Levi had been feeling all night crept up the back of his throat like bile. A log cracked in the fire, and Levi got up to go add more wood, taking more time than was strictly necessary shoving the logs around with the fireplace poker.

But when he got back to the couch, Elinor's much-too-perceptive eyes were still watching him. "Are you okay?"

"I'm fine."

"Levi."

He met her eyes, the truth pulled out of him like taffy, reluctant and stretching. "He should have a mother."

Her eyes widened and she opened her mouth—undoubtedly to say something sympathetic, but now that he'd told her, he needed her to know all of it.

"I was called out to Britt Wells's place over a year ago—before...Well. Before. It wasn't the first time. Brayden was already living with his grandparents, so at least he didn't see it, but she was a mess." He closed his eyes remembering the scene. "I thought if I—she'd already been in and out of rehab. I knew she tried to stay clean for Brayden, but she never quite could. I thought if she was in jail, at least she wouldn't be using. Brought her in on possession charges. Six months. And then the day after she got out—"

"She ODed."

He nodded. "I should have done more. I didn't know what to do, so I just...I failed her."

"You weren't the only one who tried to help her. It wasn't your fault any more than it was her parents' or anyone else's in this town. Or hers. She was sick. And it killed her. Not you."

He swallowed, looking at the fire when he couldn't look at her, the logs glowing bright beneath the flames.

"Is this why you've been...?"

"Going to therapy?" he finished for her. "Part of it..."

"And the other part?"

He met her eyes then. Eyes that had always seen more in him than he saw in himself. They were wide and brown, framed by the same dark-framed glasses she'd had for nearly a decade. Her lashes were thick, her eyebrows always giving her mood away—pulling in tight when she was angry. Or lifting ever so slightly when she was pleading with him— as she was now. As if she could beg him to open up to her with just her eyes.

And she could. Elinor always could.

"I guess I had some things to talk about." He glanced down at his hands, not uncomfortable so much as uncomfortable with the fact that he wasn't uncomfortable. "Some mistakes I made. Things I regret."

When he looked up her eyes were huge, her lips slightly parted. She'd always had a slight overbite, and he could just see the tips of her front teeth. She'd hated it when they were younger, claiming she looked like a chipmunk, but he'd always loved her mouth. Her smile. The way she nibbled her lower lip when she was thinking. Or when she was nervous.

Her tongue slipped out to wet the lip she'd been biting, but she still didn't say a word—and Levi, for once in his life, wanted to fill the silence.

"At first I went to placate Marjorie and Elton. I didn't think I needed...Jackson men are strong, right? We don't need therapy."

"Sometimes I hate your father," she said with quiet feeling.

"Don't go getting all vengeful on me. You're supposed to be the nice one," he tried to joke, though the words fell flat.

"I'm not the nice one." Elinor's eyes were full of fire, that look she got when she was defending him, even to himself. "*You're* the nice one. You do more for others than anyone I've ever met."

"You know what I mean."

"You mean how you're incapable of seeing your virtues? You just take responsibility for every bad thing that ever happens in this town, but none of the good things could possibly be because of you?"

"That's a little dramatic, don't you think?" he asked— before he realized his error. A wise man did not tell the woman he loved that she was being dramatic.

Her eyes narrowed. "So it's dramatic for me to want you to stop seeing yourself as the little boy who acted out in class so no one would realize he wasn't perfect in every way?"

"Perfect was always more your thing than mine."

"Oh, please." Her eyes rolled. "You forget I know you, Levi. You're so scared people will figure out you aren't smart, but that's ridiculous. You're the man who invented strip *Jeopardy*. And you always won."

"I was motivated."

"You're *smart*."

He shook his head, the movement automatic. "Not in the way people care about."

"Because you didn't go to college?"

"Because I can barely read, Elinor," he snapped. His face immediately heated, shame a poison coating his throat.

"You listen to thousands of books on tape. You remember everything. You care about everyone. And the way you see yourself drives me crazy. I could never get you to see what I see—"

"Because your rose-colored glasses distort your vision."

"No. I see *you*, Levi. I always have." Her eyes met his, piercing and unwavering. Suddenly he knew what she was going to say even before her lips formed the words. "I love you."

He couldn't look away—and a truth he'd never quite acknowledge slipped out unguarded. "And I always thought you were wrong to."

Chapter Thirty-Two

It's amazing the truths that can come out with the snow.

—*Pine Hollow Newsletter*,
Thursday, January 27

Elinor's heart broke a little as she held Levi's gaze, refusing to flinch. That was it, right there. The thing that had broken them apart. The thing she'd never been able to understand. He'd always loved her. She'd always loved him. But he hadn't been willing to let her. If she couldn't change the way he saw himself, could she ever have a prayer of convincing him to accept her feelings? Were they back at the same impasse they'd always been?

"You were never supposed to end up with me," he said—as if reminding her of a fact they both knew to be true.

"Why not?" she challenged.

"The pride of Pine Hollow?"

"That wasn't all I was. And sometimes it felt like you and Katie were the only ones who knew that. Who saw the imperfect me and liked me anyway."

"But *everyone* saw the imperfect me," he growled. "Everyone knew I wasn't good enough for you."

"*Levi.*"

"It's true," he argued, before she could contradict him again. "Do you remember your prom? When I took you to the inn for dinner beforehand?"

"Of course I remember." He'd saved up for months. Neither of them had been able to afford the prices at the Pine Hollow Inn's fancy restaurant, but he'd been so determined to take her to the best restaurant in town, even if she would have been perfectly happy with burgers from Gwennie's, the dive that had become the Tipsy Moose when Gwennie retired.

"Everyone stared at us." His voice was clipped. "Patronizing me. They knew I didn't belong there with you."

"Levi, of course they stared. Neither of us belonged there. We were sixteen, dressed up for prom, and trying to pretend we knew what foie gras was. They probably thought we were adorable. And clueless. Which we were."

He shook his head. "You can't understand. This is your town. Everyone has always loved you."

"It's your town too!" She realized she'd raised her voice and glanced over her shoulder toward the bedroom door, behind which Dory was guarding Brayden's sleep, but there was no sound from the other side.

Levi's brow pulled down. "I couldn't wait to get out of here."

"Then why didn't you?"

He shook his head again, as if he hadn't had a choice. "Elton offered me a job. It wasn't like a kid who barely finished high school had a lot of options. Not like you. You could have gone anywhere. I've never understood why you didn't put this place in your rearview mirror and never look back. Get away from all these people with their fixed ideas of who you are. Locked in at age ten and never changing."

"I know what it feels like to have the whole town expecting something from you." She twisted to face him, gripping the back of the couch as she talked. "And yes, I know it must be worse when they're waiting for you to screw up instead of always assuming you'll be perfect. And that does suck, but this is home. I love Pine Hollow. I don't want to be anywhere else. I know you've never understood why I came back when I could have left, but I didn't *want* to stay away. I was so lonely at school—maybe because I was younger than everyone else, maybe because I just didn't let myself be a part of things, but being off in the world wasn't *better* for me, no matter what you thought. You were the one who wanted to get away from here. To get away from the idea everyone had of you. But, Levi, you've done that! You've changed the way people see you. You're the chief of police now. You're respected and admired. People in small towns have long memories, but if they remember that kid who always got into trouble, it's only so they can talk about how far you've come."

He'd gone quiet, watching her impassioned speech, and when she stopped her face was warm, as if she'd been running. He studied her. Like he was trying to see if she really believed what she'd said to him. Trying to decide if he could let himself believe it. How could she convince him?

Elinor took a deep breath. "The other day I was listening to this—"

"Podcast?"

She narrowed her eyes at him in mock irritation. "You don't know me as well as you think you do, Levi Jackson."

Except he did. He really did.

"My apologies. What were you listening to?"

Her smile twisted ruefully. "A podcast." He snorted, and she pressed on—relieved that his guard seemed to be lowering. "It was actually about appreciation—how you want to do things for people who express gratitude. It made me think of my dad and Anne and how I always want to do whatever they ask, but as soon as Charlotte asks me for the littlest thing I have to control my urge to grumble at her because it feels like she just accepts it as her due. But then I realized that even when she does thank me, it's like I can't hear her. And I don't know why that is. So what I'm getting at is, is the problem that the town doesn't appreciate you? That they don't admire you? Or that you can't hear it when they do?"

He swallowed, shaking his head. She wasn't sure she knew the answer to those questions, either. But there was something else she suddenly needed to say to him.

"I was listening to another podcast," she began, her nerves slowing the words. "It had this quote that's been stuck in my mind. I can't seem to stop thinking about it. 'Love is a collaborative work of art.'" She wet her lips, forcing herself not to look away from the pale gray eyes that were watching her steadily. Levi had always been amazing at paying attention.

"I'd never thought of it that way," she admitted. "It was always this big thing I felt for you. This force of nature, right? Like it was pushing me from the outside and the inside at the same time, *making* me feel, making me act a certain way, but it wasn't something we did together. It wasn't something we crafted and perfected as a team."

"Love isn't something we do to other people. It's something we do with them," he said softly—and Elinor sat up a little straighter, excitement making her lean toward him.

"Yes! Exactly. We loved each other so much, but it was like we were throwing all our emotion at each other rather than trying to build this thing. And so it was easy to blame you completely for breaking up with me, because it wasn't anything I had done. But it was actually something I didn't do. I let you get to the point where you thought I didn't need you. Where you thought I was better without you."

"You always deserved someone better." His voice was low and raspy.

"*Levi.*" She reached out, grabbing his forearm, gripping the muscle through his flannel shirt. "There was never anyone better for me than you."

He searched her eyes, always searching for the truth, and she tried to let him see how much she meant it. Tried to make him *believe* it.

"Do you know what I realized?" she asked softly, still holding his arm. "When we were driving around tonight, looking for Dory? I kept thinking how sure I was that you would help when I called you. How even if it had been the worst part of our breakup, when I thought I hated you and things were terrible between us, you still would have come. Like you came when Katie died. Because when I need you, you are *always* there for me. And I want to be that for you."

She didn't realize her eyes had started leaking until Levi lifted his hand—on the arm she wasn't still gripping—and gently brushed his thumb across her cheek, catching a drop of moisture.

"You've always taken care of me," Elinor whispered, the words halting. "Do you think you could let me take care of you, too? Because I love you, Levi Jackson. I don't know how to stop loving you. I don't think I ever will. But you have to let me. I don't want to be blindsided again if you decide one day that you aren't good enough for me. I wouldn't let you go so easily this time. I would fight you until you knew you were the best damn person I know. Until you saw yourself the way I see you. But you have to see it. Do you understand? Love is a collaborative work of art. And I can't do it if you won't do it with me."

Levi wet his lips—and Elinor held her breath. He was getting ready to say something. Something that she *knew* would change her life. But for the better or the worse? Was he going to tell her he didn't love her anymore? That he was only taking care of her because that was what he did for everyone? Or would he keep insisting she was better off without him? She needed him to say something, but she was also terrified that this was about to hurt.

She took her hand back, bracing herself against the corner of the couch.

Levi took a breath.

Please, she silently pleaded, barely resisting the urge to close her eyes to give the one-word prayer a little extra potency.

"I always felt like I was playing pretend," Levi said slowly. "Playing the part of the perfect boyfriend for you. I wanted to take you to the fancy restaurant at the inn and give you whatever the perfect guy would give you. But it always felt like this role I was playing that didn't quite fit, and if I stopped, you would realize I wasn't what you thought. I thought I was fooling you. Like it was a bluff I'd gotten away with. I never thought I deserved you. So when my dad and Katie basically told me you'd be better off without me, it just confirmed what I already wanted to believe. And it felt like the only way to be good enough for you, to actually be this hero you thought I was, was to make the sacrifice to let you go. I didn't think it would hurt you. Not in the long run. Because I always thought you'd fallen in love with a lie—and breaking up would show you that."

Another log cracked in the fire, and he looked toward the sound, watching the logs shift and resettle. "I don't think I could have said that to you three years ago. Or even last year." He looked back at her, holding her gaze. "I don't know how to prove to you that I've changed. That I *am* changing. I don't know how to show you that I would never do that to you again. To us. The guys were trying to help me brainstorm big romantic gestures that would, I don't know, be like the end of some romantic movie, but I couldn't come up with anything that would undo the last three years."

"I don't need romantic gestures, Levi. I just need this. I just need you to talk to me. To be in this with me."

He reached out, almost hesitant, and brushed her fingertips, not quite taking her hand, just playing his fingers against hers. An invitation. She tightened her fingers around his.

"Do you think you might be willing to give us another try?" he asked softly.

He hadn't actually said the words. The three little ones everyone made out to be the be-all, end-all. But she knew. It was there on his face when she nodded—the relief. The hope. The fear.

The love.

They would build it together.

Elinor pulled him toward her across the couch, her hand cupping the firm angle of his jaw, drawing her down to him. And answered him with a kiss.

Chapter Thirty-Three

…and the shenanigans people get up to
during a power outage…
—*Pine Hollow Newsletter*,
Thursday, January 27

Nothing happened, of course. There was only so much Elinor was willing to do on a lumpy couch during a snowstorm with one of her students sleeping twenty feet away. But even making out with Levi like teenagers and falling asleep on the couch with her head on his chest felt like coming home.

In the morning, Dory woke them both by taking a running leap onto the couch the second Brayden opened the bedroom door. Levi had always woken up quickly. He was on his feet while Elinor was still rubbing at the creases his shirt had left on her face.

Brayden stood in the doorway of the bedroom, his narrow shoulders braced as if for the punishment he hadn't received last night—but Levi was so calm and Dory so infectious that before long he was smiling shyly as Levi filled bowls with cereal for breakfast.

It was all surprisingly normal. Domestic. Levi checked in with his office while they ate, then announced he was going outside to check the conditions. The snow had stopped sometime during the night, but it was hard to judge how deep it was from the side-facing windows.

Brayden watched intently while Levi pulled on his boots, until Elinor suggested lightly, "Brayden, why don't you borrow a coat and help Levi dig us out? You can keep Dory from driving him crazy."

Levi glanced at her in surprise, but when she gave him a pointed look he caught on quickly. "I could use a hand, if you like," he offered, nodding to his old parkas hanging on the hooks beside the door in a ragged row. "They're all gonna be big on you, but they're warm. Take your pick."

Elinor stayed inside while they went out to survey the terrain. Dory leapt off the porch and disappeared into a snowbank in a puff of white. Brayden laughed, the sound echoed by Levi's rusty-sounding chuckle, and Elinor bit her lip, closing the door and moving to the kitchen so she could watch them through the narrow window above the sink.

As much as she wanted to believe that last night had magically settled everything, she was still worried. She and Levi were together again—that much she knew—but it felt tentative. And fragile.

She wanted this. She hadn't really admitted to herself how badly she wanted it, but now she chewed on her lower lip and watched Levi talking to Brayden outside, and her heart ached with want. They both looked so serious. There was something so similar about them, the big, strong sheriff and the scrawny little boy. She didn't know what they were talking about out there, but something about the scene caught her right in the chest, and she finally had to turn away from the window so she wouldn't be a maudlin mess.

School had been canceled for the snow day, though Levi announced the plows had already been through his street when he and Brayden entered, stomping the snow from their boots.

"We dug enough of a path to get the Explorer out," Levi explained, unzipping his coat but not taking it off. "You about ready? I wanna get Brayden home. I know his grandparents were worried."

Elinor quickly gathered up her things—which pretty much consisted of putting on her coat. Brayden started to shrug off the borrowed parka, but Levi stopped him with a matter-of-fact "Hang on to that for now. I have others. Car'll be cold."

Elinor didn't know what Brayden's grandparents' situation was, but she knew Levi was already planning to send Marjorie out to talk to them, to find out what they needed. She'd never seen him come to school without the proper winter gear, or someone would have flagged him for a visit already, but now he wouldn't slip through the cracks again.

They were lucky they'd found him last night.

The SUV was quiet as they drove through the peaceful, snow-covered streets of Pine Hollow, each of them preoccupied with their thoughts. Even Dory curled up on Elinor's lap rather than pushing her nose against the windows. After they dropped Brayden off and Levi spoke briefly with his grandparents, they were back in the Explorer on their way to her house, and silence reigned again.

When they pulled into her driveway and she opened the door, Dory bounded out to romp through the new snow, but Elinor hesitated. Levi had put the SUV in park, but he hadn't turned off the engine.

She met his eyes, this new thing between them humming in the air. "Would you like to come in?"

His silver gaze locked onto hers. "You have no idea how much."

But he wasn't going to. It was obvious in his voice. "But?"

"The roads are being cleared, but there's always a lot to do the day after a big snow and a power outage. We've got to help anyone with caved-in roofs or frozen pipes. And I want to talk to Marjorie about Brayden as soon as possible."

She nodded. "I saw you talking to his grandparents."

"They didn't even know he was gone last night until Kaye called them. Apparently he's been going into his room, locking the door, and blasting video games. They were trying to give him space to process and never suspected he was going out the window at night. He left without his winter coat, and then got caught in the storm. At least that's what he admitted when we were shoveling."

"You were good with him," she whispered, thinking again of the similarities between them.

He shook his head, dismissing the praise as always, and she opened her mouth to argue with him, to push him to accept the compliment—but his gaze was fixed on the rearview mirror.

"You have company."

A small crossover SUV parked at the curb rather than trying to drive through the deep snow of her driveway.

Elinor twisted for a better look. "That's Charlotte's car."

"You two talking again?"

"Not as of last night." She frowned. Charlotte opened

her car door and Dory bounded through the snow to greet her, barking happily. "I should…"

"Go on," he encouraged. "I've gotta get to work. We can talk later."

Elinor unbuckled her seat belt, unsure whether they were at the casual-kiss-goodbye stage right now. Everything felt so uncertain in the light of day. Her instinct was to lean over—but Charlotte was right there, coming up the drive, and so she just flashed him a quick smile and mumbled "Bye" as she hopped out of the Explorer, feeling as awkward as when he'd dropped her off after their very first official date, the one where he'd held her hand all through *Charlie's Angels* and she'd barely been able to concentrate on the movie.

She slammed the door and gave another awkward wave as Charlotte arrived at her side—and the awkwardness shifted toward a new target.

"Hey," Charlotte muttered, reflecting her discomfort back at her.

"Hey," Elinor replied brilliantly. She caught Dory's collar to keep her from getting in the way of the Explorer as Levi backed out of the driveway, the snow crunching and creaking beneath his tires. "You want some cocoa?"

Charlotte rolled her eyes. "I'm not five, Elinor."

"I know," she snapped, then immediately regretted her tone, softening it as she continued, "I could just really use a nice comforting cup of cocoa right now. You can do tequila shots if you want, but I want cocoa."

Charlotte had the grace to flush. "Sorry. Cocoa sounds good."

After Dory took a moment to create some yellow snow, they all retreated inside. Elinor knew she looked a little ragged after a night sleeping in her clothes, but she didn't want to take the time to change. Not when it felt like Charlotte might bail at a moment's notice. They needed to sort things out. She needed to apologize.

But before she could, while she was still getting out cocoa makings, Charlotte blurted, "So, Levi again, huh?"

Elinor sighed. "Please don't. I can't handle anyone picking us apart right now."

"Sorry," Charlotte murmured, sounding like she actually meant it. "I heard Dory got out during the storm and Levi was helping you look."

Elinor frowned at her sister. "How did you hear about that already?"

"Magda called me this morning. Kaye called her to see if she was going to open the bakery today. She wanted pastries for the rescue squad because she figured they'd be busy all day and Levi had already been out half the night looking for Dory with you. She didn't tell Magda that you'd found Dory—obviously you did. But I figured if she was still missing I could, you know... help, or whatever."

Suddenly, stupidly, there were tears in Elinor's eyes. "Thank you. I'm lucky to have you as my sister, you know that?"

Charlotte pressed her lips together, tightening the leash on her own emotion. "Likewise," she whispered.

"I'm sorry, kiddo." Elinor cringed. "God, and I just did it again. I know you're an adult. And I know you are capable and competent and brilliant, and I never want you to feel like I don't see that."

"No, it's my fault. I'm too defensive," Charlotte insisted, dramatically flopping onto one of the barstools at the island. "You're the best pseudo-mom ever, and I've been a brat."

"I shouldn't have been trying to tell you what to do about

Warren. And I shouldn't have brushed off how you've always come through when I need you, no matter what. Like showing up today. And after Katie died—I know you didn't move in just to save money. And I know you gave yourself a crappy commute for the last year of your residency so you could be closer to me. And I love you. Even when you drive me crazy."

"Likewise," Charlotte said again, her throat working as she looked away.

"I'm going to stop trying to fix everything. Or at least try really hard."

"I know you only do it because you love me," Charlotte said, then grimaced. "But yes, please?"

Elinor laughed. "Really, *really* hard. I promise."

The tension that had been hanging in the air released, and Elinor refocused on making the cocoa as Charlotte told her about the latest gossip up at the Estates. It was much later, when they were both on their second cup and Dory was asleep in front of the fire, that Charlotte caught her glancing at her phone.

"So, Levi…" Charlotte prompted gently.

Elinor flipped her phone over and shoved it under her leg so she would stop checking it every five seconds for a text that wasn't going to come in. "He'll be busy for hours. Whenever there's a big snow—"

"That's not what I was asking."

Elinor felt her face heating. "I know."

"You don't have to tell me."

"No, I want to, I just…" Elinor squeezed her mug between her hands, staring into it as if it would somehow provide the answers to all the questions she didn't know how to put into words. "I'm not sure I know what we are right now. Last night we talked and we..." She blushed. "We kissed, and we agreed we want to try again, but then this morning we didn't really talk about it. There wasn't a chance, and Levi's never really been a talker—and I'm probably overthinking this, because I'm always overthinking things, but it still feels like it could all vanish in a second."

"That makes sense. It will probably take a while to feel secure in it, after what happened."

Elinor narrowed her eyes. "Why aren't you telling me to run in the other direction? I thought you were Team Closure and Moving on with Your Life."

"I'm Team Whatever Makes My Sister Happy," Charlotte corrected. "I thought that was getting over Levi, but now..." She shrugged. "It's obvious you still love him."

Elinor chewed her lower lip. "Is that enough?"

"I hope so. Because it would really suck to go to prison for murdering the chief of police, and I'm going to have to, if he breaks your heart again."

"Please try to restrain your murderous impulses."

"I'll try," Charlotte agreed. "If only because you two are boomerangs. Always coming back to one another. I'd hate to murder him while he's on the return trajectory."

Elinor laughed, like she knew Charlotte wanted her to, but she still couldn't ignore the whisper of doubt in the back of her mind. Had they come back to one another to stay? Or was Levi going to go boomeranging away again the second she let herself get comfortable?

Could she really let herself believe that this time it was different? Or was she always going to be waiting for the other shoe to drop?

Chapter Thirty-Four

This morning, the snow is being cleared away to reveal the true Pine Hollow beneath—and this author is finally able to reveal another truth. One that has remained secret for far too long...

—*Pine Hollow Newsletter*, Friday, January 28

The day after a big snowfall was always a nonstop litany of headaches and minor disasters as the town put itself back to rights—but no matter how busy he was, or how frustrating it was to be dealing with town business when he really wanted to be playing hooky with Elinor, Levi still walked into the rescue squad station that afternoon with a feeling of quiet satisfaction.

Something that had been out of sync for the last three years—hell, much longer than that—had finally clicked fully into place last night. He had Elinor back, but it wasn't just that. It was a certainty he'd never had before that they were right together, and this time it would stick. He'd told her things last night he'd never told anyone—and far from making him feel stripped bare, he'd felt lighter, freer.

But he still just grunted when Kaye called out, "Hey, Chief," as he walked through the door. He wasn't a completely different person, after all.

Kaye's gaze rarely lifted from her books for long when he walked in the door, but she was watching him now, studying him as if trying to see some secret message on his face. It was disconcerting—for the two seconds it took him to realize she, and everyone else at the station, had undoubtedly figured out he'd spent the night with Elinor at his cabin. Apparently the fact that they'd been chaperoned by an eleven-year-old didn't make much difference when it came to town gossip.

"No comment," he said before she could ask him, moving steadily toward his office. He still needed to talk to Marjorie about Brayden.

Kaye's eyes flared with surprise—and something like relief. "So you already saw the newsletter?"

He hadn't, but he could imagine every word. He just grunted again. The last thing he needed was Linda Hilson's editorial comments on his love life. He knew where he and Elinor stood—and it was no one's business but their own.

Two of the volunteer firefighters who had come in to help dig people out lingered in the hallway with cups of coffee. They stopped talking as soon as they saw Levi, openly staring, and Levi mentally rolled his eyes. He'd be relieved when he and Elinor were old news again and could go about their lives in peace.

He closed the door to his office to shut out the gawking and shot Marjorie a quick message to ask when she was available to talk about Brayden. She wasn't always the fastest with replies, so he expected to wait awhile for a response, but he was still hanging up his coat when a knock sounded on his door.

"Come in."

Marjorie stepped inside, her expression far too serious as she quickly closed the door behind her. "Levi. How are you?"

Suspicion stirred, and he realized the gossip in the newsletter might be of the inaccurate variety. Marjorie studied him like she was braced for the worst.

Just what had Linda said happened last night? He might have to open his email and read the damn newsletter for himself.

But first, Brayden.

"I'm good," Levi assured Marjorie, leaving that statement to contradict whatever rumors Linda had started in the newsletter and getting down to more important matters. "Have you had a chance to talk to Brayden Wells's grandparents?"

Marjorie didn't miss a beat, quickly settling into the chair opposite him to discuss their local artist.

Levi focused on the task at hand, but during the entire conversation part of his mind was working the puzzle of the newsletter. Obviously everyone thought *something* had happened, and he needed to know what it was, if only so he knew whether it was a rumor he needed to defuse or one that would die on its own when everyone realized it was nonsense.

As soon as Marjorie left, he pulled out his phone and pulled up the email, activating his text reader.

The digital voice was clear, but the words refused to compute. He expected some bullshit story. Some fiction about how Elinor had dropped him for good and run off with George. He'd expected lies.

But what he heard was true.

And it wasn't about Elinor.

🐾

"Oh my God."

Elinor stared at the town newsletter on her phone, hoping if she stared at it long enough the words would change and she would realize she'd been hallucinating.

"No," she whispered as she read the words over and over. "No, no, no."

"Is that an it's-all-lies no or an oh-crap-how-did-she-find-out no?" Charlotte asked from across the counter, where she was reading the same newsletter.

Anne had arrived moments ago, her face tight with worry, and asked them if they'd seen the newsletter. She was now pacing in front of the fireplace, Dory dancing excitedly around her feet.

"It's true, isn't it?" Anne asked softly.

Elinor closed her eyes miserably. For once, Linda Hilson had gotten it right. And Levi...Levi would *hate* this.

If there was one secret in his life he'd always worked hardest to hide—even from his closest friends—it was what he'd always thought of as his great inadequacy. And now Linda Hilson had printed it in her damn newsletter. Elinor could strangle the woman.

"How did no one know he was dyslexic?" Charlotte asked, her tone arguing that the email had to be wrong—and Elinor almost leapt on that. Almost lied to her sisters. But once the rumor started, the truth was undoubtedly going to come out.

"He's very good at hiding it," she murmured, not looking up.

"Why?" Charlotte seemed genuinely puzzled. "Lots of people have learning disabilities. And he obviously overcame it." She waved her phone. "Half the newsletter is about how *heroic* he is for conquering it."

Elinor just shook her head. Levi wouldn't see it that way. He never had.

He only saw his failures, never his successes.

"It doesn't matter what we think," Anne said quietly— once again proving she was the wisest of the three of them. "All that matters is how Levi feels about it, and he's private about absolutely everything. He's obviously been private about this as well, and now the whole town knows."

"I really hate that woman," Elinor growled.

"I'm sure she didn't mean it like that—" Charlotte began.

Elinor cut her off with her iciest glare. "We are *not* taking Linda Hilson's side right now. At the moment, I hope Levi arrests her for invasion of privacy."

"I'm not sure he can legally—"

"Charlotte, stop defending her," Elinor snapped. "He's always trying to be perfect for the town, and that woman just told everyone he knows the one thing he sees as his great imperfection."

"I just think it's not such a terrible secret—"

Elinor turned to Anne. "Can you take her out of here before I kill her?"

"Okay! Fine!" Charlotte held up her hands. "I'm on Team Levi, too. I just don't see why this has to be a tragedy."

"It doesn't," Anne assured them both in her steady way, but Elinor was too busy panicking for the words to land.

This was her fault.

As she'd read the newsletter, a sinking feeling had taken hold in her gut. She'd blurted it out a couple of weeks ago while they were at the Cup. Then, when she'd rushed out of the bathroom hallway after he'd kissed her, she'd seen Linda lurking nearby and wondered how much she'd overheard of their conversation, but she hadn't suspected Linda had eavesdropped on that part. Or that she would even care.

It hadn't occurred to her that Linda was doing some sleuthing. That she would track down one of Levi's old teachers with loose lips and get corroboration. She'd never shown any particular journalistic impulses before, just repeating rumors, but somehow *this* she'd turned into a whole exposé.

And Elinor was the one who'd given her the idea.

He was never going to forgive her.

Her sisters were discussing the newsletter—Charlotte on the opposite side of the island and Anne now perched on the edge of the couch in the living area—but Elinor didn't hear them anymore. He would hate this. The whole town talking about him. Even if it was just because he'd surprised them.

Elinor turned her back to her sisters and swiped through her phone until she got away from the newsletter and pulled up her contacts. She considered texting—telling herself not to make it into a big deal if it wasn't one for him, not to blow things out of proportion and make him uncomfortable—but she didn't know what she would even say in a text, so she called instead, pacing with her head down as the phone rang. And rang.

It went through to voice mail and she hung up before she could say the wrong thing.

Okay. She needed a plan. Something to show him that he wasn't still the kid who felt like he needed to hide all his supposed weaknesses. He was valued. He was appreciated. He was so much more to this town. And to her.

Her phone binged with a text, and she frantically opened it, her heart in her throat, but it was just Connor.

Are you with Levi?

The text kicked her spiraling thoughts to the curb and replaced them with a single certainty: She needed to go to the station. She needed to see him.

She'd known Levi a long time. She knew he tended to pull back, to retreat. He'd broken up with her last time over *nothing*, and this time she'd actually done something. She'd exposed his secret, no matter how inadvertently. He was going to find out it was her. Linda had never kept her mouth shut in her life. He was going to retreat, and it was going to be her fault this time.

"I have to go," she announced to her sisters, already moving toward the door. Dory barked once, racing ahead of her. Elinor shoved her feet into her boots as she texted Connor back.

I'm on my way.

🐾

Levi had sometimes envisioned what it would feel like if the entire town suddenly figured out he'd been hiding the fact that he was a moron. He'd expected to be swamped by shame. By embarrassment. He'd worked so hard not to let anyone see the dyslexia.

It still felt like such a foreign word. *Dyslexia.* Like it didn't really apply to him. Like it never had.

His phone began buzzing with texts and calls, proof that more and more people were opening and reading the newsletter. Since he was physically at the rescue station and he'd hear about any emergencies through the intercom, he silenced his phone to quiet the repetitive notifications.

He had work to do.

Marjorie had invited the Wells family in this afternoon to discuss Brayden's upcoming apology tour and next steps moving forward. Levi needed to be focused on making sure the kid got pointed in the right direction and not on some ridiculous newsletter.

But it was hard to ignore it when the second he stepped out of his office, Aaron was strolling back in after a call, his coat still dusted with snow from digging Mrs. Robinson out.

"Hey, Chief!" he called out, his voice ringing through the station. "I had no idea you were dyslexic! I have a little cousin going to special classes for that. I'll have to tell him my boss's brain works like his. He'll love that."

Aaron was smiling, cheerful. Levi had been braced for grating patronization, but Aaron was the same as always, surfer-happy and wandering back to the lounge to check out the pastries Kaye had picked up for the crew today.

The door to Marjorie's office opened before he reached it. "Oh, Levi, there you are. I was just going to look for you. Did you get my text? About the Wellses asking if we could meet at their place so Brayden would feel more comfortable?"

"Sorry, I didn't get it, but that's fine. What time should we head over?"

"Are you free now?"

Levi nodded and they headed toward the front, where Kaye was still giving him that cautious, searching look—the one Levi now had a feeling had nothing to do with Elinor. He told Kaye how to reach them, reluctantly turned the notifications on his phone back on, and held open the door for Marjorie.

"Okay to drive separately?" she asked as she headed for her worn-in Volkswagen. "I have a few people I'd like to look in on after."

Levi grunted the affirmative and headed for his Explorer as another car pulled into the lot beside it. Kaitlyn Devers, who had been flirting with the fire chief for months, popped out of her car with her little dog tucked under one arm and a Magda's box under the other. She'd be disappointed that Kaye had already beaten her to the punch when it came to wooing Dean with pastries. But then her eyes lit on him, and her absent expression changed to an avid one.

"Levi! Oh my gosh, I was just talking about you!"

He winced internally at the reminder that he was currently the hot topic and gave her the barest nod of greeting before continuing to his SUV. Until she literally put herself in his path.

Silently, he weighed how rude he wanted to be. How quickly would it get around town if he just stepped around her and kept walking? Was it likely to affect his appointment as chief of police? Probably not any more than the fact that the entire town now thought he was illiterate.

"You're all anyone can talk about. I was just reading that column, and it makes so much sense!"

And that was his cue to leave. "I'm sorry, Kaitlyn. I have work to do."

"Oh! Right!" She bounced out of his way and he climbed into his Explorer, trying to ignore the echo of her words.

All anyone can talk about. It makes so much sense.

He barely remembered the short drive to the Wells place.

Marjorie's car was already in the driveway, and she must have beaten him by several minutes because there was no sign of her or Brayden's grandparents on the front porch. Just the boy, waiting for him in his winter gear, slumping with his hands in his pockets.

"Brayden." Levi jutted his chin at the kid as he climbed the porch steps.

The boy's mouth twisted to one side like he'd tasted something sour. "My grandma wants me to tell you I'm sorry about the paint and promise to clean it up or whatever people want to make it mends."

Levi stopped on the porch, nodding soberly.

Brayden fidgeted with his zipper, making no move to go inside, where Levi could see his grandparents and Marjorie moving around through the front window. Levi had always trusted his instincts, and right now they were telling him that the kid had more to say, so he waited him out. His patience was his superpower, and no eleven-year-old was a match for it.

Brayden proved that within moments, blurting out, "Can you really not read?"

Thanks to years of practice, Levi managed not to flinch with surprise, keeping his expression calm. Unflappable. "I can. But I'm not very good at it," he admitted. "I had a lot of trouble when I was younger, and so I found a lot of ways to get around it. I still avoid it. Probably more than I should. I don't like to let people see the things I have a hard time with."

"But you're the chief of police."

"I am."

"Don't you have to read to do that?"

"I do. And I manage. Turns out the things you struggle

with don't have to define you. Took me a long time to learn that." He was still learning it, some days. "My mentor used to say it's not about the hand you're dealt, it's how you play it."

The kid cocked his head, frowning. "That sounds like the stuff grown-ups tell you that they don't really believe."

Levi met his eyes. This kid was far too old for eleven. "Do you think I believe it?"

Brayden studied him, his mouth twisting in that sour way again. "You really couldn't read?"

"I could. Slow. And I never wanted people to think I was stupid, so I mouthed off to my teachers in class whenever they asked me to read aloud and got sent to the principal instead." Levi fixed him with a hard look. "*Don't* do that. And don't paint any more buildings. I'm not the one who needs an apology and amends. You're going to have your work cut out for you convincing the folks at the Pine Hollow Inn not to press charges. That building is historic. They're pretty mad. You wanna tell me why you did it?"

The kid shook his head. And Levi nodded. He hadn't really expected an answer.

He jerked his chin toward the door. "Come on. Time to face the music."

Brayden headed inside, but Levi was still on the porch when another car pulled into the driveway. He turned, letting the screen door fall shut again and faced the newcomer, a frown pulling at his brow. "What are you doing here?"

Chapter Thirty-Five

It turns out our chief has been hiding
something from us for nearly three
decades...

—*Pine Hollow Newsletter*,
Friday, January 28

Connor walked toward the porch steps as Ben and Mac climbed out of the car behind him, all three of them frowning—even Mac.

"Kaye told us where you were," Ben explained.

"Because you've been ignoring all our texts," Connor added.

"And we were worried," Mac finished.

"I'm fine," he assured the trio. "But I can't talk right now."

"This won't take long," Connor assured him. "I just want to know if I need to draw up papers to sue Linda Hilson for libel."

Levi snorted. "No lawsuits. I just want it to go away."

He wanted everyone to stop talking about it, but that didn't look like it was going to happen anytime soon when Ben asked softly, "Why didn't you tell us?"

"How did we not know?" Mac added.

"I didn't want you to. I didn't want anyone to. Outside me, my parents, and a couple of my teachers, only Elinor knew." Which did make him wonder how Linda Hilson had figured it out, but that was a question for another time. "It's not a big deal."

Which, strangely, felt like the truth. An odd feeling, when for the longest time it had felt like the biggest deal. His great secret. When had that changed?

The things he'd been saying to Brayden hadn't been platitudes to make him feel better. He really didn't have to define himself by his weaknesses, not anymore.

He looked at his friends, these three guys who had always shown up for him.

"Look, guys, I've gotta work, but we'll talk later, okay? And I'm sorry I hid it from you. It wasn't that I didn't trust you. I just didn't want anyone to see me the way I saw myself. I had to sort that out first."

"You realize the whole town thinks you're even more badass now?" Connor asked.

"I'd rather the whole town not talk about me at all." But it could have been worse.

"We're talking later," Ben insisted—and Levi felt their care pushing at him. He loved these guys. They were more his family than his blood relatives.

But if he told them that, he'd probably start blubbering, and that was the last thing he needed before going inside and discussing junior probation for their town's amateur artist. So he just nodded. And his best friends nodded, too. And then they turned toward Connor's Tesla SUV and he turned toward the house.

But it felt unfinished. It felt like it wasn't enough.

He turned back toward them.

"Guys. Thanks for coming."

Connor's jaw worked as he nodded. Ben shoved his hands in his pockets. And Mac—the asshole—just grinned the biggest damn grin of his life. "Love you too, Chief."

Levi rolled his eyes, shaking his head, but he was smiling as he turned back to the door.

And thirty minutes later, the memory of smart-ass Mac had him smiling again as he made his way back to his car.

His friends knew him. They knew the newsletter would make him feel exposed, and they'd come to check on him. That was what you did for the people you loved. You showed up.

You didn't make them feel like they weren't good enough.

Levi drove through town on autopilot, ending up back at the mill. He parked his Explorer in front and stared at the falling-down building before reaching for his cell phone.

His mother answered on the third ring. "Levi? This is a nice surprise!"

"Is Dad dyslexic, too?" The pause showed he'd startled her with the blunt question and lack of greeting, but he didn't wait for an answer before going on. "It would explain a lot. How you were always making allowances for him. Why he hated it so much that I wasn't better in school. Is that why he always made all those cracks about how alike we were? The ones that always felt like he was insulting us both?"

"Levi. Your father is a very complicated man."

"I know. And he made me complicated, too."

"He wanted you to have realistic expectations for life. He'd been so disappointed, and he didn't want that for you—"

Levi cut her off. "He told me I was stupid."

Silence. Finally broken by, "If you could just understand—"

"I'm trying to. That's why I called. It was never about me, was it? It was always about him."

"He didn't have it easy—"

"No one is guaranteed easy. That isn't an excuse. Why are you still making excuses for him?"

She sighed softly. "He's my husband."

"And I'm your son."

"Levi. I would never choose one of you over the other. You know that."

He did know. His mother was Switzerland. And she had tried. She really had. She'd tried to soften the blows, dull the damage of his father's words. But somehow that hadn't made it any better. It had made him believe it more. Because it felt like she was agreeing with the old man. Like she was only telling him those stories that adults tell kids, like Brayden had said. He'd learned to believe the negative and doubt the positive—and it was taking him a lifetime to unlearn that. But he wanted to. He'd never wanted to be his father in any way. And he refused to be like him in this.

He wasn't going to sabotage the best things in his life because he thought he didn't deserve them. He wasn't going to hide behind an emotionless façade. His father was only one of the people in his life who had shaped him.

Elton had been there, too; his mother had introduced them. And Marjorie. Ben and Connor and Mac.

And Elinor.

He never bothered to go back to the house he'd grown up in, but he drove past this mill at least three times a week. This was home. This was where he'd become the man he was today. Where he could become better.

"I love you, Mom. We'll talk later, okay?"

She meekly accepted his request, because that was who

she was, and he wasn't going to change her now. But he didn't need to change her to change himself.

He needed to stop hiding. Stop trying to protect himself. He needed to talk to Elinor.

There were things he hadn't said last night. Things that *needed* saying.

He threw the Explorer into reverse—

And a very familiar blue Subaru pulled into the ruts left by his tires, blocking him in. The driver's door opened. Dory leapt out.

And Levi smiled at the perfection of it.

Of course she was here. She knew him. She'd always known.

The snow was higher than her boots, and as soon as Elinor stepped out of the car, it slid down the tops, but she barely noticed. Dory sprang gleefully through the mounds of fresh powder, but Elinor had eyes only for Levi.

Her worry—and her guilt—had only grown as she'd searched for him. She'd gotten a text from Connor after her second circuit through town, saying they'd found Levi at the Wells place, but Elinor hadn't wanted to ambush him there, so she'd parked at the rescue squad building, waiting for him to come back. But he'd never appeared, even after Marjorie had returned to the station. So Elinor had gone hunting through town again—and spotted his SUV in front of the mill.

"I'm sorry," she called as she tromped toward him through the knee-deep snow.

His expression tightened the way it did when he was about to refuse sympathy, and she rushed to continue.

"I know you must hate this—the whole town speculating and talking about you—and it's all my fault. Linda Hilson must have heard me when we were talking at the Cup."

"It isn't your fault."

"Please let me say this." Elinior stopped a few feet away from him, clasping her hands at her chest. "It is my fault. And I'm so sorry. But none of that changes who you are. It never has. You've always been amazing. You fixate on your failures—but look at your successes! Look at Kaye! You helped her get out of a horrible marriage and get on her feet! Look at how you're helping Brayden—and Marjorie! Look how you've made her feel like she's essential to this town again—"

"She is."

"But you did that! This whole town is better because of you, and maybe we've been remiss in telling you that, in making sure you know what you mean to us. We love you, Levi. *I* love you. Not in spite of your dyslexia or anything else you've struggled with, but because it's part of what made you who you are. I hated the way it made you feel, but that so-called flaw you always tried to hide never made you any less wonderful in my eyes. Or any less valuable to this town. You're *better* this way. You're *real*. And more compassionate. And understanding. And I know you hate being on display, but the whole town agrees with me."

"Can I talk now?" he asked when she drew breath.

"Yes." She dropped her hands as she finished the speech that had been running circles through her head as she searched for him. "But just one more thing. You've never taken credit for the good you do. You've always taken care of this town, taken care of me, and never wanted attention or praise, but we should still thank you. I thank you. I would throw a parade for you if I thought you wouldn't hate being the center of attention. And I know you probably hate it, but if you look at the newsletter, it's actually really appreciative. Of you." She swallowed thickly. "Okay, I'm done. I just want you to see what I see when I look at you. That's all I've ever wanted."

"I do."

"Really?" Her voice squeaked with disbelief.

He smiled gently—and for the first time she looked past her panic and realized he didn't look angry or distant, like she'd expected. The expression behind his blank face was amused. Comfortable.

"Are you not upset?" she blurted.

"At first it did feel like I was on display," he admitted. "But then I started to think how exhausting it was to worry about people finding out and how I didn't have to do that anymore. Some people will think less of me. Linda apparently likes me more. But now it's just something I am, not this great hidden shame. It's kind of a relief."

Elinor's jaw dropped. "No offense, but I did not expect you to be okay with this."

"Honestly, neither did I. And a few months ago, I probably wouldn't have been. But I'm trying to be better. And Aaron said something interesting."

"Deputy Aaron?" She could hear the skepticism in her own voice, because Aaron, while sweet, was not exactly known for being profound.

"He said his little cousin who has dyslexia would love knowing his boss had it, too. Aren't you the one who's always going on about modeling and letting kids see you try and fail so they don't think they have to be perfect?"

"I didn't think you heard me."

"I always hear you. I just need to work on telling you that." He swallowed, and she could swear he flushed. "And in the interest of being better about the communication stuff, I should have told you last night..."

Nerves pitted her stomach. *Oh no.* "What?"

"I love you, Elinor. You know that, don't you? I never stopped."

"Yeah?" This time her squeak was barely audible. She'd wanted to believe that, wanted to trust it, but it was so good to hear him say the words. "It wasn't just the romance of the moment last night? Getting snowed in with the fire and—"

"No. Not even a little. For weeks I've been trying to think how I could convince you to give us another chance. A few more days and I probably would have broken Dory out just so I'd have an excuse to talk to you."

Her eyes grew damp. "Yeah?" she asked, biting her lower lip.

He closed the distance between them, his thumb brushing her lip where she'd chewed it. "I'm sorry it took me so long to get here. I've always been a slow study."

She narrowed her eyes. "Stop. You're the smartest person I know."

"Now that I've figured out I love you?"

She tipped her chin up. "I heard somewhere that love is a collaborative work of art. Maybe we could work on that together?"

He groaned through his grin. "You're going to make me listen to that podcast, aren't you?"

"I'm a big believer that we should never stop learning," she declared primly.

"Or loving," he murmured, brushing his thumb again across her lower lip.

One side of her mouth quirked up in a teasing smile. "Are you gonna kiss me or what, Levi Jackson?"

He didn't smile. He got all serious. Concentrating. Like he was trying to memorize the moment.

And then he kissed her.

And just like the first time, it was *everything*.

When he finally lifted his head, his silver-gray eyes were clear and happy. And then his lips quirked in a grin. "What do you think of buying the mill?"

She was still gripping his coat where she'd grabbed it during their kiss, and she laughed as she dropped her forehead against his chest. "You already did, didn't you?"

"I'm not saying I did. But if, hypothetically, I had bought just this plot from the family four years ago and never told you and considered selling it this year when the Keller heirs were going to sell the rest of the original property, but then decided I wasn't sure I wanted to sell anymore when I thought we might get back together…hypothetically, exactly how angry would you be?"

She stared up at him, her eyebrows drawn tight in a frown. "You bought it while we were engaged and didn't tell me?"

"It was supposed to be a wedding present. Surprise."

She huffed out a laugh. "Levi. No more major land purchases without discussing it with me. Deal?"

"Deal."

And they sealed it with a kiss.

Epilogue

One Year Later

The Second Annual Chief Appreciation Day parade was this weekend and this author is happy to report that it appears the chief has *finally* put a ring on it. Again.

—*Pine Hollow Newsletter,*
Monday, March 6

his is ridiculous."

"You know you love it." Elinor linked her arm through Levi's, smiling broadly and waving as another float rolled by.

Pine Hollow loved any excuse for a parade, so she hadn't been surprised when the impromptu Chief Appreciation Day had spawned one—though she was a little surprised that the holiday had taken on a life of its own and become an annual event. She hadn't even been involved in the planning this year. Which just made it that much more special.

She'd wanted Levi to *see* how much he meant to this town. And how much he meant to her. To have the memory of Levi Day, as she liked to think of it, to look back on whenever the residents were driving him crazy with their antics—which was still a frequent occurrence.

He liked to grumble that the first parade was just an attempt to stave off any lawsuits against the town for invasion of privacy, since the newsletter was technically a town publication—but they all knew he'd never actually planned to file a complaint. Especially after the council voted unanimously to establish an approval committee for all of Linda Hilson's newsletters. Which had reined her in. Somewhat.

This year Levi Day had become a celebration of the entire rescue squad and everything they did for the town. And Levi could grumble all he wanted, but she knew him. She saw the pride behind his stoic cop face. Sometimes a man just needed an entire town to make a fuss over him. At least that was her theory.

The middle school marching band clattered past, playing what she was pretty sure was supposed to be a rendition of "For He's a Jolly Good Fellow," though it was hard to tell.

"So how does it feel to be the pride of Pine Hollow?" Elinor asked him as the Estates float glided past, George waving cheerfully alongside the residents.

"You would know," Levi said.

"Nah. My golden child status was always provisional. Based on the assumption that someday I would achieve something. You really have."

He glanced down at her, his pale silver eyes certain. "You're going to reclaim the golden child crown. You're still at the beginning of your story."

She smiled—that had never felt more true. Like the world was full of possibilities, just opening up in front of her. Though that optimism might have had something to do with the email sitting in her inbox.

She'd gotten it yesterday and hadn't opened it yet. She'd gotten a revise-and-resubmit request from an agent last March with some great ideas to improve her book. After a *massive* rewrite, she'd resubmitted, and gotten rejected, but the agent wanted to see her next book, and *this* one, the one she'd sent last week, really *was* the best thing she'd ever done. She just *knew* this was going to be a yes, and if it wasn't, she would keep going, keep trying, keep getting better.

She and Levi were getting *very* good at celebrating her victories and rejections. She already had the champagne chilling.

But she hadn't wanted to step on his day.

The Furry Friends float came next—which was really just the decked-out Furry Friends truck with a bunch of dogs in the truck bed and some more walking alongside. Dory rode in her place of honor in the cab, her paws braced on the dashboard as she surveyed *her* town.

Dory had become the rescue squad's unofficial mascot, riding around with Levi every day. They'd even put together an obstacle course for her in the fire truck bay and started training her for search and rescue. Elinor teased him regularly that he'd stolen her dog, but as long as they both came home to her each night, she couldn't complain.

And if they both snuck Dory extra treats, she'd earned them by bringing them back together.

"Is that Charlotte?"

Elinor followed Levi's gaze to the volunteers in Furry Friends T-shirts walking behind the decorated truck, each carrying one of the shelter's latest litter of puppies. Her eyes widened when she spotted her sister. "She said she was swearing off men and getting a puppy after the breakup with Jerkface Jeff, but I didn't think she actually meant it."

"Which part, the swearing off men or the puppy?"

"Both. Either." Her sister had *finally* split up with the latest in a long line of asshole boyfriends—and Elinor had managed not to interfere this time. Mostly.

"Looks like she meant it," Levi commented, nodding toward Charlotte, who was so busy cooing at the puppy in her arms that she didn't seem to notice there was a parade going on around them.

"She's always been a sucker for Dory. Maybe a puppy is just what she needs." Elinor felt a little spoiled—since she already had everything she needed.

Levi grunted. "Just try not to tell her how to train it."

"Hey. She only called me controlling and threw tinsel in my face *once* this Christmas. That's a new record."

At her side, he snorted. Then his expression darkened as the next float rolled by—with Linda Hilson on it. Since the town council had started monitoring her newsletters, she'd restricted herself to only printing the gossip that had been cleared with the involved parties, but Levi was still holding a grudge.

"I don't know why you told her she could put our engagement in her damn newsletter," he grouched.

"Would you rather have everyone in town asking us about it individually as the gossip spreads the old-fashioned way?"

He grimaced, not deigning to answer.

He'd proposed again on Valentine's Day. She'd teased him about being a creature of habit—because he'd given her the promise ring on the Valentine's when they were fifteen,

and proposed again on a Valentine's Day in their twenties—
but she also hadn't been able to say yes fast enough.

It felt different this time. *They* felt different. No longer
relying on the magic or fate of their relationship, but con-
tinually committing to one another. Committing to work
together. Maybe they'd finally grown up.

And if Levi was going to ask her to marry him over and
over again on Valentine's, at least it was a better tradition
than Deenie and Connor's of watching horror movies and
eating pizza. She happened to love that there was a sappy
romantic underneath the stoic chief of police.

And if he wasn't as stoic as he wanted everyone to think,
if she caught him sniffling a little as his rescue squad cadets
marched past, waving little Pine Hollow flags, that was
their secret.

"They look really good."

"Yeah," he managed, still choked up.

Elinor gave his biceps a squeeze and rested her head
against his shoulder. She'd fallen in love with him when she
was barely older than any of those cadets, but it had taken
them a while longer to figure out how to love each other. It
was a collaborative work of art, after all. And she and Levi?
Together, they were getting better every day.

And they were just getting started.

Don't miss Charlotte's story in
Pride and Puppies,
coming in Fall 2022

Acknowledgments

Two years ago, when I started researching for *The Twelve Dogs of Christmas*, I visited several shelters and in the process met a sweet, shy Australian shepherd who clearly needed to come home with us. Gracie quickly proved to be as clever as she is sweet—she really can open doors—and became the inspiration for Dory, the escape artist Aussie. So special thanks to Kris and Gracie for all the good memories—and the great puppy material.

I also owe a debt of gratitude to my incredible grand-mother. She worked as an advocate for children for decades, championing hundreds of kids, many of whose brains worked a little differently, including those in my own family. Thank you for helping us all to shine. (And I'm so glad I can visit you again!)

Thank you to my tier of best friends for being generally awesome. You know who you are. And major thanks to my beta readers, who patiently reassure me along the way that no, the book does not, in fact, suck.

I'm always grateful for my agent, Michelle, who is incredibly patient with my author neuroses and obsession with lists—and who is always fun to have on an escape room team. Also huge thanks to my amazing Forever team, including Sabrina, Joelle, Lori, Stacey, and Estelle—it takes a village to launch a book into the world, and I'm so lucky to have you shepherding mine.

Special thanks to my amazing editor, Leah, who didn't even blink when I started nerding out about *Doctor Who* in the middle of a book. (Rory is a prince among men, and I will aggressively debate all who claim otherwise.) Thank you for having *excellent* taste in your nerd obsessions and for letting me cram a bunch of them into this book!

And finally, huge thanks go to the podcasters. Like Elinor, I am a magpie for information and utterly addicted to the podcast format. All of the podcasts referenced in this book are 100 percent real—and absolutely fascinating. I've included a list of those referenced below.

And *finally* finally, I need to thank my readers, without whom this series would not be able to continue. I'm so delighted that you keep coming back to Pine Hollow with me.

PODCASTS BIBLIOGRAPHY

The grandma benches in Zimbabwe (a concept I fell in love with the first time I heard about it) are from NPR's *TED Radio Hour* podcast episode "Erasing the Stigma," specifically the section with Dixon Chibanda titled "How Can a Team of Grandmothers Make Therapy Accessible to All?"

The synthesized happiness podcast Elinor references multiple times is also a *TED Radio Hour* episode, "Simply Happy," namely the section with Professor Dan Gilbert titled "How Does Misfortune Affect Long-Term Happiness?"

Elinor's infamous love podcast is another *TED Radio Hour* keeper episode, "In & Out of Love," specifically the section with Mandy Len Catron titled "Can You Jumpstart Love?"

I didn't want to call out a specific podcasting agent as being the one who had quickly rejected Elinor, but I figured, as an aspiring YA author, she would be a big fan of both the *KT Literary Podcast* and *Literaticast*.

Levi would have listened to several podcasts on rejection, including the episode "Five Ways to Handle Rejection in Publishing" by *The Gatecrashers Podcast*.

And finally, when Elinor discussed appreciation, she was referencing the "Approaching with Kindness" episode of the *TED Radio Hour*.

About the Author

A lifelong movie lover and book nerd, Lizzie Shane graduated from Northwestern University and headed off to forge her way in the entertainment industry—an attempt that lasted about five seconds. Following her brief jaunt into showbiz, Lizzie traveled extensively while pursuing her other great love—writing romance novels—and has now written her way through all fifty states and over fifty countries. Lizzie is a three-time finalist for RWA's RITA® Award and also writes for Hallmark Publishing, but her favorite claim to fame is that she lost on *Jeopardy!*

She is currently based in Alaska and can be found on Facebook, Twitter, or Instagram gushing about her favorite books...and her favorite dogs.

Learn more at:

LizzieShane.com

Twitter @LizzieShaneAK

Facebook.com/LizzieShaneAuthor

Instagram @LizzieShaneAK

Keep reading for the bonus novella
I'll Be Home for Christmas
by Hope Ramsay.

After ignoring the advice of Miz Miriam
Randall, local matchmaker, Annie
Roberts expects another humdrum
holiday in Last Chance, South Carolina.
But when a stray cat arrives in the arms
of Army sergeant Matt Jasper, a calico
named Holly just may be the best
matchmaker of all.

FOREVER

I'll Be Home for Christmas

♥

Baby Jesus wailed loud enough to be heard in the next county. His floodlit manger rocked back and forth while a group of gaily painted plaster wisemen looked on. Staff Sergeant Matt Jasper took a few hesitant steps toward the crèche and wondered if PTSD had finally found him. He peeked into the wobbling manger.

A pair of golden eyes stared back.

He let go of the breath he'd been holding. It was a cat, not a baby. Thank goodness. He knew how to handle a cat. A baby would have scared him silly.

"What're you doing in there with Jesus?" he said as he scooped up the animal and cradled it against his chest. It sank its claws into the fabric of his combat uniform and ducked its head under his chin.

It started to purr, its body shaking with the effort.

He looked down at the animal. The markings on its face weren't quite symmetrical—a little patch of brown fur by its white nose made its face look dirty. The cat stared back at him as if it could see things beyond Matt's vision.

Then it let go of its claws and settled down into his big hands as if it believed it had found a permanent home.

Stupid cat. It should know better than to settle on him. He didn't have a permanent home. He was as much a stray as the animal in his hands.

He didn't need a cat right now.

He just needed to deliver Nick's present—the last one he'd bought for his grandmother. And once Matt finished that errand, he could think about the future—preferably without any animals in it.

Annie Roberts sang the closing lyrics to "Watchman, Tell Us of the Night," her solo scheduled for tomorrow night's Christmas Eve service. Dale Pontius, the Christ Church choir director, sat in the back pew listening and nodding his head.

Pride rushed through her. She had a very good singing voice, and she loved this particular carol. She was looking forward to singing it for everyone at tomorrow night's services. Singing on Christmas Eve was one of Annie's greatest joys. She'd been singing in the Christ Church choir since she'd returned home from college, almost fifteen years before.

Just as the closing notes of the guitar accompaniment faded, a soldier in fatigues with a big pack on his back entered the sanctuary through the front doors. He strolled down the center aisle a few steps, the sound of his boot heels echoing. He stared up at the choir and Annie in particular.

He had forgotten to take off his dark beret, and a shadow of day-old beard colored his cheeks. He looked hard and worn around the edges.

"Who the dickens are you?" Dale said from his place in the back pew.

The soldier looked over one broad shoulder. "I'm Staff Sergeant Matt Jasper, sir," he said in a deep voice. "I was wondering if anyone had lost a cat. And also I need some directions."

It was only then that Annie noticed the ball of orange, white, and brown fur resting in Sergeant Jasper's hands.

"Good heavens, get that mangy thing out of here. I'm allergic." Dale stood up and gestured toward the door.

Millie Polk, standing behind Annie in the alto section, whispered, *sotto voce*, "Maybe he'll have a sneezing fit, and we'll all get to go home to our gift wrapping and cooking."

This elicited several chortles of laughter from the vicinity of the sopranos. Annie loved choir practice, but she had to admit that Dale was a real taskmaster this time of year. And, like Millie Polk, she had a long list of Christmas errands she needed to get done before tomorrow afternoon.

"You think a cat in this sanctuary is funny?" Dale said, turning toward the soprano section. "Did ya'll have any idea how lacking your performance of the 'Hallelujah Chorus' was this evening? There is nothing funny about this situation."

Dale turned toward the soldier. "I am very grateful for your service to the country, but this is a closed rehearsal. I would appreciate it if you would leave and take the cat with you."

It was almost comical the way Dale managed to stare down his nose while simultaneously looking up at the sergeant holding the kitten. The situation was sort of like a Chihuahua playing alpha dog to an adorable collie.

Matt Jasper wasn't intimidated by Dale though. He simply stared down at the choir director out of a pair of dark, almost black eyes. His eyebrows waggled. "Sorry to bust up your choir practice, sir, but I found this cat in your manger. If I hadn't picked it up, it probably would have broken your Baby Jesus. So I figure the cat's yours. I need to get going. I've got an errand to run, and I—"

"Well, it's not *my* cat." Dale turned to the choir. "Did any of you bring your cat to choir practice?" There was no mistaking the scorn in Dale's voice.

The choir got really quiet. Nobody liked it when Dale lost his temper.

"See? The cat doesn't belong to anyone." Dale gazed at the bundle of fur in the soldier's hands and sniffed. "It's probably a stray. Why don't you leave it outside and get on with your errand?"

"He can't do that," Annie said, and then immediately regretted her words. She did not *want* a cat, no matter how lonely she felt sometimes.

On the other hand, she wasn't going to stand by and let Dale Pontius and Sergeant Jasper drop a stray in the churchyard and walk away. That was inhumane.

Dale turned toward Annie, his displeasure evident in his scowl. Dale could be a tyrant. She should keep her mouth shut. But for some reason, the little bundle of fur in the big soldier's hands made her brave. "It's cold outside. It's supposed to rain."

She pulled her gaze away from Dale and gave the soldier the stink eye. She wasn't intimidated by that uniform or his broad shoulders. He needed to know that she frowned on people leaving stray cats in the neighborhood.

Jasper's full mouth twitched a little at the corner. "Ma'am," he said, "you can rest easy. I'm not going to leave it outside to wander. I'd like to find it a good home." His gaze never wavered. His eyes were deep and dark and sad, like a puppy dog's eyes.

She didn't need a puppy either.

The cat issued a big, loud meow that reverberated in the empty sanctuary. The church's amazing acoustic qualities magnified the meow to monumental proportions.

"Get that thing out of here." Dale was working himself into a tizzy.

"Uh, look," the soldier said, "can anyone here tell me where I might find Ruth Clausen? I went to what I thought was her address, but the house is all boarded up."

The choir shifted uneasily. "Ruth's in a nursing home," Annie said.

The soldier's thick eyebrows almost met in the middle when he frowned. "In a nursing home?"

"Yes, she's very old and quite ill," Dale said. "Now, if you don't mind, I have a choir practice to get on with." Dale strode past the man in the aisle and back to the front of the church.

"That was very nice, Annie, Clay." Dale turned toward Clay Rhodes, the choir's main instrumentalist. "I'd like one more run-through on the Handel."

Annie resumed her place with the altos, and Clay put his guitar in its stand and took his place at the organ. He flipped through a few pages of music and began the opening chords of the "Hallelujah Chorus."

Annie sang her part and watched as the cat-packing soldier ignored Dale's request and took a seat in the back pew. Halfway through the choir's performance, Sergeant Jasper must have remembered that he was in a church, because he finally took off his beret. His hair was salt-and-pepper and cut military short.

For some reason, Annie couldn't keep her eyes off him. She wondered if he might have been one of Nick's friends.

It seemed likely, since he'd come in here asking after Ruth, Nick's grandmother. She didn't want to be the one to tell him that he'd come on a fool's errand.

Matt settled back in the pew and listened to the music. This little town was way in the boonies, but the choir sounded pretty good. Not that he was a student of religious Christmas music. Matt had never been to church on Christmas. In fact, he'd pretty much never been to church in his life.

Not like Nick Clausen. If Nick's stories were to be believed, his folks had practically lived at church.

That's why Matt had come here to the church after he'd discovered that Ruth's house was boarded up. He'd known that someone at this church would know where to find Nick's grandmother.

Just like he'd known that the altar would have big bunches of poinsettias all over it, and the stained-glass window would have a picture of Jesus up on his cross.

It struck him, sitting there, that Nick had gone to Sunday school here. Nick had been confirmed here. He'd come here on Christmas Eve.

Matt took a deep breath. Boy, Nick sure had loved Christmas. Matt could kind of understand it, too, listening to the choir.

Matt's Christmases had been spent in a crummy apartment in Chicago while his mother and father got drunk.

He closed his eyes and let the music carry him away from those memories. He'd gotten over his childhood. He'd found a home in the army. He'd made something of himself.

He buried his fingers in the stray's soft fur. It licked his hand with a rough tongue.

He needed to find the local animal shelter, followed by the nursing home. Then he planned to get the hell out of Dodge before the urge to stay overwhelmed him. Because a guy like him didn't belong in a place like this. This was Nick's place, not his.

The music ended, and the choir director finally let everyone go. Matt stood up and slung his pack over his shoulder. Maybe the brown-haired woman with the amazing voice could help him. He'd heard her singing from out on the lawn, after the cat had stopped howling. The sound had called to him, and he'd followed it right into the church.

The choir members seemed thrilled to be dismissed. Probably because the choir director was a jerk, and they had shopping, and cooking, and a lot of other holiday crap to do. People in Last Chance would be busy like that, cooking big meals, wrapping presents, decorating trees, and stuff.

He found the brown-haired woman who'd spoken up in the cat's defense. "Ma'am, I was wondering, could you help me, please?"

She was shrugging into a big dark coat that had a sparkly Christmas tree pin on its collar. She gazed at him out of a pair of dark blue eyes. She had very pale skin, a long nose, and a thin face.

"I'm not taking your cat," she said in a defensive voice. "But if you're looking for Ruth, she's in the Golden Years Nursing Home up in Orangeburg."

He frowned. "Where's that?"

"You're not from around here, are you?"

"No, ma'am. I'm originally from Chicago. Since I joined up, I'm from wherever they station me." Except, of course, that wasn't true anymore. He hadn't re-upped this time, and he had nowhere permanent to go. He'd come to deliver Nick's present, and then he had some vague plans for spending New Year's on a beach somewhere—maybe Miami.

"Well, Orangeburg is about twenty miles north of here. But I need to warn you, Ruth's been in the nursing home for the last year, and she's pretty ill. I know because I work for her doctor."

"I see."

"Are you a friend of Nick's?" she asked.

He smiled. "Yes. Did you know him too?"

"I went to high school with him. I had a bit of a crush on him." She blushed when she said it.

"And you are?"

"I'm Annie Roberts."

He blinked and almost said *I know you*. But of course he didn't know Annie, except from the things Nick had told him. Annie had been Nick's girlfriend in high school. They had broken up the night of their senior prom.

"You studied nursing at the University of Michigan," he said.

"How did you—Oh, Nick told you that, didn't he?"

He grinned. "He told me you were looking forward to going someplace where it snows."

She frowned at him. "Why are you here? Nick died more than a year ago."

"I know. I was with him when it happened."

"Oh."

He shouldn't have said that. People always got that look on their faces when he spoke about this crap. No one back home really understood.

She squared her shoulders. "I'm so sorry. Are you a member of the Army Engineers K-9 team too?"

He continued to stroke the cat. "I was. As of yesterday, I'm officially a civilian."

The words came out easy. It took everything he had to hide the emotions behind them.

"And you came here? Right before Christmas? Don't you have a family someplace?"

He shrugged. "I have Nick's last Christmas present—you know, the one he intended to send home to his grand-mother. I need to deliver it."

Her gaze pierced him for a moment. It was almost as if she could read all of his thoughts and emotions. A muscle ticked in her cheek, and she seemed to be weighing some-thing in her mind.

She must have decided that he wasn't a threat because she let go of a long breath and gave the kitten a little stroke. "Poor thing. She looks half starved."

"How do you know it's a female?"

"How do you know it's not?"

He shifted the animal so he could actually inspect it. "Well, you were right. It's a girl. Means she'll have to be fixed. Is there an animal shelter somewhere?"

"Yes. In Allenberg. But it's probably closed."

His frustration with the situation mounted. "Uh, look, Annie, I just got in on the bus from Charlotte. I don't have a car. And now I need to find a home for this kitten, as well as a place to stay for the night. It's probably too late to go visiting at a nursing home twenty miles away."

She buttoned up her coat. "Boy, you're in a fix, aren't you?"

"Is there a hotel somewhere?"

Her cheeks colored just the slightest bit. "Well, the only

place in town is the Peach Blossom Motor Court. They would probably allow you to keep the cat."

"I've heard about the Peach Blossom Motor Court," he blurted and then remembered the story. "Oh, crap. That was stupid."

Annie's cheeks reddened further. "I guess guys in the army have nothing better to do than talk."

"Yes, ma'am. And believe me, being in the army can be really boring at times. Guys talk about home all the time. I'm sorry. I should have kept my mouth shut."

"Don't be sorry. What happened between me and Nick the night of senior prom happened almost twenty years ago."

"I guess he never told you about me, did he?" Matt asked.

She shook her head. "Why would he? He and I parted ways that night. He went off to join the army and see the world. I went off to college to see the snow. I guess I saw him that Christmas right after he went through basic training, but I wasn't speaking with him at the time." She hugged herself, and Matt noticed that she wasn't wearing a wedding ring.

So the girl Nick had never forgotten was unmarried.

She gave him a smile that didn't show any teeth. A few lines bunched at the corner of her eyes. She wasn't young. But she was pretty.

And Matt knew that she was sweet. He had a lot of Nick's stories filed away in his head. Nick had been a real good storyteller when things got slow.

Annie studied the cat sleeping in his hands and then nodded her head as if she'd come to a decision. "Look, you can't stay at the Peach Blossom. It probably has bedbugs. It's just an awful place. So you might as well come on home with me. I've got a perfectly fine guest room where you can sleep, and in the morning, we can figure something out. I'm sure I can find someone to run you up to Orangeburg, or I can do it myself."

"How about a friend who wants to adopt Fluffy?" He held up the cat in his hands.

"Fluffy?" She gave him a funny look. "That is a stupid name for a cat."

"Why? She's kind of fluffy."

"Yeah, but everyone names their cat Fluffy. There must be five Fluffys living here in Last Chance, and they all belong to single women. Please don't name the cat Fluffy."

"Okay, I won't," Matt said. "I thought you didn't care about this cat."

"Well, no, but you found it in a manger a couple days before Christmas, didn't you?"

"Yeah."

"Well, then, it needs a better name than Fluffy. Something holiday-related, like Noel."

He looked down at the slightly scruffy kitten. "That's a pretty pretentious name for this particular cat, don't you think? Of course, if you were going to adopt it, you could name it anything you wanted."

She scowled at him. "I'm not adopting any cats, understand?"

"Yes, ma'am."

Annie should have her head examined. She could almost hear Mother's voice outlining all the reasons she should send Sergeant Matt Jasper off to the Peach Blossom Motor Court. Mother would start with the fact that he was male, and then move right on to the worry that he was secretly either a pervert or an ax murderer.

Mother had trust issues.

But Annie could not, for the life of her, believe that a man with Matt's warm, dark eyes was either a pervert or a murderer. And besides, he knew how to handle the cat. His hands were big and gentle. And that uniform seemed to be tailor made for him.

She led him down the aisle and out the door and into the blustery December evening.

"Feels like snow," he said.

She laughed. "I don't think so. We don't ever get snow here."

"It seems like you should." They headed across Palmetto Avenue and down Julia Street.

"Snow in South Carolina? Not happening."

He shifted the cat in his arms. "Nick used to talk about Christmas in Last Chance all the time. I always kind of imagined the place with a dusting of snow."

She snorted. "Nick sure could tell stories. But I can only remember one year when we got a dusting of snow. It was pitiful by snow standards. And it didn't last very long."

"Well, I'm from Chicago, you know."

"So I reckon ya'll have snow on the ground at Christmas all the time."

"Yeah. But in the city it doesn't take very long for the snow to get dirty and gray. I always kind of imagined Last Chance covered in pristine white."

"Well, that's a fantasy." She reached her mother's house on Oak Street. The old place needed a coat of paint, and a few of the porch balusters needed replacing. Annie ought to sell the place and move to Orangeburg or Columbia. A registered nurse could get a job just about anywhere these days. And her social life might improve if she moved to a bigger town.

But she'd have to leave home. She'd have to leave friends. She'd have to leave the choir and the book club, not to mention Doc Cooper and the clinic.

No wonder Miriam Randall had told her to get a cat. If she wanted to deal with her loneliness in Last Chance, a cat was probably her best bet.

She pushed open the door and hit the switch for the hall and porch lights. Her Christmas lights—the same strand of large-bulbed lights that Mother had used for decades—blinked on.

"Oh," Matt said. It was less than a word and more than an exhalation.

"I'm afraid it's not much of a display. Nothing like the lights the Canadays put out every year."

She looked over her shoulder. Matt was smiling, the lights twinkling merrily in his eyes. A strange heat flowed through Annie that she recognized as attraction.

Boy, she was really pathetic, wasn't she?

She shucked out of her coat and hung it on one of the pegs by the door.

"It smells wonderful in here," Matt said. He strolled past her into the front parlor. His presence filled up the space and made the large room seem smaller by half. He made a full three-sixty, inspecting everything, from the old upright piano to Grandmother's ancient mohair furniture.

Crap. Her house look like it belonged to a little old lady. Which, in fact, it had, until last spring, when Mother died. Suddenly the cabbage rose wallpaper and the thread-bare carpet made Annie feel like a spinster. The cat would complete the picture.

Matt stopped and cocked his head. "You have a tree."

"Of course I have a tree. Mother would—" She cut herself off. The last thing Matt wanted to hear about was what Mother expected out of Christmas. This year, Annie planned to make a few changes.

But she'd still put out Mother's old Christmas lights. And she had still bought a Douglas fir instead of a blue spruce.

And she'd made the annual climb up to the attic for the ornaments. But when she'd gotten the boxes down to the front parlor, she'd lost the will to decorate. One look at her mother's faded decorations, and she'd felt like her life was in a big rut.

She'd done the unthinkable—she'd carried all those old boxes right back up to the attic. If she'd been a braver woman, she would have carried them to the curb for the trashman.

Of course, she hadn't done one thing about replacements. She had been putting all of that off. And suddenly she realized that if she was going to take Matt up to Orangeburg tomorrow to visit Ruth, and still host a party for her friends from the book club, she was going to have to get her fanny in gear.

Matt pulled in a deep breath, drinking in the Christmas tree aroma. He squeezed his eyes closed and could almost hear Nick's voice, talking about how he'd helped his grandmother trim her tree.

Annie's tree was naked.

He put the cat down on the carpet. She darted under the sofa, where she crouched, looking up at him as if he'd abandoned her.

Stupid cat. She should realize that she had found a

better home than he could provide. Annie's house was like something out of a picture postcard. If Matt had had a grandmother, this is precisely the way he'd want her house to look.

Matt had a feeling that Nick's grandma's house had been like this too.

He turned back toward Annie. She looked like a picture postcard too. Like Mom and apple pie. Like home.

"So," he said on a deep breath, "your tree needs help, Annie Roberts."

She gave him a bashful smile. "I guess it does."

"I'm willing to work for my room and board. Just point me in the direction of the lights."

She laughed. "Everything is up in the attic. Wait a sec, and I'll go get the boxes."

She scurried away up the stairs in the main hall, and he amused himself watching her shapely backside, clad in a pair of blue jeans, as she climbed to the second story.

Oh yeah, Annie Roberts was more than pretty. She was built. He could understand why Nick had had trouble forgetting her.

"No, cat!" Annie tried to pull the feline away from the string of lights that Matt was hanging on the tree.

"Maybe we should call her Pouncy," he said with a deep, rumbling laugh.

He stood rock steady on the stepladder. He'd taken off his army jacket and wore only a tan-colored T-shirt that hugged his torso. He looked fit.

Okay, she was understating the fact. Matt looked gorgeous, and ripped, and competent, standing there hanging tree lights.

The cat, on the other hand, looked like a menace on four feet. The kitten had gotten over her fear of the new environment and had decided that the Christmas tree and anything associated with it was her personal play toy.

Matt was no good at discouraging her either. He kept tugging on the string of lights, making them move suddenly in a way that the cat found irresistible. The kitten pounced ferociously on them and then backed up and pounced again.

The cat was growing on Annie.

But not as much as the man.

"So, you said you have a Christmas gift for Ruth?" she asked, purposefully raising the specter of Nick. She really needed to remember that Matt had come to do something that was going to make Ruth unspeakably sad. And then he would go away, just like Nick had done. Best to keep her distance.

"Yeah. Nick bought it for her a year and a half ago."

"What is it?"

"I have no idea. I don't even know where he bought it. I just know that I found it with his stuff after he died. I took it before the CO could lay his hands on it. Not exactly regulation, I know, but I kept thinking about Ruth getting Nick's effects and finding it there. I thought it would be really crummy to get a gift and not have Nick there, you know? I thought it would be better to bring it myself."

She studied him for a very long time. He was a pretty sensitive guy for a soldier. Her opinion of him rose a little more. "You waited a long time."

He finished putting the lights on the tree and stepped down from the stepladder. "I was in Afghanistan. It was a long deployment."

Annie unwrapped the angel that Mother always put on the top of the tree. The angel wore yellow velvet with gold trim, and her halo had been broken years and years ago. She handed the tree topper to Matt, and their fingers touched. Heat flooded through her, and the look of longing in Matt's eyes told her that the reaction was mutual. Matt let go of a big breath, as if he'd been holding something inside. They stood there for the longest moment, their fingers touching across the angel. Eventually Annie let go, and Matt turned, stepped up the ladder, and put the angel in her place.

For some reason, the angel, even with her bent wings and broken halo, looked beautiful up there. Once, a long time ago, Annie had thought the angel was the most beautiful Christmas ornament ever. How had she forgotten that?

Matt turned back toward her, his eyes filled with joy. "I love doing this," he said. "I haven't had much experience trimming trees. My folks used to put a little fake tree on the kitchen table when I was a kid. We always lived in a pretty small apartment."

Annie turned away, suddenly overcome by emotions she couldn't name. Who was this stranger who had walked into her house with a cat and a heaping dose of holiday spirit?

He was the man who'd come to give Ruth a present she didn't need or want.

But Annie could hardly explain that to Matt, could she? He'd come here first thing after the army let him go. Like delivering his gift was a kind of obligation.

She held her tongue and picked up a cardboard box filled with slightly tarnished glass balls. "Here, make yourself busy."

He took the box and immediately set to work. She

362 Hope Ramsay

watched him for the longest moment before she said, "You know, Ruth isn't in her right mind."

He stopped. Turned. "No?"

Annie shook her head. "Hasn't been since those army men came to her door with the news."

He pressed his lips together. "I'm sorry."

"What do you have to be sorry about? It's just the way it is. She's been in a nursing home for more than a year. And according to what I heard from Doc Cooper, she's not expected to live past New Year's. She's got congestive heart failure. It's only a matter of time. But, you know, she's alone now and almost ninety."

He startled. His hands reflexively squeezed the box of ornaments.

Annie stood up. "Can I get you something? A cup of coffee? Some hot chocolate?"

He stood there, looking a little confused, his eyebrows cocked at a funny angle. "Uh, yeah. Some hot chocolate would be great."

What was he doing here? He looked up at the little angel atop the tree. She didn't seem to have an answer.

Just then the cat attacked his bootlace. He bent down and picked Pouncy up.

Annie was right. Pouncy was a stupid name. One day the kitten would grow up and quit pouncing on everything in sight.

He cuddled her closer and sat in the big armchair facing the front window. The lights on the tree looked festive. The cat curled up in his lap.

"Poor little stray, born out of season. Were you abandoned?" he asked the cat.

The cat only purred in response.

He let go of a long sigh. He wondered what was in that gaily wrapped package at the bottom of his knapsack. Maybe it would be better if he left town tomorrow and didn't bother.

"Here you go." Annie came into the room bearing a tray and a bright smile. "Hot chocolate, made with real milk."

She bent over to put the tray down on the coffee table, giving Matt a great view of her backside. Unwanted desire tugged at him with a vengeance.

He shouldn't be getting the hots for Nick's old high school flame. Even if she and Nick had broken up twenty years ago. It seemed forbidden somehow.

And yet attraction was there as clear as a bell. Annie was everything Nick had said she was, and more. And her home was...

Well, he didn't want to delve too deeply into that. Especially since he felt like he'd walked right into one of Nick's Christmas stories.

Annie handed him a cup of chocolate, their fingers touched again, and the heat curled up in his chest.

He took the mug from her and lifted it to his mouth. The chocolate was warm and rich and sweet. A lot like the woman who had made it.

She turned away and put her hands on her hips. "We still have a lot of work to do."

She picked up another box of ornaments and began digging through tissue. "These are my mother's birds," she said.

She pulled out a delicate red glass bird and clipped it to a branch.

"I take it your mother is gone?" he asked.

She nodded, her shoulders stiff. "Yeah, she died last spring. This is my first Christmas without her."

"I'm sorry."

"Well, she's in a happier place. She was always sick, and she missed my father." Annie stopped and turned and gave him a very serious stare. "Sort of like Ruth these last few years."

"You think I shouldn't deliver my present?"

"Depends on the reason you want to deliver it."

Before he could answer, the kitten got up and stretched, then bounded off Matt's lap. It pranced over to a box laden with decorations and dived right into it. Pouncy stalked and jumped and pussyfooted while Matt and Annie watched her and laughed.

Finally she lifted her "dirty" face over the lip of the cardboard as she ferociously batted at the red ribbon she'd managed to entangle herself in.

"I think we should name you Holly," Annie said on a laugh.

"Holly's a good name for a cat that was found two days before Christmas," Matt agreed.

Annie turned her head, and they gazed at each other for the longest moment. She finally blushed, and an answering heat rose like a column right through him. He stood up, drawn to her by some force he didn't quite understand. "Annie Roberts," he said, "I feel like I've known you all my life."

She blinked at him. "Uh. That's not possible. It's probably just because Nick talked about me."

"Maybe, but that's not quite it. Do you believe in love at first sight?"

She blanched. "No. No, I don't." She turned a suddenly

nervous gaze on the kitten who had curled up under the coffee table.

She stepped back toward the hallway. "Uh, I'm going to go check the guest bedroom—make sure the bed in there has clean sheets."

She turned and escaped.

Matt stood by the tree watching her run.

Boy, he was an idiot. He should have kept his feelings inside. He glanced around the room, filled with Christmas decorations that had been carefully handed down through the generations.

Annie was like Nick. She had traditions and a place where she fit. Matt wanted all that. He could tell himself he'd come to deliver a Christmas gift, but that would be a lie.

He'd come to Last Chance in the hope that Ruth might invite him in and give him a taste of what Nick had known growing up. The truth was, Matt envied Nick's childhood.

But Matt was just a stray, like the cat. And Annie had made it clear that she wasn't interested in taking in any strays.

Christmas Eve day dawned gray. Annie awakened just before seven. She snuggled down under the covers and listened to the rain pinging against the tin roof.

She didn't realize she had company until Holly pranced across Grandmother's quilt, her little claws pulling at the fabric. Annie started to scold and then held her tongue.

The old quilt was nearly a rag anyway. She slept under it only as a matter of habit. For months now, she'd been telling herself that she'd make a run down to Target and buy herself something new.

Why had she been putting that off? Why hadn't she gone down to Target earlier in the week and purchased new ornaments for the tree?

Why had she run away from Matt last night?

The kitten wormed its body up against her chest, curled itself into a little ball, and started to purr.

If she was going to keep it, she'd need to get a litter box. She stopped herself in midthought.

She was not keeping this cat. No matter what. The cat was like an emblem for everything that was wrong in her life. If she took responsibility for a cat, like she'd taken responsibility for Mother all those years ago, how was she ever going to escape and find her own life?

She was getting old. She wanted children. She wanted a family of her own—someone she could hand the old ornaments off to. But if she accepted that cat, she was accepting the end of that dream.

No way. She pushed the cat aside. It didn't get the message. It came right back at her, cute as a button and looking for love.

Matt looked up from his cup of coffee as Annie stepped into the kitchen. She looked like something out of a Christmas movie in a red-and-white snowflake sweater, her hair in a ponytail with a red ribbon.

"Thanks for all your help last night," she said as she leaned in the kitchen doorway. "I just checked in with the nursing home. They open for nonfamily visiting hours at ten a.m. I've got an early appointment at the beauty shop, and after that, I can run you up to Orangeburg. I've got some last-minute shopping to do; then I have to get back here to cook before my friends arrive for Christmas Eve dinner."

"I've been an imposition, haven't I?"

"No, it's all right." She seemed so nervous with her arms

crossed over her breasts, as if she were trying to shield herself from him.

He came to the decision he'd been mulling over for most of the night. "Look, I've been thinking about what you said last night, about Ruth's present."

"Oh? What did I say? I don't remember saying anything in particular."

"You asked me why I wanted to deliver a present that's probably going to make her very sad."

"I asked that? I mean, I think you should think about what you're doing. After all, Ruth is ill and she's not entirely with it, you know."

"Okay, maybe you didn't. But it's still a good question, isn't it? I've been trying to decide why I wanted to come here and deliver that stupid gift. And, well, the thing is, I'm not sure I came here for the right reasons."

"What do you think are the right reasons, Matt?" Her gaze seemed to focus on him, as if she really cared about his answer.

He shrugged. "When I took that present from out of Nick's effects, I told myself I was going to do his grandmother a favor. I thought it might be hard for her to get a Christmas present from a person who had died. I thought maybe I could come and say a couple of words to her, you know, about what a great buddy Nick had been."

"That seems like a good reason, Matt."

He nodded. "Yeah, but there was something else. I realized it last night while I was helping you with the tree."

"What?"

"The thing is, my Christmases as a kid were crummy. They sucked. But Nick used to talk about Christmas all the time. He used to tell stories about how his grandmother made a big roast with mashed potatoes. He used to talk about his parents kissing under the mistletoe, before they died." Matt's voice wavered, and he stopped and took a big breath.

"So you thought you'd come and experience that?" Annie said.

He turned away and looked out the window that opened on to the backyard. The window had lacy curtains, and outside the rain was pouring down.

"My dog died three weeks ago," he said in a voice that he could barely control. "They shipped me home, and because the dog died, they let me out a little early. I had already told them I wasn't going to re-up. Now I just want..." He shook his head and pressed his lips together.

"Oh, Matt, I'm so sorry. I didn't know."

Then he turned back toward Annie. "Losing the dog was hard. He wasn't killed in action. He just got sick and had to be put down. He was getting old anyway, and I had planned for the two of us to retire together. But now I'm alone. And being a soldier is the only thing I know how to be."

"Matt, every returning soldier has an adjustment period."

"I know. But I came here looking for Ruth. I thought maybe she would have some wisdom for me, or at least maybe a slice of her apple pie. God, Nick used to talk about that pie all the time, especially when we were stuck eating MREs. And then I found her house all boarded up, and I was lost. I went to the church because I knew she was a member there. To be honest, I heard the cat yowling, and Holly kind of led me right there."

"Really?"

He gave her a short nod. "And then I heard you sing-ing, and it was like, for an instant I felt like I'd...well, hell...I don't...like I'd come home. And that's ridiculous because I don't belong in Last Chance. I'm a street kid from Chicago."

She blinked down at him but didn't say a word.

"I've scared you again, haven't I?"

"No, it's more like I'm a little surprised. What was your dog's name?"

"Murphy. He had liver failure. He'd been a pretty hard worker for six years. He saved a whole lot of lives over there, sniffing out IEDs. He was a good, hardworking war dog." Matt swallowed before the emotion ate him up.

"I'm sure he was. You know, you should take Holly. She'd be a comfort to you."

He nodded and took a calming sip of his coffee. Annie really didn't want that cat, did she?

"So, uh," Annie said, "I have an early appointment at the Cut 'n' Curl. I won't be more than an hour at most." She turned on her heel and strode out of the room like she was trying to escape his toxic emotions.

Matt watched her go. He really needed to get a grip. He probably needed to put that stupid gift under Annie's tree and go see about taking a bus to someplace warm and sunny.

Annie's appointment at the Cut 'n' Curl was for nine in the morning, and even at that early hour several members of the Christ Church Ladies Auxiliary were already present and accounted for. It being both Saturday and Christmas Eve, Ruby Rhodes, Last Chance's main hairdresser, had opened up an hour early.

Thelma Hanks was having her roots touched up. Lessie Anderson was in Ruby's chair getting a wash and set, and Jane Rhodes, Ruby's new daughter-in-law, was giving Miriam Randall a manicure.

"Hey, Annie," Thelma Hanks said after Annie had hung her coat in the closet. Thelma had just looked up from one of those romance books Ruby kept on a shelf at the back of the shop. This particular book had a cover featuring a naked male torso.

"How are you doing, honey? Everything okay?" Thelma's voice was laden with concern. All the women in the shop stopped what they were doing and watched Annie as she sat down in one of the dryer chairs. "What?" she asked, flicking her gaze from one woman to another.

"We're just concerned, sugar," Ruby said.

Ruby and her customers had been Mother's friends. Mother had been an active member of the Auxiliary. She had a standing Wednesday appointment at the Cut 'n' Curl, so it was just natural that they would be worried about Annie this Christmastime.

It was her first Christmas alone. And everyone seemed to be working hard to make sure she didn't have a minute to be sad about it. She'd received invitations to Christmas Eve and Christmas Day dinner from Ruby, Lessie, Thelma, Miriam, and several of Mother's other friends. She had declined them all and had invited some of the members of the book club to dinner instead.

Mother had not fully approved of the book club. She was living in the last century and looked down her nose at Nita and Kaylee, because of their race. But Annie had always counted them as friends, even in the face of Mother's disapproval. And now Annie could invite whomever she wanted to dinner, without hearing Mother's ugly complaints.

"I'm fine," she said to the ladies in the beauty parlor. "I've got my tree all trimmed, and I'm going up to the Target in Orangeburg for some shopping this afternoon, and then Nita and Jenny and a few other friends from the book club are coming over for dinner before midnight services."

"I'm so glad to hear that," Ruby said, "what with Nita's daughter being off in Atlanta this year. It's nice the two of you are spending time together."

"So, honey, have you taken my advice yet?" Miriam asked from her place at the manicure station.

Everyone turned to stare at Miriam. Today the little old lady was dressed in a pair of red plaid slacks and a red sweatshirt with a big graphic of Rudolph on its front. She had a pair of dangly Christmas tree earrings in her ears. Her eyes twinkled behind her 1950s-style trifocals.

Miriam was about eighty-five years old and widely regarded as Allenberg County's premier matchmaker. Not that Miriam considered *herself* a matchmaker. She always told folks she was a match *finder*. She said God made the matches, but sometimes He would clue her in.

Her matchmaking advice sometimes resembled the messages you might find inside a fortune cookie. But the weird thing about Miriam's marital forecasts was that they almost always came true.

"I declare," Ruby said to Miriam, "when did you give Annie any advice?"

"Oh, I think it was last week after church."

"And what advice did you give Annie?" Thelma leaned forward, her romance book forgotten.

"I told her to get a cat."

"What?" Lessie turned her head, and the roller Ruby was trying to secure came undone.

"And I told her that I wasn't so lonely that I needed a cat." Annie folded her arms across her chest. "I need to get out and have a social life now that Mother's gone. I don't need a cat."

"Miriam," Ruby said, "you didn't really tell Annie she needed a cat, did you?"

"What's wrong with suggesting that she get a cat?" Miriam looked honestly surprised.

"Because you don't tell a single lady of a certain age that she needs a cat. It's, well . . . " Ruby's voice trailed off.

"It's pitiful," Annie said into the silence. "It's bad enough that I'm sleeping under a quilt my grandmother made and living in a house with old-fashioned mohair furniture. Getting a cat would be like sealing my fate."

"Yes, exactly," Miriam said.

Ruby, Lessie, and Thelma stared at Miriam as if she'd lost her mind. Miriam was a little quirky, but she'd never been mean.

Jane pulled Miriam's hand out of the soaking solution and said, "Clay said something about a big soldier finding a cat in the manger down at the church last night. This guy came strolling into the sanctuary with a little kitten, interrupting choir practice, and Dale almost had a stroke."

"Really?" Miriam asked. Somehow Miriam didn't sound very surprised.

Everyone turned toward Annie. Her face flamed. "His name is Matt Jasper, and he did find a cat in the manger. He came in on the bus from Charlotte last night, and he was looking for Ruth Clausen."

"Oh dear," Ruby said. "Is he one of Nick's army friends?"

"Yes, he is. He's come here to deliver Nick's last Christmas gift."

"What?" the women asked in unison.

"Evidently, Nick bought Ruth's present before he died last year. Matt has been carrying it around Afghanistan for a long time."

"Oh my," Thelma said. "He has no clue, does he?"

"No, he doesn't."

"Did you tell him about Ruth?" Thelma asked.

"Well, I told him that she'd been sick and a little out of it. But I didn't say anything else. He's committed to making this delivery. It's kind of sweet, actually. His heart's in the right place."

"So he didn't spend the night at the motel, did he?" Jane asked.

"Uh, no, he didn't."

Miriam snorted. "See, I told ya'll. Annie needed to get a cat. The Lord was very specific about that part."

While Annie went to her appointment at the beauty shop, Matt showered and shaved and put on his civvies. Holly kept him company, trailing after him like a little lost soul.

He and the cat were kind of alike. If anyone could understand how a man could come looking for a warm place by a holiday fire, it would be a stray cat.

But he didn't really belong by Annie's fire, did he? And what was the point of delivering Nick's gift to his grandmother if she was senile and sick? How could that possibly brighten her day?

He'd come for his own selfish reasons, not to do any favors for Nick. And now, here he was, staying at Annie Roberts's house, thinking things about her that he had no right to think.

He should leave, right now, and take the cat with him as

a consolation prize. He started packing his bag. He had just brought the bag downstairs and set it in the corner when Annie's key slipped into the front door.

She came prancing into the foyer like a young girl. She stopped just a few feet from where he was standing and gave him the biggest grin. She was red cheeked from the cold outside, and there was a spark of something in her eyes that hadn't been there last night or even this morning. Something had changed. She seemed lit up from the inside.

"Uh," he said, suddenly tongue-tied, "I was thinking that with Ruth so ill, it might be best if I just..." He couldn't finish the sentence.

Holly pussyfooted across the floorboards and meowed a welcome. She rubbed up against Annie's legs and tried to wrap herself around both of them simultaneously.

Annie laughed. The sound was so merry and full of life. She bent down and picked up the kitten. "You need some cat food and a litter box," she said to Holly. "I hope you're housebroken."

She glanced up at Matt, and he had a feeling Annie was talking about something other than the cat.

"I understand your hesitation about Ruth," she said, her blue eyes darkening with some emotion he couldn't quite fathom. "But there's no rush. The Ladies Auxiliary always visits up there on Christmas morning, and you could tag along with them. I offered to drive Miriam Randall and the rest of the ladies up there, since I don't have a big family. So, if you want, we can all go together tomorrow morning. In the meantime, if you came to Last Chance for a Christmas like Nick loved, you're free to stay here at my place. In fact, I could use some help with my errands."

The tension he'd felt all morning suddenly eased. He'd

been given permission to live out his deepest fantasy and let tomorrow slide. War had taught him the benefits of living in the moment. He didn't have to think very hard about her offer.

"I'd be happy to help. But I'm warning you, I'm really inexperienced in this whole Christmas thing."

"It's okay. There are plenty of people in Last Chance willing to give you pointers on how to celebrate the season."

Annie held out her hand, and he took it. It was small and warm, and it seemed to fit in his like it had been custom made.

They went to Orangeburg and practically bought out the Target there. Annie seemed to be hell-bent on taking advantage of every cut-rate deal on Christmas decorations. It being Christmas Eve, she made a few spectacular bargains—especially on a glow-from-the-inside snowman that had caught Matt's fancy. She had refused to let him buy it for her. She told him she needed to spruce up her lighting display before the neighbors complained about her lack of imagination.

She also bought some new sheets and a blanket—a move that made Matt just a little bit uncomfortable, since she asked his opinion on every choice. When he'd wrinkled his nose at the girly flowers on one set of sheets, she'd changed her mind about them.

Shopping for sheets with Annie was definitely sexier than it probably should be. He kept thinking about what it might be like to lie down on those new sheets with this amazing woman.

He needed to watch it. She had been Nick's girlfriend, and he was already perilously close to losing his grip on the real world.

♥

Annie was brimming over with good cheer. Her day with
Holly and Matt had been so happy. But then she could
hardly fail. Miriam Randall hadn't been speaking literally
last week in church. She'd been finding Annie a match.

And Annie couldn't be more pleased with the way things
were going. Matt was tall, dark, and handsome. He was
kind, and he seemed to understand the inherent problem
associated with his grim chore. And yet she got the feeling
he still wanted to deliver that present, even if he wondered
whether it was the right thing to do. His conflict made
him all the more loveable. And she knew she was falling
for him. Maybe she did believe in love at first sight
after all.

When they got home from shopping, she put him to
work finishing the decorating and setting up the big glow-
in-the-dark snowman they had purchased.

The snowman was silly and a little tacky. But it reminded
her of the few years she'd spent in Michigan at college.
Those had been happy years, before Mother had come down
with rheumatoid arthritis. Before Dad had died. Before
her future had been hijacked by circumstances beyond her
control.

Matt had fallen in love with the snowman too. He said if
he couldn't have real snow in Last Chance, he'd go for the
fake kind.

Of course, Mother would never have approved of the
snowman, the cat, or the soldier, which made all of them
welcome additions to Annie's holiday. Nothing about this
Christmas was going to be like last year.

And having Matt around, lapping up all the holiday

cheer, made everything seem a little more joyful. He had so many reasons to be sad, having lost his dog this year and his best friend last year, but he seemed determined to let the joy of Christmas in. And his joy was infectious.

Nita Wills was the first member of the book club to arrive at Annie's dinner party, with Cathy close on her heels. Both of them seemed more impressed and surprised by the snowman than the cat or the soldier.

"Well, Annie," Nita said as she put a plate of gingerbread cookies on the buffet table, "it sure does look like Santa has been good to you this Christmas."

Annie didn't have a minute to respond before Elsie and Lola May arrived, followed very closely by Jenny Carpenter. Jenny, of course, came bearing apple and shepherd's pies. Jenny's pies were to die for, and Matt seemed more than a little interested in both of her offerings.

Annie stifled the strange, unwanted wave of jealousy. And she was soon busy playing hostess when Kaylee and Nomi arrived each bearing matching bean casseroles.

The women gathered around the buffet and filled their cups with eggnog and Christmas punch—two things Mother would never have allowed in her home at holiday time. They laughed and chatted about Barbara Kingsolver's latest book. All in all, the house hadn't seen so many people in years, and Annie was feeling happy and free and flushed with Christmas spirit.

Then Nita scooped Holly up from the easy chair and sat down. She held the kitten up for inspection. "Well, aren't you just the cutest, dirty-faced matchmaker in Last Chance?" she said aloud.

The women of the book club collectively laughed, and Annie felt suddenly stripped naked. She glanced over at

Matt to see if he'd heard what Last Chance's librarian had said.

Apparently he had, because Nita hadn't used her librarian voice. Matt's dark stare zeroed in on Nita, and his eyebrows bunched up in the middle.

Elsie gave him a pat on the back. "Don't you mind Nita, now. She's just talking about how Miriam Randall told Annie that she needed to get a cat."

Matt's frown deepened.

"See," Cathy explained, "Miriam has a pipeline to the Lord, and when she gives advice, it's always right."

"Exactly," Lola May said. "And that just means that you and Annie are a match made in heaven."

Matt turned his dark gaze on Annie. Her heartbeat raced, but whether in embarrassment or desire she wasn't sure. It was insane to think that Matt was destined to become her lover, just because he'd found a cat in a manger.

But hadn't she been behaving like that all day?

"Uh, ladies, I think there's been some kind of misunderstanding," Matt said. "I just came here to deliver a gift to Ruth Clausen."

"And have you delivered it yet?" Nita asked.

Matt scratched the back of his head and glanced at Annie. "Uh, no. I kind of got involved with a bunch of errands. I'm going up to Orangeburg tomorrow for that chore."

Nita spoke again. "Do you think that's wise?"

"I don't know. But I've been lugging that thing all over Afghanistan. I think it needs to find its way home."

Nita nodded. "Well, I guess I can understand that. And I admire you for bringing it to Ruth personally. You didn't have to do that." She gazed at the kitten. "Well, one thing is for sure, this cat is cute," she said.

The members of the book club went back to chatting and grazing at the buffet.

Matt strolled over to where Annie was standing, his dark eyes filled with emotions that weren't very merry.

"I can explain about the matchmaker," she said. "See—"

"I know all about Miriam Randall," he murmured.

"What?"

"Nick told me all about her. He seemed to think she was infallible. He told me once that he was very sorry Miriam hadn't matched him up permanently with you. You should know that Nick really regretted what happened between the two of you."

"He wanted to be a soldier. He wanted to leave this town, Matt. That's all he ever talked about. And I wasn't sure I wanted to be in love with a soldier or a man with wanderlust in his soul."

"I know all about what happened. I know how you guys fought that night at the motel. I know how he walked away in a huff. He told me everything."

"He told you all that?"

"He told me a lot of things. You talk about things when you're getting shot at. And God knows, we got shot at a lot when we were in Baghdad on our first deployment. You were the girl he never forgot, Annie. You're the girl he regretted. The one he missed. He never married, you know."

They stared at each other for a long emotion-filled moment; then he leaned in to kiss her on the cheek. She saw what was coming and turned her head to meet his lips. It was a pretty brazen thing to do, given the fact that Matt had been talking about how Nick had loved her. But Nick had walked away twenty years ago and never come back.

Annie tried, for all she was worth, to take the kiss a little deeper, but Matt pulled back. He looked up. "So, ah, that's what mistletoe is all about, huh?"

Annie followed his gaze. Sure enough they were standing under a sprig of the stuff. Disappointment swallowed up her Christmas merriment.

"Sorry, I couldn't resist," he said in a voice loud enough for everyone in the room to hear, "seeing as you were standing there under the mistletoe."

"Do you remember what you said last night?" she whispered.

"Yeah, I remember. I was insane last night. I don't know what came over me." He let go of a long breath and turned to look at her mother's parlor, filled with the members of the book club. "I don't belong here. This is Nick's place, not mine."

"But—"

He turned and held up his hand. "I'm a guy from Chicago, Annie. And they don't have snow here. I'll probably go back to the Midwest and see if I can get a job as a dog handler someplace like Milwaukee or St. Louis. There isn't anything for me in Last Chance. I just came here because I wanted to see if Nick's stories were true. I wanted to meet his grandmother. So I'm going to go up there to the nursing home tomorrow. I'll pay my respects, deliver Nick's present, and be on my way."

"But—"

"Annie, I'm not your soul mate, no matter what Miriam Randall says. And don't you go mistaking me for Nick Clausen either. Because I'm not him. If you believe in what they say about Miriam, you should keep the cat. I'm guessing that there's a handsome veterinarian in your future."

Matt went to midnight services along with all the

members of the book club. He sat in the back of the church. He wasn't a believer. He was out of step with the people who came to celebrate the birth of Jesus that night.

The only thing that kept him in his place was the choir.

When they sang the "Hallelujah Chorus," Matt's skin prickled. But that reaction was nothing compared to what happened when Annie sang her solo, especially when she got to the last couple of lines.

> *Traveler, darkness takes its flight,*
> *Doubt and terror are withdrawn.*
> *Watchman, let thy wanderings cease;*
> *Hie thee to thy quiet home.*
> *Traveler, lo! the Prince of Peace,*
> *Lo! the Son of God is come!*

There seemed to be a message in that song, even for an unbeliever. He needed to firm his resolve, push his own needs aside, and visit Ruth tomorrow. Nick had wanted his grandmother to have a Christmas gift last year, and Matt had kept it from her. He needed to go and let her know just what a good friend Nick had been.

Early the next morning, after a night of very little sleep, Matt found himself in the Christ Church van, sandwiched between Miriam Randall and another, equally ancient church lady. Making good on her promises, as Matt suspected she always did, Annie took the wheel of the van and drove everyone up to Orangeburg.

The church ladies came laden down with gifts like the wisemen. They carried cookies and gingerbread and a bundle of quilts the size of pillowcases that they called prayer blankets. He was literally surrounded by a bevy of ancient angels of mercy.

Within an hour, he stood alone on the threshold of Ruth Clausen's room at the nursing home, holding a brightly wrapped shirt box in his hands. The box wasn't very heavy, nor did it rattle. It was surely something to wear—something Ruth Clausen, now consigned to this small room, didn't need anymore.

He stepped up to the bed. The old lady looked pale and tiny, her gray hair thin. She had an oxygen tube hooked over her ears. She seemed to be having trouble breathing.

"Ruth," Matt said gently.

She opened a pair of hazel eyes, the exact same color as Nick's. Man, staring into those eyes threw him for a loop. They seemed clear and aware and alive.

A little smile quivered at the corner of her lips. "Nicky, you're home," she said.

Matt opened his mouth to correct her. But just as he was about to speak, something came over him. He flashed on the sound of Annie's voice singing that carol from the night before. He said not one word.

Instead, he pulled up the chair and took Ruth's hand in his. Her skin was paper-thin, her hand cold. He rubbed it between his.

"I've missed you so much," Ruth said.

"Me too, but you didn't expect me to miss Christmas, did you?"

"Christmas?" Ruth's voice sounded frail and confused. Her eyes dulled a little.

"Yes, Grandma, it's Christmas. The best time of year. You remember that year when we had the snow?"

She nodded, and her lips quivered. "It wasn't really snow, Nicky, just a dusting."

"I made a snowman."

"It was three inches tall."

"It was still a snowman. Size is not that important, Grandma."

She laughed and squeezed his hand. "I love you, boy, you know that?"

"Yes, ma'am, I do," Matt said; then he launched into one of Nick's favorite Christmas stories that involved a dog named Gonzo and an apple pie that disappeared when no one was looking.

Ruth enjoyed that story, and the five other Christmas stories Matt told her as if they belonged to him.

At some point, just as Ruth was beginning to fade off into sleep, he became aware of someone behind him. He turned and found Annie and Miriam standing in the doorway of the room. He had no idea how long they had been there listening. Both of them had tears in their eyes.

"So," Miriam whispered, "you going to give her that present or not?"

Matt realized that he hadn't said a word about Nick's present. It still rested on his lap.

Suddenly the present seemed kind of stupid. Ruth didn't need or want a present like this. All Ruth wanted for Christmas was Nick. And in a way Nick lived on, in the stories he'd told when the bullets had been flying or the boredom had set in. Matt knew them all by heart.

He couldn't bear to look at Annie or Miriam because his own eyes were overflowing with the tears he'd been holding back for a long, long time.

Annie strode into the room, bent over, and put her arms

around his shoulders. Her hair spilled over him like a veil. "You're staying, of course," she murmured in his ear. "I couldn't imagine Christmas without you."

"But—"

"But nothing. You aren't Nick. I know that even if Ruth doesn't. You're kinder than Nick ever was. And you came home, when all Nick ever wanted was to wander the world. He may have told great stories, Matt, but he left Ruth alone. He walked away from me and everyone he loved in Last Chance. He never came back to visit, even when he wasn't on deployment. Instead, every year, he sent Ruth a Christmas present, as if that were enough. They came like clockwork. She always put them in the charity box. She never even unwrapped them."

"You knew this all along and you didn't tell me?"

"We all knew it. Why do you think I asked you about your reasons for coming? Why do you think Nita questioned your motives last night? I guess once you explained yourself everyone understood that you'd come here looking for something Nick had thrown away without really looking back. No one wanted to dash your illusions. Not after what you'd been through."

"And," Miriam said, "it sure does look like Nick's last present was maybe the best one he ever sent home."

Matt closed his eyes and leaned in to Annie. Miriam was wrong. If there had been a gift given this Christmas, it had been what Annie had given him the last few days—a Christmas he would never forget.

And a warm, welcoming place to come home to.

About the Author

Hope Ramsay is a *USA Today* bestselling author of heart-warming contemporary romances set below the Mason-Dixon Line. Her children are grown, but she has a couple of fur babies who keep her entertained. Pete the cat, named after the cat in the children's books, thinks he's a dog, and Daisy the dog thinks Pete is her best friend except when he decides her wagging tail is a cat toy. Hope lives in the medium-sized town of Fredericksburg, Virginia, and when she's not writing or walking the dog, she spends her time knitting and noodling around on her collection of guitars.

You can learn more at:
HopeRamsay.com
Twitter @HopeRamsay
Facebook.com/Hope.Ramsay

READ MORE IN HOPE RAMSAY'S CHARMING LAST CHANCE SERIES

The Last Chance series

*Can't get enough of that small-town charm?
Forever has you covered with these
heartwarming contemporary romances!*

ONLY FOR YOU
by Barb Curtis

After Emily Holland's friend gets his heart broken on national TV, he proposes a plan to stop town gossip: a fake relationship with *her*. Emily has secretly wanted Tim Fraser for years, but pretending her feelings are only for show never factored into her fantasy. Still, her long-standing crush makes it impossible to say no. But with each date, the lines between pretend and reality blur, giving Tim and Emily a tantalizing taste of life outside the friend zone... Can they find the courage to give *real* love a real chance?

THE HOUSE ON SUNSHINE CORNER
by Phoebe Mills

Abby Engel has a great life. She's the owner of Sunshine Corner, the daycare she runs with her girlfriends; she has the most adoring grandmother (aka the Baby Whisperer); and she lives in a hidden gem of a town. All that's missing is love. Then her ex returns home to win back the one woman he's never been able to forget. But after breaking her heart years ago, can Carter convince Abby that he's her happily-ever-after?

THE AMISH BABY FINDS A HOME
by Barbara Cameron

Amish woodworker Gideon Troyer is ready to share his full life with someone special. And his friendship with Hannah Stoltzfus, the lovely owner of a quilt shop, is growing into something deeper. But before Gideon can tell Hannah how he feels, she makes a discovery in his shop: a baby…one sharing an unmistakable Troyer family resemblance. As they care for the sweet abandoned *boppli* and search for his family, will they find they're ready for a *familye* of their own?

NO ORDINARY CHRISTMAS
by Belle Calhoune

Mistletoe, Maine, is buzzing, and not just because Christmas is near! Dante West, local cutie turned Hollywood hunk, is returning home to make his next movie. Everyone in town is excited except librarian Lucy Marshall, whose heart was broken when Dante took off for LA. But Dante makes an offer Lucy's struggling library can't refuse: a major donation in exchange for allowing them to film on site. Will this holiday season give their first love a second chance?

THE INN ON SWEETBRIAR LANE
by Jeannie Chin

June Wu is in over her head. Her family's inn is empty, and the surly stranger next door is driving away her last guests! But when ex-soldier Clay Hawthorne asks for June's help, she can't say no. The town leaders are trying to stop his bar from opening, and June thinks his new venture is just what Blue Cedar Falls needs to bring in more tourists. But can two total opposites really learn to meet each other in the middle? Includes a bonus story by Annie Rains!

TO ALL THE DOGS I'VE LOVED BEFORE
by Lizzie Shane

The last person librarian Elinor Rodriguez wants to see at her door is her first love, town sheriff Levi Jackson, but her mischievous rescue dog has other ideas. Without fail, Dory slips from the house whenever Elinor's back is turned—and it's up to Levi to bring her back. The quietly intense lawman broke Elinor's heart years ago, and she's determined to move on, no matter how much she misses him. But will this four-legged friend prove that a second chance is in store? Includes a bonus story by Hope Ramsay!

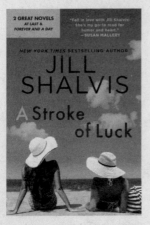

A STROKE OF LUCK
(2-IN-1 EDITION)
by Jill Shalvis

Get swept off your feet with two Lucky Harbor novels! In *At Last*, a weekend hike for Amy Michaels accidentally gets her up close and personal with forest ranger Matt Bowers. Will Matt be able to convince Amy that they can build a future together? In *Forever and a Day*, single dad and ER doctor Josh Scott has no time for anything outside of his clinic and son—until the beautiful Grace Brooks arrives in town and becomes his new nanny. And in a town like Lucky Harbor, a lifetime of love can start with just one kiss.

DREAM KEEPER
by Kristen Ashley

Single mom Pepper Hannigan has sworn off romance because she refuses to put the heart of her daughter, Juno, at risk. Only Juno thinks her mom and August Hero are meant to be. Despite his name, the serious, stern commando is anything *but* a knight in shining armor. However, he can't deny how much he wants to take care of Pepper and her little girl. And when Juno's matchmaking brings danger close to home, August will need to save both Pepper and Juno to prove that happy endings aren't just for fairy tales.